C

I.

II.

III.

IV.

A Torrent

Best Scienc

Mr

They Shall Have Stars

A SCIENCE FICTION NOVEL

by

JAMES BLISH

*

And death shall have no dominion
Dead men naked they shall be one
With the man in the wind and the west moon;
When their bones are picked clean and the
*   clean bones gone,*
They shall have stars at elbow and foot . . .
                    DYLAN THOMAS

FABER AND FABER LTD
3 Queen Square
London

First published in 1956
by Faber and Faber Limited
3 Queen Square, London WC1
Reprinted 1965, 1968 and 1974
Printed in Great Britain by
Whitstable Litho Straker Brothers Ltd.
All rights reserved

ISBN 0 571 06264 4

To
FREDERIK POHL

Author's Note

This first volume of *Cities in Flight* is a prologue to the work as a whole, and hence contains neither any flying cities nor any characters in common with the remaining three volumes. Instead, it undertakes to show the circumstances under which the two fundamental inventions which made the Okie cities possible were discovered—and the reasons why the cities found the nearer stars already scattered with colonists, ready to employ them, when the time for their own diaspora came round.

We begin in 2018 A.D.—imminent enough so that my "Premier Erdsenov" might be Brezhnev-Kosygin's successor—and the events here cover about two years. There is a leap of several centuries before *Cities in Flight* proper begins, and thereafter the action is continuous through the remaining three volumes, all the way to 4004 A.D. For what happened in the interim, and for a general skeleton of all the important events, the reader is referred to the overall Chronology at the end of this volume.

The writing of *Cities in Flight* occupied me, off and on, from 1948 to 1962, and like many such long projects, the order of composition of its parts wasn't orderly at all, and was further complicated by the publishing history (which is also appended). Briefly, however, the third volume, *Earthman, Come Home*, was written first, and was followed by the first volume—this one—to provide a "prequel." Then I wrote the ending, *A Clash of Cymbals*, and backtracked to the second volume, *A Life For The Stars*. Thus the novel as a whole contains some reminders of preceding events which economy would say it does not now need. But then, so does *The Ring of the Nibelung*, for similar reasons though to far nobler effect.

JAMES BLISH

New York
1964

6

A.D.

2012 Bliss Wagoner elected Senator (D.) from Alaska. Dr. Guiseppi Corsi drummed out of the U.S. Bureau of Standards as a security risk.

2013 Joint Senate-House Committee on Space Flight launches the Jupiter Project. Department of Health, Education, Welfare and Security underwrites international conference on degenerative disease.

2015 Investigating subcommittee of the Senate Finance Committee votes to investigate the Bridge.

2016 Construction of the Proserpine Station begun.

2018 Bliss Wagoner re-elected. Discovery of ascomycin.

2019 Publication of the report on the Bridge investigation. Discovery of the Dillon–Wagoner graviton-polarity generator.

2020 Second investigation of the Bridge. Flight of Wagoner. The Believer Riots. The Orders of Extradition. Fall of the Bridge.

2021 Escape of the "Colonials" from the Jovian system. Trial and death of Wagoner. Death of Corsi, under questioning.

2022 The MacHinery–Erdsenov Agreement. The Cold Peace.

2027 Assassination of MacHinery. The Erdsenov Proclamation.

2032 Assassination of Erdsenov. The Terror. The Hamiltonian Exodus.

7

2039 Banning of space flight and all associated sciences on Earth, by the Krushchevgrad Proclamation.

2105 Fall of the West (an agreed arbitrary date).

2289 First colonial contact with the Vegan Tyranny.

2310 The Battle of Altair, first engagement of the Vegan War.

2375 Rediscovery of the spindizzy. Escape from Earth of the Thorium Trust's Plant No. 8.

2394 Height of the Earth Exodus. Rape of Thor V by the Interstellar Master Traders (*orig.* Gravitogorsk–Mars).

2413 Investment of Vega. Battle of the Forts. Scorching of the Vegan system by the Third Colonial Navy, under Adm. Hrunta.

2451 Alois Hrunta found guilty *in absentia* of atrocities and attempted genocide by the Colonial Court, Judge Schmitz presiding.

2464 Battle of BD 40°4048′. Alois Hrunta declares himself Emperor of Space.

2522 Collapse of the Bureaucratic State. The Police Interregnum. Proclamation of amnesty to the colonists. Beginning of the Empty Years.

2998 Birth of John Amalfi.

3089 Amalfi becomes mayor of Manhattan. Poisoning of Alois Hrunta. Balkanization of the Hruntan Empire.

3111 Manhattan leaves the Earth. Arpad Hrunta installed as Emperor of Space.

3200 Birth of Mark Hazleton. Anti-Earth pogrom in the Malar system; colonization of the Acolyte cluster.

3301 Manhattan violates its contract on Epoch; deFord is shot, and Hazleton becomes city manager.

3548 Escape of Squadron 32 of the Hruntan Navy from the Battle of Procyon. Founding of the Duchy of Gort.

3571 Interception of the war between Gort and Utopia.

3602 Reduction of Gort and Utopia by the Earth police. Second Hamiltonian Exodus. Death of Arpad Hrunta; dissolution of the Empire. Escape of Manhattan.

8

3844 The crossing of the Rift. First contact with the planet of He.

3850 The tipping of He; beginning of the first intergalactic crossing.

3900 Collapse of the germanium standard.

3905 Battle of the Jungle, in the Acolyte cluster. Lt. Lerner named Acolyte-Regent. Beginning of the March on Earth.

3910 Acolyte-Regent Lerner proclaims himself Emperor of Space.

3911 The flight of Hern VI. Annihilation of the Acolyte fleet by the Earth police. Death of Emperor Lerner, under an overdose of wisdom-weed, in a slum on Murphy.

3913 The Battle of Earth. Last stand of the Vegan Tyranny.

3917 Hern VI leaves the galaxy.

3918 Manhattan leaves the galaxy. Re-election of Mayor Amalfi.

3925 Passage of the anti-Okie bill.

3944 Discovery of the Interstellar Master Traders. Colonization of the Greater Magellanic Cloud.

3948 The Battle of the Blasted Heath. Destruction of IMT by the Earth police. Abandonment by Earth of the Clouds.

3949 Founding of New Earth.

4000 Assimilation by the Web of Hercules of the Earth culture; emergence of the Milky Way's IVth great civilization. The return of He.

4002 The Jehad of Jorn. Conquest and recovery of New Earth.

4004 The Ginnunga-Gap.

". . . While Vegan civilization was undergoing this peculiar decline in influence, while at the height of its political and military power, the culture which was eventually to replace it was beginning to unfold. The reader should bear in mind that at that time nobody had ever heard of the Earth, and the planet's sun, Sol, was known only as an undistinguished type Go star in the Draco sector. It is possible—although highly unlikely—that Vega knew that the Earth had developed space flight some time before the events we have just reviewed here. It was, however, only local interplanetary flight; up to this period, Earth had taken no part in Galactic history. It was inevitable, however, that Earth should make the two crucial discoveries which would bring it on to that starry stage. We may be very sure that Vega, had she known that Earth was to be her successor, would have exerted all of her enormous might to prevent it. That Vega failed to do so is evidence enough that she had no real idea of what was happening on Earth at this time. . . ."

—ACREFF-MONALES: *The Milky Way: Five Cultural Portraits*

BOOK ONE

*

PRELUDE

The shadows flickered on the walls to his left and right, just inside the edges of his vision, like shapes stepping quickly back into invisible doorways. Despite his bone-deep weariness, they made him nervous, almost made him wish that Dr. Corsi would put out the fire. Nevertheless, he remained staring into the leaping orange light, feeling the heat tightening his cheeks and the skin around his eyes, and soaking into his chest.

Corsi stirred a little beside him, but Senator Wagoner's own weight on the sofa seemed to have been increasing ever since he had first sat down. He felt drained, lethargic, as old and heavy as a stone despite his forty-eight years; it had been a bad day in a long succession of bad days. Good days in Washington were the ones you slept through.

Next to him Corsi, for all that he was twenty years older, formerly Director of the Bureau of Standards, formerly Director of the World Health Organization, and presently head man of the American Association for the Advancement of Science (usually referred to in Washington as "the left-wing Triple-A-S"), felt as light and restless and quick as a chameleon.

"I suppose you know what a chance you're taking, coming to see me," Corsi said in his dry, whispery

13

voice. "I wouldn't be in Washington at all if I didn't think the interests of the AAAS required it. Not after the drubbing I've taken at MacHinery's hands. Even outside the government, it's like living in an aquarium —in a tank labelled 'Pirhana'. But you know about all that."

"I know," the senator agreed. The shadows jumped forward and retreated. "I was followed here myself. MacHinery's gumshoes have been trying to get something on me for a long time. But I had to talk to you, Seppi. I've done my best to understand everything I've found in the committee's files since I was made chairman—but a non-scientist has inherent limitations. And I didn't want to ask revealing questions of any of the boys on my staff. That would be a sure way to a leak— probably straight to MacHinery."

"That's the definition of a government expert these days," Corsi said, even more dryly. "A man of whom you don't dare ask an important question."

"Or who'll give you only the answer he thinks you want to hear," Wagoner said heavily. "I've hit that, too. Working for the government isn't a pink tea for a senator, either. Don't think I haven't wanted to be back in Alaska more than once; I've got a cabin on Kadiak where I can *enjoy* an open fire, without wondering if the shadows it throws carry notebooks. But that's enough self-pity. I ran for the office and I mean to be good at it, as good as I can be, anyhow."

"Which is good enough," Corsi said unexpectedly, taking the brandy snifter out of Wagoner's lax hand and replenishing the little amber lake at the bottom of it. The vapours came welling up over his cupped hand, heavy and rich. "Bliss, when I first heard that the Joint Congressional Committee on Space Flight was going to

14

fall into the hands of a freshman senator, one who'd been nothing but a press agent before his election——"

"Please," Wagoner said, wincing with mock tenderness. "A public relations counsel."

"As you like. Still and all, I turned the air blue. I knew it wouldn't have happened if any senator with seniority had wanted the committee, and the fact that none of them did seemed to me to be the worst indictment of the present Congress anyone could ask for. Every word I said was taken down, of course, and will be used against you, sooner or later. It's already been used against me, and thank God *that's* over. But I was wrong about you. You've done a whale of a good job; you've learned like magic. So if you want to cut your political throat by asking me for advice, then by God I'll give it to you."

Corsi thrust the snifter back into Wagoner's hand with something more than mock fury. "That goes for you, and for nobody else," he added. "I wouldn't tell anybody else in government the best way to pound sand —not unless the AAAS asked me to."

"I know you wouldn't, Seppi. That's part of our trouble. Thanks, anyhow." He swirled the brandy reflectively. "All right, then, tell me this: What's the matter with space flight?"

"The Army," Corsi said promptly.

"Yes, but that's not all. Not by a long shot. Sure, the Army Space Service is graft-ridden, shot through with jealousy, and gone rigid in the brains. But it was far worse back in the days when half a dozen branches of government were working on space-flight at the same time—the Weather Bureau, the Navy, your bureau, the Air Force and so on. I've seen some documents dating back that far. The Earth Satellite Programme was announced in 1944; we didn't actually get SV-1 up there until 1962, after the Army was given full jurisdiction. They couldn't even get the damned thing off the drawing boards; every Rear-Admiral insisted that the plans include a parking place for his pet launch. At least now we *have* space-flight.

"But there's something far more radically wrong now. If space flight were still a live proposition, by now some of it would have been taken away from the Army again. There'd be some merchant shipping, maybe; or even small passenger lines for the luxury trade, for the kind of people who'll go in uncomfortable ways to unliveable places just because it's horribly expensive." He chuckled heavily. "Like fox-hunting in England a hundred years ago; some Irish senator, Gogarty I think it was, called it 'the pursuit of the inedible by the unspeakable'."

"Isn't it still a little early for that?" Corsi said.

"In 2013? I don't think so. But if I'm rushing us on that one point, I can mention others. Why have there been no major exploratory expeditions for the past fifteen years? I should have thought that as soon as that tenth planet, Proserpine, was discovered, some university or foundation would have wanted to go there. It has a big fat moon that would make a fine base—no weather exists at those temperatures—there's no sun in the sky out there to louse up photographic plates, it's only another zero-magnitude star—and so on. That kind of thing used to be meat and drink to private explorers. Given a millionaire with a thirst for science, like old Hale, and a sturdy organizer with a little grandstand in him—a Byrd-type—and we should have had a Proserpine Two station long ago. Yet space has been dead since Titan Station was set up in 1981. Why?"

He watched the flames a moment.

"Then", he said, "there's the whole question of invention in the field. It's stopped, Seppi. Stopped cold."

Corsi said: "I seem to remember a paper from the boys on Titan not so long ago——"

"On xenobacteriology. Sure. That's not space flight, Seppi; space flight only made it possible; their results don't update space flight itself, don't improve it, make it more attractive. Those guys aren't even interested in it. *Nobody* is any more. That's why it's stopped changing.

"For instance: we're still using ion-rockets, driven by an atomic pile. It works, and there are a thousand minor variations on the principle; but the principle itself was described by Coupling in 1954! Think of it, Seppi—not one single new, basic engine design in *fifty years!* And what about hull design? That's still based on von Braun's work—older even than Coupling's. Is it really possible that there's nothing better than those frameworks of hitched onions? Or those powered gliders that act as ferries for them? Yet I can't find anything in the committee's files that looks any better."

"Are you sure you'd know a minor change from a major one?"

"You be the judge," Wagoner said grimly. "The hottest thing in current spaceship design is a new elliptically wound spring for acceleration couches. It drags like a leaf-spring with gravity, and pushes like a coil-spring against it. The design wastes energy in one direction, stores it in the other. At last reports, couches made with it feel like sacks stuffed with green tomatoes, but we think we'll have the bugs worked out of it soon. Tomato bugs, I suppose. Top Secret."

"There's one more Top Secret I'm not supposed to know," Corsi said. "Luckily it'll be no trouble to forget."

"All right, try this one. We have a new water-bottle for ships' stores. It's made of aluminium foil, to be collapsed from the bottom like a toothpaste tube to feed the water into the man's mouth."

"But a plastic membrane collapsed by air-pressure is handier, weighs less——"

"Sure it does. And this foil tube is already standard for paste rations. All that's new about this thing is the proposal that we use it for water too. The proposal came to us from a lobbyist for CanAm Metals, with strong endorsements by a couple of senators from the Pacific north-west. You can guess what we did with it."

"I am beginning to see your drift."

"Then I'll wind it up as fast as I can," Wagoner said. "What it all comes to is that the whole structure of space flight as it stands now is creaking, obsolescent, over-elaborate, decaying. The field is static; no, worse than that, it's losing ground. By this time, our ships ought to be sleeker and faster, and able to carry bigger payloads. We ought to have done away with this dichotomy between ships that can land on a planet, and ships that can fly from one planet to another.

"The whole question of *using* the planets for something—something, that is, besides research—ought to be within sight of settlement. Instead, nobody even discusses it any more. And our chances to settle it grow worse every year. Our appropriations are dwindling, as it gets harder and harder to convince the Congress that space flight is really good for anything. You can't sell the Congress on the long-range rewards of basic research, anyhow; Representatives have to stand for election every two years, Senators every six years; that's just about as far ahead as most of them are prepared to look. And suppose we tried to explain to them the basic research we're doing? We couldn't; it's classified!

"And above all, Seppi—this may be only my personal ignorance speaking, but if so, I'm stuck with it—above all, I think that by now we ought to have some slight clue toward an inter*stellar* drive. We ought even to have a model, no matter how crude—as crude as a Fourth-of-July rocket compared to a Coupling engine, but with the principle visible. But we don't. As a matter of fact, we've written off the stars. Nobody I can talk to thinks we'll ever reach them."

Corsi got up and walked lightly to the window, where he stood with his back to the room, as though trying to look through the light-tight blind down on to the deserted street. While he stood there, a shot blatted not far away, and the echoes bounded back at them from the face of the embassy across the street. It was not a common sound in Washington, but neither was it unusual: it was almost surely one of the city's thousands of anonymous snoopers firing at a counter-agent, a cop, or a shadow.

Corsi made no responding movement. To Wagoner's fire-hazed eyes, he was scarcely more than a shadow himself. The senator found himself thinking, for perhaps the twentieth time in the past six months, that Corsi might even be glad to be out of it all, branded unreliable though he was. Then, again for at least the twentieth time, Wagoner remembered the repeated clearance hearings, the oceans of dubious testimony and gossip from witnesses with no faces or names, the clamour in the press when Corsi was found to have roomed in college with a man suspected of being an ex-YPSL member, the denunciation on the Senate floor by one of MacHinery's captive solons, more hearings, the endless barrage of vilification and hatred, the letters beginning "Dear Doctor Corsets, You bum," and signed "True American". . . . To get out of it that way was worse than enduring it, no matter how stoutly most of your fellow scholars stood by you afterwards.

"I shan't be the first to say so to you," the physicist said, turning at last. "I don't think we'll ever reach the stars either, Bliss. And I am not very conservative, as physicists go. We just don't live long enough for us to become a star-travelling race. A mortal man limited to speeds below that of light is as unsuited to interstellar travel as a moth would be to crossing the Atlantic. I'm sorry to believe that, certainly; but I do believe it."

Wagoner nodded and filed the speech away. On that subject, he had expected even less than Corsi had given him.

"But", Corsi said, lifting his snifter from the table, "it isn't impossible that inter*planetary* flight could be bettered. I agree with you that it's rotting away now. I'd suspected that it might be, and your showing to-night is conclusive."

"Then why is it happening?" Wagoner demanded.

"Because scientific method doesn't work any more."

"*What!* Excuse me, Seppi, but that's sort of like hearing an Archbishop say that Christianity doesn't work any more. What do you mean?"

Corsi smiled sourly. "Perhaps I was overdramatic. But it's true that, under present conditions, scientific method is a blind alley. It depends on freedom of information, and we deliberately killed that. In my bureau, when it was mine, we seldom knew who was working on what project at any given time; we seldom knew whether or not somebody else in the bureau was duplicating it; we never knew whether or not some other

20

department might be duplicating it. All we could be sure of was that many men, working in similar fields, were stamping their results *Secret* because that was the easy way—not only to keep the work out of Russian hands, but to keep the workers in the clear if their own government should investigate them. How can you apply scientific method to a problem when you're forbidden to see the data?

"Then there's the calibre of scientist we have working for the government now. The few first-rate men we have are so harassed by the security set-up—and by the constant suspicion that's focused on them because they *are* top men in their fields, and hence anything they might leak would be particularly valuable—that it takes them years to solve what used to be very simple problems. As for the rest—well, our staff at Standards consisted almost entirely of third-raters: some of them were very dogged and patient men indeed, but low on courage and even lower on imagination. They spent all their time operating mechanically by the cook-book— the routine of scientific method—and had less to show for it every year."

"Everything you've said could be applied to the space-flight research that's going on now, without changing a comma," Wagoner said. "But Seppi, if scientific method used to be sound, it should still be sound. It ought to work for anybody, even third-raters. Why has it suddenly turned sour now—after centuries of unbroken successes?"

"The time lapse", Corsi said sombrely, "is of the first importance. Remember, Bliss, that scientific method is *not* a natural law. It doesn't exist in nature, but only in our heads; in short, it's a way of thinking about things —a way of sifting evidence. It was bound to become

21

obsolescent sooner or later, just as sorites and paradigms and syllogisms became obsolete before it. Scientific method works fine while there are thousands of
obvious facts lying about for the taking—facts as obvious and measurable as how fast a stone falls, or what
the order of the colours is in a rainbow. But the more
subtle the facts to be discovered become—the more they
retreat into the realms of the invisible, the intangible,
the unweighable, the sub-microscopic, the abstract—
the more expensive and time-consuming it is to investigate them by scientific method.

"And when you reach a stage where the *only* research
worth doing costs millions of dollars per experiment,
then those experiments can be paid for only by government. Governments can make the best use only of third-
rate men, men who can't leaven the instructions in the
cook-book with the flashes of insight you need to make
basic discoveries. The result is what you see: sterility,
stasis, dry rot."

"Then what's left?" Wagoner said. "What are we
going to do now? I know you well enough to suspect
that you're not giving up all hope."

"No," Corsi said, "I haven't given up, but I'm quite
helpless to change the situation you're complaining
about. After all, I'm on the outside. Which is probably
good for me." He paused, and then said suddenly:
"There's no hope of getting the government to drop the
security system completely?"

"Completely?"

"Nothing else would do."

"No," Wagoner said. "Not even partially, I'm afraid.
Not any longer."

Corsi sat down and leaned forward, his elbows on his
knobby knees, staring into the dying coals. "Then I

have two pieces of advice to give you, Bliss. Actually they're two sides of the same coin. First of all, begin by abandoning these multi-million-dollar, Manhattan-District approaches. We don't need a newer, still finer measurement of electron resonance one-tenth so badly as we need new pathways, new categories of knowledge. The colossal research project is defunct; what we need now is pure skullwork."

"From *my* staff?"

"From wherever you can get it. That's the other half of my recommendation. If I were you, I would go to the crackpots."

Wagoner waited. Corsi said these things for effect; he liked drama, in small doses. He would explain in a moment.

"Of course I don't mean total crackpots," Corsi said. "But you'll have to draw the line yourself. You need marginal contributors, scientists of good reputation generally whose obsessions don't strike fire with other members of their profession. Like the Crehore atom, or old Ehrenhaft's theory of magnetic currents, or the Milne cosmology—you'll have to find the fruitful one yourself. Look for discards, and then find out whether or not the idea deserved to be *totally* discarded. And—don't accept the first 'expert' opinion that you get."

"Winnow chaff, in other words."

"What else is there to winnow?" Corsi said. "Of course it's a long chance, but you can't turn to scientists of real stature now; it's too late for that. Now you'll have to use sports, freaks, near-misses."

"Starting where?"

"Oh," said Corsi, "how about gravity? I don't know any other subject that's attracted a greater quota of idiot speculations. Yet the acceptable theories of what

23

gravity is are of no practical use to us. They can't be put to work to help lift a spaceship. We can't manipulate gravity as a field; we don't even have a set of equations for it that we can agree upon. No more will we find such a set by spending fortunes and decades on the project. The law of diminishing returns has washed that approach out."

Wagoner got up. "You don't leave me much," he said glumly.

"No," Corsi agreed. "I leave you only what you started with. That's more than most of us are left with, Bliss."

Wagoner grinned tightly at him and the two men shook hands. As Wagoner left, he saw Corsi again silhouetted against the fire, his back to the door, his shoulders bent. The senator closed the door quietly.

He was shadowed all the way back to his own apartment, but this time he hardly noticed. He was thinking about an immortal man who flew from star to star faster than light.

*

* 1 *

The parade of celebrities, notorieties, and just plain
brass that passed through the reception-room of Jno.
Pfitzner & Sons, Inc., was marvellous to behold. During the hour and a half that Col. Paige Russell had been
cooling his heels, he had identified the following
publicity-saints:

Senator Bliss Wagoner (Dem., Alaska), chairman of
the Joint Congressional Committee on Space Flight;

Dr. Guiseppi Corsi, president of the American
Association for the Advancement of Science, and a
former Director of the World Health Organization; and,

Francis Xavier MacHinery, hereditary head of the
FBI.

He had seen also a number of other notables, of
lesser calibre, but whose business at a firm which made
biologicals was an equally improper subject for guessing
games. He fidgeted.

At the present moment, the girl at the desk was talking softly with a seven-star general, which was a rank
nearly as high as a man could rise in the Army. The
general was so preoccupied that he had failed completely to recognize Paige's salute. He was passed
through swiftly. One of the two swinging doors with the
glass ports let into them moved outward behind the
desk, and Paige caught a glimpse of a stocky, dark-

25

haired, pleasant-faced man in a conservative grosse-pointilliste suit.

"Gen. Horsefield, glad to see you. Come in."

The door closed, leaving Paige once more with nothing to look at but the motto written over the entrance in German black-letter:

Wider den Tod ist kein Krautlein gewachsen!

Since he did not know the language, he had already translated this by the If-only-it-were-English system, which made it come out, "The fatter toad is waxing on the kine's cole-slaw." This did not seem to fit what little he knew about the eating habits of either animal, and it was certainly no fit admonition for workers in the main plant of the world's largest producers of biological drugs.

Of course, Paige could always look at the receptionist —but after an hour and a half he had about plumbed the uttermost depths of that ecstasy. The girl was pretty in a way, but hardly striking, even to a recently returned spaceman. Perhaps if someone would yank those black-rimmed pixie glasses away from her and undo that bun at the back of her head, she might pass, at least in the light of a whale-oil lamp in an igloo during a record blizzard.

This too was odd now that he thought about it. A firm as large as Pfitzner could have its pick of the glossiest of office girls, especially these days.

All in all, Paige was thoroughly well past mere mild annoyance with being stalled. He was, after all, here at these people's specific request, doing them a small favour for which they had asked him—and soaking up good leave-time in the process. Abruptly he got up and strode to the desk.

"Excuse me, miss," he said, "but I think you're being

26

goddamned impolite. As a matter of fact, I'm beginning to think you people are making a fool of me. Do you want these, or don't you?"

He unbuttoned his right breast pocket and pulled out three little pliofilm packets, heat-sealed to plastic mailing tags. Each packet contained a small spoonful of dirt. The tags were addressed to Jno. Pfitzner & Sons, Inc., The Bronx 153, WPO 249920, Earth; and each carried a $25 rocket-mail stamp for which Pfitzner had paid, still uncancelled.

"Colonel Russell, I agree with you," the girl said, looking up at him seriously. She looked even less glamorous than she had at a distance, but she did have a pert and interesting nose, and the current royal-purple lip-shade suited her better than it did most of the novalettes to be seen on 3–V these days. "It's just that you've caught us on a very bad day. We do want the samples, of course. They're very important to us, otherwise we wouldn't have put you to the trouble of collecting them for us."

"Then why can't I give them to someone?"

"You could give them to me," the girl suggested gently. "I'll pass them along faithfully, I promise you."

Paige shook his head. "Not after this run-around. I did just what your firm asked me to do, and I'm here to see the results. I picked up soils from every one of my ports of call, even when it was a nuisance to do it. I mailed in a lot of them; these are only the last of a series. Do you know where these bits of dirt came from?"

"I'm sorry, it's slipped my mind. It's been a very busy day."

"Two of them are from Ganymede; and the other one is from Jupiter V, right in the shadow of the Bridge gang's shack. The normal temperature on both satellites is about two hundred degrees below Fahrenheit zero. Ever try to swing a pick against ground frozen that solid—working inside a spacesuit? But I got the dirt for you. Now I want to see why Pfitzner wants dirt."

The girl shrugged. "I'm sure you were told why before you even left Earth."

"Supposing I was? I know that you people get drugs out of dirt. But aren't the guys who bring in the samples entitled to see how the process works? What if Pfitzner gets some new wonder-drug out of one of my samples—couldn't I have a sentence or two of explanation to pass on to my kids?"

The swinging doors bobbed open, and the affable face of the stocky man was thrust into the room.

"Dr. Abbott not here yet, Anne?" he said.

"Not yet, Mr. Gunn. I'll call you the minute he arrives."

"But you'll keep me sitting at least another ninety minutes," Paige said flatly. Gunn looked him over, starting at the colonel's eagle on his collar and stopping at the winged crescent pinned over his pocket.

"Apologies, Colonel, but we're having ourselves a small crisis today," he said, smiling tentatively. "I gather you've brought us some samples from space. If you could possibly come back tomorrow, I'd be happy to give you all the time in the world. But right now——"

Gunn ducked his head in apology and pulled it in, as though he had just cuckooed 2400 and had to go somewhere and lie down until 0100. Just before the door came to rest behind him, a faint but unmistakable sound slipped through it.

Somewhere in the laboratories of Jno. Pfitzner & Sons, Inc. a baby was crying.

Paige listened, blinking, until the sound was damped off. When he looked back down at the desk again, the expression of the girl behind it seemed distinctly warier.

"Look," he said. "I'm not asking a great favour of you. I don't want to know anything I shouldn't know. All I want to know is how you plan to process my packets of soil. It's just simple curiosity—backed up by a trip that covered a few hundred millions of miles. Am I entitled to know for my trouble, or not?"

"You are and you aren't," the girl said steadily. "We want your samples, and we'll agree that they're unusually interesting to us because they came from the Jovian system—the first such that we've ever gotten. But that's no guarantee that we'll find anything useful in them."

"It isn't?"

"No. Colonel Russell, you're not the first man to come here with soil samples, believe me. We've asked virtually every space-pilot, every Witness missionary, every commercial traveller, every explorer, every foreign correspondent to scoop up soil samples for us, wherever they may go. Before we discovered ascomycin, we had to screen *one hundred thousand* soil samples, including several hundred from Mars and nearly five thousand from the Moon. And do you know where we found the organism that produces ascomycin? On an over-ripe peach one of our detail men picked up from a peddler's stall in Baltimore!"

"I see the point," Paige said reluctantly. "What's ascomycin, by the way?"

The girl looked down at her desk and moved a piece of paper from *here* to *there*. "It's a new antibiotic," she said. "We'll be marketing it soon. But I could tell you the same kind of story about other such drugs."

"I see." Paige was not quite sure he did see, however, after all. He had heard the name of Pfitzner fall from some very unlikely lips during his many months in space. As far as he had been able to determine after he had become sensitized to the sound, about every third person on the planets was either collecting samples for the firm or knew somebody who was. The grapevine, which among spacemen was the only trusted medium of communication, had it that the company was doing important government work. That, of course, was nothing unusual in the Age of Defence, but Paige had heard enough to suspect that Pfitzner was something special —something as big, perhaps, as the historic Manhattan District and at least twice as secret.

The door opened and emitted Gunn for the third time hand-running, this time all the way.

"Not yet?" he said to the girl. "Evidently he isn't going to make it. Unfortunate. But I've some spare time now, Colonel——"

"Russell, Paige Russell, Army Space Corps."

"Thank you. If you'll accept my apologies for our preoccupation, Colonel Russell, I'll be glad to show you around our little establishment. My name, by the way, is Truman Gunn, vice-president in charge of exports."

"I'm importing at the moment," Paige said, holding out the soil samples. Gunn took them reverently and dropped them in a pocket of his jacket. "But I'd enjoy seeing the labs."

He nodded to the girl and the doors closed between them. He was inside.

The place was at least as fascinating as he had expected it to be. Gunn showed him, first, the rooms where the incoming samples were classified and then distributed to the laboratories proper. In the first of these, a measured fraction of a sample was dropped into a one-litre flask of sterile distilled water, swirled to distribute it evenly, and then passed through a series of dilutions. The final suspensions were then used to inoculate test-tube slants and petri plates containing a wide variety of nutrient media, which went into the incubator.

"In the next lab here—Dr. Aquino isn't in at the moment, so we mustn't touch anything, but you can see through the glass quite clearly—we transfer from the plates and agar slants to a new set of media," Gunn explained. "But here each organism found in the sample has a set of cultures of its own, so that if it secretes anything into one of the media, that something won't be contaminated."

"If it does, the amount must be very tiny," Paige said. "How do you detect it?"

"Directly, by its action. Do you see the rows of plates with the white paper discs in their centres, and the four furrows in the agar radiating from the discs? Well, each one of those furrows is impregnated with culture medium from one of the pure cultures. If all four streaks grow thriving bacterial colonies, then the medium on the paper disc contains no antibiotic against those four germs. If one or more of the streaks fails to grow, or is retarded compared to the others, then we have hope."

In the succeeding laboratory, antibiotics which had been found by the disc method were pitted against a whole spectrum of dangerous organisms. About 90 per cent of the discoveries were eliminated here, Gunn explained, either because they were insufficiently active or because they duplicated the antibiotic spectra of already known drugs. "What we call 'insufficiently active' varies with the circumstances, however," he added. "An antibiotic which shows *any* activity against tuberculosis or against Hansen's disease—leprosy—is always of interest to us, even if it attacks no other germ at all."

A few antibiotics which passed their spectrum tests went on to a miniature pilot plant, where the organisms that produced them were set to work in a deep-aerated fermentation tank. From this bubbling liquor, comparatively large amounts of the crude drug were extracted, purified, and sent to the pharmacology lab for tests on animals.

"We lose a lot of otherwise promising antibiotics here, too," Gunn said. "Most of them turn out to be too toxic to be used in—or even on—the human body. We've had Hansen's bacillus knocked out a thousand times in the test-tube, only to find here that the antibiotic is much more quickly fatal *in vivo* than is leprosy itself. But once we're sure that the drug isn't toxic, or that its toxicity is outweighed by its therapeutic efficacy, it goes out of our shop entirely, to hospitals and to individual doctors for clinical trial. We also have a virology lab in Vermont where we test our new drugs against virus diseases like the 'flu and polio—it isn't safe to operate such a lab in a large city like The Bronx."

"It's much more elaborate than I would have imagined," Paige said. "But I can see that it's well worth the trouble. Did you work out this sample-screening technique here?"

"Oh, my, no," Gunn said, smiling indulgently. "Waksman, the discoverer of streptomycin, laid down the essential procedure decades ago. We aren't even the first firm to use it on a large scale; one of our competitors did that, and found a broad-spectrum antibiotic called chloramphenicol with it, scarcely a year after they'd begun. That was what convinced the rest of us that we'd better adopt the technique, before we got shut out of the market entirely. A good thing, too; otherwise we'd none of us have discovered tetracycline, which turned out to be the most versatile antibiotic ever tested."

Farther down the corridor a door opened. The squall of a baby came out of it, much louder than before. It was not the sustained crying of a child who had had a year or so to practise, but the short-breathed "ah-la, ah-la, ah-la" of a newborn infant.

Paige raised his eyebrows. "Is that one of your experimental animals?"

"Ha, ha," Gunn said. "We're enthusiasts in this business, Colonel, but we must draw the line somewhere. No, one of our technicians has a baby-sitting problem, and so we've given her permission to bring the child to work with her, until she's worked out a better solution."

Paige had to admit that Gunn thought fast on his feet. That story had come reeling out of him like so much ticker tape, without the slightest sign of a preliminary double-take. It was not Gunn's fault that Paige, who had been through a marriage which had lasted five years before he had taken to space, could distinguish the cry of a baby old enough to be out of a hospital nursery from that of one only days old.

"Isn't this", Paige said, "a rather dangerous place to park an infant—with so many disease germs, poisonous disinfectants, and such things all around?"

"Oh, we take all proper precautions. I daresay our staff has a lower yearly sickness rate than you'll find in industrial plants of comparable size, simply because we're more aware of the problem. Now if we go through this door, Colonel Russell, we'll see the final step, the main plant where we turn out drugs in quantity after they've proved themselves."

"Yes, I'd like that. Do you have ascomycin in production now?"

This time, Gunn looked at him sharply and without any attempt to disguise his interest. "No," he said, "that's still out on clinical trial. May I ask you, Colonel Russell, just how you happened to——"

The question, which Paige realized belatedly would have been rather sticky to answer, never did get all the way asked. Over Truman Gunn's head, a squawk-box said, "Mr. Gunn, Dr. Abbott has just arrived."

Gunn turned away from the door that, he had said, led out to the main plant, with just the proper modicum of polite regret. "There's my man," he said. "I'm afraid I'm going to have to cut this tour short, Colonel Russell. You may have seen what a collection of important people we have in the plant today; we've been waiting only for Dr. Abbott to begin a very important meeting. If you'll oblige me——"

Paige could say nothing but: "Certainly." After what seemed only a few seconds, Gunn deposited him smoothly in the reception room from which he had started.

"Did you see what you wanted to see?" the receptionist said.

"I think so," Paige said thoughtfully. "Except that what I wanted to see sort of changed in mid-flight. Miss Anne, I have a petition to put before you. Would you be kind enough to have dinner with me this evening?"

"No," the girl said. "I've seen quite a few spacemen, Colonel Russell, and I'm no longer impressed. Furthermore, I shan't tell you anything you haven't heard from Mr. Gunn, so there's no need for you to spend your money or your leave-time on me. Good-bye."

"Not so fast," Paige said. "I mean business—or, if you like, I mean to make trouble. If you've met spacemen before, you know that they like to be independent —not much like the conformists who never leave the ground. I'm not after your maidenly laughter, either. I'm after information."

"Not interested," the girl said. "Save your breath."

"MacHinery is here," Paige said quietly. "So is Senator Wagoner, and some other people who have influence. Suppose I should collar any one of those people and accuse Pfitzner of conducting human vivisection?"

That told: Paige could see the girl's knuckles whitening. "You don't know what you're talking about," she said.

"That's my complaint. And I take it seriously. There were some things Mr. Gunn wasn't able to conceal from me, though he tried very hard. Now, am I going to put my suspicions through channels—and get Pfitzner investigated—or would you rather be sociable, over a fine flounder broiled in paprika butter?"

The look she gave him back was one of almost pure hatred. She seemed able to muster no other answer. The expression did not at all suit her; as a matter of fact, she looked less like someone he would want to date than any other girl he could remember. Why *should* he spend his money or his leave-time on her? There were, after all, about five millions of surplus women in the United States by the Census of 2000, and at least 4,999,950 of them must be prettier and less recalcitrant than this one.

"All right," she said abruptly. "Your natural charm

35

has swept me off my feet, Colonel. For the record, there's no other reason for my acceptance. It would be even funnier to call your bluff and see how far you'd get with that vivisection tale, but I don't care to tie my company up in a personal joke."

"Good enough," Paige said, uncomfortably aware that his bluff in fact *had* been called. "Suppose I pick you up——"

He broke off, suddenly noticing that voices were rising behind the double doors. An instant later, General Horsefield bulled into the reception room, closely followed by Gunn.

"I want it clearly understood, once and for all," Horsefield was rumbling, "that this entire project is going to wind up under military control unless we can show results before it's time to ask for a new appropriation. There's still a lot going on here that the Pentagon will regard as piddling inefficiency and highbrow theorizing. And if that's what the Pentagon reports, you know what the Treasury will do—or Congress will do it for them. We're going to have to cut back, Gunn. Understand? Cut right back to basics!"

"General, we're as far back to basics as we possibly can get," Truman Gunn said, placatingly enough, but with considerable firmness as well. "We're not going to put a gram of that drug into production until we're satisfied with it on all counts. Any other course would be suicide."

"You know I'm on your side," Horsefield said, his voice becoming somewhat less threatening. "So is General Alsos, for that matter. But this is a war we're fighting, whether the public understands it or not. And on as sensitive a matter as these death-dopes, we can't afford——"

36

Gunn, who had spotted Paige belatedly at the conclusion of his own speech, had been signalling Horsefield ever since with his eyebrows, and suddenly it took. The general swung around and glared at Paige, who, since he was uncovered now, was relieved of the necessity for saluting. Despite the sudden freezing silence, it was evident that Gunn was trying to retain in his manner toward Paige some shreds of professional cordiality—a courtesy which Paige was not too sure he merited, considering the course his conversation with the girl had taken.

As for Horsefield, he relegated Paige to the ghetto of "unauthorized persons" with a single look. Paige had no intention of remaining in that classification for a second longer than it would take him to get out of it, preferably without having been asked his name; it was deadly dangerous. With a mumbled "—at eight, then," to the girl, Paige sidled ingloriously out of the Pfitzner reception room and beat it.

He was, he reflected later in the afternoon before his shaving mirror, subjecting himself to an extraordinary series of small humiliations, to get closer to a matter which was none of his business. Worse: it was obviously Top Secret, which made it potentially lethal even for everyone authorized to know about it, let alone for rank snoopers. In the Age of Defence, to know was to be suspect, in the West as in the USSR; the two great nation-complexes had been becoming more and more alike in their treatment of "security" for the past fifty years. It had even been a mistake to mention the Bridge on Jupiter to the girl—for despite the fact that everyone knew that the Bridge existed, anyone who spoke of it with familiarity could quickly earn the label

37

of being dangerously flap-jawed. Especially if the speaker, like Paige, had actually been stationed in the Jovian system for a while, whether he had had access to information about the Bridge or not.

And especially if the talker, like Paige, had actually spoken to the Bridge gang, worked with them on marginal projects, was known to have talked to Charity Dillon, the Bridge foreman. More especially if he held military rank, making it possible for him to sell security files to Congressmen, the traditional way of advancing a military career ahead of normal promotion schedules.

And most especially if the man was discovered nosing about a new and different classified project, one to which he hadn't even been assigned.

Why, after all, was he taking the risk? He didn't even know the substance of the matter; he was no biologist. To all outside eyes the Pfitzner project was simply another piece of research in antibiotics, and a rather routinized research project at that. Why should a spaceman like Paige find himself flying so close to the candle already?

He wiped the depilatory cream off his face into a paper towel, and saw his own eyes looking back at him from the concave mirror, as magnified as an owl's. The image, however, was only his own, despite the distortion. It gave him back no answer.

★

★ 2 ★

A screeching tornado was rocking the Bridge when the alarm sounded; it was making the whole structure shudder and sway. This was normal, and Robert Helmuth barely noticed it. There was always a tornado shaking the Bridge. The whole planet was enswathed in tornadoes, and worse.

The scanner on the foreman's board had given 114 as the sector where the trouble was. That was at the north-western end of the Bridge, where it broke off, leaving nothing but the raging clouds of ammonia crystals and methane, and a sheer drop thirty miles down to the invisible surface. There were no ultraphone "eyes" at that end to show a general view of the area—in so far as any general view was possible—because both ends of the Bridge were incomplete.

With a sigh, Helmuth put the beetle into motion. The little car, as flat-bottomed and thin through as a bedbug, got slowly under way on its ball-bearing races, guided and held firmly to the surface of the Bridge by ten close-set flanged rails. Even so, the hydrogen gales made a terrific siren-like shrieking between the edge of the vehicle and the deck, and the impact of the falling drops of ammonia upon the curved roof was as heavy and deafening as a rain of cannon balls. As a matter of fact, the drops weighed almost as much as cannon-balls here under Jupiter's two-and-a-half-fold gravity, although they were not much bigger than ordinary raindrops. Every so often, too, there was a blast, accompanied by a dull orange glare, which made the car, the deck, and the Bridge itself buck savagely; even a small shock wave travelled through the incredibly dense atmosphere of the planet like the armour-plate of a bursting battleship.

These blasts were below, however, on the surface. While they shook the structure of the Bridge heavily, they almost never interfered with its functioning. And they could not, in the very nature of things, do Helmuth any harm.

Helmuth, after all, was not on Jupiter—though that was becoming harder and harder for him to bear in mind. Nobody was on Jupiter; had any real damage ever been done to the Bridge, it probably would never have been repaired. There was nobody on Jupiter to repair it; only the machines which were themselves part of the Bridge.

The Bridge was building itself. Massive, alone, and lifeless, it grew in the black deeps of Jupiter.

It had been well planned. From Helmuth's point of view—that of the scanners on the beetle—almost nothing could be seen of it, for the beetle tracks ran down the centre of the deck, and in the darkness and perpetual storm even ultrawave-assisted vision could not penetrate more than a few hundred yards at the most. The width of the Bridge, which no one would ever see, was eleven miles; its height, as incomprehensible to the Bridge gang as a skyscraper to an ant, thirty miles; its length, deliberately unspecified in the plans, fifty-four miles at the moment and still increasing—a squat, colossal structure, built with engineering principles, methods, materials and tools never touched before now. . . .

For the very good reason that they would have been impossible anywhere else. Most of the Bridge, for instance, was made of ice: a marvellous structural material under a pressure of a million atmospheres, at a temperature of 94 degrees below Fahrenheit zero. Under such conditions, the best structural steel is a friable, talc-like powder, and aluminium becomes a peculiar transparent substance that splits at a tap; water, on the other hand, becomes Ice IV, a dense, opaque white medium which will deform to a heavy stress, but will break only under impacts huge enough to lay whole Earthly cities waste. Never mind that it took millions of megawatts of power to keep the Bridge up and growing every hour of the day; the winds on Jupiter blow at velocities up to twenty-five thousand miles per hour, and will never stop blowing, as they may have been blowing for more than four billion years; there is power enough.

Back home, Helmuth remembered, there had been talk of starting another Bridge on Saturn, and perhaps, later still, on Uranus too. But that had been politicians' talk. The Bridge was almost five thousand miles below the visible surface of Jupiter's atmosphere—luckily in a way, for at the top of that atmosphere the temperature was 76 Fahrenheit degrees colder than it was down by the Bridge, but even with that differential the Bridge's mechanisms were just barely manageable. The bottom of Saturn's atmosphere, if the radiosonde readings could be trusted, was just 16,878 miles below the top of the Saturnian clouds one could see through the telescope, and the temperature down there was below − 150° C. Under those conditions, even pressure-ice would be

41

immovable, and could not be worked with anything softer than itself.

And as for a Bridge on Uranus. . . . As far as Helmuth was concerned, Jupiter was quite bad enough.

The beetle crept within sight of the end of the Bridge and stopped automatically. Helmuth set the vehicle's "eyes" for highest penetration, and examined the nearby I-beams.

The great bars were as close-set as screening. They had to be, in order to support even their own weight, let alone the weight of the components of the Bridge. The gravity down here was two and a half times as great as Earth's.

Even under that load, the whole webwork of girders was flexing and fluctuating to the harpist-fingered gale. It had been designed to do that, but Helmuth could never help being alarmed by the movement. Habit alone assured him that he had nothing to fear from it.

He took the automatic cut-out out of the circuit and inched the beetle forward on manual control. This was only Sector 113, and the Bridge's own Wheatstone scanning system—there was no electronic device anywhere on the Bridge, since it was impossible to maintain a vacuum on Jupiter—said that the trouble was in Sector 114. The boundary of that sector was still fully fifty feet away.

It was a bad sign. Helmuth scratched nervously in his red beard. Evidently there was cause for alarm—real alarm, not just the deep grinding depression which he always felt while working on the Bridge. Any damage serious enough to halt the beetle a full sector short of the trouble area was bound to be major.

It might even turn out to be the disaster which he had felt lurking ahead of him ever since he had been made foreman of the Bridge—that disaster which the Bridge itself could not repair, sending man reeling home from Jupiter in defeat.

The secondaries cut in, and the beetle hunkered down once more against the deck, the ball-bearings on which it rode frozen magnetically to the rails. Grimly, Helmuth cut the power to the magnet windings and urged the flat craft inch by inch across the danger line.

Almost at once, the car tilted just perceptibly to the left, and the screaming of the winds between its edges and the deck shot up the scale, sirening in and out of the soundless-dogwhistle range with an eeriness which set Helmuth's teeth on edge. The beetle itself fluttered and chattered like an alarm-clock hammer between the surface of the deck and the flanges of the tracks.

Ahead there was still nothing to be seen but the horizontal driving of the clouds and the hail, roaring along the length of the Bridge, out of the blackness into the beetle's fanlights, and onward into blackness again toward the horizon which, like the Bridge itself, no eye would ever see.

Thirty miles below, the fusillade of hydrogen explosions continued. Evidently something really wild was going on on the surface. Helmuth could not remember having heard so much vulcanism in years.

There was a flat, especially heavy crash, and a long line of fuming orange fire came pouring down the seething air into the depths, feathering horizontally like the mane of a Lipizzan stallion, directly in front of Helmuth. Instinctively, he winced and drew back from the board, although that stream of flame actually was only a little less cold than the rest of the storming, streaming gases, and far too cold to injure the Bridge.

In the momentary glare, however, he saw something:

an upward twisting of shadows, patterned but obviously unfinished, fluttering in silhouette against the lurid light of the hydrogen cataract.

The end of the Bridge.

Wrecked.

Helmuth grunted involuntarily and backed the beetle away. The flare dimmed; the light poured down the sky and fell away into the raging sea of liquid hydrogen thirty miles below. The scanner clucked with satisfaction as the beetle recrossed the danger line into Sector 113.

Helmuth turned the body of the vehicle 180 degrees on its chassis, presenting its back to the dying orange torrent. There was nothing further that he could do at the moment on the Bridge. He searched his control board—a ghost image of which was cast on the screen across the scene on the Bridge—for the blue button marked *Garage*, punched it savagely, and tore off his foreman's helmet.

Obediently, the Bridge vanished.

The girl—whose full name, Paige found, was Anne Abbott—looked moderately acceptable in her summer suit, on the left lapel of which she wore a model of the tetracycline molecule with the atoms picked out in tiny synthetic gems. But she was even less inclined to talk when he picked her up than she had been in Pfitzner's reception room. Paige himself had never been expert at making small talk, and in the face of her obvious, continuing resentment, his parched spring of social invention went underground completely.

Five minutes later, all talk became impossible, anyhow. The route to the restaurant Paige had chosen lay across Foley Square, where there turned out to be a Witness Mission going. The Caddy Paige had hired—at nearly a quarter of his leave-pay, for commercial kerosene-fuelled taxis were strictly a rich man's occasional luxury—was bogged down almost at once in the groaning, swaying crowd.

The main noise came from the big plastic proscenium, where one of the lay preachers was exhorting the crowd in a voice so heavily amplified as to be nearly unintelligible. Witnesses with portable tape recorders, bags of tracts and magazines, sandwich-boards lettered with fluorescent inks, confessions for sinners to sign, and green baize pokes for collections were well scattered among the pedestrians, and the streets were crossed about every fifteen feet with the straight black snakes of compressed-air triggers.

As the Caddy pulled up for the second time, a nozzle was thrust into the rear window and a stream of iridescent bubbles poured across the back seat directly under Paige's and Anne's noses. As each bubble burst, there was a wave of perfume—evidently it was "Celestial Joy" the Witnesses were using this year—and a sweet voice said:

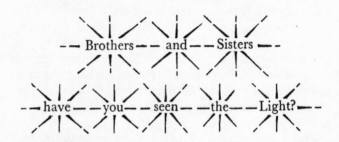

Paige fought at the bubbles with futile windmillings, while Anne Abbott leaned back against the cushions of the Caddy and watched him, with a faint smile of contemptuous amusement. The last bubble contained no word, but only an overpowering burst of odour. Despite herself, the girl's smile deepened: the perfume, in addition to being powerfully euphoric, was slightly aphrodisiac as well. This year, apparently, the Witnesses were readier than ever to use any means that came to hand.

The driver lurched the Caddy ahead. Then, before Paige could begin to grasp what was happening, the car stopped, the door next to the steering wheel was wrenched open, and four spidery, many-fingered arms

46

plucked the driver neatly from his seat and deposited him on his knees on the asphalt outside.

"SHAME! SHAME!" the popai-robot thundered. "YOUR SINS HAVE FOUND YOU OUT! REPENT, AND FIND FORGIVENESS!"

A thin glass globe of some gas, evidently a narco-synthetic, broke beside the car, and not only the unfortunate chauffeur but also the part of the crowd which had begun to collect about him—mostly women, of course—began to weep convulsively.

"REPENT!" the robot intoned, over a sneaked-in choir now singing "Ah-ah-ah-ah-ah-h-h-h-h" somewhere in the warm evening air. "REPENT, FOR THE TIME IS AT HAND!"

Paige, astonished to find himself choking with sourceless, maudlin self-pity, flung himself out of the Caddy in search of a nose to break. But there were no live Witnesses in sight. The members of the order, all of whom were charged with spreading the good work by whatever means seemed good to them, had learned decades ago that their proselytizing was often resented, and had substituted technology for personal salesmanship wherever possible.

Their machines, too, had been forced to learn. The point-of-purchase robot retreated as Paige bore down upon it. The thing had been conditioned against allowing itself to be broken.

The Caddy's driver, rescued, blew his nose resentfully and started the car again. The wordless choir, with its eternal bridge-passage straight out of the compositions of Dmitri Tiomkin, diminished behind them, and the voice of the lay preacher came roaring back through to them over the fading, characterless music.

"I say to you," the p.a. system was moaning unctuously, like a lady hippopotamus reading A. E. Housman, "I say to you, the world and the things which are the world's come to an end and a quick end. In his overweening pride, man has sought even to wrest the stars from their courses, but the stars are not man's, and he shall rue that day. Ah, vanity of vanities, all is vanity (Preacher V: 796). Even on mighty Jove man dared to erect a great Bridge, as once in Babel he sought to build a tower to heaven. But this also is vanity, it is vicious pride and defiance, and it too shall bring calamity upon men. Pull down thy vanity, I say pull down! (Ezra lxxxi, 99.) Let there be an end to pride, and there shall be peace. Let there be love, and there shall be understanding. I say to you——"

At this point, the Witnesses' over-enthusiastic booby-trapping of the square cut off whatever the preacher was going to say next, as far as the occupants of the Caddy were concerned. The car passed over another trigger, and there was a blinding, rose-coloured flash. When Paige could see again, the car seemed to be floating in mid-air, and there were actual angels flapping solemnly around it. The *vox humana* of a Hammond organ sobbed among the clouds.

Paige supposed that the Witnesses had managed to crystallize temporarily, perhaps with a supersonic pulse, the glass of the windows, which he had rolled up to prevent another intromission of bubbles, and to project a 3-V tape against the glass crystals with polarized ultraviolet light. The random distribution of fluorescent trace compounds in ordinary window glass would account for the odd way the "angels" changed colour as they moved.

Understanding the vision's probable *modus operandi*

left Paige no less furious at the new delay, but luckily the thing turned out to be a trick left over from last year's Revival, for which the Caddy was prepared. The driver touched something on the dash and the saccharine scene vanished, hymns and all. The car lunged abruptly through an opening in the crowd, and a moment later the square was behind them.

"Whew!" Paige said, leaning back at last. "Now I understand why taxi depots have vending machines for trip-insurance policies. The Witnesses weren't much in evidence the last time I was on Earth."

"Every tenth person you meet is a Witness now," Anne said. "And eight of the other nine claim that they've given up religion as a bad job. While you're caught in the middle of one of those Revivals, though, it's hard to believe the complaints you read about our times—that people have no faith and so on."

"I don't find it so," Paige said reflectively. This certainly did not strike him as light social conversation, but since it was instead a kind of talk he much more enjoyed—talk which was about something—he could only be delighted that the ice was broken. "I've no religion of my own, but I think that when the experts talk about 'faith' they mean something different than the shouting kind, the kind the Witnesses have. Shouting religions always strike me as essentially like pep-meetings among salesmen; their ceremonies and their manners are so aggressive because they don't really believe the code themselves. Real faith is so much a part of the world you live in that you seldom notice it, and it isn't always religious in the formal sense. Mathematics is based on faith, for instance, for those who know it."

"I should have said that it was based on the antithesis of faith," Anne said, turning a little cooler. "Have you had any experience in the field, Colonel?"

"Some," he said, without rancour. "I'd never have been allowed to pilot a ship outside the orbit of the Moon without knowing tensors, and if I expect to get my next promotion, I'm going to have to know spinor calculus as well—which I do."

"Oh," the girl said. She sounded faintly dashed. "Go on; I'm sorry I interrupted."

"You were right to interrupt; I made my point badly. I meant to say that the mathematician's belief that there is some relationship between maths and the real world is a faith; it can't be proven, but he feels it very strongly. For that matter, the totally irreligious man's belief that there even *is* a real world, corresponding to what his senses show him, can't be proven. John Doe and the most brilliant of physicists both have to take that on faith."

"And they don't conduct ceremonies symbolizing the belief," Anne added, "and train specialists to reassure them of it every seven days."

"That's right. In the same way, John Doe used to feel that the basic religions of the West had some relationship to the real world which was valid, even though it couldn't be proven. And that includes Communism, which was born in the West, after all. John Doe doesn't feel that way any more—and by my guess, neither do the Witnesses, or they wouldn't be shouting so loud. In that sense, there's not much faith lying around loose these days anywhere, as far as I can see. None for me to pick up, that much I've found out the hard way."

"Har y'are," the chauffeur said.

Paige helped the girl out of the car, trying not to notice how much fare he had to pay, and the two were shown to a table in the restaurant. Anne was silent again for a while after they were seated. Paige had about decided that she had chosen to freeze up once more, and had begun to wonder if he could arrange to have the place invaded by Witnesses to start the conversation again, when she said:

"You seem to have been thinking about faith quite a bit. You talk as though the problem meant something to you. Could you tell me why?"

"I'd be glad to try," he said slowly. "The standard answer would be that while you're out in space you have lots of time to think—but people use thinking-time differently. I suppose I've been looking for some frame of reference that could be mine ever since I was four, when my father and mother split up. She was a Christian Scientist and he was a Dianeticist, so they had a lot to fight about. There was a court battle over custody that lasted for nearly five years.

"I joined the Army when I was seventeen, and it didn't take me very long to find out that the Army is no substitute for a family, let alone a church. Then I volunteered for space service school. That was no church either. The Army got jurisdiction over space travel when the whole field was just a baby, because it had a long tradition of grafting off land-grants, and it didn't want the Navy or the Air Force to grab off the gravy from any such grants that might be made on the planets. I spent more time helping the Army space-travel department fight unification with the space arms of the other services than I did doing real work in space. That was what I was ordered to do—but it didn't help me to think of space as the ultimate cathedral. . . .

"Somewhere along in there, I got married and we had one son; he was born the same day I entered space school.

Two years later, the marriage was annulled. That sounds funny, I know, but the circumstances were unusual.

"When Pfitzner approached me and asked me to pick up soil samples for them, I suppose I saw another church with which I could identify myself—something humanitarian, long-range, impersonal. And when I found this afternoon that the new church wasn't going to welcome the convert with glad cries—well, the result is that I'm now weeping on your shoulder." He smiled. "That's hardly flattering, I know. But you've already helped me to talk myself into a spot where the only next step is to apologize, which I hereby do. I hope you'll accept it."

"I think I will," she said, and then, tentatively, she smiled back. The result made him tingle as though the air-pressure had dropped suddenly by five pounds per square inch. Anne Abbott was one of those exceedingly rare plain girls whose smiles completely transform them, as abruptly as the bursting of a star-shell. When she wore her normal, rather sullen expression, no one would ever notice her—but a man who had seen her smile might well be willing to kill himself working to make her smile again, as often as possible. A woman who was beautiful all the time, Paige thought, probably never could know the devotion Anne Abbott would be given, when she found that man.

"Thank you," Paige said, rather inadequately. "Let's order, and then I'd like to hear you talk. I dumped the Story of My Life into your lap rather early in the game, I'm afraid."

"You order," she said. "You talked about seafood this afternoon, so you must know the menu here—and you handed me out of the Caddy so nicely that I'd like to preserve the illusion."

"Illusion?"

"Don't make me explain," she said, colouring faintly. "But. . . . Well, the illusion of there being one or two cavaliers in the world still. Since you haven't been a surplus woman on a planet full of lazy males, you wouldn't understand the value of a small courtesy or two. Most men I meet want to be shown my garters before they'll bother to learn my last name."

Paige's surprised shout of laughter made heads turn all over the restaurant. He throttled it hurriedly, afraid that it would embarrass the girl, but she was smiling again, making him feel instead as though he had just had three whiskies in quick succession.

"That's a quick transformation for me," he said. "This afternoon I was a blackmailer, and by my own intention, too. Very well, then, let's have the flounder; it's a speciality of the house. I had visions of it, while I was on Ganymede munching my concentrates."

"I think you had the right idea about Pfitzner," Anne said slowly when the waiter had gone. "I can't tell you any secrets about it, but maybe I can tell you some bits of common knowledge that you evidently don't know. The project the plant is working on now seems to me to fit your description exactly: it's humanitarian, impersonal, and just about as long-range as any project I can imagine. I feel rather religious about it, in your sense. It's something to tie to, and it's better for me than being a Witness or a WAC. And I think you could understand why I feel that way—better than either Tru Gunn or I thought you could."

It was his turn to be embarrassed. He covered by dosing his Blue Points with Worcestershire until they flinched visibly. "I'd like to know."

"It goes like this," she said. "In between 1940 and

53

1960, a big change took place in Western medicine. Before 1940—in the early part of the century—the infectious diseases were major killers. By 1960 they were all but knocked out of the running. The change started with the sulfa drugs; then came Fleming and Florey and mass production of penicillin during World War II. After that war we found a whole arsenal of new drugs against tuberculosis, which had really never been treated successfully before—streptomycin, PAS, isoniazid, viomycin, and so on, right up to Bloch's isolation of the TB toxins and the development of the metabolic blocking agents.

"Then came the broad-spectrum antibiotics, like terramycin, which attacked some virus diseases, protozoan diseases, even worm diseases; that gave us a huge clue to a whole set of tough problems. The last major infectious disease—bilharzia, or schistosomiasis—was reduced to the status of a nuisance by 1966."

"But we still have infectious diseases," Paige objected.

"Of course we do," the girl said, the little atom-points in her brooch picking up the candle-light as she leaned forward. "No drug ever wipes out a disease, because it's impossible to kill all the dangerous organisms in the world just by treating the patients they invade. But you can reduce the danger. In the 1950s, for instance, malaria was the world's greatest killer. Now it's as rare as diphtheria. We still have both diseases with us—but how long has it been since you heard of a case of either?"

"You're asking the wrong man—germ diseases aren't common on space vessels. But you win the point, all the same. Go on. What happened then?"

"Something kind of ominous. Life insurance companies, and other people who kept records, began to be

54

alarmed at the way the degenerative diseases were coming to the fore. Those are such ailments as hardening of the arteries, coronary heart disease, embolisms, and almost all the many forms of cancer—diseases where one or another body mechanism suddenly goes haywire, without any visible cause."

"Isn't old age the cause?"

"*No*," the girl said forcefully. "Old age is just the *age*; it's not a thing in itself, it's just the time of life when most degenerative diseases strike. Some of them prefer children—leukemia, for instance. When the actuaries first began to notice that the degenerative diseases were on the rise, they thought that it was just a sort of side-effect of the decline of the infectious diseases. They thought that cancer was increasing because more people were living long enough to come down with it. Also, the reporting of the degenerative diseases was improving, and so part of the rise in incidence really was an illusion—it just meant that more cases than before were being detected.

"But that wasn't all there was to it. Lung cancer and stomach cancer in particular continued to creep up the statistical tables, far beyond the point which could have been accounted for by better reporting, or by the increase in the average life-span, either. Then the same thing took place in malignant hypertension, in Parkinsonism and other failures of the central nervous system, in muscular dystrophy, and so on, and so on. It began to look very much as though we'd exchanged a devil we knew for a devil we didn't.

"So there was quite a long search for a possible infectious origin for each of the degenerative diseases. Because some animal tumours, like poultry sarcoma, are caused by viruses, a lot of people set to work hunt-

55

ing like mad for all kinds of cancer viruses. There was a concerted attempt to implicate a group called the pleuropneumonia-like organisms as the cause of the arthritic diseases. The vascular diseases, like hypertension and thrombosis, got blamed on everything from your diet to your grandmother.

"And it all came to very little. Oh, we did find that *some* viruses did cause *some* types of cancer, leukemia among them. The PPLO group does cause *a* type of arthritis, too, but only the type associated with a venereal disease called essential urethritis. And we found that the commonest of the three types of lung cancer was being caused by the radio-potassium content of tobacco smoke; it was the lip and mouth cancers that were caused by the tars. But for the most part, we found out just what we had known before—that the degenerative diseases weren't infectious. We'd already been down *that* dead end.

"About there was when Pfitzner got into the picture. The NHS, the National Health Service, got alarmed enough about the rising incidence-curves to call the first really major world congress on the degenerative diseases. The U.S. paid part of the bill because the armed services were getting nervous about the rising rate of draft rejections they were being forced to return. It doesn't seem unusual now that 10 per cent of a given class of men in their twenties should be rejected for what we still call 'diseases of old age', but in those days it was shocking."

"It shocks me right now," Paige admitted.

"Only because it's new to you, I'm afraid. It's old stuff to the armed services' medical departments now. Anyhow, the result of the congress was that the U.S. Department of Health, Welfare and Security somehow got a billion-dollar appropriation for a real mass attack on the degenerative diseases. In case you drop zeros as easily as I do, that was about half what had been spent to produce the first atomic bomb. Since then, the appropriation has been added to once, and it's due for renewal again now.

"Pfitzner holds the major contract on that project, and we're well enough staffed and equipped to handle it so that we've had to do very little sub-contracting. We simply share the appropriation with three other producers of biologicals, two of whom are producers only and so have no hand in the research; the third firm has done as much research as we have, but we know—because this is supposed to be a co-ordinated effort with sharing of knowledge among the contractors—that they're far gone down another blind alley. We would have told them so, but after one look at what *we'd* found, the government decided that the fewer people who knew about it, the better. We didn't mind; after all, we're in business to make a profit, too. But that's one reason why you saw so many government people on our necks this afternoon."

The girl broke off abruptly and delved into her pocket-book, producing a flat compact which she opened and inspected intently. Since she wore almost no make-up, it was hard to imagine the reason for the sudden examination; but after a brief, odd smile at one corner of her mouth, she tucked the compact away again.

"The other reason," she said "is even simpler, now that you have the background. *We've just found what we think may be a major key to the whole problem.*"

"Wow," Paige said, inelegantly but *affetuoso*.

"Or zowie, or biff-bam-krunk," Anne agreed calmly,

"or maybe God-help-us-every-one. But so far the thing's held up. It's passed every test. If it keeps up that performance, Pfitzner will get the whole of the new appropriation—and if it doesn't, there may not be any appropriation at all, not only for Pfitzner, but for the other firms that have been helping on the project.

"The whole question of whether or not we lick the degenerative diseases hangs on those two things: the validity of the solution we've found, and the money. If one goes, the other goes. And we'll have to tell Horsefield and MacHinery and the others what we've found some time this month, because the old appropriation lapses after that."

The girl leaned back and seemed to notice for the first time that she had finished her dinner. "And that," she said, pushing regretfully at the sprig of parsley with her fork, "isn't exactly public knowledge yet! I think I'd better shut up."

"Thank you," Paige said gravely. "It's obviously more than I deserve to know."

"Well," Anne said, "you can tell *me* something, if you will. It's about this Bridge that's being built on Jupiter. Is it worth all the money that they're pouring into it? Nobody seems to be able to explain what it's good for. And now there's talk that another Bridge'll be started on Saturn, when this one's finished!"

"You needn't worry," Paige said. "Understand, I've no connection with the Bridge, though I do know some people on the Bridge gang, so I haven't any inside information. I do have some public knowledge, just like yours—meaning knowledge that anyone can have, if he has the training to know where to look for it. As I understand it, the Bridge on Jupiter is a research project, designed to answer some questions—just what questions, nobody's bothered to tell me, and I've been careful not to ask; you can see Francis X. MacHinery's face in the constellations if you look carefully enough. But this much I know: the conditions of the research demand the use of the largest planet in the system. That's Jupiter, so it would be senseless to build another Bridge on a smaller planet, like Saturn. The Bridge gang will keep the present structure going until they've found out what they want to know. Then the project will almost surely be discontinued—not because the Bridge is 'finished', but because it will have served its purpose."

"I suppose I'm showing my ignorance," Anne said, "but it sounds idiotic to me. All those millions and millions of dollars—that *we* could be saving lives with!"

"If the choice were mine," Paige agreed, "I'd award the money to you, not to Charity Dillon and his crew. But then, I know almost as little about the Bridge as you do, so perhaps it's just as well that I'm not allowed to route the check. Is it my turn to ask a question? I still have a small one."

"Your witness," Anne said, smiling her altogether lovely smile.

"This afternoon, while I was in the labs, I twice heard a baby crying—and I think it was actually two different babies. I asked your Mr. Gunn about it, and he told me an obvious fairy-story." He paused. Anne's eyes had already begun to glitter.

"You're on dangerous ground, Colonel Russell," she said.

"I can tell. But I mean to ask my question anyhow. When I pulled my absurd vivisection threat on you later, I was out-and-out flabbergasted that it worked, but it set me to thinking. Can you explain—and if so, would you?"

59

Anne got out her compact again and seemed to consult it, warily. At last she said: "I suppose I've forgiven you, more or less. Anyhow, I'll answer. It's very simple: the babies *are* being used as experimental animals. We have a pipeline to the local foundling home. It's all only technically legal, and had you actually brought charges of human vivisection against us, you probably could have made them stick."

His coffee cup clattered into its saucer. "Great God, Anne. Isn't it dangerous to make such a joke these days —especially with a man you've known only half a day? Or are you trying to startle me into admitting I'm a stoolie?"

"I'm not joking and I don't think you're a stoolie," she said calmly. "What I said was perfectly true—oh, I souped up the way I put it just a little, maybe because I haven't *entirely* forgiven you for that bit of successful blackmail, and I wanted to see you jump. And for other reasons. But it's true."

"But Anne—why?"

"Look, Paige," she said. "It was fifty years ago that we found that if we added minute amounts of certain antibiotics, really just traces, to animal feeds, the addition brought the critters to market months ahead of normally-fed animals. For that matter, it even provokes growth spurts in plants under special conditions; and it works for poultry, piglets, calves, mink cubs, a whole spectrum of animals. It was logical to suspect that it might work in newborn humans, too."

"And you're trying that?" Paige leaned back and poured himself another glass of Chilean Rhine. "I'd say you souped up your revelation quite a bit, all right."

"Don't be so ready to accept the obvious, and listen to me. We are *not* doing that. It was done decades ago,

60

regularly and above the board, by students of Paul György and half a hundred other nutrition experts. Those people used only very widely known and tested antibiotics, drugs that had already been used on literally millions of farm animals, dosages worked out to the milligram of drug per kilogram of body weight, and so on. But this particular growth-stimulating effect of antibiotics happens to be a major clue to whether or not a given drug has the kind of biological activity *we* want— and we have to know whether or not it shows that activity *in human beings*. So we screen new drugs on the kids, as fast as they're found and pass certain other tests. We have to."

"I see," Paige said. "I see."

"The children are 'volunteered' by the foundling home, and we could make a show of legality if it came to a court fight," Anne said. "The precedent was established in 1952, when Pearl River Labs used children of its own workers to test its polio vaccine—which worked, by the way. But it isn't the legality of it that's important. It's the question of how soon and how thoroughly we're going to lick the degenerative diseases."

"You seem to be defending it to me," Paige said slowly, "as though you cared what I thought about it. So I'll tell you what I think: it seems mighty damned cold-blooded to me. It's the kind of thing of which ugly myths are made. If ten years from now there's a pogrom against biologists because people think they eat babies, I'll know why."

"Nonsense," Anne said. "It takes centuries to build up that kind of myth. You're over-reacting."

"On the contrary. I'm being as honest with you as you were with me. I'm astonished and somewhat repelled by what you've told me. That's all."

61

The girl, her lips slightly thinned, dipped and dried her fingertips and began to draw on her gloves. "Then we'll say no more about it," she said. "I think we'd better leave now."

"Certainly, as soon as I pay the check. Which reminds me: do you have any interest in Pfitzner, Anne—a personal interest, I mean?"

"No. No more interest than any human being with a moment's understanding of the implications would have. And I think that's a rather ugly sort of question."

"I thought you might take it that way, but I really wasn't accusing you of being a profiteer. I just wondered whether or not you were related to the Dr. Abbott that Gunn and the rest were waiting for this afternoon."

She got out the compact again and looked carefully into it. "Abbott's a common enough name."

"Sure. Still, *some* Abbotts are related. And it seems to make sense."

"Let's hear you do that. I'd be interested."

"All right," he said, beginning to become angry himself. "The receptionist at Pfitzner, ideally, should know exactly what is going on in the plant at all times, so as to be able to assess accurately the intentions of every visitor—just as you did with me. But at the same time, she has to be an absolutely flawless security risk, or otherwise she couldn't be trusted with enough knowledge to be that kind of a receptionist. The best way to make sure of the security angle is to hire someone with a blood tie to another person on the project. That adds up to *two* people who are being careful. A classical Soviet form of blackmail, as I recall.

"That much is theory. There's fact, too. You certainly explained the Pfitzner project to me this evening from a broad base of knowledge that nobody could expect to find in an ordinary receptionist. On top of that, you took policy risks that, properly, only an officer of Pfitzner should be empowered to take. I conclude that you're not *only* a receptionist; your name is Abbott; and . . . there we have it, it seems to me."

"Do we?" the girl said, standing abruptly in a white fury. "Not quite! Also, I'm not pretty, and a receptionist for a firm as big as Pfitzner is usually pretty striking. Striking enough to resist being pumped by the first man to notice her, at least. Go ahead, complete the list! Tell the whole truth!"

"How can I?" Paige said, rising also and looking squarely at her, his fingers closing slowly. "If I told you honestly just what I think of your looks—and by God I will, I think the most beautiful woman in the world would bathe every day in fuming nitric acid just to duplicate your smile—you'd hate me more than ever. You'd think I was mocking you. Now you tell me the rest of the truth. You *are* related to Dr. Abbott."

"Patly enough," the girl said, each word cut out of smoking-dry ice, "Dr. Abbott is my father. And I insist upon being allowed to go home now, Colonel Russell. Not ten seconds from now, but *now*."

The Bridge vanished. Helmuth set the heavy helmet carefully in its niche and felt of his temples, feeling the blood passing under his fingertips. Then he turned.

Dillon was looking at him.

"Well?" the civil engineer said. "What's the matter, Bob? Is it bad——?"

Helmuth did not reply for a moment. The abrupt transition from the storm-ravaged deck of the Bridge to the quiet, placid air of the operations shack on Jupiter's fifth moon was always a shock. He had never been able to anticipate it, let alone become accustomed to it; it was worse each time, not better.

He pulled the jacks from the foreman's board and let them flick back into the desk on their alive, elastic cables, and then got up from the bucket seat, moving carefully upon shaky legs, feeling implicit in his own body the enormous weights and pressures his guiding intelligence had just quitted. The fact that the gravity on the foreman's deck was as weak as that of most of the habitable asteroids only made the contrast greater, and his need for caution in walking more extreme.

He went to the big porthole and looked out. The unworn, tumbled, monotonous surface of airless Jupiter V looked almost homey after the perpetual holocaust of Jupiter itself. But there was an overpowering reminder of that holocaust—for through the thick quartz of the porthole, the face of the giant planet stared at Helmuth, across only 112,600 miles, less than half the distance between Earth's moon and Earth; a sphere-section occupying almost all of the sky, except the near horizon, where one could see a few first-magnitude stars. The rest of the sky was crawling with colour, striped and blotched with the eternal, frigid, poisonous storming of Jupiter's atmosphere, spotted with the deep-black, planet-sized shadows of moons closer to the sun than Jupiter V.

Somewhere down there, six thousand miles below the clouds that boiled in Helmuth's face, was the Bridge. The Bridge was thirty miles high and eleven miles wide and fifty-four miles long—but it was only a sliver, an intricate and fragile arrangement of ice-crystals beneath the bulging, racing tornadoes.

On Earth, even in the West, the Bridge would have been the mightiest engineering achievement of all history, could the Earth have borne its weight at all. But on Jupiter, the Bridge was as precarious and perishable as a snowflake.

"Bob?" Dillon's voice asked. "What is it? You seem more upset than usual. Is it serious?"

Helmuth looked up. His superior's worn young face, lantern-jawed and crowned by black hair already beginning to grey at the temples, was alight both with love for the Bridge and with the consuming ardour of the responsibility he had to bear. As always, it touched Helmuth, and reminded him that the implacable universe had, after all, provided one warm corner in which human beings might huddle together.

"Serious enough," he said, forming the words with difficulty against the frozen inarticulateness Jupiter had forced upon him. "But not fatal, as far as I could see. There's a lot of hydrogen vulcanism on the surface, especially at the north-west end, and it looks like there must have been a big blast under the cliffs. I saw what looked like the last of a series of fire-falls."

Dillon's face relaxed while Helmuth was talking, slowly, line by engraved line. "Oh. It was just a flying chunk, then."

"I'm almost sure that was what it was. The cross-draughts are heavy now. The Spot and the STD are due to pass each other some time next month, aren't they? I haven't checked, but I can feel the difference in the storms."

"So the chunk got picked up and thrown through the end of the Bridge. A big piece?"

Helmuth shrugged. "That end is all twisted away to the left, and the deck is burst into matchwood. The scaffolding is all gone, too, of course. A pretty big piece, all right, Charity—two miles through at a minimum."

Dillon sighed. He, too, went to the window, and looked out. Helmuth did not need to be a mind reader to know what he was looking at. Out there, across the stony waste of Jupiter V plus 112,600 miles of space, the South Tropical Disturbance was streaming toward the Great Red Spot, and would soon overtake it. When the whirling funnel of the STD—more than big enough to suck three Earths into deep-freeze—passed the planetary island of sodium-tainted ice which was the Red Spot, the Spot would follow it for a few thousand miles, at the same time rising closer to the surface of the atmosphere.

Then the Spot would sink again, drifting back toward the incredible jet of stress-fluid which kept it in being— a jet fed by no one knew what forces at Jupiter's hot, rocky, 22,000-mile core, compacted down there under

66

16,000 miles of eternal ice. During the entire passage, the storms all over Jupiter became especially violent; and the Bridge had been forced to locate in anything but the calmest spot on the planet, thanks to the uneven distribution of the few "permanent" land-masses.

But—"permanent"? The quote-marks Helmuth's thinking always put around that word were there for a very good reason, he knew, but he could not quite remember the reason. It was the damned conditioning showing itself again, creating another of the thousand small irreconcilables which contributed to the tension.

Helmuth watched Dillon with a certain compassion, tempered with mild envy. Charity Dillon's unfortunate given name betrayed him as the son of a hangover, the only male child of a Witness family which dated back long before the current resurgence of the Witnesses. He was one of the hundreds of government-drafted experts who had planned the Bridge, and he was as obsessed by the Bridge as Helmuth was—but for different reasons. It was widely believed among the Bridge gang that Dillon, alone among them, had not been given the conditioning, but there was no way to test that.

Helmuth moved back to the port, dropping his hand gently on Dillon's shoulder. Together they looked at the screaming straw yellows, brick reds, pinks, oranges, browns, even blues and greens that Jupiter threw across the ruined stone of its innermost satellite. On Jupiter V, even the shadows had colour.

Dillon did not move. He said at last: "Are you pleased, Bob?"

"Pleased?" Helmuth said in astonishment. "No. It scares me white; you know that. I'm just glad that the whole Bridge didn't go."

"You're quite sure?" Dillon said quietly.

Helmuth took his hand from Dillon's shoulder and returned to his seat at the central desk. "You've no right to needle me for something I can't help," he said, his voice even lower than Dillon's. "I work on Jupiter four hours a day—not actually, because we can't keep a man alive for more than a split second down there— but my eyes and my ears and my mind are there, on the Bridge, four hours a day. Jupiter is not a nice place. I don't like it. I won't pretend I do.

"Spending four hours a day in an environment like that over a period of years—well, the human mind instinctively tries to adapt, even to the unthinkable. Sometimes I wonder how I'll behave when I'm put back in Chicago again. Sometimes I can't remember anything about Chicago except vague generalities, sometimes I can't even believe there is such a place as Earth —how could there be, when the rest of the universe is like Jupiter, or worse?"

"I know," Dillon said. "I've tried several times to show you that isn't a very reasonable frame of mind."

"I know it isn't. But I can't help how I feel. For all I know it isn't even my own frame of mind—though the part of my mind that keeps saying 'The Bridge *must* stand' is more likely to be the conditioned part. No, I don't think the Bridge will last. It can't last; it's all wrong. But I don't *want* to see it go. I've just got sense enough to know that one of these days Jupiter is going to sweep it away."

He wiped an open palm across the control boards, snapping all the toggles to "Off" with a sound like the fall of a double-handful of marbles on a pane of glass. "Like that, Charity! And I work four hours a day, every day, on the Bridge. One of these days, Jupiter is going to destroy the Bridge. It'll go flying away in little flinders, into the storms. My mind will be there, supervising some puny job, and my mind will go flying away along with my mechanical eyes and ears and hands—still trying to adapt to the unthinkable, tumbling away into the winds and the flames and the rains and the darkness and the pressure and the cold——"

"Bob, you're deliberately running away with yourself. Cut it out. Cut it out, I say!"

Helmuth shrugged, putting a trembling hand on the edge of the board to steady himself. "All right. I'm all right, Charity. I'm here, aren't I? Right here on Jupiter V, in no danger, in no danger at all. The Bridge is one hundred and twelve thousand six hundred miles away from here, and I'll never be an inch closer to it. But when the day comes that the Bridge is swept away——

"Charity, sometimes I imagine you ferrying my body back to the cosy nook it came from, while my soul goes tumbling and tumbling through millions of cubic miles of poison. . . . All right, Charity, I'll be good. I won't think about it out loud, but you can't expect me to forget it. It's on my mind; I can't help it, and you should know that."

"I do," Dillon said, with a kind of eagerness. "I do, Bob. I'm only trying to help, to make you see the problem as it is. The Bridge isn't really that awful, it isn't worth a single nightmare."

"Oh, it isn't the Bridge that makes me yell out when I'm sleeping," Helmuth said, smiling bitterly. "I'm not that ridden by it yet. It's while I'm awake that I'm afraid the Bridge will be swept away. What I sleep with is a fear of myself."

"That's a sane fear. You're as sane as any of us," Dillon insisted, fiercely solemn. "Look, Bob. The Bridge isn't a monster. It's a way we've developed for studying the behaviour of materials under specific conditions of pressure, temperature and gravity. Jupiter isn't Hell, either; it's a set of conditions. The Bridge is the laboratory we set up to work with those conditions."

"It isn't going anywhere. It's a bridge to noplace."

"There aren't many *places* on Jupiter," Dillon said, missing Helmuth's meaning entirely. "We put the Bridge on an island in the local sea because we needed solid ice we could sink the foundation in. Otherwise, it wouldn't have mattered where we put it. We could have floated the caissons on the sea itself, if we hadn't wanted a fixed point from which to measure storm velocities and such things."

"I know that," Helmuth said.

"But Bob, you don't show any signs of understanding it. Why, for instance, should the Bridge *go* any place? It isn't even, properly speaking, a bridge at all. We only call it that because we used some bridge engineering principles in building it. Actually, it's much more like a travelling crane—an extremely heavy-duty overhead rail line. It isn't going anywhere because it hasn't any place interesting to go to, that's all. We're extending it to cover as much territory as possible, and to increase its stability, not to span the distance between places. There's no point to reproaching it because it doesn't span a real gap—between, say, Dover and Calais. It's a bridge to knowledge, and that's far more important. Why can't you see that?"

"I can see that; that's what I was talking about," Helmuth said, trying to control his impatience. "I have at least as much common sense as the average child. What I was trying to point out is that meeting colossalness with colossalness—out here—is a mug's game. It's a game Jupiter will always win, without the

70

slightest effort. What if the engineers who built the Dover-Calais bridge had been limited to broom-straws for their structural members? They could have got the bridge up somehow, sure, and made it strong enough to carry light traffic on a fair day. But what would you have had left of it after the first winter storm came down the Channel from the North Sea? The whole approach is idiotic!"

"All right," Dillon said reasonably. "You have a point. Now you're being reasonable. What better approach have you to suggest? Should we abandon Jupiter entirely because it's too big for us?"

"No," Helmuth said. "Or maybe, yes. I don't know. I don't have any easy answer. I just know that this one is no answer at all—it's just a cumbersome evasion."

Dillon smiled. "You're depressed, and no wonder. Sleep it off, Bob, if you can—you might even come up with that answer. In the meantime—well, when you stop to think about it, the surface of Jupiter isn't any more hostile, inherently, than the surface of Jupiter V, except in degree. If you stepped out of this building naked, you'd die just as fast as you would on Jupiter. Try to look at it that way."

Helmuth, looking forward into another night of dreams, said: "That's the way I look at it now."

BOOK TWO

★

INTERMEZZO

The report of the investigating sub-committee of the Senate Finance Committee on the Jupiter Project was a massive document, especially so in the mimeographed, uncorrected form in which it had been rushed to Wagoner's desk. In its printed form—not due for another two weeks—the report would be considerably less bulky, but it would probably be more unreadable. In addition, it would be tempered in spots by the cautious second thoughts of its seven authors; Wagoner needed to see their opinions in the raw or "for colleagues only" version.

Not that the printed version would get a much wider circulation. Even the mimeographed document was stamped "Top Secret". It had been years since anything about the government's security system had amused Wagoner in the slightest, but he could not repress a wry grin now. Of course the Bridge itself was Top Secret; but had the sub-committee's report been ready only a little over a year ago, everybody in the country would have heard about it, and selected passages would have been printed in the newspapers. He could think offhand of at least ten opposition senators, and two or three more inside his own party, who had been determined to use the report to prevent his re-election—or any parts of the report that might have been turned to that purpose. Unhappily for them, the report had been still only a third finished when election day had come, and Alaska had sent Wagoner back to Washington by a very comfortable plurality.

And, as he turned the stiff legal-length pages slowly, with the pleasant smoky odour of duplicator ink rising from them as he turned, it became clear that the report would have made pretty poor campaign material anyhow. Much of it was highly technical, and had obviously been written by staff advisers, not by the investigating senators themselves. The public might be impressed by, but it could not read and would not read, such a show of erudition. Besides, it was only a show; nearly all the technical discussions of the Bridge's problems petered out into meaningless generalities. In most such instances Wagoner was able to put a mental finger on the missing fact, the ignorance or the withholding of which had left the chain of reasoning suspended in mid-air.

Against the actual operation of the Bridge the senators had been able to find nothing of substance to say. Given in advance the fact that the taxpayers had wanted to spend so much money to build a Bridge on Jupiter—which is to say, somebody (Wagoner himself) had decided that for them, without confusing them by bringing the proposition to their attention—then even the opposition senators had had to agree that it had been built as economically as possible, and was still being built that way.

Of course, there had been small grafts waiting to be discovered, and the investigators had discovered them. One of the supply-ship captains had been selling cakes of soap to the crew on Ganymede at incredible prices, with the co-operation of the stores clerk there. But that was nothing more than a book-keeper's crime, on a project the size of the Bridge. Wagoner a little admired the supply-ship captain's ingenuity—or had it been the stores clerk's?—in discovering an item wanted badly enough on Ganymede, and small enough, and light enough, to be worth smuggling. The men on the Bridge gang banked most of their salaries automatically on Earth without ever seeing them; there was very little worth buying, or selling, on the moons of Jupiter.

Of major graft, however, there had been no trace. No steel company had sold the Bridge any sub-standard castings, because there was no steel in the Bridge. A Jovian might have made a good thing of selling the Bridge sub-standard Ice IV—but as far as anyone could know there were no Jovians, so the Bridge got its Ice IV for nothing but the cost of cutting it. Wagoner's office had been very strict about the handling of the lesser contracts—for prefabricated moon huts, for supply ferry fuel, for equipment—and had policed not only its own deals, but all the Army Space Service sub-contracts connected with the Bridge.

As for Charity Dillon and his foremen, they were rigidly efficient—partly because it was in their natures to work that way, and partly because of the intensive conditioning they had all been given before being shipped to the Jovian system. There was no waste to be found in anything that they supervised, and if they had occasionally been guilty of bad engineering judgment, no outside engineer would be likely to detect it. The engineering principles by which the Bridge operated did not hold true anywhere but on Jupiter.

The hugest loss of money the whole Jupiter Project had yet sustained had been accompanied by such carnage that it fell—in the senators' minds—in the category of warfare. When a soldier is killed by enemy action, nobody asks how much money his death cost the government through the loss of his gear. The part of the report which described the placing of the Bridge's foundation mentioned reverently the heroism of the lost two hundred and thirty-one crewmen; it said nothing about the cost of the nine specially-designed space tugs which now floated in silhouette, as flat as so many tin cut-outs under six million pounds per square inch of pressure, somewhere at the bottom of Jupiter's atmosphere— floated with eight thousand vertical miles of eternally roaring poisons between them and the eyes of the living.

Had those crewmen been heroes? They had been enlisted men and officers of the Army Space Service, acting under orders. While doing what they had been ordered to do, they had been killed. Wagoner could not remember whether or not the survivors of that operation had also been called heroes. Oh, they had certainly been decorated—the Army liked its men to wear as much fruit salad on their chests as it could possibly spoon out to them, because it was good public relations —but they were not mentioned in the report.

This much was certain: the dead men had died because of Wagoner. He had known, generally at least, that many of them would die, but he had gone ahead anyhow. He knew now that there might be worse to come. Nevertheless, he would proceed, because he thought that—in the long run—it would be worth it. He knew well enough that the end cannot justify the means; but if there are *no* other means, and the end is necessary. . . .

But from time to time he thought of Dostoievski, and the Grand Inquisitor. Would the Millennium be worth having, if it could be ushered in only by the torturing to death of a single child? What Wagoner foresaw and planned for was by no means the Millennium; and while the children at Jno. Pfitzner & Sons were certainly not being tortured or even harmed, their experiences there were at least not normal for children. And there were two hundred and thirty-one men frozen solid somewhere in the bottomless hell of Jupiter, men who had had to obey their orders even more helplessly than children.

Wagoner had not been cut out to be a general.

The report praised the lost men's heroism. Wagoner lifted the heavy pages one after another, looking for a word from the investigating senators about the cause those deaths had served. There was nothing there—nothing but the conventional phrases, "for their country", "for the cause of peace", "for the future". High-order abstractions—blabs. The senators had no notion of what the Bridge was for. They had looked, but they hadn't seen. Even with a total of four years to think back on the experience, they hadn't seen. The very size of the Bridge evidently had convinced them that it was a form of weapons research—so much for "for the cause of peace"—and that it would be better for them not to know the nature of the weapon until an official announcement was circulated to them.

They were right. The Bridge was assuredly a weapon. But in neglecting to wonder what kind of a weapon it might be, the senators had also neglected to wonder at whom it was pointed. Wagoner was glad that they had.

The report did not even touch upon those two years of exploration, of search for some project which might be worth attacking, which had preceded even the notion of the Bridge. Wagoner had had a special staff of four devoted men at work during every minute of those

79

two years, checking patents that had been granted but not sequestered, published scientific papers containing suggestions other scientists had decided not to explore, articles in the lay press about incipient miracles which hadn't come off, science-fiction stories by practising scientists, anything and everything that might lead somewhere. The four men had worked under orders to avoid telling anybody what they were looking for, and to stay strictly away from the main currents of modern scientific thought on the subject; but no secret is ever truly safe; no fact in nature is ever truly a secret.

Somewhere, for instance, in the files of the FBI, was a tape recording of the conversation he had had with the chief of the four-man team, in his office, the day the break came. The man had said, not only to Wagoner, but to the attentive FBI microphones no senator dared to seek out and muffle: "This looks like a real line, Bliss. On Subject G." (Something on gravity, chief.)

"Keep it to the point." (A reminder: Keep it too technical to interest a casual eavesdropper—if you *have* to talk about it here, with all these bugs to pick it up.)

"Sure. It's a thing called the Blackett equation. Deals with a possible relationship between electron-spin and magnetic moment. I understand Dirac did some work on that, too. There's a G in the equation, and with one simple algebraic manipulation you can isolate the G on one side of the equals-sign, and all the other elements on the other." (Not a crackpot notion this time. Real scientists have been interested in it. There's math to go with it.)

"Status?" (Why was it never followed, then?)

"The original equation is about status seven, but there's no way anybody knows that it could be subjected to an operational test. The manipulated equation is called the Locke Derivation, and our boys say that a little dimensional analysis will show that it's wrong; but they're not entirely sure. However, it *is* subject to an operational test if we want to pay for it, where the original Blackett formula isn't." (Nobody's sure what it means yet. It may mean nothing. It would cost a hell of a lot to find out.)

"Do we have the facilities?" (Just how much?)

"Only the beginnings." (About four billion dollars, Bliss.)

"Conservatively?" (Why so much?)

"Yes. Field strength again."

(That was shorthand for the only problem that mattered, in the long run, if you wanted to work with gravity. Whether you thought of it, like Newton, as a force, or like Faraday as a field, or like Einstein as a condition in space, gravity was incredibly weak. It was so weak that, although theoretically it was a property of every bit of matter in the universe no matter how small, it could not be worked with in the laboratory. Two magnetized needles will rush toward each other over a distance as great as an inch; so will two balls of pith as small as peas if they bear opposite electrical charges. Two ceramet magnets no bigger than doughnuts can be so strongly charged that it is impossible to push them together by hand when their like poles are opposed, and impossible for a strong man to hold them apart when their unlike poles approach each other. Two spheres of metal of any size, if they bear opposite electrical charges, will mate in a fat spark across the insulating air, if there is no other way that they can neutralize each other.

(But gravity—theoretically one in kind with electricity and magnetism—cannot be charged on to any object. It produces no sparks. There is no such thing as an insulation against it—a di-gravitic. It remains beyond detection as a force, between bodies as small as peas or doughnuts. Two objects as huge as skyscrapers and as massive as lead will take centuries to crawl into the same bed over a foot of distance, if nothing but their mutual gravitational attraction is drawing them together; even love is faster than that. Even a ball of rock eight thousand miles in diameter—the Earth—has a gravitational field too weak to prevent one single man from pole-vaulting away from it to more than four times his own height, driven by no opposing force but that of his spasming muscles.)

"Well, give me a report when you can. If necessary, we can expand." (Is it worth it?)

"I'll give you the report this week." (*Yes!*)

And that was how the Bridge had been born, though nobody had known it then, not even Wagoner. The senators who had investigated the Bridge still didn't know it. MacHinery's staff at the FBI evidently had been unable to penetrate the jargon on their recording of that conversation far enough to connect the conversation with the Bridge; otherwise MacHinery would have given the transcript to the investigators. Mac-Hinery did not exactly love Wagoner; he had been unable thus far to find any handle by which he might grasp and use the Alaskan senator.

All well and good.

And yet the investigators *had* come perilously close, just once. They had subpoenaed Guiseppi Corsi for the preliminary questioning.

Committee Counsel: Now then, Dr. Corsi, according to our records, your last interview with Senator Wagoner was in the winter of 2013. Did you discuss the Jupiter Project with him at that time?

Corsi: How could I have? It didn't exist then.

Counsel: But was it mentioned to you in any way? Did Senator Wagoner say anything about plans to start such a project?

Corsi: No.

Counsel: You didn't yourself suggest it to Senator Wagoner?

Corsi: Certainly not. It was a total surprise to me, when it was announced afterwards.

Counsel: But I suppose you know what it is.

Corsi: I know only what the general public has been told. We're building a Bridge on Jupiter. It's very costly and ambitious. What it's for is a secret. That's all.

Counsel: You're sure you don't know what it's for?

Corsi: For research.

Counsel: Yes, but research for what? Surely you have some clues.

Corsi: I don't have any clues, and Senator Wagoner didn't give me any. The only facts I have are those I read in the press. Naturally I have some conjectures. But all I *know* is what is indicated, or hinted at, in the official announcements. Those seem to convey the impression that the Bridge is for weapons research.

Counsel: But you think that maybe it isn't?

Corsi: I—I'm not in a position to discuss government projects about which I know nothing.

Counsel: You could give us your opinion.

Corsi: If you want my opinion as an expert, I'll have my office go into the subject and let you know later what such an opinion would cost.

Senator Billings: Dr. Corsi, do we understand that you refuse to answer the question? It seems to me that in view of your past record you might be better advised——

Corsi: I haven't refused to answer, senator. I make part of my living by consultation. If the government wishes to use me in that capacity, it's my right to ask to be paid. You have no right to deprive me of my livelihood, or any part of it.

Senator Croft: The government made up its mind about employing you some time back, Dr. Corsi. And rightly, in my opinion.

Corsi: That is the government's privilege.

Senator Croft: —but you are being questioned now by the Senate of the United States. If you refuse to answer, you may be held in contempt.

Corsi: For refusing to state an opinion?

Counsel: If you will pardon me, Senator Croft, the witness may refuse to offer an opinion—or withhold such an opinion, pending payment. He can be held in contempt only for declining to state the facts, as he knows them.

Senator Croft: All right, let's get some facts, and stop the pussyfooting.

Counsel: Dr. Corsi, was anything said during your last meeting with Senator Wagoner which might have had any bearing on the Jupiter Project?

Corsi: Well, yes. But only negatively. I did counsel him against any such project. Rather emphatically, as I recall.

Counsel: I thought you said that the Bridge hadn't been mentioned.

Corsi: It hadn't. Senator Wagoner and I were discussing research methods in general. I told him that I thought research projects of the Bridge's order of magnitude were no longer fruitful.

84

Senator Billings: Did you charge Senator Wagoner for that opinion, Dr. Corsi?

Corsi: No, senator. Sometimes I don't.

Senator Billings: Perhaps you should have. Wagoner didn't follow your free advice.

Senator Croft: It looks like he considered the source.

Corsi: There's nothing compulsory about advice. I gave him my best opinion at the time. What he did with it was up to him.

Counsel: Would you tell us if that is your best opinion now? That research projects the size of the Bridge are —I believe your phrase was, "no longer fruitful"?

Corsi: That is still my opinion.

Senator Billings: Which you give us free of charge . . . ?

Corsi: It is the opinion of every scientist I know. You could get it free from those who work for you. I have better sense than to charge fees for common knowledge.

It had been a near thing. Perhaps, Wagoner thought, Corsi had after all remembered the really crucial part of that interview, and had decided not to reveal it to the sub-committee. It was more likely, however, that those few words that Corsi had thrown off while standing at the blinded window of his apartment would not have stuck in his memory, as they had stuck in Wagoner's.

Yet surely Corsi knew, at least in part, what the Bridge was for. He must have remembered the part of that conversation which had dealt with gravity. By now he would have reasoned his way from those words all the difficult way to the Bridge—after all, the Bridge was not a difficult object for an understanding like Corsi's.

But he had said nothing about it. That had been a crucial silence.

Wagoner wondered if it would ever be possible for him to show his gratitude to the ageing physicist. Not now. Possibly never. The pain and the puzzlement in Corsi's mind stood forth in what he had said, even over the gap of years, even through the coldness of the official transcript. Wagoner badly wanted to assuage both. But he couldn't. He could only hope that Corsi would see it whole, and understand it whole, when the time came.

The page turned on Corsi. Now there was another question which had to be answered. Was there a single hint, anywhere in the sixteen hundred mimeographed pages of the report, that the Bridge was incomplete without what was going on at Jno. Pfitzner & Sons? . . .

No, there was not. Wagoner let the report fall, with a sigh of relief of which he was hardly conscious. That was that.

He filed the report, and reached into his "In" basket for the dossier on Paige Russell, Colonel, Army Space Corps, which had come in from the Pfitzner plant only a week ago. He was tired, and he did not want to perform an act of judgment on another man for the rest of his life—but he had asked for the job, and now he had to work at it.

Bliss Wagoner had not been cut out to be a general. As a god he was even more inept.

★
★ 5 ★

It took Paige no more than Anne's mandatory ten seconds, during breakfast of the next day in his snuggery at the Spaceman's Haven, to decide that he was going back to the Pfitzner plant and apologize. He didn't quite understand why the date had ended as catastrophically as it had, but of one thing he was nearly certain: the fiasco had had something to do with his space-rusty manners, and if it were to be mended, he had to be the one to tool up for it.

And now that he came to think of it over his cold egg, it seemed obvious in essence. By his last line of questioning, Paige had broken the delicate shell of the evening and spilled the contents all over the restaurant table. He had left the more or less safe womb of technicalities, and had begun, by implication at least, to call Anne's ethics into question—first by making clear his first reaction to the business about the experimental infants, and then by pressing home her irregular marriage to her firm.

In this world called Earth of disintegrating faiths, one didn't call personal ethical codes into question without getting into trouble. Such codes, where they could be found at all, obviously had cost their adherents too much pain to be open for any new probing. Faith had once been self-evident; now it was desperate. Those

87

who still had it—or had made it, chunk by fragment by shard—wanted nothing but to be allowed to hold it.

As for why he wanted to set matters right with Anne Abbott, Paige was less clear. His leave was passing him by rapidly, and thus far he had done little more than stroll while it passed—especially if he measured it against the desperate meter-stick established by his last two leaves, the two after his marriage had shattered and he had been alone again. After the present leave was over, there was a good chance that he would be assigned to the Proserpine station, which was now about finished and which had no competitors for the title of the most forsaken outpost of the solar system. None, at least, until somebody should discover an 11th planet.

Nevertheless, he was going to go out to the Pfitzner plant again, out to the scenic Bronx, to revel among research scientists, business executives, government brass, and a frozen-voiced girl with a figure like an ironing-board, to kick up his heels on a reception-room rug in the sight of gay steel engravings of the Founders, cheered on by a motto which might or might not be Dionysiac, if he could only read it. Great. Just great. If he played his cards right, he could go on duty at the Proserpine station with fine memories: perhaps the Vice-President in Charge of Export would let Paige call him "Tru", or maybe even "Bubbles".

Maybe it was a matter of religion, after all. Like everyone else in the world, Paige thought, he was still looking for something bigger than himself, bigger than family, Army, marriage, fatherhood, space itself, or the pub-crawls and tyrannically meaningless sexual spasms of a spaceman's leave. Quite obviously the project at Pfitzner, with its air of mystery and selflessness, had touched that very vulnerable nerve in him once more.

Anne Abbott's own dedication was merely the touch-stone, the key. . . . . No, he hadn't the right word for it yet, but her attitude somehow fitted into an empty, jagged-edge blemish in his own soul like—like . . . yes, that was it: like a jigsaw-puzzle piece.

And besides, he wanted to see that sunburst smile again.

Because of the way her desk was placed, she was the first thing he saw as he came into Pfitzner's reception room. Her expression was even stranger than he had expected, and she seemed to be making some kind of covert gesture, as though she were flicking dust off the top of her desk toward him with the tips of all her fingers. He took several slower and slower steps into the room and stopped, finally baffled.

Someone rose from a chair which he had not been able to see from the door, and quartered down on him. The pad of the steps on the carpet and the odd crouch of the shape in the corner of Paige's eye were unpleasantly stealthy. Paige turned, unconsciously closing his hands.

"Haven't we seen this officer before, Miss Abbott? What's his business here—or has he any?"

The man in the eager semi-crouch was Francis X. MacHinery.

Like his unforgettable grandfather, Francis X. Mac-Hinery was a beetle-browed, heavy-faced man who seemed always in need of a shave. Though he would have been easy to dismiss on first glance as a not very bright truck driver, MacHinery was as full of cunning as a wolverine, and he had managed times without number to land on his feet regardless of what political disasters had been planned for him. And he was, as Paige was now discovering, the man for whom the

89

metaphor "gimlet-eyed" had all unknowingly been invented.

"Well, Miss Abbott?"

"Colonel Russell was here yesterday," Anne said. "You may have seen him then."

The swinging doors opened and Horsefield and Gunn came in. MacHinery paid no attention to them. He said: "What's your name, soldier?"

"I'm a spaceman," Paige said stiffly. "Colonel Paige Russell, Army Space Corps."

"What are you doing here?"

"I'm on leave."

"Will you answer the question?" MacHinery said. He was, Paige noticed, not looking at Paige at all, but over his shoulder, as though he were actually paying no real heed to the conversation. "What are you doing at the Pfitzner plant?"

"I happen to be in love with Miss Abbott," Paige said sharply, to his own black and utter astonishment. "I came here to see her. We had a quarrel last night and I wanted to apologize. That's all."

Anne straightened behind her desk as though a curtain rod had been driven up her spine, turning toward Paige a pair of blindly blazing eyes and a rigidly unreadable expression. Even Gunn's mouth sagged slightly to one side; he looked first at Anne, then at Paige, as if he were abruptly uncertain that he had ever seen either of them before.

MacHinery, however, shot only one quick look at Anne, and his eyes seemed to turn into bottle-glass. "I'm not interested in your personal life," he said, in a tone which, indeed, suggested active boredom. "I will put the question another way, so that there'll be no excuse for evading it. Why did you come to the plant in the first place? What is your *business* at Pfitzner, soldier?"

Paige tried to pick his next words carefully. Actually it would hardly matter what he said, once MacHinery developed a real interest in him; an accusation from the FBI had nearly the force of law. Everything depended upon so conducting himself as to be of no interest to MacHinery to begin with—an exercise at which, fortunately up to now, Paige had had no more practice than had any other spaceman.

He said: "I brought in some soil samples from the Jovian system. Pfitzner asked me to do it, as part of their research programme."

"And you brought these samples in yesterday, you told me."

"No, I didn't tell you. But as a matter of fact I did bring them in yesterday."

"And you're still bringing them in today, I see." MacHinery jerked his chin over his shoulder toward Horsefield, whose face had frozen into complete tetany as soon as he had shown signs of realizing what was going on. "What about this, Horsefield? Is this one of your men that you haven't told me about?"

"No," Horsefield said, but putting a sort of a question-mark into the way he spoke the word, as though he did not mean to deny anything which he might later be expected to affirm. "Saw the man yesterday, I think. For the first time, to the best of my knowledge."

"I see. Would you say, General, that this man is no part of the Army's assigned complement on the project?"

"I can't say that for sure," Horsefield said, his voice sounding more positive now that he was voicing a doubt. "I'd have to consult my T.O. Perhaps he's somebody new in Alsos' group. He's not part of my staff, though—doesn't claim that he is, does he?"

"Gunn, what about this man? Did you people take him on without checking with me? Does he have security clearance?"

"Well, we did in a way, but he didn't need to be cleared," Gunn said. "He's just a field collector, hasn't any real part in the research work, no official connection. These field people are all volunteers; you know that."

MacHinery's brows were drawing closer and closer together. With only a few more of these questions, Paige knew even from the few newspapers which had reached him in space, he would have material enough for an arrest and a sensation—the kind of sensation which would pillory Pfitzner, destroy every civilian working for Pfitzner, trigger a long chain of courts martial among the military assignees, ruin the politicians who had sponsored the research, and thicken MacHinery's scrapbook of headlines about himself by at least three inches. That last outcome was the only one in which MacHinery was really interested; that the project itself would die was a side-effect which, though nearly inevitable, could hardly have interested him less.

"Excuse me, Mr. Gunn," Anne said quietly. "I don't think you're quite as familiar with Colonel Russell's status as I am. He's just come in from deep space, and his security record has been in the 'Clean and Routine' file for years; he's not one of our ordinary field collectors."

"Ah," Gunn said. "I'd forgotten, but that's quite true." Since it was both true and perfectly irrelevant, Paige could not understand why Gunn was quite so hearty about agreeing to it. Did he think Anne was stalling?

"As a matter of fact," Anne proceeded steadily,

"Colonel Russell is a planetary ecologist specializing in the satellites; he's been doing important work for us. He's quite well known in space, and has many friends on the Bridge team and elsewhere. That's correct, isn't it, Colonel Russell?"

"I know most of the Bridge gang," Paige agreed, but he barely managed to make his assent audible. What the girl was saying added up to something very like a big, black lie. And lying to MacHinery was a short cut to ruin; only MacHinery had the privilege of lying, never his witnesses.

"The samples Colonel Russell brought us yesterday contained crucial material," Anne said. "That's why I asked him to come back; we needed his advice. And if his samples turn out to be as important as they seem, they'll save the taxpayer quite a lot of money—they may help us close out the project a long time in advance of the projected closing date. If that's to be possible, Colonel Russell will have to guide the last steps of the work personally; he's the only one who knows the microflora of the Jovian satellites well enough to interpret the results."

MacHinery looked dubiously over Paige's shoulder. It was hard to tell whether or not he had heard a word. Nevertheless, it was evident that Anne had chosen her final approach with great care, for if MacHinery had any weakness at all, it was the enormous cost of his continual, overlapping investigations. Lately he had begun to be nearly as sure death on "waste in government" as he was traditionally on "subversives". He said at last:

"There's obviously something irregular here. If all that's so, why did the man say what he said in the beginning?"

"Perhaps because it's also true," Paige said sharply.

MacHinery ignored him. "We'll check the records and call anyone we need. Horsefield, let's go."

The general trailed him out, his back very stiff, after a glare at Paige which failed to be in the least convincing, and an outrageously stagey wink at Anne. The moment the outer door closed behind the two, the reception-room seemed to explode. Gunn swung on Anne with a motion astonishingly tiger-like for so mild-faced a man. Anne was already rising from behind her desk, her face twisted with fear and fury. Both of them were shouting at once.

"Now see what you've done with your damned nosiness——"

"What in the world did you want to tell MacHinery a tale like that for——"

"—even a spaceman should know better than to hang around a defence area——"

"—you know as well as I do that those Ganymede samples are trash——"

"—you've probably cost us our whole appropriation with your snooping——"

"—we've never hired a 'Clean and Routine' man since the project began——"

"—I hope you're satisfied——"

"—I would have thought you'd have better sense by now——"

"*Quiet!*" Paige shouted over them, with the authentic parade-ground blare. He had never found any use for it in deep space, but it worked now. Both of them looked at him, their mouths still incongruously half-opened, their faces white as milk. "You act like a pair of hysterical chickens, both of you! I'm sorry if I got you into trouble—but I didn't ask Anne to lie in my behalf—and I didn't ask you to go along with it, either,

Gunn! Maybe you'd best stop yelling accusations and try to think the thing through. I'll try to help, for whatever that's worth—but not if you're going to scream and weep at each other and at me!"

The girl bared her teeth at him in a real snarl, the first time he had ever seen a human being mount such an expression and mean it. She sat down, however, swiping at her patchily red cheeks with a piece of cleansing tissue. Gunn looked down at the carpet and just breathed noisily for a moment, putting the palms of his hands together solemnly before his white lips.

"I quite agree," Gunn said after a moment, as calmly as if nothing had happened. "We'll have to get to work and work fast. Anne, please tell me: why was it necessary for you to say that Colonel Russell was essential to the project? I'm not accusing you of anything, but we need to know the facts."

"I went to dinner with Colonel Russell last night," Anne said. "I was somewhat indiscreet about the project. At the end of the evening we had a quarrel which was probably overheard by at least two of MacHinery's amateur informers in the restaurant. I had to lie for my own protection, as well as Colonel Russell's."

"But you have an Eavesdropper! If you knew that you might be overheard——"

"I knew it well enough. But I lost my temper. You know how these things go."

It all came out as emotionlessly as a tape recording. Told in these terms, the incident sounded to Paige like something that had happened to someone whom he had never met, whose name he could not even pronounce with certainty. Only the fact that Anne's eyes were reddened with furious tears offered any bridge between the cold narrative and the charged memory.

"Yes; nasty," Gunn said reflectively. "Colonel Russell, *do* you know the Bridge team?"

"I know some of them quite well, Charity Dillon in particular; after all, I was stationed in the Jovian system for a while. MacHinery's check will show that I've no official connection with the Bridge, however."

"Good, good," Gunn said, beginning to brighten. "That widens MacHinery's check to include the Bridge too, and dilutes it from Pfitzner's point of view—gives us more time, though I'm sorry for the Bridge men. The Bridge and the Pfitzner project both suspect—yes, that's a big mouthful even for MacHinery; it will take him months. And the Bridge is Senator Wagoner's pet project, so he'll have to go slowly; he can't assassinate Wagoner's reputation as rapidly as he could some other senator's. Hmm. The question now is, just how are we going to use the time?"

"When you calm down, you calm right down to the bottom," Paige said, grinning wryly.

"I'm a salesman," Gunn said. "Maybe more creative than some, but at heart a salesman. In that profession you have to suit the mood to the occasion, just like actors do. Now about those samples——"

"I shouldn't have thrown that in," Anne said. "I'm afraid it was one good touch too many."

"On the contrary, it may be the only out we have. MacHinery is a 'practical' man. Results are what count with him. So suppose we take Colonel Russell's samples out of the regular testing order and run them through right now, issuing special orders to the staff that they are to find something in them—anything that looks at all decent."

"The staff won't fake," Anne said, frowning.

"My dear Anne, who said anything about faking?

Nearly every batch of samples contains some organism of interest, even if it isn't good enough to wind up among our choicest cultures. You see? MacHinery will be contented by results if we can show them to him, even though the results may have been made possible by an unauthorized person; otherwise he'd have to assemble a committee of experts to assess the evidence, and that costs money. All this, of course, is predicated on whether or not we have any results by the time MacHinery finds out Colonel Russell *is* an unauthorized person."

"There's just one other thing," Anne said. "To make good on what I told MacHinery, we're going to have to turn Colonel Russell into a convincing planetary ecologist—*and* tell him just what the Pfitzner project is."

Gunn's face fell momentarily. "Anne," he said, "I want you to observe what a nasty situation that strong-arm man has gotten us into. In order to protect our legitimate interests from our own government, we're about to commit a real, serious breach of security— which would never have happened if MacHinery hadn't thrown his weight around."

"Quite true," Anne said. She looked, however, rather poker-faced, Paige thought. Possibly she was enjoying Gunn's discomfiture; he was not exactly the first man one would suspect of disloyalty or of being a security risk.

"Colonel Russell, there is no faint chance, I suppose, that you *are* a planetary ecologist? Most spacemen with ranks as high as yours are scientists of some kind."

"No, sorry," Paige said. "Ballistics is my field."

"Well, you do have to know something about the planets, at least. Anne, I suggest that you take charge now, I'll have to do some fast covering. Your father would probably be the best man to brief Colonel Russell. And, Colonel, would you bear in mind that from now on, every piece of information that you're given in our plant might have the giver jailed or even shot, if MacHinery were to find out about it?"

"I'll keep my mouth shut," Paige said. "I'm enough at fault in this mess to be willing to do all I can to help —and my curiosity has been killing me anyhow. But there's something you'd better know, too, Mr. Gunn."

"And that is——"

"That the time you're counting on just doesn't exist. My leave expires in ten days. If you think you can make a planetary ecologist out of me in that length of time, I'll do my part."

"Ulp," Gunn said. "Anne, get to work." He bolted through the swinging doors.

The two looked at each other for a starchy moment, and then Anne smiled. Paige felt like another man at once.

"Is it really true—what you said?" Anne said, almost shyly.

"Yes. I didn't know it until I said it, but it's true. I'm really sorry that I had to say it at such a spectacularly bad moment; I only came over to apologize for my part in last night's quarrel. Now it seems that I've a bigger hassel to account for."

"Your curiosity is really your major talent, do you know?" she said, smiling again. "It took you only two days to find out just what you wanted to know—even though it's about the most closely guarded secret in the world."

"But I don't know it yet. Can you tell me here—or is the place wired?"

The girl laughed. "Do you think Tru and I would

have cussed each other out like that if the place were wired? No, it's clean, we inspect it daily. I'll tell you the central fact, and then my father can give you the details. The truth is that the Pfitzner project isn't out to conquer the degenerative diseases alone. It's aimed at the end-product of those diseases, too. *We're looking for the answer to death itself.*"

Paige sat down slowly in the nearest chair. "I don't believe it can be done," he whispered at last.

"That's what we all used to think, Paige. That's what that says." She pointed to the motto in German above the swinging doors. "*Wider den Tod ist kein Krautlein gewachsen.*" " 'Against Death doth no simple grow.' That was a law of nature, the old German herbalists thought. But now it's only a challenge. Somewhere in nature there *are* herbs and simples against death—and we're going to find them."

Anne's father seemed both preoccupied and a little worried to be talking to Paige at all, but it nevertheless took him only one day to explain the basic reasoning behind the project vividly enough so that Paige could understand it. In another day of simple helping around the part of the Pfitzner labs which was running his soil samples—help which consisted mostly of bottle-washing and making dilutions—Paige learned the reasoning well enough to put forward a version of it himself. He practised it on Anne over dinner.

"It all rests on our way of thinking about why antibiotics work," he said, while the girl listened with an attentiveness just this side of mockery. "What good are they to the organisms that produce them? We assumed that the organism secretes the antibiotic to kill or inhibit competing organisms, even though we were never able to show that enough antibiotic for the purpose is actually produced in the organism's natural medium, that is, the soil. In other words, we figured, the wider the range of the antibiotic, the less competition the producer had."

"Watch out for teleology," Anne warned. "That's not *why* the organism secretes it. It's just the result. Function, not purpose."

"Fair enough. But right there is the borderline in our thinking about antibiosis. What is an antibiotic to the organism it *kills*? Obviously, it's a poison, a toxin. But some bacteria always are naturally resistant to a given antibiotic, and through—what did your father call it?— through clone-variation and selection, the resistant cells may take over a whole colony. Equally obviously, those resistant cells would seem to produce an anti-toxin. An example would be the bacteria that secrete penicillinase, which is an enzyme that destroys penicillin. To those bacteria, penicillin is a toxin, and penicillinase is an antitoxin—isn't that right?"

"Right as rain. Go on, Paige."

"So now we add to that still another fact: that both penicillin and tetracycline are not only antibiotics— which makes them toxic to many bacteria—but *antitoxins* as well. Both of them neutralize the placental toxin that causes the eclampsia of pregnancy. Now, tetracycline is a broad-range antibiotic; is there such a thing as a broad-range antitoxin, too? Is the resistance to tetracycline that many different kinds of bacteria can develop all derived from a single counteracting substance? The answer, we know now, is Yes. We've also found another kind of broad-range antitoxin—one which protects the organism against many different kinds of antibiotics. I'm told that it's a whole new field of research and that we've just begun to scratch the surface.

"Ergo: Find the broad-range antitoxin that acts against the toxins of the human body which accumulate after growth stops—as penicillin and tetracycline act against the pregnancy toxin—and you've got your magic machine-gun against degenerative disease. Pfitzner already has found that antitoxin: its name is ascomycin. . . . How'd I do?" he added anxiously, getting his breath back.

"Beautifully. It's perhaps a little too condensed for MacHinery to follow, but maybe that's all to the good —it wouldn't sound authoritative to him if he could understand it all the way through. Still it might pay to be just a little more roundabout when you talk to him." The girl had the compact out again, and was peering into it intently. "But you covered only the degenerative diseases, and that's just background material. Now tell me about the direct attack on death."

Paige looked at the compact and then at the girl, but her expression was too studied to convey much. He said slowly: "I'll go into that if you like. But your father told me that that element of the work was secret even from the government. Should I discuss it in a restaurant?"

Anne turned the small, compact-like object around, so that he could see that it was in fact a meter of some sort. Its needle was in uncertain motion, but near the zero-point. "There's no mike close enough to pick you up," Anne said, snapping the device shut and restoring it to her purse. "Go ahead."

"All right. Some day you're going to have to explain to me why you allowed yourself to get into that first fight with me here, when you had that Eavesdropper with you all the time. Right at the moment I'm too busy being a phony ecologist.

"The death end of the research began back in 1952, with an anatomist named Lansing. He was the first man to show that complex animals—it was rotifers he used—produce a definite ageing toxin as a normal part of their growth, and that it gets passed on to the off-spring. He bred something like fifty generations of rotifers from adolescent mothers, and got an increase in the life-span in every new generation. He ran 'em up from a natural average span of 24 days to one of 104 days. Then he reversed the process, by breeding consistently from old mothers, and cut the life-span of the final generation way *below* the natural average."

"And now," Anne said, "you know more about the babies in our labs than I told you before—or you should. The foundling home that supplies them specializes in the illegitimates of juvenile delinquents—the younger, for our purposes, the better."

"Sorry, but you can't needle me with that any longer, Anne. I know now that it's a blind alley. Breeding for longevity in humans isn't practicable; all that those infants can supply to the project is a set of comparative readings on their death-toxin blood-levels. What we want now is something much more direct: an antitoxin against the ageing toxin of humans. We know that the ageing toxin exists in all complex animals. We know that it's a single, specific substance, quite distinct from the poisons that cause the degenerative diseases. And we know that it can be neutralized. When your lab animals were given ascomycin, they didn't develop a single degenerative disease—but they died anyhow, at about the usual time, as if they'd been set, like a clock, at birth. Which, in effect, they had, by the amount of ageing toxin passed on to them by their mothers.

"So what we're looking for now is not an antibiotic— an anti-life drug—but an anti-agathic, an anti-death drug. We're running on borrowed time, because asco- mycin already satisfies the conditions of our develop- ment contract with the government. As soon as we get ascomycin into production, our government money will be cut down to a trickle. But if we can hold back on ascomycin long enough to keep the money coming in, we'll have our anti-agathic too."

"Bravo," Anne said. "You sound just like father. I wanted you to raise that last point in particular, Paige, because it's the most important single thing you should remember. If there's the slightest suspicion that we're systematically dragging our feet on releasing ascomycin —that we're taking money from the government to do something the government has no idea can be done— there'll be hell to pay. We're so close to running down our anti-agathic now that it would be heart-breaking to have to stop, not only heart-breaking for us, but for humanity at large."

"The end justifies the means," Paige murmured.

"It does in this case. I know secrecy's a fetish in our society these days—but here secrecy will serve everyone in the long run, and it's *got* to be maintained."

"I'll maintain it," Paige said. He had been referring, not to secrecy, but to cheating on government money; but he saw no point in bringing that up. As for secrecy, he had no practical faith in it—especially now that he had seen how well it worked.

For in the two days that he had been working inside Pfitzner, he had already found an inarguable spy at the very heart of the project.

★
★ 6 ★

There were three yellow "Critical" signals lit on the long gangboard when Helmuth passed through the gang deck on the way back to duty. All of them, as usual, were concentrated on Panel 9, where Eva Chavez worked.

Eva, despite her Latin name—such once-valid tickets no longer meant anything among the West's uniformly mixed-race population—was a big girl, vaguely blonde, who cherished a passion for the Bridge. Unfortunately, she was apt to become enthralled by the sheer Cosmicness of It All, precisely at the moment when cold analysis and split-second decisions were most crucial.

Helmuth reached over her shoulder, cut her out of the circuit except as an observer, and donned the co-operator's helmet. The incomplete new shoals caisson sprang into being around him. Breakers of boiling hydrogen seethed seven hundred feet up along its slanted sides—breakers that never subsided, but simply were torn away into flying spray.

There was a spot of dull orange near the top of the north face of the caisson, crawling slowly toward the pediment of the nearest truss. Catalysis——

Or cancer, as Helmuth could not help but think of it. On this bitter, violent monster of a planet, even tiny specks of calcium carbide were deadly, that same calcium carbide which had produced acetylene gas for buggy lamps two centuries ago on Earth. At these wind velocities, such specks imbedded themselves deeply in anything they struck; and at fifteen million p.s.i of pressure, under the catalysis of sodium, pressure-ice took up ammonia and carbon dioxide, building protein-like compounds in a rapid, voracious chain of decay:

For a moment, Helmuth watched it grow. It was, after all, one of the incredible possibilities the Bridge had been built to study. On Earth, such a compound, had it occurred at all, might have grown porous, hard, and as strong as rhinocerous-horn. Here, under nearly three times Earth's gravity, the molecules were forced to assemble in strict aliphatic order, but in cross section their arrangement was hexagonal, as though the stuff would become an aromatic compound if only it could. Even here it was moderately strong in cross section—

but along the long axis it smeared like graphite, the calcium and sulphur atoms readily changing their minds as to which was to act as the metal of the pair, surrendering their pressure-driven holds on one carbon atom to grab hopefully for the next one in line, or giving up altogether to become incorporated instead in a radical with a self-contained double sulphur bond, rather like cystine. . . .

It was not too far from the truth to call it a form of cancer. The compound seemed to be as close as Jupiter came to an indigenous form of life. It grew, fed, reproduced itself, and showed something of the characteristic structure of an Earthly virus, such as tobacco-mosaic. Of course it grew from outside, by accretion like any non-living crystal, rather than from inside, by intussusception, like a cell; but viruses grew that way too, at least *in vitro*.

It was no stuff to hold up the piers of humanity's greatest engineering project, that much was sure. Perhaps it was a suitable ground-substance for the ribs of some Jovian jellyfish; but in a Bridge-caisson, it was cancer.

There was a scraper mechanism working on the edge of the lesion, flaking away the shearing aminos and laying down new ice. In the meantime, the decay in the caisson-face was working deeper. The scraper could not possibly get at the core of the trouble—which was not the calcium carbide dust, with which the atmosphere was charged beyond redemption, but was instead one imbedded speck of metallic sodium which was taking no part in the reaction—fast enough to extirpate it. It could barely keep pace with the surface spread of the disease.

And laying new ice over the surface of the wound was

worthless, as Eva should have known. At this rate, the whole caisson would slough away and melt like butter, within an hour, under the weight of the Bridge above it.

Helmuth sent the futile scraper aloft. Drill for the speck of metal? No—it was far too deeply buried already, and its location was unknown.

Quickly he called two borers up from the shoals below, where constant blasting was taking the foundation of the caisson deeper and deeper into Jupiter's dubious "soil". He drove both blind, fire-snouted machines down into the lesion.

The bottom of that sore turned out to be forty-five metres within the immense block of ice. Helmuth pushed the red button all the same.

The borers blew up, with a heavy, quite invisible blast, as they had been designed to do. A pit appeared on the face of the caisson.

The nearest truss bent upward in the wind. It fluttered for a moment, trying to resist. It bent farther.

Deprived of its major attachment, it tore free suddenly, and went whirling away into the blackness. A sudden flash of lightning picked it out for a moment, and Helmuth saw it dwindling like a bat with torn wings being borne away by a cyclone.

The scraper scuttled down into the pit and began to fill it with ice from the bottom. Helmuth ordered down a new truss and a squad of scaffolders. Damage of this order of magnitude took time to repair. He watched the tornado tearing ragged chunks from the edges of the pit until he was sure that the catalysis-cancer had been stopped. Then—suddenly, prematurely, dismally tired —he took off the helmet.

He was astounded by the white fury that masked Eva's big-boned, mildly pretty face.

"You'll blow the Bridge up yet, won't you?" she said, evenly, without preamble. "Any pretext will do!"

Baffled, Helmuth turned his head helplessly away; but that was no better. The suffused face of Jupiter peered swollenly through the picture-port, just as it did on the foreman's deck.

He and Eva and Charity and the gang and the whole of satellite V were falling forward toward Jupiter; their uneventful, cooped-up lives on Jupiter V were utterly unreal compared to the four hours of each changeless day spent on Jupiter's ever-changing surface. Every new day brought their minds, like ships out of control, closer and closer to that gaudy inferno.

There was no other way for a man—or a woman—on Jupiter V to look at the giant planet. It was simple experience, shared by all of them, that planets do not occupy four-fifths of the whole sky, unless the observer is himself up there in that planet's sky, falling toward it, falling faster and faster——

"I have no intention," he said tiredly, "of blowing up the Bridge. I wish you could get it through your head that I want the Bridge to stay up—even though I'm not starry-eyed to the point of incompetence about the project. Did you think that that rotten spot was going to go away by itself after you'd painted it over? Didn't you know that——"

Several helmeted, masked heads near by turned blindly toward the sound of his voice. Helmuth shut up. Any distracting conversation or other activity was taboo, down here on the gang deck. He motioned Eva back to duty.

The girl donned her helmet obediently enough, but it was plain from the way that her normally full lips were thinned that she thought Helmuth had ended the argument only in order to have the last word.

Helmuth strode to the thick pillar which ran down the central axis of the operations shack, and mounted the spiralling cleats toward his own foreman's cubicle. Already he felt in anticipation the weight of the helmet upon his own head.

Charity Dillon, however, was already wearing the helmet. He was sitting in Helmuth's chair.

Charity was characteristically oblivious of Helmuth's entrance. The Bridge operator must learn to ignore, to be utterly unconscious of anything happening about his body except the inhuman sounds of signals; must learn to heed only those senses which report something going on thousands and hundreds of thousands of miles away.

Helmuth knew better than to interrupt him. Instead, he watched Dillon's white, blade-like fingers roving with blind sureness over the controls.

Dillon, evidently, was making a complete tour of the Bridge—not only from end to end, but up and down, too. The tally board showed that he had already activated nearly two-thirds of the ultraphone eyes. That meant that he had been up all night at the job; had begun it immediately after he had last relieved Helmuth.

Why?

With a thrill of unfocused apprehension, Helmuth looked at the foreman's jack, which allowed the operator here in the cubicle to communicate with the gang when necessary, and which kept him aware of anything said or done on the gang boards.

It was plugged in.

Dillon sighed suddenly, took the helmet off, and turned.

"Hello, Bob," he said. "It's funny about this job. You can't see, you can't hear, but when somebody's watching you, you feel a sort of pressure on the back of your neck. Extra-sensory perception, maybe. Ever felt it?"

"Pretty often, lately. Why the grand tour, Charity?"

"There's to be an inspection," Dillon said. His eyes met Helmuth's. They were frank and transparent. "A couple of Senate sub-committee chairmen, coming to see that their eight billion dollars isn't being wasted. Naturally, I'm a little anxious to see to it that they find everything in order."

"I see," Helmuth said. "First time in five years, isn't it?"

"Just about. What was that dust-up down below just now? Somebody—you, I'm sure, from the drastic handiwork involved—bailed Eva out of a mess, and then I heard her talk about your wanting to blow up the Bridge. I checked the area when I heard the fracas start, and it did seem as if she had let things go rather far, but—— What was it all about?"

Dillon ordinarily hadn't the guile for cat-and-mouse games, and he had never looked less guileful than now. Helmuth said carefully: "Eva was upset, I suppose. On the subject of Jupiter we're all of us cracked by now, in our different ways. The way she was dealing with the catalysis didn't look to me to be suitable—a difference of opinion, resolved in my favour because I had the authority, Eva didn't. That's all."

"Kind of an expensive difference, Bob. I'm not niggling by nature, you know that. But an incident like that while the sub-committees are here——"

"The point is," said Helmuth, "are we going to spend an extra ten thousand, or whatever it costs to replace a truss and reinforce a caisson, or are we to lose the whole caisson—and as much as a third of the whole Bridge along with it?"

"Yes, you're right there, of course. That could be explained, even to a pack of senators. But—it would be difficult to have to explain it very often. Well, the board's yours, Bob; you could continue my spot-check, if you've time."

Dillon got up. Then he added suddenly, as though it were forced out of him:

"Bob, I'm trying to understand your state of mind. From what Eva said, I gather that you've made it fairly public. I . . . I don't think it's a good idea to infect your fellow workers with your own pessimism. It leads to sloppy work. I know that you won't countenance sloppy work, regardless of your own feelings, but one foreman can do only so much. And you're making extra work for yourself—not for me, but for yourself— by being openly gloomy about the Bridge.

"It strikes me that maybe you could use a breather, maybe a week's junket to Ganymede or something like that. You're the best man on the Bridge, Bob, for all your grousing about the job, and your assorted misgivings. I'd hate to see you replaced."

"A threat, Charity?" Helmuth said softly.

"*No.* I wouldn't replace you unless you actually went nuts, and I firmly believe that your fears in that respect are groundless. It's a commonplace that only sane men suspect their own sanity, isn't it?"

"It's a common misconception. Most psychopathic obsessions begin with a mild worry—one that can't be shaken."

Dillon made as if to brush that subject away. "Anyhow, I'm not threatening; I'd fight to keep you here.

But my say-so only covers Jupiter V and the Bridge; there are people higher up on Ganymede, and people higher yet back in Washington—and in this inspecting commission.

"Why don't you try to look on the bright side for a change? Obviously the Bridge isn't ever going to inspire you. But you might at least try thinking about all those dollars piling up in your account back home, every hour you're on this job. And about the bridges and ships and who knows what-all that you'll be building, at any fee you ask, when you get back down to Earth. All under the magic words: 'One of the men who built the Bridge on Jupiter'!"

Charity was bright red with embarrassment and enthusiasm. Helmuth smiled.

"I'll try to bear it in mind, Charity," he said. "And I think I'll pass up a vacation for the time being. When is this gaggle of senators due to arrive?"

"That's hard to say. They'll be coming to Ganymede directly from Washington, without any routing, and they'll stop there a while. I suppose they'll also make a stop at Callisto before they come here. They've got something new on their ship, I'm told, that lets them flit about more freely than the usual uphill transport can."

An icy lizard suddenly was nesting in Helmuth's stomach, coiling and coiling but never settling itself. The persistent nightmare began to seep back into his blood; it was almost engulfing him—already.

"Something . . . new?" he echoed, his voice as flat and non-committal as he could make it. "Do you know what it is?"

"Well, yes. But I think I'd better keep quiet about it until——"

"Charity, nobody on this deserted rock-heap could possibly be a Soviet spy. The whole habit of 'security' is idiotic out here. Tell me now and save me the trouble of dealing with senators; or tell me at least that you know I know. *They have antigravity!* Isn't that it?"

One word from Dillon, and the nightmare would be real.

"Yes," Dillon said. "How did you know? Of course, it couldn't be a complete gravity screen by any means. But it seems to be a good long step toward it. We've waited a long time to see that dream come true——

"But you're the last man in the world to take pride in the achievement, so there's no sense in exulting about it to you. I'll let you know when I get a definite arrival date. In the meantime, will you think about what I said before?"

"Yes, I will." Helmuth took the seat before the board.

"Good. With you, I have to be grateful for small victories. Good trick, Bob."

"Good trick, Charity."

Paige's gift for putting two and two together and getting 22 was in part responsible for the discovery of the spy, but the almost incredible clumsiness of the man made the chief contribution to it. Paige could hardly believe that nobody had spotted the agent before. True, he was only one of some two dozen technicians in the processing lab where Paige had been working; but his almost open habit of slipping notes inside his lab apron, and his painful furtiveness every time he left the Pfitzner laboratory building for the night, should have aroused someone's suspicions long before this.

It was a fine example, Paige thought, of the way the blunderbus investigation methods currently popular in Washington allowed the really dangerous man a thousand opportunities to slip away unnoticed. As was usual among groups of scientists, too, there was an unspoken covenant among Pfitzner's technicians—against informing on each other. It protected the guilty as well as the innocent, but it would never have arisen at all under any fair system of juridical defence.

Paige had not the smallest idea what to do with his fish once he had hooked it. He took an evening—which he greatly begrudged—away from seeing Anne, in order to trace the man's movements after a day which had produced two exciting advances in the research, on the hunch that the spy would want to ferry the information out at once.

This hunch proved out beautifully, at least at first. Nor was the man difficult to follow; his habit of glancing continually over first one shoulder and then the other, evidently to make sure that he was not being followed, made him easy to spot over long distances, even in a crowd. He left the city by train to Hoboken, where he rented a bicycle and pedalled directly to the cross-roads town of Secaucus, which called itself—accurately, to judge by the smell—"The Biggest Little Piggery On Earth". It was a long pull, but not at all difficult otherwise.

Outside Secaucus, however, Paige nearly lost his man for the first and last time. The cross-roads, which lay across New Jersey Route 3 to the Lincoln Tunnel, turned out also to be the site of the temporary trailer city of the Witnesses—nearly 300,000 of them, or almost half of the 700,000 who had been pouring into town for two weeks now for the Revival. Among the trailers Paige saw licence plates from as far away as Eritrea.

The trailer city was far bigger than any nearby town except Passaic. It included a score of supermarkets, all going full blast even in the middle of the night, and about as many coin-in-slot laundries, equally wide open. There were at least a hundred public baths, and close to 360 public toilets. Paige counted ten cafeterias, and twice that many hamburger stands and one-arm joints, each of the stands no less than a hundred feet long; at one of these he stopped long enough to buy a "Texas wiener" nearly as long as his forearm, covered with mustard, meat sauce, sauerkraut, corn relish, and pic-calilli. There were ten highly conspicuous hospital tents, too—and after eating the Texas wiener Paige thought he knew why—the smallest of them perfectly capable of housing a one-ring circus.

And, of course, there were the trailers, of which Paige guessed the number at sixty thousand, from two-wheeled jobs to Packards, in all stages of repair and shininess. Luckily, the city was well lit, and since everyone living in it was a Witness, there were no booby-traps or other forms of proselytizing. Paige's man, after a little thoroughly elementary doubling on his tracks and setting up false trails, ducked into a trailer with a Latvian licence plate. After half an hour—at exactly 0200—the trailer ran up a stubby VHF radio antenna as thick through as Paige's wrist.

And the rest, Paige thought grimly, climbing back on to his own rented bicycle, is up to the FBI—if I tell them.

But what would he say? He had every good reason of his own to stay as far out of sight of the FBI as possible. Furthermore, if he informed on the man now, it would mean immediate curtains on the search for the anti-agathic, and a gross betrayal of the trust, enforced though it had been, that Anne and Gunn had placed in him. On the other hand, to remain silent would give the Soviets the drug at the same time that Pfitzner found it—in other words, before the West had it as a government. And it would mean, too, that he himself would have to forego an important chance to prove that he was loyal, when the inevitable showdown with Mac-Hinery came around.

By the next day, however, he had hit upon what should have been the obvious course in the beginning. He took a second evening to rifle his fish's laboratory bench—the incredible idiot had stuffed it to bulging with incriminating photomicrograph negatives, and

116

with bits of paper bearing the symbols of a simple substitution code once circulated to Tom Mix's Square Shooters on behalf of Shredded Ralston—and a third to take step-by-step photos of the hegira to the Witness trailer city, and of the radio-transmitter-equipped trailer with the buffer-state licence. Assembling everything into a neat dossier, Paige cornered Gunn in his office and dropped the whole mess squarely in the vice-president's lap.

"My goodness," Gunn said, blinking. "Curiosity is a disease with you, isn't it, Colonel Russell? And I really doubt that even Pfitzner will ever find the antidote for that."

"Curiosity has very little to do with it. As you'll see in the folder, the man's an amateur—evidently a volunteer from the Party, like the Rosenbergs, rather than a paid expert. He practically led me by the nose."

"Yes, I see he's clumsy," Gunn agreed. "And he's been reported to us before, Colonel Russell. As a matter of fact, on several occasions we've had to protect him from his own clumsiness."

"But why?" Paige demanded. "Why haven't you cracked down on him?"

"Because we can't afford to," Gunn said. "A spy scandal in the plant now would kill the work just where it stands. Oh, we'll report him sooner or later, and the work you've done here on him will be very useful then —to all of us, yourself included. But there's no hurry."

"No hurry!"

"No," Gunn said. "The material he's ferrying out now is of no particular consequence. When we actually have the drug——"

"But he'll already know the production method by that time. Identifying the drug is a routine job for any team of chemists—your Dr. Agnew taught me that much."

"I suppose that's so," Gunn said. "Well, I'll think it over, Colonel. Don't worry about it, we'll deal with it when the time seems ripe."

And that was every bit of satisfaction that Paige could extract from Gunn. It was small recompense for his lost sleep, his lost dates, the care he had taken to inform Pfitzner first, or the soul-searching it had cost him to put the interests of the project ahead of his officer's oath and of his own safety. That evening he said as much to Anne Abbott, and with considerable force.

"Calm down," Anne said. "If you're going to mix into the politics of this work, Paige, you're going to get burnt right up to the armpits. When we do find what we're looking for, it's going to create the biggest political explosion in history. I'd advise you to stand well back."

"I've been burned already," Paige said hotly. "How the hell can I stand back now? And tolerating a spy isn't just politics. It's treason, not only by rumour, but in fact. Are you deliberately putting everyone's head in the noose?"

"Quite deliberately. Paige, this project is for everyone—every man, woman and child on the Earth and in space. The fact that the West is putting up the money is incidental. What we're doing here is in every respect just as anti-West as it is anti-Soviet. We're out to lick death for human beings, not just for the armed forces of some one military coalition. What do we care who gets it first? We want everyone to have it."

"Does Gunn agree with that?"

"It's company policy. It may even have been Tru's own idea, though he has different reasons, different

118

justifications. Have you any idea what will happen when a death-curing drug hits a totalitarian society—a drug available in limited quantities only? It won't prove fatal to the Soviets, of course, but it ought to make the struggle for succession over there considerably bloodier than it is already. That's essentially the way Tru seems to look at it."

"And you don't," Paige said grimly.

"No, Paige, I don't. I can see well enough what's going to happen right here at home when this thing gets out. Think for a moment of what it will do to the religious people alone. What happens to the after-life if you never need to leave this one? Look at the Witnesses. They believe in the literal truth of everything in the Bible—that's why they revise the book every year. And this story is going to break before their Jubilee year is over. Did you know that their motto is: 'Millions now living will never die'? They mean themselves, but what if it turns out to be *everybody*?

"And that's only the beginning. Think of what the insurance companies are going to say. And what's going to happen to the whole structure of compound interest. Wells's old yarn about the man who lived so long that his savings came to dominate the world's whole financial structure—*When the Sleeper Wakes*, wasn't it?—well, that's going to be theoretically possible for *everybody* with the patience and the capital to let his money sit still. Or think of the whole corpus of the inheritance laws. It's going to be the biggest, blackest social explosion the West ever had to take. We'll be much too busy digging in to care about what's happening to the Central Committee in Moscow."

"You seem to care enough to be protecting the Central Committee's interests, or at least what they probably think of as their interests," Paige said slowly. "After all, there is a possibility of keeping the secret, instead of letting it leak."

"There is no such possibility," Anne said. "Natural laws can't be kept secret. Once you give a scientist the idea that a certain goal can be reached, you've given him more than half of the information he needs. Once he gets the idea that the conquest of death is possible, no power on Earth can stop him from finding out how it's done—the 'know-how' we make so many fatuous noises about is the most minor part of research, it's even a matter of total indifference to the essence of the question."

"I don't see that."

"Then let's go back to the fission bomb again for a moment. The only way we could have kept that a secret was to have failed to drop it at all, or even test-fire it. Once the secret was out that the bomb existed—and you'll remember that we announced that before hundreds of thousands of people in Hiroshima—we had no secrets in that field worth protecting. The biggest mystery in the Smyth report was the specific method by which uranium slugs were 'canned' in a protective jacket; it was one of the toughest problems the project had to lick, but at the same time it's exactly the kind of problem you'd assign to an engineer, and confidently expect a solution inside of a year.

"The fact of the matter, Paige, is that you can't keep scientific matters a secret from the other guy without keeping them a secret from yourself. A scientific secret is something that some other scientist can't *contribute to*, any more than he can profit by it. Contrariwise, if you arm yourself through discoveries in natural law, you also arm the other guy. Either you give him the information, or you cut your own throat; there aren't any other courses possible.

"And let me ask you this, Paige: should we give the USSR the advantage—temporary though it'll be—of having to get along *without* the anti-agathics for a while? By their very nature, the drugs will do more damage to the West than they will to the USSR. After all, in the Soviet Union one isn't permitted to inherit money, or to exercise any real control over economic forces just because one's lived a long time. If both major powers are given control over death at the same time, the West will be at a natural disadvantage. If we give control over death to the West alone, we'll be sabotaging our own civilization without putting the USSR under any comparable handicap. Is that sensible?"

The picture was staggering, to say the least. It gave Paige an impression of Gunn decidedly at variance with the mask of salesman-turned-executive which the man himself wore. But it was otherwise self-consistent; that, he knew, was supposed to be enough for him.

"How could I tell?" he said coldly. "All I can see is that every day I stick with you, I get in deeper. First I pose for the FBI as something that I'm not. Next I'm given possession of information that it's unlawful for me to have. And now I'm helping you two conceal the evidence of a high crime. It looks more and more to me as though I was supposed to be involved in this thing from the beginning. I don't see how you could have done so thorough a job on me without planning it."

"You needn't deny that you asked for it, Paige."

"I don't deny that," he said. "You don't deny deliberately involving me, either, I notice."

"No. It was deliberate, all right. I thought you'd have suspected it before. And if you're planning to ask me why, save your breath. I'm not permitted to tell you. You'll find out in due course."

"You two——"

"No. Tru had nothing to do with involving you. That was my idea. He only agreed to it—and he had to be convinced from considerably higher up."

"You two," Paige said through almost motionless lips, "don't hesitate to trample on the bystanders, do you? If I didn't know before that Pfitzner was run by a pack of idealists, I'd know it now. You've got the characteristic ruthlessness."

"That," Anne said in a level voice, "is what it takes."

★

★ 8 ★

Instead of sleeping after his trick—for now Helmuth knew that he was really afraid—he sat up in the reading chair in his cabin. The illuminated microfilmed pages of a book flicked by across the surface of the wall opposite him, timed precisely to the reading rate most comfortable for him, and he had several weeks' worry-conserved alcohol and smoke rations for ready consumption.

But Helmuth let his mix go flat, and did not notice the book, which had turned itself on, at the page where he had abandoned it last, when he had fitted himself into the chair. Instead, he listened to the radio.

There was always a great deal of ham radio activity in the Jovian system. The conditions were good for it, since there was plenty of power available, few impeding atmosphere layers and those thin, no Heaviside layers, and few official and no commercial channels with which the hams could interfere.

And there were plenty of people scattered about the satellites who needed the sound of a voice.

". . . anybody know whether or not the senators are coming here? Doc Barth put in a report a while back on a fossil plant he found here, at least he thinks it was a plant. Maybe they'd like a look at it."

"It's the Bridge team they're coming to see." A strong voice, and the impression of a strong transmitter wavering in and out to the currents of an atmosphere; that would be Sweeney, on Ganymede. "Sorry to throw the wet blanket, boys, but I don't think the senators'll be interested in our rock-balls for their own lumpy selves. They're only scheduled to stay here three days."

Helmuth thought greyly: *Then they'll stay on Callisto only one.*

"Is that you, Sweeney? Where's the Bridge tonight?"

"Dillon's on duty," a very distant transmitter said. "Try to raise Helmuth, Sweeney."

"Helmuth, Helmuth, you gloomy beetle-gooser! Come in, Helmuth!"

"Sure, Bob, come in and dampen us a little. We're feeling cheerful."

Sluggishly, Helmuth reached out to take the mike, from where it lay clipped to one arm of the chair. But before he had completed the gesture, the door to his room swung open.

Eva came in.

She said: "Bob, I want to tell you something."

"His voice is changing!" the voice of the Callisto operator said. "Sweeney, ask him what he's drinking!"

Helmuth cut the radio out. The girl was freshly dressed—in so far as anybody dressed in anything on Jupiter V—and Helmuth wondered why she was prowling the decks at this hour, half-way between her sleep period and her trick. Her hair was hazy against the light from the corridor, and she looked less mannish than usual. She reminded him a little of the way she had looked when they had first met, before the Bridge had come to bestride his bed instead. He put the memory aside.

"All right," he said. "I owe you a mix, I guess. Citric, sugar and the other stuff are in the locker . . . you know where it is. Shot-cans are there, too."

The girl shut the door and sat down on the bunk, with a free litheness that was almost grace, but with a determination which, Helmuth knew, meant that she had just decided to do something silly for all the right reasons.

"I don't need a drink," she said. "As a matter of fact, I've been turning my lux-R's back to the common pool. I suppose you did that for me—by showing me what a mind looks like that's hiding from itself."

"Evita, stop sounding like a tract. Obviously you've advanced to a higher, more Jovian plane of existence, but won't you still need your metabolism? Or have you decided that vitamins are all-in-the-mind?"

"Now you're being superior. Anyhow, alcohol isn't a vitamin. And I didn't come to talk about that. I came to tell you something I think you ought to know."

"Which is——?"

She said: "Bob, I mean to have a child here."

A bark of laughter, part sheer hysteria and part exasperation, jack-knifed Helmuth into a sitting position. A red arrow bloomed on the far wall, obediently marking the paragraph which, supposedly, he had reached in his reading. Eva twisted to look at it, but the page was already dimming and vanishing.

"*Women!*" Helmuth said, when he could get his breath back. "Really, Evita, you make me feel much better. No environment can change a human being much, after all."

"Why should it?" she said suspiciously, looking back at him. "I don't see the joke. Shouldn't a woman want to have a child?"

"Of course she should," he said, settling back. The pages began to flip across the wall again. "It's quite ordinary. All women want to have children. All women dream of the day they can turn a child out to play in an airless rock-garden like Jupiter V, to pluck fossils and make dust-castles and get quaintly star-burned. How cosy to tuck the blue little body back into its corner that night, and give it its oxygen bottle, promptly at the sound of the trick-change bell! Why, it's as natural as Jupiter-light—as Western as freeze-dried apple pie."

He turned his head casually away. "Congratulations. As for me, though, Eva, I'd much prefer that you take your ghostly little pretext out of here."

Eva surged to her feet in one furious motion. Her fingers grasped him by the beard and jerked his head painfully around again.

"You reedy male platitude!" she said, in a low grinding voice. "How you could see almost the whole point, and make so little of it—*Women*, is it? So you think I came creeping in here, full of humbleness, to settle our technical differences in bed!"

He closed his hand on her wrist and twisted it away. "What else?" he demanded, trying to imagine how it would feel to stay reasonable for five minutes at a time with these Bridge-robots. "None of us need bother with games and excuses. We're here, we're isolated, we were all chosen because, among other things, we were judged incapable of forming permanent emotional attachments, and capable of any alliances we liked—without going unbalanced when the attraction died and the alliance came unstuck. None of us have to pretend that our living arrangements would keep us out of jail in Boston, or that they have to involve any Earth-normal excuses."

She said nothing. After a while he asked, gently: "Isn't that so?"

"Of course it's not so," Eva said. She was frowning at him; he had the absurd impression that she was pitying him. "If we were really incapable of making any permanent attachment, we'd never have been chosen. A cast of mind like that is a mental disease, Bob; it's anti-survival from the ground up. It's the conditioning that made us this way. Didn't you know?"

Helmuth hadn't known; or if he had, he had been conditioned to forget it. He gripped the arms of the chair tighter.

"Anyhow," he said, "that's the way we are."

"Yes, it is. Also it has nothing to do with the matter."

"It doesn't? How stupid do you think I am? *I* don't care whether or not you've decided to have a child here, if you really mean what you say."

She, too, seemed to be trembling. "You really don't, too. The decision means nothing to you."

"Well, if I liked children, I'd be sorry for the child. But as it happens, I can't stand children—and if that's the conditioning, too, I can't do a thing about it. In short, Eva, as far as I'm concerned you can have as many kids as you want, and to me you'll *still* be the worst operator on the Bridge."

"I'll bear that in mind," she said. At this moment she seemed to have been cut from pressure-ice. "I'll leave you something to charge your mind with, too, Robert Helmuth. I'll leave you sprawled here under your precious book . . . what is Madame Bovary to you, anyhow, you unadventurous turtle? . . . to think about a man who believes that children must always be born into warm cradles—a man who thinks that men have to huddle on warm worlds, or they won't survive. A man with no ears, no eyes, scarcely any head. A man in terror, a man crying: Mamma! *Mamma!* all the stellar days and nights long!"

"Parlour diagnosis."

127

"Parlour labelling! Good trick, Bob. Draw your warm woolly blanket in tight around your brains, or some little sneeze of sense might creep in, and impair your—efficiency!"

The door closed sharply after her.

A million pounds of fatigue crashed down without warning on the back of Helmuth's neck, and he fell back into the reading chair with a gasp. The roots of his beard ached, and Jupiters bloomed and wavered away before his closed eyes.

He struggled once, and fell asleep.

Instantly he was in the grip of the dream.

It started, as always, with commonplaces, almost realistic enough to be a documentary film-strip—except for the appalling sense of pressure, and the distorted emotional significance with which the least word, the smallest movement was invested.

It was the sinking of the first caisson of the Bridge. The actual event had been bad enough. The job demanded enough exactness of placement to require that manned ships enter Jupiter's atmosphere itself: a squadron of twenty of the most powerful ships ever built, with the five-million-ton asteroid, trimmed and shaped in space, slung beneath them in an immense cat's-cradle.

Four times that squadron had disappeared beneath the racing clouds; four times the tense voices of pilots and engineers had muttered in Helmuth's ears, and he had whispered back, trying to guide them by what he could see of the conflicting trade-blasts from Jupiter V; four times there were shouts and futile orders and the snapping of cables and men screaming endlessly against the eternal howl of the Jovian sky.

It had cost, altogether, nine ships, and two hundred

thirty-one men, to get one of five laboriously-shaped asteroids planted in the shifting slush that was Jupiter's surface. Until that had been accomplished, the Bridge could never have been more than a dream. While the Great Red Spot had shown astronomers that some structures on Jupiter could last for long periods of time —long enough, at least, to be seen by many generations of human beings—it had been equally well known that nothing on Jupiter could be really permanent. The planet did not even have a "surface" in the usual sense; instead, the bottom of the atmosphere merged more or less smoothly into a high-pressure sludge, which in turn thickened as it went deeper into solid pressure-ice. At no point on the way down was there any interface between one layer and another, except in the rare areas where a part of the deeper, more "solid" medium had been thrust far up out of its normal level, to form a continent which might last as long as two years, or two hundred. It was on to one of these great ribs of bulging ice that the ships had tried to plant their asteroid—and, after four tries, had succeeded.

Helmuth had helped to supervise all five operations, counting the successful one, from his desk on Jupiter V. But in the dream he was not in the control shack, but instead on shipboard, in one of the ships that was never to come back——

Then, without transition, but without any sense of discontinuity either, he was on the Bridge itself. Not *in absentia*, as the remote guiding intelligence of a beetle, but in person, in an ovular, tank-like suit the details of which would never come clear. The high brass had discovered antigravity, and had asked for volunteers to man the Bridge. Helmuth had volunteered.

Looking back on it, in the dream, he did not understand why he had volunteered. It had simply seemed expected of him, and he had not been able to help it, even though he had known to begin with what it would be like. He belonged on the Bridge, though he hated it —he had been doomed to go there, from the first.

And there was . . . something wrong . . . with the antigravity. The high brass had asked for its volunteers before the research work had been completed. The present antigravity fields were weak, and there was some basic flaw in the theory. Generators broke down after only short periods of use; burned out, unpredictably, sometimes only moments after having passed their production tests with perfect scores. In waking life, vacuum tubes behaved in that unpredictable way; there were no vacuum tubes anywhere on Jupiter, but machines on Jupiter burned out all the same, burned out at temperatures which would freeze Helmuth solid in an instant.

That was what Helmuth's antigravity set was about to do. He crouched inside his personal womb, above the boiling sea, the clouds raging by him in little scouring crystals which wore at the chorion protecting him, lit by a plume of hydrogen flame—and waited to feel his weight suddenly become three times greater than normal, the pressure on his body go from sixteen pounds per square inch to fifteen million, the air around him take on the searing stink of poisons, the whole of Jupiter come pressing its burden upon him.

He knew what would happen to him then.

It happened.

Helmuth greeted "morning" on Jupiter V with his customary scream.

130

BOOK THREE

★

ENTR'ACTE

Dear Seppi,

Lord knows I have better sense than to mail this, send it to you by messenger, or leave it anywhere in the files—or indeed on the premises—of the Joint Committee; but if one is sensible about such matters these days, one never puts anything on paper at all, and then burns the carbons. As a bad compromise, I am filing this among my personal papers, where it will be found, opened and sent to you only after I will be beyond reprisals.

That's not meant to sound as ominous as, upon re-reading, I see it does. By the time you have this letter, abundant details of what I've been up to should be available to you, not only through the usual press garble, but through verbatim testimony. You will have worked out, by now, a rational explanation of my conduct since my re-election (and before it, for that matter). At the very least, I hope you now know why I authorized such a monstrosity as the Bridge, even against your very good advice.

All that is water over the dam (or ether over the Bridge, if you boys are following Dirac's lead back to the ether these days. How do I know about that? You'll see in a moment.) I don't mean to rehash it here. What I want to do in this letter is to leave you a more specialized memo, telling you in detail just how well the research system you suggested to me worked out for us.

Despite my surface appearance of ignoring that advice, we were following your suggestion, and very closely. I took a particular interest in your hunch that there might be "crackpot" ideas on gravity which needed investigation. Frankly, I had no hope of finding anything, but that would have left me no worse off than I had been before I talked to you. And actually it wasn't very long before my research chief came up with the Locke Derivation.

The research papers which finally emerged from this particular investigation are still in the Graveyard file, and I have no hope that they'll be released to non-government physicists within the foreseeable future. If you don't get the story from me, you'll never get it from anyone; and I've enough on my conscience now to be indifferent to a small crime like breaking Security. Besides, as usual, this particular "secret" has been available for the taking for years. A man named Schuster—you may know more about him than I do— wondered out loud about it as far back as 1891, before anybody had thought of trying to keep scientific matters a secret. He wanted to know whether or not every large rotating mass, like the Sun for instance, was a natural magnet. (That was before the sun's magnetic field had been discovered, too.) And by the 1940s it was clearly established for *small* rotating bodies like electrons—a thing called the Lande factor with which I'm sure you're familiar. I myself don't understand Word One of it. (Dirac was associated with much of that part of the work.) Finally, a man named W. H. Babcock, of Mount Wilson, pointed out in the 1940s that the Lande factor for the Earth, the Sun, and a star named 78 Virginius was identical, or damned close to it.

Now all this seemed to me to have nothing to do at all with gravity, and I said so to my team chief, who brought the thing to my attention. But I was wrong (I suppose you're already ahead of me by now). Another man, Prof. P. M. S. Blackett, whose name was even familiar to *me*, had pointed out the relationship. Suppose, Blackett said (I am copying from my notes now), we let P be magnetic moment, or what I have to think of as the leverage effect of a magnet—the product of the strength of the charge times the distance between the poles. Let U be angular momentum—rotation to a slob like me; angular speed times moment of inertia to you. Then if C is the velocity of light, and G is the acceleration of gravity (and they always are in equations like this, I'm told), then:

$$P = \frac{BG^{\frac{1}{2}}U}{2C}$$

(B is supposed to be a constant amounting to about 0·25. Don't ask me why.) Admittedly this was all speculative; there would be no way to test it, except on another planet with a stronger magnetic field than Earth's—preferably about a hundred times as strong. The closest we could come to that would be Jupiter, where the speed of rotation is about 25,000 miles an hour at the equator—and that was obviously out of the question.

Or was it? I confess that I never thought of using Jupiter, except in wish-fulfilment daydreams, until this matter of the Locke Derivation came up. It seems that by a simple algebraic manipulation, you can stick G on one side of the equation, and all the other terms on the other, and come up with this:

$$G=\left(\frac{2PC}{BU}\right)^2$$

To test that, you need a gravitational field little more than twice the strength of Earth's. And there, of course, is Jupiter again. None of my experts would give the notion a nickel—they said, among other things, that nobody even knew who Locke was, which is true, and that his algebraic trick wouldn't stand up under dimensional analysis, which turned out to be also true—but irrelevant. (We *did* have to monkey with it a little after the experimental results were in.) What counted was that we could make a practical use of this relationship.

Once we tried that, I should add, we were astonished at the accompanying effects: the abolition of the Lorentz-Fitzgerald relationship inside the field, the intolerance of the field itself to matter outside its influence, and so on; not only at their occurring at all—the formula doesn't predict them—but at their order of magnitude. I'm told that when this thing gets out, dimensional analysis isn't the only scholium that's going to have to be revamped. It's going to be the greatest headache for physicists since the Einstein theory; I don't know whether you'll relish this premonitory twinge or not.

Pretty good going for a "crackpot" notion, though.

After that, the Bridge was inevitable. As soon as it became clear that we could perform the necessary tests only on the surface of Jupiter itself, we had to have the Bridge. It also became clear that the Bridge would have to be a dynamic structure. It couldn't be built to a certain size and stopped there. The moment it was stopped, Jupiter would tear it to shreds. We had to build it to grow—to do more than just resist Jupiter—to push back against Jupiter, instead. It's double the size that it needed to be to test the Locke Derivation, now, and I still don't know how much longer we're going to have to keep it growing. Not long, I hope; the thing's a monster already.

But Seppi, let me ask you this: Does the Bridge really fall under the interdict you uttered against gigantic research projects? It's gigantic, all right. But—is it gigantic *on Jupiter?* I say it isn't. It's peanuts. A piece of attic gadgetry and nothing more. And we couldn't have performed the necessary experiments on any other planet.

Not all the wealth of Ormus or of Ind, or of all the world down all the ages, could have paid for a Manhattan District scaled to Jupiter's size.

In addition—though this was incidental—the apparent giganticism involved was a useful piece of misdirection. Elephantine research projects may be just about played out, but government budgetry agencies are used to them and think them normal. Getting the Joint Committee involved in one helped to revive the committeemen from their comatose state, as nothing else could have. It got us appropriations we never could have corralled otherwise, because people associate such projects with weapons research. And—forgive me, but there is a sort of science to politics too—it seemed to show graphically that I was *not* following the suspect advice of the suspect, Dr. Corsi. I owed you that, though it's hardly as large a payment as I would like to make.

But I don't mean to talk about the politics of crackpot-mining here; only about the concrete results. You should be warned, too, that the method has its pitfalls.

You will know by now about the anti-agathic research, and what we got out of it. I talked to people who might know what the chances were, and got general agreement from them as to how we should proceed. This straight-line approach looked good to me from the beginning —I set the Pfitzner people to work on it at once, since they already had that HWS appropriation for similar research, and HWS wouldn't be alert enough to detect the moment when Pfitzner's target changed from just plain old age to death itself. But we didn't overlook the crackpots—and before long we found a real dilly.

This was a man named Lyons, who insisted that the standard Lansing hypothesis, which postulates the existence of an ageing-toxin, was exactly the opposite of the truth. (I go into this subject with a certain relish, because I suspect that you know as little about it as I do; it's not often that I find myself in that situation.) Instead, he said, what happens is that it's the *young* mothers who pass on to their offspring some substance which makes them long-lived. Lansing's notion that the old mothers were the ones who did the passing along, and that the substance passed along speeding up ageing, was unproven, Lyons said.

Well, that threw us into something of a spiral. Lansing's Law—"Senescence begins when growth ends"— had been regarded as gospel in gerontology for decades. But Lyons had a good hypothetical case. He pointed out that, among other things, all of Lansing's long-lived rotifers showed characteristics in common with polyploid individuals. In addition to being hardy and long-lived, they were of unusually large size, and they were less fertile than normal rotifers. Suppose that the substance which was passed along from one generation to another was a chromosome-doubler, like colchicine?

We put that question to Lansing's only surviving student, a living crotchet named MacDougal. He wouldn't hear of it; to him it was like questioning the Word of God. Besides, he said, if Lyons is right, how do you propose to test it? Rotifers are microscopic animals. Except for their eggs, their body-cells are invisible even under the microscope. It would be quite a few months of Sundays before we ever got a look at a rotifer chromosome.

Lyons thought he had an answer for that. He proposed to develop a technique of microtome preparation which would make, not one, but several different slices through a rotifer's egg. With any sort of luck, he said, we might be able to extend the technique to rotifer spores, and maybe even to the adult critters.

We thought we ought to try it. Without telling Pfitzner about it, we gave Pearl River Labs that headache. We put Lyons himself in charge, and assigned Mac-Dougal to act as a consultant (which he did by sniping and scoffing every minute of the day, until not only Lyons, but everybody else in the plant hated him). It was awful. Rotifers, it turns out, are incredibly delicate animals, just about impossible to preserve after they're dead, no matter what stage of their development you catch them in. Time and time again, Lyons came up with microscope slides which, he said, *proved* that the long-lived rotifers were at least triploid—three labelled chromosomes per body-cell instead of two—and maybe even tetraploid. Every other expert in the Pearl River plant looked at them, and saw nothing but a blur which might have been rotifer chromosomes, and might equally well have been a newspaper halftone of a grey cat walking over a fur rug in a thick fog. The comparative tests—producing polyploid rotifers and other critters with drugs like colchicine, and comparing them with the critters produced by Lansing's and Mac-Dougal's classical breeding methods—were just as indecisive. Lyons finally decided that what he needed to prove his case was the world's biggest and most expensive X-ray microscope, and right then we shut him down.

MacDougal had been right all the time. Lyons was a crackpot with a plausible line of chatter, enough of a technique at microdissection to compel respect, and a real and commendable eagerness to explore his idea right down to the bottom. MacDougal was a frozen-brained old man with far too much reverence for his teacher, a man far too ready to say that a respected notion was right because it was respected, and a man who had performed no actual experiments himself since his student days. But he had been right—purely intuitively—in predicting that Lyons' inversion of Lansing's Law would come to nothing. I gather that victory in the sciences doesn't always go to the most personable man, any more than it does in any other field. I'm glad to know it; I'm always glad to find some small area of human endeavour which resists the con-man and the sales-talk.

When Pfitzner discovered ascomycin, we had HWS close Pearl River out entirely.

Negative results of this kind are valuable for scientists too, I'm told. How you will evaluate your proposed research method in the light of these two experiences is unknown to me; I can only tell you what I think *I* learned. I am convinced that we must be much slower, in the future, to ignore the fringe notion and the marginal theorist. One of the virtues of these crackpots—if that is what they are—is that they tend to cling to ideas

140

which can be tested. That's worth hanging on to, in a world where scientific ideas have become so abstract that even their originators can't suggest ways to test them. Whoever Locke was, I suppose he hadn't put a thousandth as much time into thinking about gravity as Blackett had; yet Blackett couldn't suggest a way to test his equation, whereas the Locke Derivation was testable (on Jupiter) and turned out to be right. As for Lyons, his notion was wrong; but it too fell down because it failed the operational test, the very test it proposed to pass; until we performed that test, we had no real assessment of Lansing's Law, which had been travelling for years on prestige because of the "impossibility" of weighing any contrary hypothesis. Lyons forced us to do that, and enlarged our knowledge.

And so, take it from there; I've tried to give back as good as I have gotten. I'm not going to discuss the politics of this whole conspiracy with you, nor do I want you to concern yourself with them. Politics is death. Above all, I beg you—if you're at all pleased with this report—not to be distressed over the situation I will probably be in by the time this reaches you. I've been ruthless with your reputation to advance my purposes; I've been ruthless with the careers of some other people; I've been quite ruthless in sending some men—some hundreds of men—to deaths they could surely have avoided had it not been for me; I've put many others, including a number of children, into considerable jeopardy. With all this written against my name, I'd think it a monstrous injustice to get off scot-free.

And that is all I can say; I have an appointment in a few minutes. Thank you for your friendship and your help.

BLISS WAGONER

★
★ 9 ★

Ruthlessness, Anne had said, is what it takes. But—Paige thought afterwards—is it?

Does faith add up to its own flat violation? It was all well enough to have something in which you could believe. But when a faith in humanity-in-general automatically results in casual inhumanity toward individual people, something must have gone awry. Should the temple bell be struck so continually that it has to shatter, and make all its worshippers ill with terror until it is silenced?

Silence. The usual answer. Or was the fault not in faith itself, but in the faithful? The faithful were usually pretty frightening as people, Witnesses and humanitarians alike.

Paige's time to debate the point with himself had already almost run out—and with it, his time to protect himself, if he could. Nothing had emerged from his soil samples. Evidently bacterial life on the Jovian moons had never at any time been profuse, and consisted now only of a few hardy spores of common species, like *Bacillus subtilis*, which occurred on every Earth-like world and sometimes even in meteors. The samples plated out sparsely and yielded nothing which had not been known for decades—as, indeed, the statistics of this kind of research had predicted from the beginning.

142

It was now known around the Bronx plant that some sort of investigation of the Pfitzner project was rolling, and was already moving too fast to be derailed by any method the company's executives could work out. Daily reports from Pfitzner's Washington office—actually the Washington branch of Interplanet Press, the public relations agency Pfitzner maintained—were filed in the plant, but they were apparently not very informative. Paige gathered that there was some mystery about the investigation at the source, though neither Gunn nor Anne would say so in so many words.

And, finally, Paige's leave was to be over, day after tomorrow. After that, the Proserpine station—and probably an order to follow, emerging out of the investigation, which would maroon him there for the rest of his life in the service.

And it wasn't worth it.

That realization had been staring him in the eyes all along. For Anne and Gunn, perhaps, the price was worth paying, the tricks were worth playing, the lying and the cheating and the risking of the lives of others were necessary and just to the end in view. But when the last card was down, Paige knew that he himself lacked the necessary dedication. Like every other road toward dedication that he had assayed, this one had turned out to have been paved with pure lead—and had left him with no better emblem of conduct than the miserable one which had kept him going all the same: self-preservation.

He knew then, with cold disgust toward himself, that he was going to use what he knew to clear himself, as soon as the investigation hit the plant. Senator Wagoner, the grapevine said, would be conducting it—oddly enough, for Wagoner and MacHinery were deadly political enemies; had MacHinery gotten the jump on him at last?—and would arrive tomorrow. If Paige timed himself very carefully, he could lay down the facts, leave the plant for ever, and be out in space without having to face Tru Gunn or Anne Abbott at all. What would happen to the Pfitzner project thereafter would be old news by the time he landed at the Proserpine station—more than three months old.

And by that time, he told himself, he would no longer care.

Nevertheless, when the quick morrow came, he marched in to Gunn's office—which Wagoner had taken over—like a man going before a firing squad.

A moment later, he felt as though he had been shot down while still crossing the door-sill. Even before he realized that Anne was already in the room, he heard Wagoner say:

"Colonel Russell, sit down. I'm glad to see you. I have a security clearance for you, and a new set of orders; you can forget Proserpine. You and Miss Abbott and I are leaving for Jupiter. Tonight."

It was like a dream after that. In the Caddy on the way to the spaceport, Wagoner said nothing. As for Anne, she seemed to be in a state of slight shock. From what little Paige thought he had learned about her— and it was very little—he deduced that she had expected this as little as he had. Her face as he had entered Gunn's office had been guarded, eager, and slightly smug all at once, as though she had thought she'd know what Wagoner would say. But when Wagoner had mentioned Jupiter, she'd turned to look at him as though he'd been turned from a senator into a boxing kangaroo, in the plain sight of the Pfitzner

144

Founders. Something was wrong. After the long catalogue of things already visibly wrong, the statement didn't mean very much. But something had clearly gone wrong.

There were fireworks in the sky to the south, visible from the right side of the Caddy where Paige sat as the car turned east on to the parkway. They were big and spectacular, and seemed to be going up from the heart of Manhattan. Paige was puzzled until he remembered, like a fact recalled from the heart of an absurd dream, that this was the last night of the Witness Revival, being held in the stadium on Randalls Island. The fireworks celebrated the Second Coming, which the Witnesses were confident could not now be long delayed.

> *Gewiss, gewiss, es naht noch heut'*
> *und kann nicht lang mehr säumen. . . .*

Paige could remember having heard his father, an ardent Wagnerian, singing that; it was from *Tristan.* But he thought instead of those frightening medieval paintings of the Second Coming, in which Christ stands ignored in a corner of the canvas while the people flock reverently to the feet of the Anti-Christ, whose face, in the dim composite of Paige's memory, was a curious mixture of Francis X. MacHinery and Bliss Wagoner.

Words began to bloom along the black sky at the hearts of starshells:

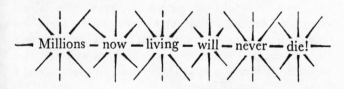

— Millions — now — living — will — never — die! —

No doubt, Paige thought bleakly. The Witnesses also believed that the Earth was flat; but Paige was on his way to Jupiter—not exactly a round planet, but rounder than the Witnesses' Earth. In quest, if you please, of immortality, in which he too had believed. Tasting bile, he thought, *It takes all kinds*.

A final starshell, so brilliant even at this distance that the word inside it was almost dazzled out, burst soundlessly into blue-white fire above the city. It said:

Paige swung his head abruptly and looked at Anne. Her face, a ghostly blur in the dying light of the shell, was turned raptly toward the window; she had been watching, too. He leaned forward and kissed her slightly parted lips, gently, forgetting all about Wagoner. After a frozen moment he could feel her mouth smiling against his, the smile which had astonished him so when he had seen it first, but softened, transformed, giving. The world went away for a while.

Then she touched his cheeks with her fingertips and sank back against the cushions; the Caddy swung sharply north off the parkway; and the spark of radiance which was the last retinal image of the shell vanished into drifting purple blotches, like aftervisions of the sun—or of Jupiter seen close-on. Anne had no way of knowing, of course, that he had been running away from her, toward the Proserpine station, when he had been cornered in this Caddy instead. *Anne, Anne, I believe; help me in mine unbelief.*

The Caddy was passed through the spaceport gates after a brief, whispered consultation between the chauffeur and the guards. Instead of driving directly for the Administration Building, however, it turned craftily to the left and ran along the inside of the wire fence, back toward the city and into the dark reaches of the emergency landing pits. It was not totally dark there, however; there was a pool of light on an apron some distance ahead, with a needle of glare pointing straight up from its centre.

Paige leaned forward and peered through the double glass barrier—one pane between himself and the driver, the other between the driver and the world. The needle of light was a ship, but it was not one he recognized. It was a single-stage job: a ferry, then, designed to take them out no farther than to Satellite Vehicle One, where they would be transferred to a proper interplanetary vessel. But it was small, even for a ferry.

"How do you like her, Colonel?" Wagoner's voice said, unexpectedly, from the black corner where he sat.

"All right," Paige said. "She's a little small, isn't she?"

Wagoner chuckled. "Pretty damn small," he said, and fell silent again. Alarmed, Paige began to wonder if the senator was feeling entirely well. He turned to look at Anne, but he could not even see her face now. He groped for her hand; she responded with a feverish, rigid grip.

The Caddy shot abruptly away from the fence, with a smoothness and a silence that bespoke gasolene in the fuel tank, not kerosene. It bore down on the pool of light. Paige could see several marines standing on the apron at the tail of the ship. Absurdly, the vessel looked even smaller as it came closer.

"All right," Wagoner said. "Out of here, both of you. We'll be taking off in ten minutes. The crewmen will show you your quarters."

"Crewmen?" Paige said. "Senator, that ship won't hold more than four people, and one of them has to be the tube-man. That leaves nobody to pilot her but me."

"Not this trip," Wagoner said, following him out of the car. "We're only passengers, you and I and Miss Abbott, and of course the marines. The *Per Aspera* has a separate crew of five. Let's not waste time, please."

It was impossible. On the cleats, Paige felt as though he were trying to climb into a ·22 calibre long-rifle cartridge. To get ten people into this tiny shell, you'd have to turn them into some sort of human concentrate and pour them in, like powdered coffee.

Nevertheless, one of the marines met him in the airlock, and within another minute he was strapping himself down inside a windowless cabin as big as any he'd ever seen on board a standard interplanetary vessel—far bigger than any ferry could acccommodate. The intercom box at the head of his hammock was already calling the clearance routine.

"Dog down and make all fast. Airlock will cycle in one minute."

What had happened to Anne? She had come up the cleats after him, of that he was sure——

"All fast. Take-off in one minute. Passengers 'ware G's."

——but he'd been hustled down to this nonsensical cabin too fast to look back. There was something very wrong. Was Wagoner——

"Thirty seconds. 'Ware G's."

——making some sort of a getaway? Bur from what?

148

And why did he want to take Paige and Anne with him? As hostages they were——

"Twenty seconds."

——worthless, since they were of no value to the government, had no money, knew nothing damning about Wagoner——

"Fifteen seconds."

But wait a minute. Anne knew something about Wagoner, or thought she did.

"Ten seconds. Stand by."

The call made him relax instinctively. There would be time to think about that later. At take-off——

"Five seconds."

——it didn't pay——

"Four."

——to concentrate——

"Three."

——on anything——

"Two."

——else but——

"One."

——actual——

"Zero."

——*take-off* hit him with the abrupt, bone-cracking, gut-wrenching impact of all ferry take-offs. There was nothing you could do to ameliorate it but let the strong muscles of the arms and legs and back bear it as best they could, with the automatic tetanus of the Seyle GA reaction, and concentrate on keeping your head and your abdomen in exact neutral with the acceleration thrust. The muscles you used for that were seldom called upon on the ground, even by weight-lifters, but you learned to use them or were invalided out of the service; a trained spaceman's abdominal muscles will bounce a heavy rock, and no strong man can make him turn his head if his neck muscles say *no*.

Also, it helped a little to yell. Theoretically, the yell collapses the lungs—acceleration pneumothorax, the books call it—and keeps them collapsed until the surge of powered flight is over. By that time, the carbon dioxide level of the blood has risen so high that the breathing reflex will reassert itself with an enormous gasp, even if crucial chest muscles have been torn. The yell makes sure that when next you breathe, you *breathe*.

But more importantly for Paige and every other spaceman, the yell was the only protest he could form against that murderous nine seconds of pressure; it makes you *feel* better. Paige yelled with vigour.

He was still yelling when the ship went into free fall.

Instantly, while the yell was still dying incredulously in his throat, he was clawing at his harness. All his spaceman's reflexes had gone off at once. The powered-flight period had been too short. Even the shortest possible take-off acceleration outlasts the yell. Yet the ion-rockets were obviously silenced. The little ship's power had failed—she was falling back to Earth——

"Attention, please," the intercom box said mildly. "We are now under way. Free fall will last only a few seconds. Stand by for restoration of normal gravity."

And then. . . . And then the hammock against which Paige was struggling was *down* again, as though the ship were still resting quietly on Earth. Impossible; she couldn't even be out of the atmosphere yet. Even if she were, free fall should last all the rest of the trip. Gravity in an interplanetary vessel—let alone a ferry—could be re-established only by rotating the ship around its long axis; few captains bothered with the fuel-expensive manœuvre, since hardly anybody but old hands flew between the planets. Besides, this ship—the *Per Aspera*—hadn't gone through any such manœuvre, or Paige would have detected it.

Yet his body continued to press down against the hammock with an acceleration of one Earth gravity.

"Attention, please. We will be passing the Moon in one point two minutes. The observation blister is now open to passengers. Senator Wagoner requests the presence of Miss Abbott and Colonel Russell in the blister."

There was no further sound from the ion-rockets, which had inexplicably been shut off when the *Per Aspera* could have been no more than 250 miles above the surface of the Earth. Yet she was passing the Moon now, without the slightest sensation of movement, though she must still be accelerating. What was driving her? Paige could hear nothing but the small hum of the ship's electrical generator, no louder than it would have been on the ground, unburdened of the job of RF-heating the electron-ion plasma which the rockets used. Grimly, he unsnapped the last gripper from his harness, conscious of what a baby he evidently was on board this ship, and got up.

The deck felt solid and abnormal under his feet, pressing against the soles of his shoes with a smug terrestrial pressure of one unvarying gravity. Only the habits of caution of a service lifetime prevented him from running forward up the companionway to the observation blister.

Anne and Senator Wagoner were there, the dimming moonlight bathing their backs as they looked ahead into deep space. Shining between them was a brilliant,

151

hard spot of yellow-white light, glaring into the blister through the thick, cosmics-proof glass. The spot was fixed and steady, as were all the stars looking into the blister; proof positive that the ship's gravity was not being produced by axial spin. The yellow spot itself, shining between Wagoner's elbow and Anne's upper arm, was——

Jupiter.

On either side of the planet were two smaller bright dots: the four Galilean satellites, as widely separated to Paige's naked eye as they would have looked on Earth through a telescope the size of Galileo's.

While Paige hesitated in the doorway to the blister, the little spots that were Jupiter's largest moons visibly drew apart from each other a little, until one of them went into occultation behind Anne's right shoulder. The *Per Aspera* was still accelerating; it was driving toward Jupiter at a speed nothing in Paige's experience could have prepared him for. Stunned, he made a very rough estimate in his head of the increase in parallax and tried to calculate the ship's rate of approach from that.

The little lunar ferry, humming scarcely louder than a transformer for a model railroad system, obviously incapable of carrying five people—let alone ten—as far as SV-1, was now hurtling toward Jupiter at about a quarter of the speed of light.

At least forty thousand miles per second.

And the deepening colour of Jupiter showed that the *Per Aspera* was still picking up speed.

"Come in, Colonel Russell," Wagoner's voice said, echoing slightly in the blister. "Come watch the show. We've been waiting for you."

10

The ship that landed as Helmuth was going on duty
did nothing to lighten the load on his heart. In shape it
was not distinguishable from any of the short-range
ferries which covered the Jovian satellary circuit,
carrying supplies from the regular SV-1-Mars-Belt-
Jupiter X cruiser to the inner moons—and, sometimes,
some years-old mail; but it was considerably bigger
than the usual Jovian ferry, and it grounded its outsize
mass on Jupiter V with only the briefest cough of
rockets.

That landing told Helmuth that his dream was well
on its way to coming true. If the high brass had a real
antigravity, there would have been no reason why the
ion-streams should have been necessary at all. Obviously, what had been discovered was some sort of partial
gravity screen, which allowed a ship to operate with
far less rocket thrust than was usual, but which still left
it subject to a sizeable fraction of the universal G, the
inherent stress of space.

Nothing less than a complete, and completely con-
trollable gravity screen would do, on Jupiter.

And theory said that a complete gravity screen was
impossible. Once you set one up—even supposing that
you could—you would be unable to enter it or leave it.
Crossing a boundary-line between a one G field and a

no-G field would be precisely as difficult as surmounting a high-jump with the bar set at infinity, and for the same reasons. If you crossed it from the other direction, you would hit the ground on the other side of the line as hard as though you had fallen there from the Moon; a little harder, in fact.

Helmuth worked mechanically at the gang board, thinking. Charity was not in evidence, but there was no special reason why the foreman's board had to be manned on this trick. The work could be as easily supervised from here, and obviously Charity had expected Helmuth to do it that way, or he would have left notice. Probably Charity was already conferring with the senators, receiving what would be for him the glad news.

Helmuth realized suddenly that there was nothing left for him to do now, once this trick was over, but to cut and run.

There could be no real reason why he should be required to re-enact the entire nightmare, helplessly, event for event, like an actor committed to a role. He was awake now, in full control of his own senses, and still at least partially sane. The man in the dream had volunteered—but that man would not be Robert Helmuth. Not any longer.

While the senators were here on Jupiter V, he would turn in his resignation. Direct—over Charity's head.

The wave of relief came washing over him just as he finished resetting the circuits which would enable him to supervise from the gang board, and left him so startlingly weak that he had to put the helmet down on the ledge before he had raised it half-way to his head. So *that* had been what he had been waiting for: to quit, nothing more.

He owed it to Charity to finish the Grand Tour of the Bridge. After that, he'd be free. He would never have to see the Bridge again, not even inside a viewing helmet. A farewell tour, and then back to Chicago, if there was still such a place.

He waited until his breathing had quieted a little, scooped the helmet up on to his shoulders, and the Bridge . . .

. . . came falling into existence all around him, a Pandemonium beyond broaching and beyond hope, sealed on all sides. The drumfire of rain against his beetle's hull was so loud that it hurt his ears, even with the gain knob of his helmet backed all the way down to the thumb-stop. It was impossible to cut the audio circuit out altogether; much of his assessment of how the Bridge was responding to stress depended on sound; human eyesight on the Bridge was almost as useless as a snail's.

And the Bridge was responding now, as always, with its medley of dissonance and cacophony: *crang . . . crang . . . spungg . . . skreek . . . crang . . . ungg . . . oingg . . . skreek . . . skreek. . . .* These structural noises were the only ones that counted; they were the polyphony of the Bridge, everything else was decorative and to be ignored by the Bridge operator—the fioritura shrieking of the winds, the battery of the rain, the pedal diapason of thunder, the distant grumbling roll of the stage-hand volcanoes pushing continents back and forth on castors down below.

This time, however, at long last, it was impossible to ignore any part of this great orchestra. Its composite uproar was enormous, implacable, incredible even for Jupiter, overwhelming even in this season. The moment he heard it, Helmuth knew that he had waited too long.

The Bridge was not going to last much longer. Not unless every man and woman on Jupiter V fought without sleep to keep it up, throughout this passage of the Red Spot and the South Tropical Disturbance——

——if even that would serve. The great groans that were rising through the tornado-riven mists from the caissons were becoming steadily, spasmodically deeper; their hinges were already overloaded. And the deck of the Bridge was beginning to rise and fall a little, as though slow, frozen waves were passing along it from one unfinished end to the other. The queasy, lazy tidal swell made the beetle tip first its nose into the winds, then its tail, then back again, so that it took almost all of the current Helmuth could feed into the magnet windings to keep the craft stuck to the rails on the deck at all. Cruising the deck seemed to be out of the question; there was not enough power left over for the engines—almost every available erg had to be devoted to staying put.

But there was still the rest of the Grand Tour to be made. And still one direction which Helmuth had yet to explore:

Straight down.

Down to the ice; down to the Ninth Circle, where everything stops, and never starts again.

There was a set of tracks leading down one of the Bridge's great buttresses, on to which Helmuth could switch the beetle in nearby sector 94. It took him only a few moments to set the small craft to creeping head downward toward the surface.

The meters on the ghost board had already told him that the wind velocity fell off abruptly at twenty-one miles—that is, eleven miles down from the deck—in this sector, which was in the lee of The Glacier, a long rib of mountain-range which terminated near by. He was unprepared, however, for the near-calm itself. There was some wind, of course, as there was everywhere on Jupiter, especially at this season; but the worst gusts were little more than a few hundred miles per hour, and occasionally the meter fell as low as seventy-five.

The lull was dream-like. The beetle crawled downward through it, like a skin-diver who has already passed the safety-knot on his line, but is too drugged by the ecstasy of the depths to care. At fifteen miles, something white flashed in the fan-lights, and was gone. Then another; three more. And then, suddenly, a whole stream of them.

Belatedly, Helmuth stopped the beetle and peered ahead, but the white things were gone now. No, there were more of them, drifting quite slowly through the lights. As the wind died momentarily, they almost seemed to hover, pulsating slowly——

Helmuth heard himself grunt with astonishment. Once, in a moment of fancy, he had thought of Jovian jellyfish. That was what these looked like—jellyfish, not of the sea, but of the air. They were ten-ribbed, translucent, ranging in size from that of a closed fist to one as big as a football. They were beautiful—and looked incredibly delicate for this furious planet.

Helmuth reached forward to turn up the lights, but the wind rose just as his hand closed on the knob, and the creatures were gone. In the increased glare, Helmuth saw instead that there was a large platform jutting out from the buttress not far below him, just to one side of the rails. It was enclosed and roofed, but the material was transparent. And there was motion inside it.

He had no idea what the structure could be; evidently it was recent. Although he had never been below the deck in this sector before, he knew the plans well enough to recall that they had specified no such excresence.

For a wild instant he had thought that there was a man on Jupiter already; but as he pulled up just above the platform's roof, he realized that the moving thing inside was—of course—a robot: a misshapen, many-tentacled thing about twice the size of a man. It was working busily with bottles and flasks, of which it seemed to have thousands on benches and shelves all around it. The whole enclosure was a litter of what Helmuth took to be chemical apparatus, and off to one side was an object which might have been a microscope.

The robot looked up at him and gesticulated with two or three tentacles. At first Helmuth failed to understand; then he saw that the machine was pointing to the fan-lights, and obediently turned them almost all the way down. In the resulting Jovian gloom he could see that the laboratory—for that was obviously what it was—had plenty of artificial light of its own.

There was, of course, no way that he could talk to the robot, nor it to him. If he wanted to, he could talk to the person operating it; but he knew the assignment of every man and woman on Jupiter V, and running this thing was no part of any of their duties. There was not even any provision for it on the boards——

A white light began to wink on the ghost board. That would be the incoming line for Europa. Was somebody on that snowball in charge of this many-tentacled experimenter, using Jupiter V's booster station to amplify the signals that guided it? Curiously, he plugged the jack in.

"Hello the Bridge! Who's on duty there?"

"Hello Europa. This is Bob Helmuth. Is this your robot I'm looking at, in sector ninety-four?"

"That's me," the voice said. It was impossible to avoid thinking of it as coming from the robot itself. "This is Doc Barth. How do you like my laboratory?"

"Very cosy," Helmuth said. "I didn't even know it existed. What do you do in it?"

"We just got it installed this year. It's to study the Jovian life-forms. You've seen them?"

"You mean the jellyfish? Are they really alive?"

"Yes," the robot said. "We were keeping it under our hats until we had more data, but we knew that sooner or later one of you beetle-goosers would see them. They're alive, all right. They've got a colloidal continuum-discontinuum exactly like protoplasm—except that it uses liquid ammonia as a sol substrate, instead of water."

"But what do they live on?" Helmuth said.

"Ah, that's the question. Some form of aerial plankton, that's certain; we've found the digested remnants inside them, but haven't captured any live specimens of it yet. The digested fragments don't offer us much to go on. And what does the plankton live on? I only wish I knew."

Helmuth thought about it. Life on Jupiter. It did not matter that it was simple in structure, and virtually helpless in the winds. It was life all the same, even down here in the frozen pits of a hell no living man would ever visit. And who could know, if jellyfish rode the Jovian air, what Leviathans might not swim the Jovian seas?

"You don't seem to be much impressed," the robot

said. "Jellyfish and plankton probably aren't very exciting to a layman. But the implications are tremendous. It's going to cause quite a stir among biologists, let me tell you."

"I can believe that," Helmuth said. "I was just taken aback, that's all. We've always thought of Jupiter as lifeless——"

"That's right. But now we know better. Well, back to work; I'll be talking to you." The robot flourished its tentacles and bent over a workbench.

Abstractedly, Helmuth backed the beetle off and turned it upward again. Barth, he remembered, was the man who had found a fossil on Europa. Earlier, there had been an officer doing a tour of duty in the Jovian system who had spent some of his spare time cutting soil samples, in search of bacteria. Probably he had found some; scientists of the age before spaceflight had even found them in meteors. The Earth and Mars were not the only places in the universe that would harbour life, after all; perhaps it was—everywhere. If it could exist in a place like Jupiter, there was no logical reason to rule it out even on the Sun—some animated flame no one would recognize as life. . . .

He regained the deck and sent the beetle rumbling for the switchyard; he would need to transfer to another track before he could return the car to its garage. It had occurred to him during the ghostly proxy-conversation that he had never met Doc Barth, or many of the other men with whom he had talked so often by ham radio. Except for the Bridge operators themselves, the Jovian system was a community of disembodied voices to him. And now, he would never meet them. . . .

"Wake up, Helmuth," a voice from the gang deck snapped abruptly. "If it hadn't been for me, you'd
160

have run yourself off the end of the Bridge. You had all the automatic stops on that beetle cut out."

Helmuth reached guiltily and more than a little too late for the controls. Eva had already run his beetle back beyond the danger line.

"Sorry," he mumbled, taking the helmet off. "Thanks, Eva."

"Don't thank me. If you'd actually been in it, I'd have let it go. Less reading and more sleep is what I recommend for you, Helmuth."

"Keep your recommendations to yourself," he growled.

The incident started a new and even more disturbing chain of thought. If he were to resign now, it would be nearly a year before he could get back to Chicago. Antigravity or no antigravity, the senators' ship would have no room for unexpected extra passengers. Shipping a man back home had to be arranged far in advance. Living space had to be provided, and a cargo equivalent of the weight and space requirements he would take up on the return trip had to be dead-headed out to Jupiter V.

A year of living in the station on Jupiter V without any function—as a man whose drain on the station's supplies no longer could be justified in terms of what he did. A year of living under the eyes of Eva Chavez and Charity Dillon and the other men and women who still remained Bridge operators, men and women who would not hesitate to let him know what they thought of his quitting.

A year of living as a bystander in the feverish excitement of direct, personal exploration of Jupiter. A year of watching and hearing the inevitable deaths—while he alone stood aloof, privileged and useless. A year

L   161

during which Robert Helmuth would become the most hated living entity in the Jovian system.

And, when he got back to Chicago and went looking for a job—for his resignation from the Bridge gang would automatically take him out of government service—he would be asked why he had left the Bridge at the moment when work on the Bridge was just reaching its culmination.

He began to understand why the man in the dream had volunteered.

When the trick-change bell rang, he was still determined to resign, but he had already concluded bitterly that there were, after all, other kinds of hells besides the one on Jupiter.

He was returning the board to neutral as Charity came up the cleats. Charity's eyes were snapping like a skyful of comets. Helmuth had known that they would be.

"Senator Wagoner wants to speak to you, if you're not too tired, Bob," he said. "Go ahead; I'll finish up there."

"He does?" Helmuth frowned. The dream surged back upon him. *No.* They would not rush him any faster than he wanted to go. "What about, Charity? Am I suspected of unwestern activities? I suppose you've told them how I feel."

"I have," Dillon said, unruffled. "But we've agreed that you may not feel the same way after you've talked to Wagoner. He's in the ship, of course. I've put out a suit for you at the lock."

Charity put the helmet over his head, effectively cutting himself off from further conversation, or from any further consciousness of Helmuth at all.

Helmuth stood looking at the blind, featureless

bubble on Charity's shoulders for a moment. Then, with a convulsive shrug, he went down the cleats.

Three minutes later, he was plodding in a spacesuit across the surface of Jupiter V, with the vivid bulk of the mother planet splashing his shoulders with colour.

A courteous marine let him through the ship's airlock and deftly peeled him out of the suit. Despite a grim determination to be uninterested in the new anti-gravity and any possible consequence of it, he looked curiously about as he was conducted up toward the bow.

But the ship on the inside was like the ones that had brought him from Chicago to Jupiter V—it was like any spaceship: there was nothing in it to see but corridor walls and cleatwells, until you arrived at the cabin where you were needed.

Senator Wagoner was a surprise. He was a young man, no more than sixty at most, not at all portly, and he had the keenest pair of blue eyes that Helmuth had ever seen. The cabin in which he received Helmuth was obviously his own, a comfortable cabin as spaceship accommodations go, but neither roomy nor luxurious. The senator was hard to match up with the stories Helmuth had been hearing about the current Senate, which had been involved in scandal after scandal of more than Roman proportions.

There were only two people with him: a rather plain girl who was possibly his secretary, and a tall man wearing the uniform of the Army Space Corps and the eagles of a colonel. Helmuth realized, with a second shock of surprise, that he knew the officer: he was Paige Russell, a ballistics expert who had been stationed in the Jovian system not too long ago. The dirt-collector. He smiled rather wryly as Helmuth's eyebrows went up.

Helmuth looked back at the senator. "I thought there was a whole sub-committee here," he said.

"There is, but we left them where we found them, on Ganymede. I didn't want to give you the idea that you were facing a Grand Jury," Wagoner said, smiling. "I've been forced to sit in on most of these endless loyalty investigations back home, but I can't see any point in exporting such religious ceremonies to deep space. Do sit down, Mr. Helmuth. There are drinks coming. We have a lot to talk about."

Stiffly, Helmuth sat down.

"You know Colonel Russell, of course," Wagoner said, leaning back comfortably in his own chair. "This young lady is Anne Abbott, about whom you'll hear more shortly. Now then: Dillon tells me that your usefulness to the Bridge is about at an end. In a way, I'm sorry to hear that, for you've been one of the best men we've had on any of our planetary projects. But, in another way, I'm glad. It makes you available for something much bigger, where we need you much more."

"What do you mean by that?"

"You'll have to let me explain it in my own way. First, I'd like to talk a little about the Bridge. Please don't feel that I'm quizzing you, by the way. You're at perfect liberty to say that any given question is none of my business, and I'll take no offence and hold no grudge. Also, 'I hereby disavow the authenticity of any tape or other tapping of which this statement may be a part.' In short, our conversation is unofficial, highly so."

"Thank you."

"It's to my interest; I'm hoping that you'll talk freely to me. Of course, my disavowal means nothing, since such formal statements can always be excised from a

164

tape; but later on I'm going to tell you some things you're not supposed to know, and you'll be able to judge by what I say that anything you say to me is privileged. Paige and Anne are your witnesses. Okay?"

A steward came in silently with the drinks, and left again. Helmuth tasted his. As far as he could tell, it was exactly like many he had mixed for himself back in the control shack, from standard space rations. The only difference was that it was cold, which Helmuth found startling, but not unpleasant after the first sip. He tried to relax. "I'll do my best," he said.

"Good enough. Now: Dillon says that you regard the Bridge as a monster. I've examined your dossier pretty closely—as a matter of fact I've been studying both you and Paige far more intensively than you can imagine—and I think perhaps Dillon hasn't quite the gist of your meaning. I'd like to hear it straight from you."

"I don't think the Bridge is a monster," Helmuth said slowly. "You see, Charity is on the defensive. He takes the Bridge to be conclusive evidence that no possible set of adverse conditions will ever stop man for long, and there I'm in agreement with him. But he also thinks of it as Progress, personified. He can't admit—you asked me to speak my mind, Senator—he can't admit that the West is a decadent and dying culture. All the other evidence that's available shows that it is. Charity likes to think of the Bridge as giving the lie to that evidence."

"The West hasn't many more years," Wagoner agreed, astonishingly.

Paige Russell mopped his forehead. "I still can't hear you say that," the spaceman said, "without wanting to duck under the rug. After all, MacHinery's with that pack on Ganymede——"

"MacHinery," Wagoner said calmly, "is probably going to die of apoplexy when we spring this thing on him, and I for one won't miss him. Anyhow, it's perfectly true; the dominoes have been falling for some time now, and the explosion Anne's outfit has cooked up is going to be the final blow. Still and all, Mr. Helmuth, the West has been responsible for some really towering achievements in its time. Perhaps the Bridge could be considered as the last and mightiest of them all."

"Not by me," Helmuth said. "The building of gigantic projects for ritual purposes—doing a thing for the sake of doing it—is the last act of an already dead culture. Look at the pyramids in Egypt for an example. Or at an even more enormous and more idiotic example, bigger than anything human beings have accomplished yet—the laying out of the 'Diagram of Power' over the whole face of Mars. If the Martians had put all that energy into survival instead, they'd probably be alive yet."

"Agreed," Wagoner said, "with reservations. 'Doing a thing for the sake of doing it' is not a definition of ritual; it's a definition of science."

"All right. That doesn't greatly alter my argument. Maybe you'll also agree that the essence of a vital culture is its ability to defend itself. The West has beaten the Soviets for half a century now—but as far as I can see, the Bridge is the West's 'Diagram of Power', its pyramids, or what have you. It shows that we're mighty, but mighty in a non-survival sort of way. All the money and the resources that went into the Bridge are going to be badly needed, *and won't be there*, when the next Soviet attack comes."

"Correction: it has already come," Wagoner said.

"And it has already won. The USSR played the greatest of all von Neumann games far better than we did, because they didn't assume as we did that each side would always choose the best strategy; they played also to wear down the players. In fifty years of unrelenting pressure, they succeeded in converting the West into a system so like the Soviets' as to make direct military action unnecessary; we Sovietized ourselves, and our moves are now exactly predictable.

"So in part I agree with you. What we needed was to sink the energy and the money into the game—into social research, since the menace was social. Instead, typically, we put it into a physical research project of unprecedented size. Which was, of course, just what the theory of games said we would do. For a man who's been cut off from Earth for years, Helmuth, you seem to know more about what's going on down there than most of the general populace does."

"Nothing promotes an interest in Earth like being off it," Helmuth said. "And there's plenty of time to read out here." Either the drink was stronger than he had expected—which was reasonable, considering that he had been off the stuff for some time now—or the senator's calm concurrence in the collapse of Helmuth's entire world had given him another shove toward the abyss; his head was spinning.

Wagoner saw it. He leaned forward suddenly, catching Helmuth flat-footed. "*However*," he said, "it's difficult for me to agree that the Bridge serves, or ever did serve, a ritual purpose. The Bridge served several huge practical purposes which are now fulfilled. As a matter of fact, the Bridge, as such, is now a defunct project."

"Defunct?" Helmuth said faintly.

"Quite. Of course, we'll continue to operate it for a

167

while. You can't stop a process of that size on a dime. Besides, one of the reasons why we built the Bridge was because the USSR expected us to; the game said that we should launch another Manhattan District or H-bomb project at this point, and we hated to disappoint them. One thing we are *not* going to do this time, however, is to tell them the problem that the project was supposed to solve—let alone that it *can* be solved, and has been.

"So we'll keep the Bridge going, physically and publically. That'll be just as well, too, for people like Dillon who are emotionally tied up in it, above and beyond their conditioning to it. You're the only person in authority in the whole station who's already lost enough interest in the Bridge to make it safe for me to tell you that it's being abandoned."

"But why?"

"Because," Wagoner went on quietly, "the Bridge has now given us confirmation of a theory of stupendous importance—so important, in my opinion, that the imminent fall of the West seems like a puny event in comparison. A confirmation, incidentally, which contains in it the seeds of ultimate destruction for the Soviets, whatever they may win for themselves in the next hundred years or so."

"I suppose," Helmuth said, puzzled, "that you mean antigravity?"

For the first time, it was Wagoner's turn to be taken aback. "Man," he said at last, "do you know *everything* I want to tell you? I hope not, or my conclusions will be mighty unwelcome to both of us. Do you also know what an anti-agathic is?"

"No," Helmuth said. "I don't even recognize the root of the word."

"Well, that's a relief. But surely Charity didn't tell you we had antigravity. I strictly enjoined him not to mention it."

"No. The subject's been on my mind," Helmuth said. "But I certainly don't see why it should be so world-shaking, any more than I see how the Bridge helped to bring it about. I thought it would be developed independently, for the further exploitation of the Bridge. In other words, to put men down there, and short-circuit this remote control operation we have on Jupiter V. And I thought it would step up Bridge operation, not discontinue it."

"Not at all. Nobody in his right mind would want to put men on Jupiter, and besides, gravity isn't the main problem down there. Even eight gravities is perfectly tolerable for short periods of time—and anyhow a man in a pressure suit couldn't get five hundred miles down through that atmosphere before he'd be as buoyed up and weightless as a fish—and even more thoroughly at the mercy of the currents."

"And you can't screen out the pressure?"

"We can," Wagoner said, "but only at ruinous cost. Besides, there'd be no point in trying. The Bridge is finished. It's given us information in thousands of different categories, much of it very valuable indeed. But the one job that *only* the Bridge could do was that of confirming, or throwing out, the Blackett-Dirac equations."

"Which are——?"

"They show a relationship between magnetism and the spinning of a massive body—that much is the Dirac part of it. The Blackett Equation seemed to show that the same formula also applied to gravity; it says G equals $(2CP/BU)^2$, where C is the velocity of light, P is magnetic moment, and U is angular momentum. B is

M
169

an uncertainty correction, a constant which amounts to 0.25.

"If the figures we collected on the magnetic field strength of Jupiter forced us to retire the equations, then none of the rest of the information we've gotten from the Bridge would have been worth the money we spent to get it. On the other hand, Jupiter was the only body in the solar system available to us which was big enough in all relevant respects to make it possible for us to test those equations at all. They involve quantities of infinitesimal orders of magnitudes.

"And the figures showed that Dirac was right. *They also show that Blackett was right.* Both magnetism *and* gravity are phenomena of rotation.

"I won't bother to trace the succeeding steps, because I think you can work them out for yourself. It's enough to say that there's a drive-generator on board this ship which is the complete and final justification of all the hell you people on the Bridge have been put through. The gadget has a long technical name, but the technies who tend it have already nicknamed it the spindizzy, because of what it does to the magnetic moment of any atom—*any* atom—within its field.

"While it's in operation, it absolutely refuses to notice any atom outside its own influence. Furthermore, it will notice no other strain or influence which holds good beyond the borders of that field. It's so snooty that it has to be stopped down to almost nothing when it's brought close to a planet, or it won't let you land. But in deep space . . . well, it's impervious to meteors and such trash, of course; it's impervious to gravity; and—it hasn't the faintest interest in any legislation about top speed limits. It moves in its own continuum, not in the general frame."

"You're kidding," Helmuth said.

"Am I, now? This ship came to Ganymede directly from Earth. It did it in a little under two hours, counting manœuvring time. That means that most of the way we made about 55,000 miles per second—with the spindizzy drawing less than five watts of power out of three ordinary No. 6 dry cells."

Helmuth took a defiant pull at his drink. "This thing really has no top speed at all?" he said. "How can you be sure of that?"

"Well, we can't," Wagoner admitted. "After all, one of the unfortunate things about general mathematical formulae is that they don't contain cut-off points to warn you of areas where they don't apply. Even quantum mechanics is somewhat subject to that criticism. However, we expect to know pretty soon just how fast the spindizzy can drive an object. We expect you to tell us."

"I?"

"Yes, you, and Colonel Russell, and Miss Abbott too, I hope." Helmuth looked at the other two; both of them looked at least as stunned as he felt. He could not imagine why. "The coming débâcle on Earth makes it absolutely imperative for us—the West—to get interstellar expeditions started at once. Richardson Observatory, on the Moon, has two likely-looking systems mapped already—one at Wolf 359, the other at 61 Cygni—and there are sure to be others, hundreds of others, where Earth-like planets are highly probable.

"What we're doing, in a nutshell, is evacuating the West—not physically, of course, but in essence, in idea. We want to scatter adventurous people, people with a thoroughly indoctrinated love of being free, all over this part of the galaxy, if it can be done.

"Once they're out there, they'll be free to flourish,

with no interference from Earth. The Soviets haven't the spindizzy yet, and even after they get it, they won't dare allow it to be used. It's too good and too final an escape route for disaffected comrades.

"What we want you to do, Helmuth . . . now I'm getting to the point, you see . . . is to direct this exodus, with Colonel Russell's help. You've the intelligence and the cast of mind for it. Your analysis of the situation on Earth confirms that, if any more confirmation were needed. And—there's no future for you on Earth now."

"You'll have to excuse me for a while," Helmuth said firmly. "I'm in no condition to be reasonable now; it's been more than I could digest in a few moments. And the decision doesn't entirely rest with me, either. If I could give you an answer in . . . let me see . . . about three hours. Will that be soon enough?"

"That'll be fine," the senator said.

For a moment after the door closed behind Helmuth there was silence in the senator's cabin. At last Paige said:

"So it was long life for spacemen you were after, all the time. Long life, by God, for *me*, and for the likes of me."

Wagoner nodded. "This was the one part of this affair that I couldn't explain to you back in Tru Gunn's office," he said. "Until you had ridden in this ship, and understood as a spaceman just what kind of a thing we have in it, you wouldn't have believed me; Helmuth does, you see, because he already has the background. In the same way, I didn't go into the question of the anti-agathic with Helmuth, because that's something he's going to have to experience; you two have the background to understand that part of it through explanation alone.

172

"Now you see why I didn't give a whistle about your spy, Paige. The Soviets can have the Earth. As a matter of fact they will take it before very long, whether we give it to them or not. But we are going to scatter the West throughout the stars, scatter it with immortal people carrying immortal ideas. People like you, and Miss Abbott."

Paige looked back to Anne. She was aloofly regarding the empty space just above Wagoner's head, as though still looking at the bewhiskered picture of the Pfitzner founder which hung in Gunn's office. There was something in her face, however, that Paige could read. He smothered a grin and said: "Why me?"

"Because you're just what we need for the job. I don't mind telling you that your blundering into the Pfitzner project in the first place was an act of Providence from my point of view. When Anne first called your qualifications to my attention, I was almost prepared to believe that they'd been faked. You're going to be liaison-man between the Pfitzner side of the project and the Bridge side. We've got the total output to date of both ascomycin and the new anti-agathic salted away in the cargo-hold, and Anne's already shown you how to take the stuff and how to administer it to others. After that—just as soon as you and Helmuth can work out the details—the stars are yours."

"Anne," Paige said. She turned her head slowly toward him. "Are you with this thing?"

"I'm here," she said. "And I'd had a few inklings of what was up before. You were the one who had to be brought in, not I."

Paige thought about it a moment more. Then something both very new and very old occurred to him.

"Senator," he said, "you've gone to an immense

amount of trouble to make this whole thing possible—but I don't think you plan to go with us."

"No, Paige, I don't. For one thing, MacHinery and his crew will regard the whole project as treasonous. If it's to be carried out nevertheless, someone has to stay behind and be the goat—and after all, the idea *was* mine, so I'm the logical candidate." He felt silent for a moment. Then he added, ruminatively: "The government boys have nobody but themselves to thank for this. The whole project would never have been possible as long as the West had a government of laws and not of men, and stuck to it. It was a long while ago that some people—MacHinery's grandfather among them—set themselves up to be their own judges of whether or not a law ought to be obeyed. They had precedents. And now here we are, on the brink of the most enormous breach of our social contract the West has ever had to suffer—and the West can't stop it." He smiled suddenly. "I'll have good use for that argument in the court."

Anne was on her feet, her eyes suddenly wet, her lower lip just barely trembling. Evidently, over whatever time she had known Wagoner and had known what he had planned, it had never occurred to her that the young-old senator might stay behind.

"That's no good!" she said in a low voice. "They won't listen, and you know it. They might easily hang you for it. If they find you guilty of treason, they'll seal you up in the pile-waste dump—that's the current penalty, isn't it? You can't go back!"

"It's a phony terror. Pile wastes are quick chemical poisons; you don't last long enough to notice that they're also hot," Wagoner said. "And what difference does it make, anyhow? Nothing and nobody can harm me now. The job is done."

Anne put her hands to her face.

"Besides, Anne," Wagoner said, with gentle insistence, "the stars are for young people—eternally young people. An eternal oldster would be an anachronism."

"Why—did you do it, then?" Paige said. His own voice was none too steady.

"Why?" Wagoner said. "You know the answer to that, Paige. You've known it all your life. I could see it in your face, as soon as I told Helmuth that we were going out to the stars. Supposing you tell *me* what it is."

Anne swung her blurred eyes on Paige. He thought he knew what she expected to hear him say; they had talked about it often enough, and it was what he once would have said himself. But now another force seemed to him to be the stronger: a special thing, bearing the name of no established dogma, but nevertheless and unmistakably the force to which he had borne allegiance all his life. He in his turn could see it in Wagoner's face now, and he knew he had seen it before in Anne's.

"It's the thing that lures monkeys into cages," he said slowly. "And lures cats into open desk drawers and up telephone poles. It's driven men to conquer death, and put the stars into our hands. I suppose that I'd call it Curiosity."

Wagoner looked startled. "Is that really what you want to call it?" he said. "Somehow it seems insufficient; I should have given it another name. Perhaps you'll amend it later, somewhere, some day out by Aldebaran."

He stood up and looked at the two for a moment in silence. Then he smiled.

"And now," he said gently, "*nunc dimittis* . . . suffer thy servant to depart in peace."

11

"And so, that's the story," Helmuth said.

Eva remained silent in her chair for a long time.

"One thing I don't understand," she said at last. "Why did you come to me? I'd have thought that you'd find the whole thing terrifying."

"Oh, it's terrifying, all right," Helmuth said, with quiet exultation. "But terror and fright are two different things, as I've just discovered. We were both wrong, Evita. I was wrong in thinking that the Bridge was a dead end. You were wrong in thinking of it as an end in itself."

"I don't understand you."

"I didn't understand myself. My fears of working in person on the Bridge were irrational; they came from dreams. That should have tipped me off right away. There was really never any chance of anyone's working in person on Jupiter; but *I wanted to*. It was a death-wish, and it came directly out of the goddamned conditioning. I knew, we all knew, that the Bridge couldn't stand for ever, but we were conditioned to believe that it had to. Nothing else could justify the awful ordeal of keeping it going even one day. The result: the classical dilemma that leads to madness. It affected you, too, and your response was just as insane as mine: you wanted to have a child here.

"Now all that's changed. The work the Bridge was doing was worth while after all. I was wrong in calling it a bridge to nowhere. And Eva, you no more saw where it was going than I did, or you'd never have made it the be-all and end-all of your existence.

"Now, there's a place to go to. In fact, there are places—hundreds of places. They'll be Earthlike places. Since the Soviets are about to win the Earth, those places will be more Earthlike than Earth itself, at least for the next century or so!"

She said: "Why are you telling me this? Just to make peace between us?"

"I'm going to take on this job, Evita . . . if you'll go along."

She turned swiftly, rising out of the chair with a marvellous fluidity of motion. At the same instant, all the alarm bells in the station went off at once, filling every metal cranny with a jangle•of pure horror.

"*Posts!*" the loudspeaker above Eva's bed roared, in a distorted, gigantic caricature of Charity Dillon's voice. "*Peak storm overload! The STD is now passing the Spot. Wild velocity has already topped all previous records, and part of the land mass has begun to settle. This is an A-1 overload emergency.*"

Behind Charity's bellow, they could hear what he was hearing, the winds of Jupiter, a spectrum of continuous, insane shrieking. The Bridge was responding with monstrous groans of agony. There was another sound, too, an almost musical cacophony of sharp, percussive tones, such as a dinosaur might make pushing its way through a forest of huge steel tuning-forks. Helmuth had never heard the sound before, but he knew what it was.

The deck of the Bridge was splitting up the middle.

After a moment more, the uproar dimmed, and the speaker said, in Charity's normal voice: "Eva, you too, please. Acknowledge, please. This is it—unless everybody comes on duty at once, the Bridge may go down within the next hour."

"Let it," Eva responded quietly.

There was a brief, startled silence, and then a ghost of a human sound. The voice was Senator Wagoner's, and the sound just might have been a chuckle.

Charity's circuit clicked out.

The mighty death of the Bridge continued to resound in the little room.

After a while, the man and the woman went to the window, and looked past the discarded bulk of Jupiter at the near horizon, where there had always been visible a few stars.

CODA

★

CODA

"Every end", Wagoner wrote on the wall of his cell on the last day, "is a new beginning. Perhaps in a thousand years my Earthmen will come home again. Or in two thousand, or four, if they still remember home then. They'll come back, yes; but I hope they won't stay. I pray they will not stay."

He looked at what he had written and thought of signing his name. While he debated that, he made the mark for the last day on his calendar, and the point on his stub of pencil struck stone under the calcimine and snapped, leaving nothing behind it but a little coronet of frayed, dirty blond wood. He could wear that away against the window-ledge, at least enough to expose a little graphite, but instead he dropped the stub in the waste can.

There was writing enough in the stars that he could see, because he had written it there. There was a constellation called Wagoner, and every star in the sky belonged to it. That was surely enough.

Later that day, a man named MacHinery said: "Bliss Wagoner is dead."

As usual, MacHinery was wrong.

ATOMS, METAPHORS AND PARADOXES

ATOMS, METAPHORS AND PARADOXES

Niels Bohr and the construction of a new physics

SANDRO PETRUCCIOLI

Professor of History of Science, University of Reggio Calabria

Translated by Ian McGilvray

CAMBRIDGE
UNIVERSITY PRESS

icate of the University of Cambridge
ngton Street, Cambridge CB2 1RP
w York, NY 10011-4211, USA
eigh, Melbourne 3166, Australia

© Cambridge University Press 1993

First published 1993

Printed in Great Britain at the University Press, Cambridge

A catalogue record for this book is available from the British Library

Library of Congress cataloguing in publication data

Petruccioli, Sandro.
[Atomi, metafore, paradossi. English]
Atoms, metaphors, and paradoxes : Niels Bohr and the construction
of a new physics / Sandro Petruccioli : translated by Ian McGilvray.
p.   cm.
Translation of: Atomi, metafore, paradossi.
Includes bibliographical references and index.
ISBN 0 521 40259 X
1. Quantum theory—History.   2. Bohr, Niels Henrik David,
1885–1962.   I. Title.
QC173.98.P483   1993
530.1′2′09—dc20   93-177   CIP

ISBN 0 521 40259 X hardback

Contents

Introduction *page* 1
1   The paradigm of complementarity   10
2   Atomic model and quantum hypotheses   36
3   The principle of correspondence   78
4   The theory of virtual oscillators   111
5   The conceptual foundation of quantum mechanics   134
6   The Bohr–Einstein confrontation: phenomena and
      physical reality   183
General bibliography   218
Name index   235
General index   238

Introduction

'Quantum mechanics is very impressive. But an inner voice tells me that it is not yet the real thing. The theory produces a good deal but hardly brings us closer to the secret of the Old One'. These views were contained in a letter written by Albert Einstein to Max Born in December 1926[1]. Though the following year would see the completion of work on the theoretical foundation of the modern physics of atoms and particles, Einstein was never to change his judgement and remained firmly convinced that 'this business [...] contains some unreasonableness'. He was unwilling to sacrifice his own ideas as to the cognitive scope of science even in the face of the important results being achieved by the new theory. To the undeterministic findings of quantum mechanics he opposed his belief in the 'possibility of giving a model of reality, a theory, that is to say, which shall represent events themselves and not merely the probability of their occurrence'[2]. For this reason he chose to live with the isolation of his scepticism and dissent, ironically accepting the reputation as a obstinate heretic that he had won over the years among his colleagues, and worked to the end on his own research programme to develop a unified field theory of rigorously causal nature.

As is generally known, Einstein carried on a strong scientific and philosophical dispute with the defenders of the so-called official interpretation of quantum mechanics. Shortly before his death he again attacked Niels Bohr and the Copenhagen school for their betrayal of what he saw as constituting the programmatic aim of physics: 'the complete description of any (individual) real situation (as it supposedly exists irrespective of any act of observation or substantiation)'[3]. It can, of course, be claimed that a theory which confines itself to statistical statements about the measurable quantities of a system also provides a consistent description of reality and exhausts all possible understanding of the physical

1

world. However, Einstein saw this as possible only at a very high philosophical price, i.e. the assumption that only what is directly observable is to be regarded as real. Abraham Pais tells how once, during a conversation with Einstein on quantum theory, 'he suddenly stopped [...] and asked me if I really believed that the moon exists only if I look at it'[4].

Questions of this type, which bring science up against the classical problems of theory of knowledge, have long ceased to figure among the writings and professional interests of physicists. Gerald Holton has described the sort of cultural mutation leading in this half of our century to the appearance of a new type of scientist, one capable of making important cognitive advances without being either illuminated or led astray by epistemological debate[5]. Thus the existing situation in contemporary scientific research would itself constitute the most evident violation of Einstein's credo, according to which 'Science without epistemology is – in so far as it is thinkable at all – primitive and muddled'. Unlike those of the past, today's scientists can tackle the most complex problems of their disciplines without requiring a particular historico-epistemological competence or explicit philosophical interests, neither of which would be of any use to them. However, the past referred to in this case does not take us back to the origins of modern scientific thought, when the lines dividing science and metaphysics were still blurred and discussions about the principles of dynamics could end up in subtle questions of theology, but rather to the comparatively recent period in which the foundations were laid for the great conceptual revolutions of our century. Einstein quoted Hume; Max Planck embarked on a philosophical dispute with Ernst Mach in one of the most important German journals of physics; Werner Heisenberg used categories of clearly Kantian derivation in explaining the programme of quantum mechanics; and Bohr discussed the use of analogy in the quantum theory of the atom with the philosopher Harald Høffding.

Holton uses the testimony of theoretical physicist Sheldon Glashow and the observations of philosopher Hilary Putnam to carry out an analysis of the causes leading to the swift decline of a consolidated scientific–philosophical tradition and to the emergence of a science which, despite having lost all fruitful contact with epistemology, strikes him today as being 'as powerful and interesting as it has ever been, both as a product and as a process'. We can certainly discuss the responsibilities of the leading schools of the philosophy of science, whose attempts to bend the logic of what scientists actually do so as to fit their own ideas of method and rationality have often ended up producing caricatures of scientific procedure. However, this would do little to attenuate our feeling that the curtain has definitively fallen on such figures as Heisenberg, Bohr, Born, Pauli, Schrödinger, Einstein and de Broglie who, despite their considerable differences, 'saw themselves as both scientists and culture carriers, with the duty, or the psychological need, to fashion a coherent world picture'. The collapse of an explicit epistemological tension is thus probably insufficient to explain why the subjects that for many years animated the discussions between Bohr and Einstein and played no minor role in the elaboration of one of the most powerful frameworks for understanding the physical world should today be almost totally ignored, as though they no longer presented any problematic aspects.

According to Karl Popper, the 1930s saw the formation and rapid development of a group of physicists 'who have turned away from these discussions because they regard them, rightly, as philosophical, and because they believe, wrongly, that philosophical discussions are unimportant for physics'[6]. However, the causes of what he views as a break with the Galilean tradition are to be sought neither in the scarce relevance for science of the problems dealt with by philosophers, nor in the inevitable sociological transformations produced within the scientific community. The idea that the only thing to count in research is a mastery of mathematical formalism and its applications and that one must rid oneself of philosophical nonsense arises, in Popper's view, from within science itself, or rather from the philosophical compromises of some influential theoretical physicists and from the solutions given by them to the difficulties inherent in the interpretation of quantum mechanics: 'In 1927 Niels Bohr, one of the greatest thinkers in the field of atomic physics, introduced the so-called *principle of complementarity* into atomic physics, which amounted to a 'renunciation' of the attempt to interpret atomic theory as a description of anything'[7]. The principle was presented and defended as the most effective, and perhaps the only, means of avoiding the contradictions arising from the possibility of associating different interpretations with the theory's formalism, e.g. from the fact that, when speaking of a micro-object, this formalism may be translated into the descriptive language of either waves or particles. All the originality of Bohr's solution is thus reduced to his having postulated an unusual logical relation in defence of the internal consistency of the mathematical formalism: complementarity would, in fact, rule out in principle the possibility of comprising the different experimental applications of the formalism within a single interpretation. Bohr's

position, according to Popper's view, was based on simple recognition of
the fact that 'any two of these conflicting applications were physically
incapable of ever being combined in one experiment. Thus the result of
every single experiment was consistent with the theory, and unambiguously laid down by it. This, he said, was all we could get. The claim to get
more, and even the hope of ever getting more, we must renounce'[8].

Popper went on to say that he had explained Bohr's principle of
complementarity as he understood it after many years of effort, and
added that Einstein himself had admitted his failure to attain a sharp
formulation of it 'despite much effort which I have expended on it'.
Perhaps, however, the principle really did confine itself to imposing
severe restrictions on the rational understanding of reality. In other
words, Bohr resolved the interpretative difficulties bogging down a
particular theory in terms of a general philosophical and epistemological
viewpoint: the consistency of physics is guaranteed as long as we avoid
pushing our demand for knowledge beyond the limits permitted by the
correct application of the formalism to actually realizable situations. By
means of this clause, Bohr immunized the theory against contradiction.
However, according to Popper, he also obliged science to renounce
forever its great task of painting a consistent and comprehensible picture
of the universe and revived the old instrumentalist philosophy of Cardinal
Bellarmino and Bishop Berkeley. That the question boils down to this is
demonstrated, in Popper's view, by the fact that Bohr's principle has
proved completely sterile within physics, having 'produced nothing
except some philosophical discussions, and some arguments for the
confounding of critics (especially Einstein)'[9]. The same view has been
expressed in still stronger terms by Mario Bunge and Imre Lakatos. The
former has presented complementarity as a pseudo-principle that has
proved particularly useful 'to consecrate obscurities and inconsistencies,
much as the mystery of the Trinity subsumes many minor mysteries'[10].
The latter sees the Copenhagen interpretation of modern quantum
theory as one of the main standard-bearers of philosophical obscuran-
tism. As he put it in his most famous epistemological paper: 'In the new
theory Bohr's notorious 'complementarity principle' enthroned [weak]
inconsistency as a basic ultimate feature of nature, and merged subjecti-
vist positivism and antilogical dialectic and even ordinary language of the
philosophy into one *unholy* alliance. After 1925 Bohr and his associates
introduced a new and unprecedented lowering of critical standards for
scientific theories. This led to a defeat of reason within modern physics
and to an anarchist cult of incomprehensible chaos'[11]. The scientific

community's acceptance of the Copenhagen interpretation could be accounted for solely by their failure to realize fully that it concealed a philosophical principle and by the fact that it was presented and imposed as the orthodox view by almost all the physicists who had made major contributions to the creation of quantum mechanics. John Heilbron has spoken of the intellectual imperialism of Bohr's group during the 1930s and reconstructed in a paper the attempt made above all by Pauli, Jordan and Bohr himself to derive a universal epistemology from the Copenhagen interpretation, which they saw as confirmed by the basic problems of biology and psychology[12]. Paul Forman has laid stress on the pressure exercised by cultural climate and on the role played by a hostile intellectual environment dominated by irrationalistic orientations such as a preconceived rejection of causality and rigorous determinism. His analysis leads him to conclude that 'an acausal quantum mechanics was particularly welcome to the German physicists because of the irresistible opportunity it offered of improving their public image. Now they too could polemicize against the rigid rationalistic concept of causality and hope to recover lost prestige thereby'[13]. All this is seen as having slowly stifled the dissenting voices of those who continued to regard physics not as a tool for the prediction of results or for any other type of practical application, but as a means to understand the world in which we live.

Views such as those shown above are no exception in the contributions made by historians and philosophers of science in recent years to reconstructing the birth of quantum mechanics and clarifying its conceptual foundations. On the contrary, there seems to be broad agreement on two interpretative theses which make such judgements possible. The first claims that the idea of complementarity – by means of which Bohr believed he had definitively settled the problems raised by the dual nature of radiation and matter and by Heisenberg's indeterminacy relations – had its origin in philosophy or at any rate outside the rigorously theoretical sphere. The second seeks to present the official interpretation of quantum mechanics as the contribution of a small group of physicists led by their common cultural background or shared metaphysical standpoint to propose what amounted to turning consolidated epistemological conceptions upside-down and redefining the cognitive aims of science.

Even scholars more interested in the ways in which theories are constructed than in the contexts of their justification are ready to admit that the development of theories of mechanics of atoms and particles was the result of strong interaction between science and philosophy. Their analyses are presented as having concretely proved how hard it is in this case to make a clear distinction between the solutions to specific technical problems proposed by individual scientists and the convictions of those scientists with regard to points such as the role of models, the problem of visualization and the operational definition of concepts. However, it is when one goes on from the recognition of such an interaction to attempt to define its nature that differences of opinion and contrasts have arisen. It is possible to trace the debate that has developed around the cognitive aspects of quantum mechanics (or the disagreement still existing within the scientific community over its conceptual foundations) back to the standpoints originally adopted with regard to this problem. In any case, what is at stake here is not the acceptance or otherwise of the thesis over which epistemologists and historians are divided, i.e. the attribution of an uneliminable role to metaphysics in the most daring and creative phases of scientific endeavour. This is certainly not the type of interaction meant by those who see the Copenhagen interpretation as a variant of bad philosophies used instrumentally for scientific ends. Nor by Popper, who sees a philosophical schism as the origin of the formation of a new generation of scientists whose training in the limitations and cultural narrow-mindedness of rigid specialization leads them to an acritical acceptance of the crisis of understanding that has struck 20th century physics. Nor, finally, by those who take the opposite view that the loss of interest in the questions of foundations stems from a prudent defensive attitude seeking to avoid the transformation of physics into a labyrinth of philosophies.

All the above points of view appear to attach little importance to (or indeed to disbelieve) the accounts given by the principal figures of this story. They were convinced that the new scientific discoveries had contributed to the redefinition of philosophical problems regarded hitherto as the object of pure speculation. Bohr maintained that knowledge of the atomic world threw 'a new light on the old philosophical problem of the objective existence of phenomena independently of our observations'[14]. Pauli claimed that the gnoseological situation modern physics found itself faced with had been foreseen by no philosophical system[15]. Pursuing an analogous line of thought, Heisenberg observed: 'What was born in Copenhagen in 1927 was not only an unambiguous prescription for the interpretation of experiments, but also a language in which one spoke about Nature on the atomic scale, and in so far a part of philosophy'[16]. In a philosophical language that had frequently been considered insufficiently rigorous, they sought to assert their role as scientists whose attempt to grasp the nature of quantum processes had obliged them to question some assumptions of modern scientific thought and to tackle the classic problems of the theory of knowledge.

The theoretical and experimental developments of physics had shown the arbitrary character of certain forms of rational interpretation of reality that had remained unchanged since the time of Galileo and Newton. In particular, the concept of the quantum of action – which expressed the essential discontinuity of microscopic physical processes – had slowly led to awareness that the description of such processes was impossible in terms of the models of representation offered by classical physics. In his idea of complementarity, Bohr gave effective expression to the abandonment of the model of causal space-time description. This made it impossible to think of an electron as a physical object similar in all respects to a material body locatable in space and time and moving along a specific trajectory. The objects of microphysics are objects of a more complex nature: they populate a level of reality that obliges us not only to restructure our theoretical tools but also to reconsider many of our convictions as to the nature of phenomena, the role of the observer, and the very meaning of scientific law. Complementarity was not therefore a theoretical principle in the classical sense of the term but rather a means of fully grasping the cognitive content of the new physics. It was problems of this type that faced the physicists who helped lay the foundations of quantum mechanics in the 1920s. While the solutions they found were always rational responses to highly concrete problems, they were able to play their role as scientists consistently precisely by virtue of their understanding that such responses involved a more mature philosophical and epistemological awareness.

Acknowledgements

This essay is the result of a programme of research into Bohr's work and the birth of quantum mechanics that began around 1974 in connection with Ludovico Geymonat's seminar on the history of science at the Domus Galilaeana in Pisa. Since then I have published various papers on the subjects dealt with here (the most recent are listed in the bibliography) and have had the opportunity to discuss my theses at conferences, congresses and seminars. The debts of gratitude accumulated over the years are many and it would be impossible here to acknowledge them all fully. This does not, however, prevent me from expressing my thanks to Ludovico Geymonat, Vincenzo Cappelletti, Paolo Rossi, Catherine Chevalley, John Hendry, Arthur I. Miller, David Favrholdt, Piers Bursill-Hall, Giulio Giorello and Silvano Tagliagambe.

Mario Ageno, Enrico Bellone, Salvo D'Agostino and Catherine Chevalley read the manuscript and offered thoughtful and helpful advice that both saved me from pitfalls and improved many aspects of the argument; I thank them in particular, while obviously exempting them from any responsibility for the views put forward here. Finally, I wish to express my gratitude to Marina Frasca Spada for all her help in revising and editing the manuscript for publication.

N.B. A few commonly cited sources are given in abbreviated form in the notes. For details of the sources see the start of the bibliography on page 218. The references to previously cited works refer to the chapter and the number of the note in the present volume.

Notes

1 M. Born, ed., *The Born–Einstein Letters*, New York: Walker, 1971, 90.
2 A. Einstein, *On the Method of Theoretical Physics*, New York: Oxford University Press, 1933; republished in *Philosophy of Science* **1** (1934), 163–69: 168–69.
3 A. Einstein, 'Reply to Criticism', in P. A. Schilpp, ed., *Albert Einstein: Philosopher–Scientist*, The Library of Living Philosophers, Illinois: Evanston, 1949, 665–88: 667.
4 A. Pais, *'Subtle is the Lord...' The Science and the Life of Albert Einstein*, Oxford: Oxford University Press, 1982, 5.
5 G. Holton, 'Do Scientists Need a Philosophy?', *The Times Literary Supplement*, 2 November 1984, 257 (4), 1231–34.
6 K. Popper, *Quantum Theory and the Schism in Physics. From the Postscript to the Logic of Scientific Discovery*, London: Hutchinson, 1982, 100.
7 K. Popper, *Conjectures and Refutations. The Growth of Scientific Knowledge*, London: Routledge & Keegan Paul, 1972, 100.
8 Ibid., 100.
9 Ibid., 101.
10 M. Bunge, *Philosophy of Physics*, Dordrecht: Reidel, 1973, 116.
11 I. Lakatos, 'Falsification and the Methodology of Scientific Research Programmes', in I. Lakatos and A. Musgrave, eds., *Criticism and the Growth of Knowledge*, Cambridge: Cambridge University Press, 1970, 91–196: 145.
12 J. L. Heilbron, 'The Earliest Missionaries of the Copenhagen Spirit', *Revue d'histoire des sciences* **38** (1985), 195–230.
13 P. Forman, 'Weimar Culture, Causality and Quantum Theory 1918–1927: Adaptation by German Physicists and Mathematicians to a Hostile Intellectual Environment', *Historical Studies in the Physical Sciences* **3** (1971), 1–116: 108.
14 N. Bohr, 'Die Atomtheorie und die Prinzipien der Naturbeschreibung', *Die Naturwissenschaften* **18** (1930), 73–78.

15 W. Pauli, 'Die philosophische Bedeutung der Idee der Komplementarität', *Experientia* **6** (1950), 72–81: 73; *CSP2*, 1149–58.

16 W. Heisenberg, 'The Development of the Interpretation of the Quantum Theory', in W. Pauli, ed., *Niels Bohr and the Development of Physics*, London: Pergamon Press, 1955, 12–29: 16.

CHAPTER 1

The paradigm of complementarity

1

'The new wave mechanics gave rise to the hope that an account of atomic phenomena might be obtained which would not differ essentially from that afforded by the classical theories of electricity and magnetism. Unfortunately, Bohr's statement in the following communication of the principles underlying the description of atomic phenomena gives little, if any, encouragement in this direction.' This comment is to be found in the brief note prefaced by the editors of the British journal *Nature* to Niels Bohr's paper 'The Quantum Postulate and the Recent Development of Atomic Theory'[1] in the supplement of 14 April 1928. The article in question is the famous paper which first introduced and defined the concept of 'complementarity' and outlined the basic points of what was to become known as the Copenhagen interpretation of quantum mechanics.

In the paper, Bohr returned to the arguments contained in the paper discussed at the International Congress of Physicists held at Como in September 1927 to mark the centenary of the death of Alessandro Volta and published in the proceedings of the same congress[2]. It was probably his conviction that the new viewpoint adopted in the description of nature fully expressed the theoretical and cognitive content of quantum physics coupled with his enthusiasm at having achieved 'after many years of struggling in the dark [...] the fulfilment of the old hopes'[3] that induced him to give his work broader and more prestigious circulation. Thus in the spring of 1928, after intense efforts enabling him to make a limited but conceptually significant number of corrections to the original text, Bohr again brought his theory to the attention of the scientific community with the above-mentioned publication in *Nature* and the

German version of the paper, which appeared in volume 16 of the journal *Die Naturwissenschaften*[4].

He certainly did not expect the impact of his article to be such as to gain immediate acceptance outside a limited group of theoretical physicists, most of whom, with the important exception of P. A. M. Dirac, were directly linked with the schools of Copenhagen and Göttingen. Apart from the coolness with which his paper had been received at Como, the course of the subsequent discussion must have furnished him with concrete evidence as to just how difficult his argument was to follow in view of its lack of any significant reference to the formalism of quantum mechanics and its development around a subtly interwoven complex of conceptual questions and epistemological considerations[5].

In addition, a more severe test had been offered him at the Solvay Conference held a few weeks later in Brussels from the 24th to the 29th of October to discuss *électrons et photons*, and attended by the leading physicists of the day, in particular Einstein, who had not been present at Como[6]. During the official sessions – but especially in the evening discussions, which often lasted well into the night – Bohr had been obliged to defend the validity of his theoretical interpretation against objections intended above all to challenge its definitive character. Though this presented no easy task, he had, in fact, succeeded on that occasion in parrying all the attempted refutations advanced by Einstein, who had sought to demonstrate by means of a series of thought experiments the possibility of real physical situations in contradiction with the principles of quantum mechanics[7]. In his obstinate search for counterexamples such as would drastically weaken the logical consistency of the theory, Einstein basically showed the same feelings of scepticism and disappointment that were to prompt the editors of *Nature* to adopt an extremely prudent stance. In suggesting a possible key to the interpretation of Bohr's work, the latter did their utmost to soften the impact of ideas which, if accepted, would mean the definitive abandonment of consolidated rational criteria of representation of the physical world and the recognition of a rupture without precedent in modern science. It must, however, be recognized that they did not resort to conventionalistic expedients or rhetorical tricks and reported in sufficiently clear terms the breadth of the upheaval involved by the new ideas.

The note of the editors of *Nature* begins by pointing out that in classical mechanics the intuitive notion of the position of a particle – as of any other material object – corresponds to the condition that its spatial coordinates should be unequivocally determinable at any instant. Consequently, with the variation of time over a certain interval it makes sense to speak of the trajectory of the motion of the particle as the continuous succession of its positions and it is possible to plot the world-line of the particle itself in an abstract representation referring to four-dimensional space (the three spatial co-ordinates plus time). Moreover, when the action exercised on the particle by all external forces is taken into consideration, it is possible to determine a causal connection between the single states of the system. This type of representation, whose conceptual and theoretical roots lie in the laws of kinematics and dynamics, had taken on increasing generality over the years to become the descriptive model of classical physics. The results achieved even in widely differing sectors of experience had produced such a quantity of evidence supporting the possibility of a causal type of spatio-temporal co-ordination of physical objects that it had appeared quite natural to take this model as an essential prerequisite for all forms of scientific explanation.

In actual fact, this generalization rested upon an implicit assumption that had long appeared absolutely unproblematic: that the phenomena observed would not be influenced by the methods or instruments of measurement. To be more precise, since each quantity measured is associated by definition with an indeterminacy deriving from unavoidable errors in reading, the underlying assumption was that by perfecting our experimental apparatus it would in principle be possible to make this indeterminacy as small as desired.

Now, as the editors' note went on to underline, this assumption and the related argument about limiting indeterminacy lost all foundation in the new quantum theory since the discovery of Planck's quantum of action h obliges us to attribute an essential element of discontinuity or individuality to any phenomenon we seek to observe. The author of the note very prudently avoided making any compromising comment on the validity or even the physical significance of this conclusion and confined himself to pointing out that if it were true, as Bohr claimed, it would necessarily entail the abandonment of causal space-time co-ordination of atomic phenomena. A 'somewhat vague statistical description' would be all that remained. This would also mean the definitive abandonment of all hope of ever achieving a theoretical synthesis capable of reconciling the interpretative dualism imposed by certain experimental results that oblige us, according to circumstances, to speak of one and the same object – e.g. an electron or radiation – in the mutually incompatible languages of waves and particles. At this point all the writer's dismay at the cogency of Bohr's reasoning becomes apparent as the note repeats his arguments almost word for word to illustrate the surprising solution that, in the context of the new theory, would make it possible to reconcile such apparently contradictory images. In Bohr's view, the difficulty of the problem and its associated paradoxical consequences turn out to be more apparent than real when it is observed that the notions of 'radiation in free space' and 'isolated material particle' are pure abstractions in that, from the viewpoint of quantum mechanics, they are by their very nature inaccessible to observation. All we are left with is the view that 'it is only through their interaction with other systems that the properties of these abstractions can be defined and observed'[8], i.e. the properties of objects that, precisely by virtue of their being mere abstractions or symbols, it is possible to describe in non-contradictory but rather complementary fashion as though they were in turn both 'waves' and 'particles'. 'It must be confessed that the new quantum mechanics is far from satisfying the requirements of the layman who seeks to clothe his conceptions in figurative language. Indeed, its originators probably hold that such symbolic representation is inherently impossible. It is earnestly to be hoped that this is not their last word on the subject, and that they may yet be successful in expressing the quantum postulate in picturesque form'[9]. The note thus concluded by expressing a hope that sounds more like a call to carry on the search for an acceptable theoretical solution capable on the one hand of reconciling the postulate of the indivisibility of phenomena with the traditional principles of physics, and on the other of overcoming the conceptual obstacles of the discontinuity and the intrinsically probabilitistic nature of events in such a way as make the theory itself immediately translatable into intuitive images.

It is clear that the comment made by *Nature* was in actual fact far more severe than was immediately apparent from the prudent tone in which its judgements were expressed. While agreeing to publish Bohr's article, the journal adopted an implicitly critical stance with regard to his ideas by in fact suggesting, as though in an attempt to interpret the attitudes prevailing within the scientific community, the requirements that the new theory would have to meet, i.e. by laying down criteria for its acceptance. In this specific case, the decision can hardly have been an easy one to take. Bohr was universally regarded as one of the most brilliant and original theoretical physicists and his contributions to the foundation of atomic physics had earned him the highest scientific and academic awards of the time.

Pauli totally dismissed the claims advanced by the British editors and wrote off their comments as quite ludicrous. In a letter to Bohr he confessed that he had not laughed so much for a long time. In his view, the sense of the note was to be deciphered in the following terms: 'We British physicists would be awfully pleased if in the future the points of view advocated in the following paper should turn out not to be true. Since, however, Mr Bohr is a nice man, such a pleasure would not be kind. Since moreover he is a famous physicist and more often right than wrong, there remains only a slight chance that our hopes will be fulfilled'[10].

However, unlike his ironic young pupil, Bohr may have been inclined to give greater weight to objections which, while calling into question neither the formal consistency of the theory nor the fertility of its explanatory potential, did contain open reservations as to its epistemological defensibility. Objections of the same nature were, in fact, being raised at precisely the same time by scientific figures of greater prestige than the editors of *Nature* and who undoubtedly enjoyed his esteem and regard.

In a letter dated 5 May 1928, Schrödinger drew Bohr's attention to the difficulties arising from the limitation that had been imposed on the applicability of the old concepts of physics in the description of experience, which were closely connected with the possible co-existence of contradictory images of reality. In his view, the new situation was not one to be crystallized – as Bohr seemed to be doing – within some more or less arbitrary epistemological criterion, but rather one calling urgently for 'the introduction of new concepts, with respect to which this limitation *no longer* applies'. What Schrödinger had in mind, albeit in still indefinite terms, was a conceptual framework such as would exclude any reference whatsoever to objects or properties that are in principle unobservable. Only on these conditions would it finally be possible to speak of a theoretically adequate framework and to overcome the uneasiness aroused by the theory in its present form, where everything appeared as though 'our possibilities of experience were limited through unfavourable circumstances'. Schrödinger in no way underestimated the enormous difficulties to be met with in inventing a new conceptual framework, since this would have to involve directly 'the deepest levels of our understanding: space, time and causality'[11].

In a long letter of reply, Bohr gave the greatest attention to considerations of this nature, but declared himself from the outset in total disagreement with Schrödinger's proposal. The search for an improbable system of new concepts was, in his view, not only unadvisable because of the difficulties pointed out by Schrödinger himself, but even forbidden by deeper reasons relating to the very nature of scientific knowledge: the so-called '"old" empirical concepts appear to me to be inseparably linked to the foundations of the human means of visualization'[12]. Given these exceptional conceptual constraints, the implications of the quantum postulate as to the indivisibility of phenomena should leave no space for regret at the loss of by now superseded forms of description and representation of the physical world and provided no justification for statements about the existence of insuperable limitations for our cognitive tools. In this sense, the main aim of Bohr's paper had been to make as clear as possible 'the failure of classical pictures in the quantum theoretical treatment of the interaction problem': an irreversible failure, since 'our entire mode of visualization is based on the abstraction of free individuals – a point where [and here Bohr flatly dismissed the reservations put forward by *Nature*] the relationship between classical theory and quantum theory is particularly evident'. For the latter, a free individual is by definition unobservable and hence devoid of any interest for scientific investigation. Bohr thus reversed the perspective adopted by his critics and called for recognition that the new theoretical solutions constituted 'a philosophically consistent and hence satisfying extension of the foundations of our description of nature'[13].

In replying to Schrödinger, Bohr was also, in fact, replying to such figures as Einstein and Planck 'with whom perhaps you will discuss the content of this letter'. However, while advising him to adopt a more reserved attitude, Einstein was in full agreement with the requests advanced by Schrödinger: 'The Heisenberg–Bohr soothing-philosophy – or religion? – is so cleverly concocted that for the present it offers the believers a soft pillow of repose from which they are not so easily chased away. Let us therefore let them rest'. After acknowledging just how little impression this religion had actually made on him, he declared that he felt his brain too stale to take an active part in the dispute[14]. The kinds of reaction aroused within the community of physicists by Bohr's interpretation of quantum mechanics thus made it clear that the clash had shifted from the outset to the philosophical and epistemological terrain. In the course of 1929, Bohr was given two opportunities to return to the argument in far clearer terms: the publication of a jubilee issue of *Die Naturwissenschaften* to celebrate Max Planck's 50th doctoral anniversary, and an invitation to deliver one of the opening lectures at the Scandinavian Meeting of Natural Scientists held in Copenhagen in the last week of August.

In the first case, Bohr's contribution to the German journal consisted of an article[15] which, as Jörgen Kalckar points out, 'represents his first attempt at tracing the bearing of what he used to call 'the general lessons of quantum theory' within a wider epistemological context'[16]. He was led to take this step both by the nature of the objections raised against the idea of complementarity and more generally by the unavoidable questions posed by such a radical revision of the foundations of physics. It is, however, certain that Bohr did not feel quite at ease in this type of theorizing. After pointing out to Pauli how the article written in honour of Planck had abandoned physics completely to address itself directly to pure philosophy, he expressed all his misgivings at this step and hoped 'that the physicists will look upon it with indulgence and that Planck himself at least will appreciate how sincerely my little article was meant'[17]. Cavalier as ever and by now convinced of the validity of his mentor's views, Pauli expressed his satisfaction with the article on Planck *precisely because* all physics was omitted. For once this was something new, original and exciting!'[18].

The main interest of the second paper[19] lies instead in its attempt to fit the new ideas into a historical perspective. Though no novelty in Bohr's scientific writings, the adoption of a historical approach to the issues of budding atomic science here took on a particular importance. The paper sought to identify what had been, in Bohr's view, the most significant stages in the theoretical and experimental development leading to the conclusions arrived at of late. The result is a sort of rational reconstruction carried out in the light of the new interpretative paradigm. The following section gives this reconstruction.

2

Bohr recalled that the hypothesis of atoms to explain the variability and instability of a broad range of phenomena – i.e. the view that the causes of such phenomena were to be sought in the interaction of a large number of particles – dated back to the ancient philosophers. Reformulated again and again in the sphere of modern science, this hypothesis constituted the interpretative basis for almost all fields of human experience, from electricity to heat and light. However, it was only since the end of the 19th century that technical advances had made it possible to push the boundary of possible observations ever further forward. The conditions had thus been created for the birth of atomic physics proper, which had made it possible to carry out a systematic study of the properties of objects which, by their very nature, escape any form of immediate perception. In particular, a profound turning point in our understanding of this field had been reached with the identification of 'phenomena which with certainty may be assumed to arise from the action of a single atom, or even of a part of an atom'[20].

In the history of physics and science, the birth of new sectors of inquiry had often been characterized by an initial, perhaps lengthy, phase of gathering empirical data, of brilliant, often surprising, and almost always indecipherable experimental results. Only later would such results be encompassed within a consistent explanatory system such as would provide the basis for the theoretical and conceptual consolidation of the new discipline. In the case of atomic physics, Bohr went on, this period had been particularly fruitful. After first making it possible to eliminate any lingering doubt as to the reality of atoms, it had then contributed to the systematic formation of a sufficiently detailed understanding of their internal structure, the outcome of which was the creation of a physically reliable image. The discovery of cathode and X-rays, the study of the behaviour of radioactive substances, the identification of electrons as negative electrical charges held within the atom by a positively charged nucleus, the discovery that the properties of a substance depend on the electronic configuration of the constituent element, the discovery of atomic number – i.e. the number of elementary charges contained within the neutral atom – as the criterion ordering the natural system of classification (the so-called periodic table): all these had been regarded as sufficient evidence to conclude that the most probable picture of the atom was a mechanical system similar in all respects to the solar system.

However, it was to be precisely the analogy suggested by this picture, with its associated implications in theoretical terms, that made the search for a rational foundation of atomic physics particularly difficult. Leaving aside the pedagogical utility of the visualizable representation from which it stemmed, the development of the analogy proved more problematic than might have been expected after the initial successes and led in the end to quite unforeseeable consequences: the drastic limitation of our forms of intuition and a radical change in the basic concepts of physics.

According to Bohr, it was immediately clear that the limitation of the analogy concerned what had from the viewpoint of classical physics always been considered the highest example of the levels to be reached by human understanding. In the description of the solar system, Newton's mechanics 'has won such great triumphs and has given us a principal example of the fulfilment of the claim of causality in ordinary physics'[21], anticipating future observations but also providing exact reconstructions of what the astronomers of the past would have seen when they pointed their rudimentary telescopes toward the heavens. The most problematic point for the effectiveness of this analogy was to be represented by the condition whereby the validity of any mechanical description depended upon the completely arbitrary choice of an initial state of the system. As Bohr pointed out, this presents great difficulties when atomic structure is considered. The first intuitive difficulty would arise from the fact that if one sought to remain faithful to the original analogy and admitted the possibility within each atom of continuously varying states of motion – forming, that is, an infinite succession – it would be no easy matter to explain the existence of properties clearly marking off the differences between one element and the next. One could always adopt a statistical viewpoint and claim that such 'properties of the elements do not inform us directly of the behaviour of the single atoms but, rather, that we are always concerned only with statistical regularities holding for the average conditions of a large number of atoms'[22]. While this hypothesis had made it possible to write several important chapters of statistical mechanics, it proved immediately sterile in the face of new empirical evidence providing direct information about the states of motion of the atomic constituents. Bohr is here referring to the wealth of experimental data regarding the light which an atom can emit in certain circumstances and which possesses characteristics such as to permit the unequivocal identification of the element responsible for the emission.

In 1913 the theory of the atom started from the idea that, on the basis of the classical theory of electromagnetism, the empirical laws of spectroscopy (the values of the frequencies and of the intensities of the lines of the elements) would provide information about the motion of the electrons within the atom[23]. However, it soon became apparent that classical mechanics lacked adequate theoretical tools to decipher such information and led to nothing less than the conclusion – logically inevitable but physically unacceptable – that if a continuous variation in the states of motion of the charged particles were to exist within atoms, then we should never observe sharp spectral lines. It thus became a question of identifying a 'missing element' capable of reconciling the picture of the atom laboriously traced by physicists with a class of experimental data of no minor importance, and in addition of restoring a certain consistency to our description of nature. The missing element was to be found in the concept of the quantum of action introduced by Planck at the turn of the century, a revolutionary concept which, by no coincidence, set an insuperable limit for the validity of thermodynamics and electromagnetism in the study of black-body radiation. With Planck's discovery a crisis had been reached as regards the demand for continuity, which guarantees for any mechanical description of nature that the causal relation between the states of the system is always fulfilled.

However, the difficulties encountered by classical physics in describing the effects dependent on the action of a single atom became still more serious and quite general when it was recalled that Einstein had years before called into question a point rightly regarded as the greatest cognitive achievement of Maxwell's theory. In a paper of 1905 – known above all for its interpretation of the photoelectric effect[24] – Einstein had suggested that the idea of the electromagnetic field did not exhaust all our knowledge of the nature of radiation, which also possessed corpuscular properties. This gave rise to an embarrassing dualism between contradictory conceptions of the physical behaviour of one and the same object. For Bohr this was resolved only upon recognition of the fact it was intimately connected with a 'peculiar limitation of our forms of perception'.

The conditions were thus laid down under which it would be possible to retain the analogy and to restore some measure of heuristic utility to the picture of the atom: 'only by a conscious resignation of our usual demands for visualization and causality was it possible to make Planck's discovery fruitful in explaining the properties of the elements on the basis of our knowledge of the building stones of atoms'[25]. This was therefore the price demanded for re-establishing the foundations of our description of nature. However, while the identification of the 'missing element' had proved fairly easy, the realization that the implications of the quantization of the atom would be so far-reaching was to emerge slowly, at the end of a long period of research and close theoretical reflection, and as a result of new experimental advances.

Within the framework of Bohr's argument, this conclusion, which was in actual fact seen as a general principle of the new mechanics, is implicitly translated into a historiographical criterion. As such it proves particularly suitable for the task of filtering and reinterpreting the complex events of the early years of the development of atomic physics so as to identify the episodes which Bohr regarded as having contributed to the formation of a new model of description.

The first decisive step was to make it possible to decide which solution would be acceptable theoretically as an explanation of the absence of any relation whatsoever between the observable properties of radiation (frequencies, intensities, etc.) and the hypothetical states of motion of atomic electrons. This would definitively clarify the nature of the obstacles preventing us from extending some of the propositions of classical electromagnetic theory to the case of the atom's radiative activity. Such a step was hardly a foregone conclusion, also in view of the already consolidated quantum hypotheses. In fact, apart from requiring a drastic scaling down of the analogy with the solar system, it also entailed the introduction of physical concepts whose peculiarity lay in their being undefinable in the light of existing knowledge. It had been Bohr himself in one of his early works, utilizing or in some way inspired by the hypothesis of the quantum of action, who suggested that 'every change in the state of an atom should be regarded as an individual process, incapable of more detailed description'[26]. This meant viewing each process taking place within the atom as a transition from one stationary state to another. It is certain that, at the time when these concepts were introduced, no theory was capable of stating what such transitions between states might be or to what physical causes we should attribute the property whereby atoms were always to be found in a stationary state at the end of a transition[27].

Despite the existence of glaring theoretical shortcomings, this unusual conceptual frame offered a rational basis for the fact that the spectra of the elements provided no direct information as to the motions of atomic particles. In such a context it is, in fact, clear that if the activation of the radiation 'mechanism' coincides with the various processes of transition between stationary states, the radiation emitted or absorbed by the atom is in no position to retain any memory of the hypothetical motions of the electrons associated, according to the model, with the different stationary states. We only know, in full agreement with the empirical laws of spectroscopy, that multiplication of the frequency of the radiation by Planck's constant gives us the exact value of the variation of the atom's internal energy produced by the process of emission or absorption[28].

Despite the violence it did to any intuitive form of understanding, such a solution had the merit of suggesting a simple and particularly elegant interpretation of the laws of spectroscopy. The conviction that the new concepts were the most effective tools to achieve an understanding of the origin of spectra was later to be reinforced experimentally by the celebrated result obtained by Franck and Hertz in their investigation of collisions between atoms and free electrons. As we know, they showed that upon collision atoms and electrons exchanged only amounts of energy corresponding exactly to the values calculated by the theory for the differences permitted between stationary states. All this was to reinforce the idea that by following this path a start had been made on constructing a consistent interpretative framework to accommodate a broad range of experimental data.

Subsequent developments were, however, to frustrate all attempts to achieve a description of the individual processes of transition, and the progressive fading of hopes of identifying a possible cause of such processes in the dynamic behaviour of electrons was itself to point naturally to the next step. With a fresh contribution by Einstein, the various stationary states were associated with certain coefficients of probability[29]. These gave a symbolic translation to the idea that each electron found in one of these states may in general be said to possess 'a free choice between various possible transitions to other stationary states'[30]. The idea of probability would thus appear not only in the processes of the radioactive decay of the nucleus but in any of the atom's physical events, being endowed in this case with the non-classical property of being irreducible to the statistical behaviour of a multitude of identical, more elementary objects which, taken individually, satisfy the laws of ordinary mechanics.

On closer examination, the apparent linearity and rationality of the reasoning which Bohr saw as having guided early research in atomic physics were, however, to founder upon a methodological objection so well grounded as to make the successes achieved by the new theory in interpreting many of the properties of elements appear surprising, to say the least. The objection is specifically concerned with the change in the system of conceptual reference that had made it possible to utilize the 'missing element' within new modes of description. In view of 'the great departure from our customary physical ideas'[31] involved in this change, Bohr remarks that one might reasonably wonder how it had been possible to devise such an effective account given that our knowledge of the building stones of the atoms rests upon those very ideas. One might, that is, legitimately suspect methodological sleight of hand in the continued use of concepts like 'mass' and 'electrical charge' when it is evident that such theoretical terms imply the validity of the laws of mechanics and electromagnetism. In other words, Bohr asks whether it is legitimate to transfer concepts from one theoretical context to another when they are so far removed that the new context actually owes its birth to the negation of some of the principles upon which the older rests. According to his reconstruction, the theoretical physicists working on the construction of quantum mechanics were induced by their awareness of

this serious epistemological obstacle to devise a method without precedent in the history of science of utilizing certain concepts 'in other
fields than that in which the classical theories are valid', which consisted
'in the demand of a direct concurrence of the quantum-mechanical
description with the customary description in the border region where
the quantum of action may be neglected'[32]. It was therefore not a
question of mechanically transferring concepts: the classical concepts
would become terms of quantum theory only subsequent to an operation
reinterpreting their meaning in such a way as, on the one hand, to fulfil
this demand and, on the other, to produce results in no way conflicting
with the postulate of the indivisibility of the quantum of action. According to Bohr, it was only when this operation – suggested by the so-called
correspondence principle – had been accomplished that it was possible to
formulate a consistent quantum mechanics. It then became clear that
quantum-mechanical description had arisen as a natural generalization
of the continuous causal description of classical mechanics[33].

Bohr recalls the difficulties encountered in this work of reinterpretation or conceptual translation before arriving at a fully satisfactory
complete description, and recognizes that, without a further and truly
decisive step made possible by an ingenious approach to the problem of
quantum theory initiated by Heisenberg, all efforts in this sense would
have proved vain. Bohr credits Heisenberg with identifying a procedure
to transform the correspondence principle into a formally rigorous
criterion, which then enabled him to show that the ordinary ideas of
motion (the basic concepts of kinematics and dynamics) may be replaced
within the theory by symbols obtained through a series of mathematical
operations on the classical laws of motion. In particular, one of the most
convincing aspects of Heisenberg's result was, in Bohr's view, the
simplicity with which it surmounted the obstacle of the quantum of
action, which appeared solely in some rules of calculation satisfied
automatically by the symbols of the quantum formalism corresponding to
the old concepts. In actual fact, Heisenberg's matrix mechanics was
convincing solely at a purely logical level since – avoiding any explicit
reference to quantities which are not directly observable, such as the
orbits of electrons – it strained human powers of abstraction to the
utmost, burying every physical idea beneath a monstrous heap of
symbols[34].

The discomfort occasioned by this abstract theoretical framework was
to be partially mitigated by the discovery that it was formally equivalent
to 'new artifices which, in spite of their formal character, more closely

meet our demands for visualization'[35]. It was precisely by virtue of this characteristic that the so-called wave mechanics of de Broglie and Schrödinger exercised a profound influence on the development and conceptual clarification of quantum mechanics. Born out of the generalization of the well-known analogy existing between the laws governing the propagation of light and those governing the motion of material bodies, it made what Bohr regarded as a decisive contribution to the clarification of the concept of stationary state and gave a suggestive interpretation of the so-called quantum numbers which, since the early work of Sommerfeld and of Bohr himself, had appeared in the quantum conditions for the atom's permitted energy levels. These numbers corresponded exactly to the numbers of nodes of the standing waves associated in wave mechanics with each stationary state.

The new mechanics, the fruit of a progressive enrichment of the original quantum conceptions, had established itself immediately by virtue of its capacity to master a vast range of experience. Nevertheless, in Bohr's view, any criterion of acceptance would have to make an explicit pronouncement as to its explanatory content, i.e. on the fact that, apart from its effectiveness as a tool, 'as with classical mechanics, so quantum mechanics, too, claims to give an exhaustive description of all phenomena which come within its scope'[36]. For many physicists of the time, the most disconcerting aspect of this claim was the attempt to demonstrate conclusively that the only description admissible for atomic phenomena was of essentially statistical type. Bohr on the other hand regarded this conclusion as obvious as soon as one reflected carefully both upon the well-known limitations imposed by measurement procedures on the information obtainable experimentally on the nature of the phenomena, and upon the meaning ascribed by quantum theory to the fundamental concepts whereby such information is expressed. Anticipating the error of interpretation upon which many of the objections subsequently moved against the validity of the new descriptive model were to rest, Bohr insisted that one should never lose sight of the profound modifications demanded of our system of conceptual reference by the quantum of action. Though it embraces concepts whose meaning is wholly tied up with our customary physical ideas and which refer to theoretical contexts now superseded, the new system subjects them to a rigorous reinterpretation to ensure their compatibility with the theoretical and experimental consequences of discontinuity, a notion indecipherable in classical terms. The quantum model of description would thus stem from the simultaneous fulfilment of two conditions. The first

concerns the observational consequences of the postulate of the indivisibility of phenomena. The second demands that the classical concepts
used in this context should have full significance for quantum theory
regardless of the intuitive content they may suggest.

This is the most difficult and delicate part of Bohr's argument in that its
force would be distorted by any stress laid on either of the conditions or
any attempt of operationalistic type to establish a close interdependence
between them. In the case of observations carried out on a material
particle, the second condition tells us that: (a) when we speak of a 'space-
time relation', we implicitly admit the permanence of the particle, i.e. we
assume that it conserves its individuality, its properties of spatial localization, in time in such a way that the terms between which the relation is
established are always defined; and (b) every possible application of the
concepts of energy and momentum to our system presupposes that the
laws of conservation are rigorously satisfied in each process of interaction. In any case, we know that the quantum postulate demands in
each measurement a finite interaction between object and instrument,
whose value remains indeterminate within certain limits. In the case
under examination, the first condition of our modes of description thus
entails that, because of the indeterminate nature of the interaction, if we
carry out a measurement intended to determine the particle's space-time
co-ordination, we must renounce all claim to exact knowledge of the
exchange of energy and momentum between particle and measuring
device. Analogously, if we are to determine energy and momentum, we
must forego any attempt to fix the particle's exact space-time co-
ordination. From the simultaneous existence of the two conditions it
follows logically that, in the first case, when we choose to gather
information as to a system's space-time co-ordination, the presence of an
indeterminate interaction destroys the grounds for a consistent application of the laws of conservation and thus eliminates the classical terms
'energy' and 'momentum' from our conceptual frame of reference.
Conversely, in the second case, our choosing to determine the values of
the energy and momentum of the system precludes for analogous reasons
any determination of the particle's space-time relations and there is no
reason for retaining such terms as 'position' within our system of concepts.

It may thus be stated that, by revealing the existence of an indeterminate interaction setting limits to the divisibility of phenomena in the
sense specified above, the quantum of action draws rigid boundaries for

the information content derivable from any operation of measurement and, at the same time, defines the sphere of validity of the concepts whereby such information may be expressed without ambiguity. The mutual incompatibility – conceptual and practical – existing between space-time co-ordination and the laws of conservation destroys, as it were, the condition upon which the classical model of representation rests and thus demonstrates the need to abandon rigorously causal description for a type regarded by Bohr as richer. Heisenberg's uncertainty relations – rigorously satisfied as they are by the formalism of quantum mechanics – are seen as reinforcing this conclusion 'as a direct expression of the absolute limitation of the applicability of visualizable conceptions in the description of atomic phenomena'[37]. In other words, these relations were supposed to show that the restrictive theoretical conditions for the use of the fundamental concepts in their ordinary sense correspond exactly to the concrete physical conditions for the observation of a system.

This would appear to be one of the greatest failures in the history of science. Atomic physics was born when scientists managed to derive the most probable picture of the atomic structure from a broad range of empirical data. On the basis of this picture, they initiated a research programme supported by analogy with a range of phenomena for which the classical model of causal description had given convincing proof of its effectiveness. Despite the success achieved in constructing a consistent theory, the results of the programme now pointed to the need to renounce intuitive understanding and causal connection, i.e. they dashed all hopes of clothing the theory in figurative language.

However, Bohr countered the understandable spread of disappointment with his deep conviction that with the new concepts an essential advance had been made in our understanding. In his view, a sense of failure could arise solely from illegitimate theoretical expectations: there were no rational grounds for believing that the fundamental principles of science could be utilized in a field of experience concerned with studying the properties and behaviour of individual objects that escape immediate perception. On the contrary, with the discovery of the natural limits of classical physics science had once again made a contribution of great cultural significance, going beyond the specific sphere of its own concerns to throw 'a new light on the old philosophical problem of the objective existence of phenomena independently of our observations'[38]. This problem was now, in Bohr's view, rescued from the field of pure speculation and enriched with unforeseeable scientific connotations. The new conceptions of quantum theory had brought out a level of complexity of the process of observation obliging us both to take into account interference in the course of the phenomenon and to consider all forms of causal description as superseded. As a physicist, Bohr used philosophical language since he felt himself pushed in this direction by his desire to make clear the extraordinary lesson to be learnt from the latest developments in physics. The same desire was later to be translated into a theoretical commitment to which he would remain faithful for the rest of his life. However, almost as though glimpsing the obstacles and incomprehension that his cultural battle was destined to encounter among the community of physicists, he made the following observation in a letter written during those months to his Swedish colleague Carl Oseen: 'Far from bemoaning the fact that in atomic physics our usual wishes with respect to the description of nature cannot be fulfilled, I believe that we ought to rejoice at the new lesson concerning the limitation in the human forms of visualization that is implied by the discovery of the quantum of action'. He then went on to express his regret at the cool attitude adopted by Einstein, at his obstinacy in opposing the possibility of statistical description with his celebrated rejection of a solution that would oblige God to play dice with the universe. At bottom, according to Bohr, the difficulties that scientists had met with in the world of atoms were not all that different from those encountered by the prophets when they had sought 'to describe the nature of God on the basis of our human concepts'. It was only because Einstein remained dogmatically convinced that the whole of reality should be referred to space-time pictures and that there was in any case a strict correspondence between the manifold articulations of nature and the modes of visualization and the tools of human communication that it came naturally to him to compare the quantum laws to a game of dice. Instead, as Bohr pointed out to Oseen, it was only through recognition of the limitation in our forms of visualization implied by these laws that it had been possible to apply the concept of causality to its ultimate limit and thus save the laws of conservation[39].

Similar reflections were contained in a letter written to thank Dirac for his observations on the text of Bohr's article for *Nature*. Here he stated in still more explicit terms that 'we cannot too strongly emphasize the inadequacy of our ordinary perception when dealing with quantum problems'[40]. Bohr concluded by drawing Dirac's attention to the fact that laying stress on the subjective character of the idea of observation was essential to the understanding that statistical-quantum description was no more than a generalization of ordinary causal description. The contrast existing between the quantum-theoretical idea of the dependence of phenomena on the conditions of observation and 'the classical idea of isolated objects is decisive for the limitation which characterizes the use of all classical concepts in the quantum theory'[41]. It was for this reason that he chose to develop these ideas in public in the short paper in honour of Planck, also because of his belief that 'we can hardly escape the conviction that in the facts which are revealed to us by the quantum theory and lie outside the domain of our ordinary forms of perception we have acquired a means of elucidating general philosophical problems'[42]. The means to which Bohr referred as capable of re-establishing fruitful interaction between problems of scientific and philosophical nature was an epistemology born from the results of the new mechanics to enrich and transform the traditional philosophical views of science, the latter being largely constructed around the development of classical physics. The epistemology of quantum theory entailed the reappraisal of many of the assumptions implicit in the previous forms of scientific explanation, and above all the recognition that 'different conceptual pictures are necessary to account completely for the phenomena and to furnish a unique formulation of the statistical laws which govern the data of observation'[43]. The unusual logical relation embedded within the idea of complementarity was no more than a concise way of expressing the same concept and showing that the contradictions suggested by the many paradoxes of quantum mechanics were such in appearance only.

The primary epistemological lesson of atomic physics thus lay in the 'relative meaning of each concept', i.e. its dependence upon the arbitrary nature of the viewpoint adopted to describe nature and upon the subjective choice of the conditions of observation. This destroys the ideal of a privileged point of reference for explanation and observation, such as that in which Laplace had situated his Intelligence capable of total and definitive knowledge of the laws of nature. Thus disappears also the certainty that the aim of science is the gradual achievement of this ideal. We must instead 'be prepared to accept the fact that a complete elucidation of one and the same object may require diverse points of view which defy a unique description'[44]. Long before philosophers of science became aware of the problem, Bohr thus appears to have grasped the profound transformation involved in transition to the new model of description. In other words, he raised the problem of 'reintegrating the subject into his own descriptions' and at the same time showed that 'the knowledge possessed by gods or demons [no longer had] any heuristic value for human understanding'[45].

Bohr also regarded the same problems with acute historical sensitivity and a critical attention to the dynamics operating within the development of knowledge. This enabled him, for example, to refute the thesis that the feature peculiar to the exact sciences, the highest criterion of demarcation for science, was the constant search for solutions of a form both unequivocal and objective precisely by virtue of their lack of any reference to the perceiving subject. While this ideal of objectivity may be aspired to by a form of mathematical knowledge, where there are in principle no limits to the application of rigorous logical criteria, far different problems and difficulties arise in this respect for the natural sciences. Here, as demonstrated also in recent history, one had to be constantly ready to adjust and even to transform radically our system of conceptual reference to ensure that new facts might be accommodated rationally within the framework of previous experience. Paying homage to what he described as the extraordinary consequences of Planck's discovery, Bohr pointed out how profoundly and definitively microphysics had shaken 'the foundations underlying the building up of concepts, on which not only the classical description of physics rests but also all our ordinary mode of thinking'[46].

3

The rational reconstruction proposed by Bohr presents a consistent and apparently trouble-free picture of over a decade of theoretical research. The central thesis of his entire argument – which sees the price to pay for the quantization of the atom as the conscious renunciation of the customary demands for intuition and causal connection – ends by asserting itself with such strength as to make any objection appear a romantic hangover from the reductionist attitudes belonging to the mechanistic tradition of the 19th century.

However, as in every rational reconstruction, Bohr's argument is concerned not so much with real history and its problematic and conflicting aspects, with the tortuous paths by which a new theoretical certainty was slowly to emerge, with alternative hypotheses that can be judged unproductive only *a posteriori*, or with the methodological assumptions and the metaphysics that have often made it possible to justify the irrational defence of a given programme, but rather with episodes which would, when read in a suitable light, serve to reinforce the context of justification of the new theory. And brilliant though the results achieved by his reconstruction may appear in this sense today, it is certain that at the time not all of those involved felt that they had been adequately represented. This was certainly the case of Schrödinger who, returning to a thesis maintained years before by Pauli, continued to speak of a research programme in a progressive phase aimed at the construction of a system of conceptual reference such as would re-establish the rights of reason and also the human understanding's demand for intuition. The same holds for Einstein, who years later, in 1951, went so far as to admit the failure of all attempts to give a stable foundation to atomic physics: 'All these fifty years of racking our brains have brought us no closer to answering the question: "What are light quanta?"'[47]. However, more surprisingly, Heisenberg himself may have had misgivings over Bohr's 'history' despite the latter's acknowledgement of and admiration for his fundamental contributions. He was probably unable to agree fully with the theoretical interpretation given to his uncertainty relations, where he saw not so much the conceptual aspects dear to Bohr as the physical consequence of discontinuity, a law regulating the effects of the disturbing action of the experimental apparatus on the system observed. It was not by chance that in the spring of 1927 he had presented his discovery as a solution restoring an intuitive content to the symbolism of quantum mechanics, i.e. the very requisite which Bohr regarded the quantum postulate as having expelled definitively from physics. Though forced at the time to bow to Bohr's authority, he was subsequently to arrive from a very different epistemological and philosophical viewpoint at the conclusion that 'the incomplete knowledge of a system is an essential component of any formulation of quantum theory' and that we must therefore resign ourselves to 'not being able in principle to know the present in all its details', a view which Bohr would obviously never have accepted[48].

Three authoritative physicists thus had good grounds for expressing reservations on decisive chapters of the reconstruction and were themselves the vehicles of conceptions and demands that could have given rise to reconstructions differing from Bohr's not only in the nature of the judgements expressed but also in the choice of subjects or the importance given them. It was, in fact, quite reasonable to criticize Bohr's retrospective survey for having consigned to (unwritten) footnotes problems and episodes which had polarized and fuelled theoretical debate for years: the hypothesis of light 'molecules' and the statistical approach to the study of radiation; the role of the mechanical model of the atom; and finally the ambitious project to re-establish a physics of the continuum through the consistent development of wave mechanics. Moreover, to those who had made significant contributions to the construction of atomic physics, many of Bohr's statements must have sounded if not exactly false at least highly ambiguous. And this legitimized the suspicion that they were intended to paint a convenient picture of the significant role played by Bohr himself in those years. The examples capable of arousing doubt and perplexity were by no means few in number.

Bohr claimed that as a result of the quantization of the image of the atom it had been necessary on the one hand to admit that radiation contained no significant information as to the motions of atomic particles, and on the other to introduce the undefinable concepts of stationary state and quantum transition. However, it thereby slipped his mind that in the early 1920s he had still sought to clothe these concepts with the image of electron orbits and had theorized about the existence of 'hidden mechanisms' that would make it possible to reconcile quantum jumps with the more traditional dynamic behaviour of electrons. He had been so firmly convinced of the need to leave open an interpretative perspective of the classical type as to resist stubbornly the objections of Heisenberg, who regarded any model-based approach as no longer defensible[49].

Still more suspect must have appeared the supposed methodological and epistemological awareness which he sought to attribute to the physicists of the time and saw as expressed in the heuristic content of the correspondence principle. From 1918 on, the latter is then supposed to have provided a rigorous guide in extending as far as possible the field of application of the classical concepts in the sphere of non-classical phenomena and laying down conditions so that their use would produce no serious contradictions. In actual fact, there were in those years very few physicists beside Bohr who had understood what this strange principle meant or how to use it. It was preferred to apply the far less problematic rules of quantization case by case, the end result of which was often to transform theoretical research into the sort of numerology that had aroused the disgust and irritation of the young Pauli[50]. For that matter, the real importance of the idea of correspondence for quantum theory was to become clear to Bohr only after the failures of the theory of virtual oscillators, with which he had sought in 1924 to define a model of spatio-temporal description of the process of atomic radiation. Above all, this was to become clear after Heisenberg's discovery that any attempt to reinterpret the concepts of classical physics in quantum terms had to be subordinated to the construction of a consistent mathematical formalism in which the symbols corresponding to such concepts were replaced with other symbols for which the fundamental relation of frequencies was always satisfied.

In 1927 there were therefore sufficiently valid reasons to justify the atmosphere of scepticism and distrust that generally greeted Bohr's proposed interpretation of quantum mechanics. However, there are also equally serious reasons for attempting a historical investigation in greater depth.

Notes

1 N. Bohr, 'The Quantum Postulate and the Recent Development of Atomic Theory', *Nature (Supplement)* **121** (1928), 580-90; *CW6*, 148–58. The note is entitled 'New Problems in Quantum Theory', ibid., 579; *CW6*, 52; the author is S. H. Allen, as reported by J. Kalckar, 'Introduction to Part I', *CW6*, 7–51: 51, on the basis of K. Stolzenburg, *Die Entwicklung des Bohrschen Komplementaritätgedankens in den Jahren 1924 bis 1929*, Stuttgart: Universität Stuttgart, 1977.

2 N. Bohr, 'The Quantum Postulate and the Recent Development of Atomic Theory', in *Atti del Congresso Internazionale dei Fisici*, 11–12 settembre 1927, 2 vols., Bologna: Zanichelli, 1928, vol. II, 565–88; *CW6*, 113–36. The later English versions of the article, published in *Atti del Congresso...* and *Nature* have many differences (changes in section divisions, new paragraphs, etc.). The main changes made by Bohr to the original text as it appeared in *Atti del Congresso...* are listed in *CW6*, 111–12. There are also German and Danish versions of the article: 'Das Quantenpostulat und die neuere Entwicklung der Atomistik', *Die Naturwissenschaften* **16** (1928), 245–57 and 'Kvantepostulatet og Atomteories seneste Udvikling', in *Atomteori og Naturbeskrivelse*, Copenhagen: Bianco Lunos Bogtrykkeri, 1929, 40–68.

3 Bohr to Schrödinger, 23 May 1928, *CW6*, 464–67; English trans. 48–50.

4 N. Bohr, 'Das Quantenpostulat und die neuere Entwicklung der Atomistik', *Die Naturwissenschaften* **16** (1928), 245–57. *CW6*, 111–12, presents the main variations between the text published in the *Atti del Congresso...* and that of the article published in *Nature*; there are, instead, no particular differences between the English and German editions of the paper. The same volume of the *Collected Works* also includes four previously unpublished manuscripts contained in the 'Como Lecture II (1927)' section of the Bohr archive, which represent preliminary drafts of the article (*CW6*, 57–98).

5 Those who spoke in the discussion were Born, Kramers, Heisenberg (twice), Fermi and Pauli; *Atti del Congresso...* cit. n. 2, vol. II, 589–98; *CW6*, 137–46. With regard to the reactions of the physicists of the period to Bohr's work, of particular interest is the testimony of Léon Rosenfeld, who for years collaborated closely with Bohr and was also to become a convinced supporter of complementarity: 'In fact, my own view of the Como lecture when I read it was that Bohr was just putting in a rather

heavy form things which had been expressed much more simply by Born and which were current in Göttingen at the time. I did not see, I did not feel, any of the subtlety that was in it, and I suppose that this was the general feeling in Göttingen'. (*SHQP*, interview with Rosenfeld, 1 July 1963, p. 19 of transcription.)

6 The fifth Solvay Conference was attended by: N. Bohr (Copenhagen), M. Born (Göttingen), L. de Broglie (Paris), P. Debye (Leipzig), P. A. M. Dirac (Cambridge), P. Ehrenfest (Leyden), R. H. Fowler (Cambridge), W. Heisenberg (Copenhagen), H. A. Kramers (Utrecht), I. Langmuir (Schenectady, NY), W. Pauli (Hamburg), M. Planck (Berlin), E. Schrödinger (Zurich) and C. T. R. Wilson (Cambridge). The scientific committee was chaired by Lorentz and included W. L. Bragg, M. Curie, A. Einstein, C. E. Guye, M. Knudsen, P. Langevin, O. W. Richardson and E. van Aubel. Bohr presented a paper dealing with practically the same subjects as at the Como conference and the translation of the article that had appeared in *Die Naturwissenschaften* was published in the proceedings (cf. n. 4); N. Bohr, 'Le postulat des quanta et le nouveau développement de l'atomistique', in *Electrons et photons. Rapports et discussions du cinquième Conseil de physique tenu à Bruxelles du 24 au 29 Octobre 1927*, Paris: Gauthier–Villars, 1928, 215–47. Cf. J. Mehra, *The Solvay Conferences on Physics*, Dordrecht: Reidel, 1975, ch. VI.

7 A careful reconstruction of the discussions that took place on that occasion between Bohr and Einstein is found in N. Bohr, 'Discussions with Einstein on Epistemological Problems in Atomic Physics', in P. A. Schilpp, ed., *Albert Einstein, Philosopher–Scientist*, The Library of Living Philosophers, Illinois: Evanston, 1949, 199–242, reprinted in N. Bohr, *Atomic Physics and Human Knowledge*, New York: J. Wiley & Sons, 1958, 32–66. A long letter dated 3 November from Ehrenfest to Goudsmit, Uhlenbeck and Dieke contains an interesting account of the discussions (*CW6*, 37–41). See below, ch. 5.

8 'New Problems...' cit. n. 1.

9 Ibid.

10 Pauli to Bohr, 16 June 1928, *CW6*, 438–39; English trans. 440–41; *WB*, 462–63.

11 Schrödinger to Bohr, 5 May 1928, *CW6*, 463–64; English trans. 46–48.

12 Bohr to Schrödinger, 23 May 1928, cit. n. 3. 'Anschauung' is here translated as 'visualization'. The German terms *Anschauung* and *Anschaulichkeit* (and the adjective *anschaulich*), which recur very frequently in writings on atomic physics in this period, have posed and still do pose serious problems of translation. For example, A. I. Miller ('Redefining Anschaulichkeit', in A. Shimony and H. Feshbach, eds., *Physics as Natural Philosophy. Essays in Honour of Laszlo Tisza on his Seventy-Fifth Birthday*, Cambridge (Mass.): MIT Press, 1983, 376–411) observes that *Anschauung* is untranslatable into any language without bearing in mind the context of Kant's philosophy, where it was used to indicate a form of immediate apprehension of a real object. On the contrary, *Anschaulichkeit* denotes intuition through a mechanical type of model or, more generally, all forms of visualization. Miller therefore suggests that the latter 'can be interpreted to be less abstract than *Anschauung*. *Anschaulichkeit* is a property of the object itself, while the *Anschauung* of an object results from the cognitive act of knowing the object'. In his view, these terms became problematic with the birth of atomic theory since physicists had previously dealt with

systems to which it was possible to apply the space-time pictures of classical physics derived by abstraction from visualizations of the objects of the world of perceptions. Considering the different use made of these terms by various authors – Heisenberg in particular – Miller suggests translating *Anschauung* as intuition and *Anschaulichkeit* as visualizability. Cf. also by the same author: 'Visualization Lost and Regained: The Genesis of the Quantum Theory in the Period 1913–1927', in J. Wechsler, ed., *On Aesthetics in Science*, Cambridge (Mass.): MIT Press, 1978, 73–102; *Imagery in Scientific Thought. Creating 20th Century Physics*, Boston: Birkhäuser, 1984. From a far more radical standpoint than that adopted by Miller, John Hendry rejects these semantic nuances and maintains that the loss of visualization brought about by quantum mechanics represented one of the most profound transformations undergone by science since the 17th century. In Hendry's view, the viewpoints adopted by Bohr, Pauli and Heisenberg on the most complex theoretical problems can be understood only in the context of the complete and explicit acceptance of the non-visualizability of the quantum world. He thus cuts through all knotty questions of translation. Cf. for example J. Hendry, 'The History of Complementarity: Niels Bohr and the Problem of Visualization', in *Proceedings of the International Symposium on Niels Bohr, Roma 25–27 novembre 1985, Rivista di Storia della Scienza* 2 (1985), 391–407. For the editors of Bohr's *Collected Works*, the German *anschaulich* 'means something that we can think through images'; they choose to translate the word and its Danish equivalent *anskueling* with visualizable (J. Kalckar, 'Introduction...' cit. n. 1, p. 12). Without going into the merits of the solutions suggested by these authors – which would require, at least in the first two cases, an in-depth examination of their historiographical approach – this essay will use the terms 'intuition' and 'visualization' and their derivatives according to context on the understanding that as regards Bohr's writings any reference to the intuitive or visualizable content of the theory is intended as reference to a theory which, leaving aside any model-based representation, makes possible a causal space-time description of phenomena. Different problems are posed by Heisenberg's work of 1927; see below, ch. 5.

13 Bohr to Schrödinger, cit. n. 3.

14 Einstein to Schrödinger, 31 May 1928, cit. in J. Kalckar, 'Introduction...' cit. n. 1, 51.

15 N. Bohr, 'Wirkungsquantum und Naturbeschreibung', *Die Naturwissenschaften* **17** (1929), 483–86; *CW6*, 203–6. An English translation of the article was published in N. Bohr, *Atomic Theory and the Description of Nature*, Cambridge: Cambridge University Press, 1934, 92–101; *CW6*, 208–17.

16 J. Kalckar, 'Introduction to Part II', *CW6*, 189–98: 189.

17 Bohr to Pauli, 1 June 1929, *CW6*, 441–43 (in Danish); English trans. 443–44. In thanking Bohr for his paper, Planck observed: 'The content of your article – like everything that you write – is so deeply thought out that I for my part shall not now attempt to comment on details. That could not be done without a longer discussion. [...] There still remains a rich field of reasoning here'. (Planck to Bohr, 14 July 1929, *CW6*, 456–57; English trans. 192).

18 Pauli to Bohr, 17 July 1929, *CW6*, 444–46; English trans. 446–48; *WB*, 512–14.

19 N. Bohr, 'Atomteorien og Grunprincipperne for Naturbeskrivelsen', in
    Beretning om det 18. skandinaviske Naturforskermode i Kobenhavn 26–31.
    August 1929, Copenhagen: Fredriksberg Bogtrykkeri, 1929, 71–83; *CW6*,
    223–35. Besides being published in the conference proceedings, the article
    also appeared in a special issue of the journal *Fysisk Tiddskrift* (**27** (1929),
    103–14) to celebrate the 450th anniversary of the University of Copenhagen
    (cf. J. Kalckar, 'Introduction...' cit. n. 16, 196–97). The article also
    appeared in German, 'Die Atomtheorie und die Prinzipien der
    Naturbeschreibung', *Die Naturwissenschaften* **18** (1930), 73–78, and in
    English, *The Atomic Theory and the Fundamental Principles Underlying the*
    Description of Nature, in N. Bohr, *Atomic Theory...* cit. n. 15, 102–19;
    CW6, 236–55. Because of the numerous discrepancies between this
    translation and the original – pointed out among others by J. Honner, 'The
    Transcendental Philosophy of Niels Bohr', *Studies in History and*
    Philosophy of Science **13** (1982), 1–29 – quotations will henceforth be taken
    from the German edition.
20 N. Bohr, 'Die Atomtheorie...' cit. n. 19, 73.
21 Ibid., 74.
22 Ibid.
23 Bohr is referring to the article on the quantum theory of the hydrogen atom
    ('On the Constitution of Atoms and Molecules') published in the
    Philosophical Magazine in 1913; see below, chs. 2 and 3.
24 A. Einstein, 'Über einen die Erzeugung und Verwandlung des Lichtes
    betreffenden heuristischen Gesichtspunkt', *Annalen der Physik* **17** (1905),
    132–48.
25 N. Bohr, 'Die Atomtheorie...' cit. n. 19, 75.
26 Ibid., 75.
27 See below, chs. 2 and 3.
28 The relation $h\nu = E' - E''$, between the frequency ν of the radiation emitted
    by an atom and the energies E' and E'' of the stationary states between
    which the transition takes place, takes the name of the quantum condition
    of frequency; in Bohr's writings it was defined as the theory's second
    postulate. See below, ch. 2.
29 A. Einstein, 'Zur Quantentheorie der Strahlung', *Physikalische Zeitschrift*
    18 (1917), 121–28.
30 N. Bohr, 'Die Atomtheorie...' cit. n. 19, 75. See below, ch. 4.
31 Ibid., 75.
32 Ibid.
33 The meaning of this principle will be analysed in ch. 3, also with regard to
    the view here expressed by Bohr on the relationship between classical
    mechanics and quantum mechanics.
34 Views of this type were expressed by figures such as Einstein, who wrote in
    the following terms to Besso on 25 December 1925: 'The most interesting
    recent theoretical achievement is the Heisenberg–Born–Jordan theory of
    quantum states. A real sorcerer's multiplication table, in which infinite
    determinants (matrices) replace the Cartesian coordinates. It is extremely
    ingenious, and thanks to its great complication sufficiently protected against
    disproof.' (A. Einstein and M. Besso, *Correspondance 1903–1955*, P.
    Speziali, ed., Paris: Hermann, 1972, 215–16.)
35 N. Bohr, 'Die Atomtheorie...' cit. n. 19, 75.
36 Ibid., 76.
37 Ibid.

38 Ibid., 77.
39 Bohr to Oseen, 5 November 1928, *CW6*, 430–32 (in Danish); English trans. 190–91. Carl W. Oseen was professor of mathematical physics at the University of Uppsala from 1909 to 1933 and for more than a decade (1933–44) director of the Nobel Institute. His correspondence with Bohr, to whom he became strongly attached, began in 1911, when the latter sent him a copy of his doctorate thesis.
40 Bohr to Dirac, 24 March 1928, *CW5*, 44–46.
41 Ibid.
42 N. Bohr, 'Wirkungsquantum...' cit. n. 15, 486; *CW6*, 206; English trans. 101; *CW6*, 217.
43 Ibid., 484; *CW6*, 204; English trans. 94; *CW6*, 210.
44 Ibid., 485; *CW6*, 205; English trans. 96; *CW6*, 212.
45 M. Ceruti, *Il vincolo e la possibilità*, Milano: Feltrinelli, 1986, 43 and 60. Ceruti identifies an interesting turning point in the latest studies in philosophy of science marked by the 'calling into question of the problem of Method as the search for a criterion of demarcation upon which to pass ahistorical judgement on the validity or otherwise of competing scientific theories or conceptions' (ibid., 103); attention has been turning to the far more fruitful question of 'how and how far the results of contemporary sciences can influence the formulation or reformulation of the classical problems of epistemology' (ibid., 61). In this sense we have arrived, among other things, at a re-evaluation of the general epistemological character of some specific problems posed by the interpretation of microphysics. On the epistemological bearings of contemporary physics cf. also I. Prigogine and I. Stengers, *La nouvelle alliance. Métamorphose de la science*, Paris: Gallimard, 1979; I. Prigogine, *From Being to Becoming*, San Francisco: Freeman, 1980.
46 N. Bohr, 'Wirkungsquantum...' cit. n. 15, 486; *CW6*, 206; English trans. 101; *CW6*, 217.
47 Einstein to Besso, 12 December 1951, in A. Einstein and M. Besso, *Correspondance* cit. n. 34, 453. Cf. also A. Pais, *'Subtle is the Lord...'* cit. Introduction n. 4.
48 W. Heisenberg, 'Atomforschung und Kausalgesetz', in W. Heisenberg, *Schritte über Grenzen*, München: Piper, 1971, 128–41.
49 Cf. for example J. Hendry, *The Creation of Quantum Mechanics and the Bohr–Pauli Dialogue*, Dordrecht: Reidel, 1984, esp. ch. IV.
50 As Pauli wrote to Bohr: 'The atomic physicists in Germany today fall into two groups. The one calculate a given problem first with half-integral values of the quantum numbers, and if it doesn't agree with experiment they then do it with integral quantum numbers. The others calculate first with whole numbers, and if it doesn't agree then they calculate with halves. But both groups of atomic physicists have the property in common that their theories offer no a priori reasoning which quantum numbers and which atoms should be calculated with half-integral values of the quantum numbers and which should be calculated with integral values. Instead they decide this merely a posteriori by comparison with experiment. I myself have no taste for this sort of theoretical physics and retire from it to my heat conduction of solid bodies'. (Pauli to Bohr, 21 February 1924, *WB*, 147–48.)

CHAPTER 2
Atomic model and quantum hypotheses

1

In 1913 the *Philosophical Magazine* published a long article by Bohr in three parts containing the first quantum theory of the atom. The article was entitled 'On the Constitution of Atoms and Molecules' and soon became known in the scientific circles of the day as Bohr's 'trilogy'[1]. The article provided a sound theoretical foundation for the Rutherford model of the nuclear atom that had become established in 1911 thanks to new experimental discoveries about the elementary constituents of matter. The importance and originality of Bohr's paper are usually seen as lying in his successful use of quantum concepts in the solution of problems concerning the constitution and physical properties of atoms, thereby effecting a significant extension of the scope of the quantization hypotheses first introduced by Planck at the beginning of the century. Until 1910 physicists had – with few but important exceptions (in particular Einstein, von Laue and Ehrenfest) – generally been convinced that Planck's constant h was characteristic only of the problem of heat radiation, i.e. had seen it as a particular hypothesis making possible the theoretical derivation of the black-body law[2]. Bohr's work would thus assume a two-fold importance in the evolution of 20th century physics. On the one hand, it would represent the first attempt to formulate a consistent theory of the constitution of the atom capable of explaining much of the experimental data available and of deducing empirical laws concerning the spectra of the elements. On the other, it would mark a decisive advance for quantum-theoretical conceptions by establishing their high level of generality.

However, as we shall see, on neither of these points did the trilogy lead to the establishment of a new paradigm, raising as it did far more problems than it actually solved. Its content is to be regarded rather as a demanding and ambitious research programme which was to oblige physicists after 1913 to exert themselves on the dual task of expanding our knowledge of atomic phenomena while carrying out a radical and, in some ways, then unpredictable revision of the foundations of physics. This phase of the development of atomic theory based on Bohr's 1913 programme was anything but short and in fact ended only in the autumn of 1927 when, as we have seen, Bohr himself furnished a physical interpretation of quantum mechanics based on the principle of complementarity.

Bohr's paper of 1913 is thus situated in a historical perspective extending far beyond the role it played on its first appearance with regard to the internal questions of a certain domain of physics, i.e. those concerning the nature and the observable behaviour of microscopic objects. Only in this broader context is it possible to reconstruct the complex network of conceptual and methodological relations stretching from the appearance of Planck's first quantum hypothesis to the establishment of the new mechanics during the 1920s. In fact, as Bohr later pointed out, some 30 years of research were needed to unveil the real physical significance and bring out all the conceptual implications of Planck's idea, according to which the quantity of energy exchanged between a field of radiation and an oscillator of frequency v (a charge oscillating around a position of equilibrium) is not the result of a continuous process but rather one dependent on distinct events, each involving a finite and indivisible quantity of energy.

In actual fact, this way of interpreting Planck's ideas was to remain controversial for many years, especially with regard to the inevitable, disastrous consequences for classical electrodynamics supposedly deriving from the concept of discontinuity. Planck's original formulation of black-body theory had, in fact, employed quantization as a hypothesis regarding the way in which the total energy of a system may be distributed among N oscillators of differing frequency. That is, it was used as a basis for certain probability calculations required to obtain the value of the entropy of the system and, at least until 1908, was not regarded by Planck as interpretable from a physical point of view as an application of the concept of discontinuity to atomic processes. Moreover, it did not necessarily imply that the interaction between radiation and oscillator was a process lying beyond the interpretative scope of 19th century electrodynamics, i.e. a non-classical process. The conviction that the quantum should be associated with the idea of discontinuity was to take gradual hold only later, even after the first demonstrations that the quantization of energy was applicable to other sectors of experience (e.g. in Einstein's interpretation of the photoelectric effect). In this way, a far deeper physical content came to be attributed to the quantum *h* than it had originally been assigned by Planck himself[3].

On first sight, the situation in physics in the first decades of the 20th century would appear to be characterized by growing awareness of the failure of the foundations upon which so-called classical physics had grown, i.e. Newton's mechanics and Maxwell's electrodynamics. Einstein's theory of relativity and Planck's quantum theory would appear to have wrought so much havoc within the body of acquired physical knowledge as to force the scientific community to refund the whole sector of science. Against such a background, the steps Bohr is regarded as having taken in the construction of the quantum theory of the atom would appear wholly justifiable and rationally legitimate. These include: acceptance of the Rutherford model composed of a positively charged nucleus and a number of electrons moving freely in predetermined orbits; recognition of the limitations of classical electrodynamics in accounting for the radiative stability of electrons; application of Planck's hypothesis to the model. This last step would then give rise to the following general assertions: (a) electrons can only occupy discrete orbits to which is associated a value of energy derivable from the so-called quantum condition for stationary states; (b) the atom emits and absorbs energy in the form of radiation not continuously but in quanta – to each process of radiation emission there corresponds the transition of an electron from one stationary state to another, from one orbit to another of different value of energy[4].

However, conclusions of this type, which seek to account for scientific choices by appeal to phases of sudden discontinuity in the development of our knowledge, should be subordinated to more thorough attempts to ascertain whether such choices are not rather the consequences of the concrete problems with which scientists are faced. In our case, it may be useful in this sense to try to weaken the previous assertions as to the factors supposed to have guided Bohr in the construction of atomic theory and to seek an answer to the following questions. Does the originality of Bohr's work boil down to the application of Planck's hypothesis to the problem of the atomic constitution? Can his theory therefore be seen simply as a return in a different phenomenal context to the ideas established within 'old quantum theory'? How far was this actually possible? Were Bohr and the other atomic physicists employing quantum concepts really acting in a theoretical context where the global and irreversible crisis of classical physics was admitted?

2

'This seems to be nothing else than what was to be expected, as it seems to be rigorously proved that the mechanics is not able to explain the experimental facts in problems dealing with single atoms. In analogy to what is known for other problems it seems however to be legitimate to use the mechanics in the investigation of the behaviour of a system, if we only look apart from questions of stability.' Thus Bohr explained his recourse to the hypothesis – irreducible to the laws of classical mechanics – that the ratio between the kinetic energy and the frequency of an atomic electron always has a definite value. This was Bohr's first attempt at the quantization of the model of the atom and the hypothesis is contained in a memorandum delivered to Ernest Rutherford in the summer of 1912 at the end of his studies in England, in which he outlined the plan of a subsequent paper on molecular structure and stability. In his view, this was a solution that seemed 'to offer a possibility of an explanation of the whole group of experimental results' and to confirm, to some extent, Planck and Einstein's conceptions of the mechanism of radiation[5]. As we shall see, the process of quantization submitted to Rutherford as a solution to the theoretical difficulties raised by the nuclear model was still a long way from the original application of Planck's ideas that was, within a few months, to enable Bohr to formulate the quantum theory of the hydrogen atom. Moreover, there was nothing really new in the conviction that the answer to the many problems encountered in the study of matter and involving direct reference to the atom's internal constitution were to be found in some non-mechanical hypothesis. Other physicists had advanced similar solutions[6] and Bohr had himself been gathering significant evidence in this sense ever since his doctorate thesis on the possible developments and the degree of generality of the electronic theory of metals formulated by Lorentz in 1905[7].

Bohr's thesis had arrived at highly interesting conclusions when he had, within the ambitious perspective of Lorentz's original programme, sought to extend the theory to cover problems the latter had not taken into consideration, such as heat radiation and magnetism. On the one hand, this demonstrated just how problematic it was to regard the electronic theory of metals as a sufficiently solid basis to derive the explanation of the fundamental properties of matter from the conceptions of classical physics. On the other, it showed that the failure of the programme offered indications whose generality made them still more interesting. In fact, further and in a certain sense conclusive confirmations were deduced from the already well-grounded suspicion that many of the difficulties encountered in this direction were attributable to a more general inability of electromagnetism to express the real physical nature of microscopic objects. Bohr's work on his doctorate thesis had thus been a most valuable field of research in that it had enabled him to ascertain the limitations of classical theory in the study of the new sectors of phenomena. However, it was decisive above all in view of his subsequent theoretical work in atomic physics, in that it made it possible to specify where such theories lost their interpretative effectiveness. In fact, closer examination reveals that it was Lorentz's own theory that demonstrated that classical ideas encountered no difficulties as long as the problems tackled involved no explicit reference to atomic structure, and that when this did happen our system of conceptual reference required bolstering with hypotheses irreducible to it[8].

In the autumn of 1911 Bohr arrived in Cambridge to complete his scientific training in the laboratory of J. J. Thomson, with whom he also hoped to find someone interested in discussing his ideas. After a few months he left England, having managed neither to find a journal willing to publish the translation of his doctorate thesis nor to exchange more than a few words with Thomson[9]. It had, however, been an experience that was later to prove extremely fruitful, above all for the connections he had made in one of the most vital and prestigious centres of experimental study. It is to the studies carried out during his stay in England, especially after his move to Manchester in January 1912, that we owe the publication of a paper on the decrease of velocity of charged particles on passing through matter, from which he obtained further hints for his approach to the problem of atomic structure[10]. However, the same studies are also the source of the far more important memorandum to Rutherford where, beside presenting a still provisional and largely unsatisfactory theoretical elaboration, he indicated with extreme clarity and surprising maturity what, in his view, should constitute the methodological basis for the rational foundation of atomic physics: the use of classical mechanics to study the behaviour of atomic systems even if it should also prove necessary to resort to hypotheses conflicting with it. While this epistemologically risky assumption might appear to be simply an extension of Bohr's previously expressed negative judgement as to the validity of classical physics in this sphere, he himself saw it as in some way imposed by empirical data and by the more probable picture of the atom deriving from it.

The systematic study of the configuration of atoms and investigations into phenomena connected with the distribution of their internal charges constituted a comparatively new sector of research in physics. Only after the turn of the century had the idea been definitively established that atoms were complex physical objects endowed with an internal structure. The electron too, understood as an elementary charge, was no longer a mere conjecture as to the nature of cathode rays but an object whose principal properties and physical characteristics were precisely known. In 1897, at the Cavendish Laboratory in Cambridge, Thomson's measurement of the ratio between the electron's mass and charge had confirmed previous theoretical predictions. Moreover, there appeared to be both theoretical grounds and empirical justification for the hypothesis that electrons were present within atoms and that they were situated in a state of elastic linkage forming a system of oscillating charges or charges rotating on particular orbits[11]. In December 1903 Thomson had himself proposed a model in which 'the atoms of the elements consist of a number of negatively electrified corpuscles enclosed in a sphere of uniform positive electrification'[12]. For reasons of mechanical stability he found that if the number of electrons of an element was lower than five then they occupied regular positions and lay at the same distance from the centre of the sphere. He further found that in all other cases electrons tended to be distributed on coplanar rings in a number corresponding to the position of the element in Mendeleev's periodic table. In both cases, however, Thomson's model guaranteed the stability of the electrons which, once displaced from their position of equilibrium, tended to return there. Thomson's theory accounted moreover for such important phenomena taking place in gases as the dispersion of light, the diffusion of X-rays, and the absorption of α-rays. However, as is known, new experimental results were soon to pinpoint serious interpretative difficulties in this model. In 1909, while studying the scattering of beams of charged particles (α-rays) by matter, Hans Geiger and Ernest Mardsen had observed anomalous behaviour – i.e. behaviour incompatible with current ideas of atomic configuration – in the direction of some particles after collision with heavy atoms. About two years later Rutherford, then director of the Manchester laboratories, arrived at the following conclusion: 'In order to explain these and other results, it is necessary to assume that the electrified particle passes through an intense electric field within the atom. The scattering of the electrified particles is considered for a type of atom which consists of a central electric charge concentrated at a point and surrounded by a uniform spherical distribution of opposite electricity equal in amount'[13]. On the basis of the model illustrated, he derived the formula describing the scattering of α-particles and, more importantly, the angular dependence of the distribution observed in particularly brilliant fashion and in complete agreement with the experimental data available.

It should be pointed out that at the time acceptance of Rutherford's new hypothesis was a far less automatic step than one would now expect, both on theoretical grounds – given that the model of the atom with nucleus ran up against the well-known problem of orbital stability – and for experimental reasons. In fact, Thomson's model had for years been the inspiration of much research seeking, for example, to determine the relation between the number of electrons and the atomic weights of the elements and to provide an explanation of their physical and chemical properties in relation to their position in the periodic table. And the results obtained often provided support for the original model.

When Bohr arrived in Manchester after his disappointing period at the Cavendish Laboratory, he found an environment fully prepared to accept contributions such as might enrich the research prospects opened up by the new model. For this reason Rutherford and his colleagues, though principally engaged in the search for new experiments to confirm the existence of the nucleus, immediately showed the greatest interest in the ideas of the young Danish physicist[14]. However, the question of orbital instability can hardly have loomed large in Bohr's thinking, given his firm conviction that this represented not a defect attributable to the characteristics of the model, but rather further confirmation of the already known impossibility of tackling the investigation of atomic structure with classical tools. This would explain why the procedure of quantization – the 'special hypothesis' contained in the memorandum – was not aimed, as one might naturally have expected, at providing a consistent solution to this problem. Or rather why, from that time on, he gave up any attempt to reconcile the glaring contradiction between the possibility of the orbital motion of charged particles and the Maxwell–Lorentz laws of electrodynamics. Bohr did speak of the stability of the atom, but the problem he had in mind was not concerned with the losses of radiant energy that these laws associate with the accelerated motion of electrons.

It is true, as has been observed, that in those years the question of radiative instability was, unlike that of mechanical instability, not a criterion discriminating between one picture of the atom and another, given that the same instability affected any model containing electronic charges in motion. And it is probably also true that this obstacle aroused little interest among physicists working in the field[15]. However, observations as to the prevailing climate of opinion in the scientific circles of the day are certainly insufficient to explain the reasons that drove Bohr to effect from the very outset a drastic reduction in the goals of the theory he intended to construct. Far more convincing justification of this choice is unquestionably provided by the hypothesis that in those months he had already arrived at the view of the implications of the new quantum theory that was to be given explicit statement in his subsequent work, i.e. that with Planck's concept of the quantum of action, physics had moved definitively beyond the scope of classical theory and that a new system of conceptual reference was therefore required[16]. As we shall see, in Bohr's contribution to the foundation of atomic physics this idea plays a role decidedly more important and fruitful than possible but not always simple generalizations of quantization techniques. This may have been the greatest intellectual debt he owed to Planck and Einstein.

The stability that he sought to restore to Rutherford's model of the atom so as to demonstrate its definitive superiority to Thomson's is closely connected with a difficulty encountered in the application of mechanical considerations to the study of the electron configuration: knowledge of the intensity of the central charge and of the number of electrons contained in a ring provides no useful information as to the frequencies of movement of the electrons themselves. In fact, all that can be derived from such considerations is the relation $(e^2/a^2)X = ma(2\pi\nu)^2$ between the frequency ν of revolution and the radius a of the ring, which says nothing about the possible states of oscillation of the electronic particles since with the varying of a an infinitely great number of frequencies may be obtained. Bohr thus saw it as absolutely clear that only a further non-mechanical hypothesis would be able to account for the stability characteristic of atoms existing in nature and to suggest, in particular, a rigorous criterion to distinguish out of all the mechanically possible states those physically admissible. As we have seen, the idea put forward in the memorandum is that the latter should satisfy the condition whereby the ratio between an electron's kinetic energy and its frequency assumes a definite value, which he posited as equal to a constant K. In order to justify this condition, Bohr recalled illustrious precedents which had obtained significant experimental confirmation of their way of treating the mechanics of radiation. However, little remained in this condition of Planck and Einstein's quantum hypotheses beyond a somewhat vague analogy. In fact, in this case not only had any procedure for the quantization of the oscillator's total energy disappeared to be replaced by a simple dependence of frequency on kinetic energy, but the constant of proportionality appearing in the latter relation was by no means reducible to some multiple or significant submultiple of Planck's quantum of action h.

The example of the hydrogen molecule with which Bohr sought to confirm the validity of his theoretical approach made it possible to obtain a reliable expression of the energy of the system, i.e. of the work required to remove an electron from the molecule. By using this expression of energy to determine the heat produced in the formation of a hydrogen molecule, he in fact found a value of the same order of magnitude as that obtained experimentally. It has, however, been shown that with the data available to Bohr, the best estimate of K was approximately equal to $0.6h$[17]. Despite these by no means negligible conceptual and formal obstacles, Bohr declared himself convinced, as he wrote to his brother Harald shortly before returning to Copenhagen, that he had found out something about the structure of atoms and managed to get hold of a little bit of reality[18].

On 6 March 1913 Bohr sent Rutherford the first chapter of the paper on the constitution of atoms that he had begun writing during his last weeks in Manchester. The accompanying letter expressed his hope that Rutherford would regard as reasonable the standpoint adopted as to 'the delicate question of the simultaneous use of the old mechanics and of the new assumptions introduced by Planck's theory of radiation' and his eagerness to know what Rutherford thought of it[19]. The period of time that had elapsed was comparatively short if one considers both the objective complexity of Bohr's initial programme and the fact that since his return to Copenhagen new academic commitments had taken up a considerable amount of his time[20]. However, his standpoint on the whole question showed a profound change from the solutions sketched out in the memorandum. The procedure of quantization was different (completely new, as he described it in his letter to Rutherford) and above all there appeared a problem which had been overlooked in the earlier memorandum and which entailed the redefinition and extension of the theory's very objectives: 'I have tried to show that from such a point of view it seems possible to give a simple interpretation of the law of the spectrum of hydrogen, and that the calculation affords a close quantitative agreement with experiments'[21]. As will be shown below, this change was to some extent influenced by comparison with Nicholson's theory, which suggested alternative solutions for the quantization of a Rutherford-type model of the atom, and by Bohr's 'discovery' of – or greater attention to – the empirical laws of atomic spectroscopy. However, precious little will be understood of the actual progress Bohr regarded himself as having made at that time, and even less of the apparently disconcerting developments which were to characterize his theoretical conceptions during 1913, if due attention is not paid to his reference to the 'delicate question', a point to which he again drew Rutherford's attention a few months later. At that time the problem of the atomic model and, more generally speaking, of atomic theory meant for Bohr the search for solutions such as would justify the simultaneous use of the tools of analysis and description provided by classical mechanics and quantum-theoretical hypotheses. Each stage in the construction of the theory was to be marked by what were regarded in turn as more satisfactory solutions to this problem.

Rutherford's reaction was one of admiration mingled with perplexity: 'Your ideas [...] are very ingenious and seem to work out very well; but the mixture of Planck's ideas with the old mechanics makes it very difficult to form a physical idea of what is at the basis of it all. There appears to me one grave difficulty in your hypothesis, which I have no doubt that you fully realise, namely, how does an electron decide what frequency it is going to vibrate at when it passes from one stationary state to the other? It seems to me that you have to assume that the electron knows beforehand where it is going to stop'[22]. In the following years objections of this type were to become common and to influence the willingness of many physicists to commit themselves fully to accepting the theory, despite the fact that it had, from the outset, shown considerable interpretative effectiveness. As a highly competent experimental physicist accustomed to considering the possibility of an immediate or intuitive representation of a physical system or process as a tool of inquiry every bit as fundamental as the ordinary apparatus of measurement, Rutherford immediately grasped the weak point in Bohr's theoretical proposal. While operating within the context of a model-based approach of classical type, the theory distorted its figurative content to suggest hypotheses (electrons which decide and know in advance the evolution of the process) violating common sense and imposing a limit to the formation of physical ideas, which Rutherford evidently regarded as the same thing. The latter thus appears to have grasped, and rejected, a conclusion that would become clear and inevitable to Bohr only many years later: the compatibility of classical concepts and quantum hypotheses can be established only by renouncing our traditional forms of intuition and representation of reality. Nevertheless, the theoretical proposal advanced by the young physicist appeared worthy of the closest attention in that it achieved truly brilliant results in the explanation of an important group of phenomena that had been left for decades with no interpretative basis whatsoever.

Though the discovery of the existence of the line spectra of elements dates from William Wollaston's observations on the solar spectrum in the early 19th century, over half a century was to pass before these observations could be reproduced in laboratory conditions. Working in the laboratories of Heidelberg University, the chemist Robert Bunsen and physicist Gustav Kirchhoff devised experimental apparatus making it possible to carry out systematic analysis of the spectra of the elements. The salts of certain substances were brought to an incandescent state and the light produced was made to pass through a slit before dispersion through a prism. The spectrum lines thus produced were observed through a telescope. After certain improvements, the apparatus made it possible to measure the values of the frequencies of each line to a very high degree of precision. In the decades following Bunsen and Kirchhoff's work, this experimental technique enabled scientists to observe the spectra of many elements and to collect a considerable quantity of experimental data. There was, of course, no lack of attempts to furnish a physical explanation for the existence of this phenomenon, which was apparently indecipherable in the light of contemporary knowledge. For example, in 1871 George Johnston Stonej attempted to trace the origin of the discrete spectra back to the internal movement of the molecules. He worked out a detailed mathematical theory based on the hypothesis that the cause of the series of lines of the spectrum of a gas lay in the periodic motion of the molecules of the gas in an incandescent state associated with the physical properties of the aether. While these attempts proved quite fruitless – the physics of the time possessing no conception of the constitution of atoms and molecules – it was in any case possible to recognize the existence of significant regularities in the arrangement of the lines appearing in the spectrum of one element and also in the spectra of different elements. In 1884 Johann Balmer found the empirical law for the spectrum lines of hydrogen, which was expressed by a very simple formula in which the wavelength λ of each line is a function of two whole numbers

$$1/\lambda = R(1/2^2 - 1/n^2), \qquad (2.1)$$

where R is a constant; the variation of n for values greater than 2 provides all the spectrum frequencies in the Balmer series. The same years also saw the success of attempts to derive the formulas for the spectra of other elements. The most important achievements in this direction were unquestionably those of Swedish physicist Johannes Rydberg in 1890 and the Swiss Walter Ritz in 1909. Their greatest merit was their success in finding a general expression for all spectra, a result now known as the Rydberg–Ritz principle of combination. This states that the wavelength or frequency of each line of an element's spectrum may be regarded as the difference of two terms – known as the 'spectral terms' – each of which depends on a whole number:

$$1/\lambda = F_r(n_1) - F_s(n_2), \qquad (2.2)$$

where n_1 and n_2 are integers and F a succession of functions of n. In the light of this principle some hitherto unobserved series were discovered. In particular, the hydrogen spectrum was completed with the infrared series discovered by Friedrich Paschen in 1908 and the ultraviolet discovered by Theodore Lyman in 1914. This was the situation obtaining after over half a century of research in the field of spectroscopy at the time when Bohr began his theoretical studies: a vast amount of material collected by highly skilled experimental scientists who had brought their measurements to a remarkable degree of precision; a set of empirical laws capable of correlating tables of figures distributed in apparently bizarre fashion and of furnishing reliable predictions as to the existence and position of new lines; a total lack of hypotheses as to the physical origin of these spectra and the absence of any explanation whatsoever of those laws[23].

The three parts of Bohr's article were published in volume 26 of the *Philosophical Magazine* and appeared successively in the issues of May, September and November 1913. The procedure followed in publication was always the same: Bohr submitted a draft manuscript to Rutherford and, after an exchange of letters making it possible to clear up certain points and improve the exposition, Rutherford himself drew the editors'

attention to the work of his young pupil[24]. We must be grateful to the
youthful enthusiasm of Bohr – who did not wait until the theory had taken
on definitive form before making public the results of his studies – that we
now possess documents of exceptional historical value bearing faithful
witness to the evolution of his ideas in that crucial year. It may, however,
not have been a question solely of youthful enthusiasm. In point of fact,
Bohr had very different reasons for adopting such an apparently cavalier
attitude and dashing off his work. He was fully aware both of the scientific
importance of the problems he was dealing with and of the fact that other
physicists were proposing new procedures for the quantization of the
nuclear atom model[25]. In particular, as he wrote in a long letter to
Rutherford dated 31 January 1913, he had been keenly struck by some
articles published in that period by astrophysicist J. W. Nicholson: 'In his
calculations, Nicholson deals, as I, with systems of the same constitution
as your atom-model; and in determining the dimensions and the energy of
the systems he, as I, seeks a basis in the relation between the energy and
the frequency suggested by Planck's theory of radiation'[26]. However, in
Nicholson's case reference to Planck was far more than a mere analogy
since, unlike Bohr, he obtained for the ratio between the electrons' total
energy and their frequency a series of values approximating closely to
whole multiples of the constant h [27]. This did not, of course, escape the
notice of Bohr, who however pointed out to Rutherford that the differences between the two theories were justified by the fact that Nicholson
was mainly concerned with the spectra emitted by certain gases present in
the solar corona and hence with highly unstable states of the atom in
which an element may emit radiant energy. He concluded in reassuring
tones: 'I must however remark that the considerations [regarding Nicholson's theory] play no essential part of the investigation in my paper. I do
not at all deal with the question of calculation of the frequencies
corresponding to the lines in the visible spectrum. I have only tried, on
the basis of the simple hypothesis, which I used from the beginning, to
discuss the constitution of the atoms and molecules in their permanent
state'[28]. Bohr thus believed he had picked out the weak point in
Nicholson's theory in the distinction – in his view crucial – between the
problems of the stability of the system, when it possesses the smallest
possible amount of energy, and the mechanism of radiation, which is
instead concerned with states of intrinsic instability. At the end of the
letter he announced the imminent dispatch of an article which, by further
developing the standpoint adopted in the memorandum, would make it
possible to elaborate 'a theory of the process of combining atoms into

molecules'. As mentioned above, Rutherford received this article barely a month later, but was to find in it a completely different theory.

The whole of Bohr's scientific production of 1913 is collected and analytically documented in the long paper published in the *Philosophical Magazine* and in the lecture delivered before the Danish Physical Society on 20 December 1913 and published early in the following year under the title 'Om Brintspektret' [On the Hydrogen Spectrum][29]. These texts are presented in the form of work in progress and in them it is possible to discover at least three different and mutually contradictory versions of the theory in question. The first two versions are contained in the trilogy and the third in the December paper. To anticipate a thesis that will become clearer below, it may be remarked that the three formulations differ with regard to the possibility of constructing the theory on the basis of analogy with Planck's quantum hypothesis, i.e. of using that hypothesis successfully in the description of the process regulating the emission of radiation by the atom, and thus reducing the empirical laws governing spectroscopic lines to the motions of electrons in their individual orbits. As we shall see, the more the theory sought to specify the nature of the mechanism regulating the interaction between atomic system and field of radiation, the more difficult – and in some ways theoretically sterile – any attempt to utilize the hypothesis proved, even when reduced to a simple analogous procedure.

From the letter sent to Rutherford, it may be inferred that by the beginning of the new year Bohr's programme had exhausted its original potential given the complex problems that he encountered both in his attempt to overcome the obstacle of the mechanical stability of the electronic orbits in the light of the theoretical framework outlined in the memorandum, and in relation to the quasi-classical nature of the radiation process, to which he referred explicitly in his comment on Nicholson's theory. As has been shown by Heilbron and Kuhn[30], Bohr saw this process as entailing the following two conditions.

(a) The radiation observed on spectroscopic analysis and emitted by the atom of the element under examination must be preceded by ionization. In other words, the radiation is emitted subsequent to a process involving two distinct phases. In the first, the atom is ionized and the electron removed from its initial bound state to an infinite distance from the nucleus. In the second, there takes place a process of recombination permitting the electron to return and occupy one of the possible orbits.

(b) During the process of recombination a certain quantity of energy is released in the form of radiation, which is produced by the disturbance of the electrons located in the orbits of greatest energy. These electrons vibrate transversally to their frequencies of resonance and thus behave like Planckian oscillators. This condition takes up a consequence of electromagnetic theory which Planck and Einstein had also had no need to abandon in their work in quantum physics: the existence of a correspondence between the optical frequency radiated and the atom's frequency of mechanical resonance. On the basis of this, even if we follow Planck in thinking that the emission of radiation is not a continuous phenomenon but that the energy associated with radiation is released in impulses (the quanta of energy), we are still obliged to recognize that the frequency of the radiation emitted is equal to the frequency of motion of the disturbed electrons. In other words, the frequency of each line of the spectrum is regarded as being produced by a charge vibrating with the same frequency.

It is clear that comparison of these hypotheses with the extraordinary profusion of the lines encountered even in the spectra of the simplest atoms would have obliged Bohr to admit the existence of a great number of vibrating systems within each atom, whatever its structure, which certainly did little to clarify the structural problems of the Rutherford model.

Early in February, Balmer's formula was brought to Bohr's attention almost by chance in a conversation about the problems of spectroscopy with a young colleague, Hans Hansen, who had just returned to Copenhagen after spending two years in the laboratories of the Göttingen Physics Institute. As Bohr remarked to some colleagues a few years later: 'As soon as I saw Balmer's formula, everything became clear to me'[31].

3

The trilogy opens with an introduction in which, after recalling the fundamental difference existing between Thomson's model and Rutherford's with regard to the mechanical stability of the orbits, Bohr stated the objectives he intended to achieve and at the same time laid down certain conceptual and methodological presuppositions required to justify some of the assumptions needed in constructing his theory. 'In an attempt to explain some of the properties of matter on the basis of this atom-model we meet, however, with difficulties of a serious nature arising from the apparent instability of the system of electrons [...] The way of considering a problem of this kind has, however, undergone essential alterations in recent years owing to the development of the theory of the energy radiation, and the direct affirmation of the new assumptions introduced in this theory, found by experiments on very different phenomena such as specific heats, photoelectric effect, Röntgen rays etc. The result of the discussion of these questions seems to be a general acknowledgment of the inadequacy of the classical electrodynamics in describing the behaviour of systems of atomic size'[32]. In support of the last statement, Bohr referred in a note to the proceedings of the first Solvay Conference held in Brussels in November 1911[33]. In it, however, he now saw implications of such importance as to require substantial modifications to his previous approach to the problem of the model's stability: the introduction of a quantity foreign to classical electrodynamics such as the quantum of action was in any case required by the new theory independently of the equations of motion of the electrons, which could be derived from either model. Therefore, contrary to what he had appeared to acknowledge implicitly in the memorandum, the question of the mechanical stability of the orbits had no weight in the choice of atomic model. On the contrary, he declared that this was substantially modified 'as this constant [h] is of such dimensions and magnitude that it, together with the mass and the charge of the particles, can determine a length of the order of magnitude [of the atom's linear dimensions]'[34]. The weakest point of Rutherford's model as compared to Thomson's – the impossibility of obtaining the dimensions of the atomic system through simple mechanical calculations – was solved independently of the problem of stability by means of considerations regarding the dimensions and values of fundamental quantities of *Nature*. Having thus disposed of the problem encountered by the quantization procedure suggested in the memorandum, Bohr went on to present his work as 'an attempt to show that the application of the above [quantum-theoretical] ideas to Rutherford's atom-model affords a basis for a theory of the constitution of atoms. [...] In the present first part of the paper the mechanism of the binding of electrons by a positive nucleus is discussed in relation to Planck's theory. It will be shown that it is possible from the point of view taken to account in a simple way for the law of the line spectrum of hydrogen'[35].

Bohr's research programme thus contains:

– a general theoretical problem ensuring the programme's legitimacy: to find an acceptable theoretical explanation of the atom's stability;

– the justification of recourse to quantum hypotheses as guiding the programme's positive heuristic: considerations as to the value and physical dimensions of the constant h are sufficient to obtain information about the characteristic properties of atoms;

– the explicit statement of three objectives to be achieved within the programme: (O_1) by application of quantum ideas to Rutherford's model it is possible to construct a consistent theory of the atom's constitution; this theory, understood as a development and generalization of Planck's theory, (O_2) makes it possible to illustrate the mechanism binding the electrons around the nucleus, and (O_3) supplies a simple interpretation of the line spectrum of the hydrogen atom, i.e. Balmer's formula may be derived from the theory itself. As examination of the three formulations of the theory will show, Bohr soon found himself obliged to scale down and reformulate the objectives of his programme. By the end of 1913, O_3 had been definitively jettisoned and O_1 and O_2 recast in a form much weaker as regards the role of Planck's theory but far more radical as regards the part played by discontinuity in the description of elementary physical processes.

Bohr's programme was also based on some conceptual assumptions and methodological precepts. For the most part these are not principles backed by unquestionable results but arise from judgements or rather personal convictions as to the potential for development possessed by classical conceptions and the conceptual implications of quantum physics. Bohr summarized such judgements and convictions as follows. It is almost universally admitted that classical electrodynamics is not applicable to the description of the behaviour of atomic systems. Therefore it is legitimate to adopt hypotheses which are not compatible with classical theory. Finally, though determination of the characteristics of electron orbits is made possible only by the formal tools of classical mechanics, it appears that, whatever the new equations of electron motion may be, description of their dynamical behaviour can only be achieved through the introduction of a quantity foreign to classical electrodynamics, i.e. Planck's constant.

The first version of the theory takes as its starting point the determination of the values of the frequency and the dimensions of the orbit of an electron in a generic state characterized by a given value of energy. For these purposes, the following hypotheses are introduced: (1) the mass of the electron is negligibly small in comparison with that of the nucleus ($m_e \ll 857\, M_N$); (2) the velocity of the electron is far below the speed of light

$(v_e \ll c)$, which makes it possible to rule out possible relativistic effects; (3) though possessing accelerated motion, the electron radiates no energy. In this case, the electron describes elliptical orbits and it is possible to obtain the value of the frequency of revolution by means of a simple classical calculation

$$\omega_n = \frac{\sqrt{2}}{\pi} \frac{W_n^{3/2}}{eEm^{1/2}}, \tag{2.3}$$

together with the length of the major axis a of the orbit

$$2a = \frac{eE}{W_n}. \tag{2.4}$$

Both prove to be functions of W_n, which represents the energy necessary to remove the electron from the orbit under consideration to an infinitely great distance from the nucleus. In the formulas, e and E are respectively the charges of the electron and of the nucleus; m is the mass of the electron.

The dependence of ω_n and $2a$ on W_n enables Bohr to specify in quantitative terms the problem of instability and the evident 'inapplicability of classical electrodynamics to a model like Rutherford's'. In fact, if we applied the laws of electrodynamics and consequently eliminated the third hypothesis, we would be faced with the following situation: by radiating the electron would lose energy (i.e. W_n would increase) and thus by (2.3) and (2.4) the frequency ω_n would increase and the dimensions of the elliptical orbit decrease. The process would end with the capture of the electron by the nucleus, a result in contradiction with the reality of the physical objects under consideration, which are always found in nature in a state characterized by determined electronic dimensions and frequencies and return to a state of stable equilibrium after each process of radiation.

The next step involves integration of the assumption that the electron does not radiate with a quantum condition necessary to select the possible values of the energy W_n appearing in the formulas just obtained. In this case, the quantum condition is derived through a simple process of generalizing Planck's hypothesis as to the quantization of the harmonic oscillator. As Bohr puts it: 'Now the essential point in Planck's theory of radiation is that the energy radiation from an atomic system does not take place in the continuous way assumed in the ordinary electrodynamics, but that it, on the contrary, takes place in distinctly separated emissions, the amount of energy radiated out from an atomic vibrator of frequency v in a single emission being equal to nhv, where n is an entire number and h is a universal constant'[36].

In order to obtain from this hypothesis the values of the energy of the stationary orbits, Bohr regards it as necessary to assume that the process of emission of the radiation is always accompanied by the ionization of the atom, as he had maintained in his letter to Rutherford. In the case of hydrogen, the electron, initially at rest at a great distance from the nucleus, is found after the process of interaction in a bound state n and describes a given orbit, with $\omega = \omega_n$ and with fixed energy W_n. In the process under examination, the electron loses a quantity of energy equal to the energy of ionization, which is released in the form of radiation which, given the observable characteristics of atomic spectra, must be homogeneous, i.e. possessing a sharply defined frequency v.

However, if we abandon Nicholson's hypothesis that the electrons disturbed during the process of recombination (in all respects similar to Planckian oscillators) are responsible for the radiation emitted, it is necessary to introduce into this framework a further hypothesis defining some relation between the nature of the radiation (v) and the electron's state of motion. The hypothesis resorted to by Bohr – referred to henceforth as the '1/2 hypothesis' – constitutes the first conceptual departure from the framework of classical physics effected by his theory in that it renounces definitively the assumption of the existence of an immediate relation between optical and mechanical frequencies. The '1/2 hypothesis' states that the frequency v of the homogeneous radiation emitted is equal to half the mechanical frequency that the electron possesses in the orbit occupied at the end of the binding process, $v = (1/2)\omega_n$. Consequently, since – in accordance with Planck's views – all the energy emitted by the electron is found in the form of radiation energy, we obtain

$$W_n = nh\frac{\omega_n}{2}, \tag{2.5}$$

which is precisely the condition sought for the energy of the stationary orbits. The system formed by (2.3), (2.4) and (2.5) makes it possible to obtain

$$W_n = \frac{2\pi^2 me^2 E^2}{n^2 h^2}, \tag{2.6a}$$

$$\omega_n = \frac{4\pi^2 me^2 E^2}{n^3 h^3}, \tag{2.6b}$$

$$2a = \frac{n^2 h^2}{2\pi^2 meE}. \tag{2.6c}$$

By assigning different integers to n $(1, 2, 3 \ldots)$ we obtain a succession of values of W_n, ω_n and $2a$ to which there corresponds a discrete succession of configurations of the system, of states in which there is no radiation.

In order to test the compatibility of the theoretical predictions with experimental values, Bohr takes the example of the basic state of the hydrogen atom, for which $e = E, n = 1$. Assigning the known values to e, m and h gives:

$$2a = 1.1 \times 10^{-8} \, \text{cm}, \quad \omega = 6.2 \times 10^{15} \, \text{s}^{-1}, \quad W = 13 \, \text{eV}, \tag{2.7}$$

which are compatible, within the range of experimental error, with the linear dimensions of the atom, the optical frequencies of the spectra and the potential of ionization.

Before going on to discuss the consequences deriving from these results, Bohr devotes a few words of comment to the procedure followed, both to underline its ability to overcome the obstacles encountered by Nicholson's theory, and to make explicit 'the ideas on which the written formulae rest', which take the form of two postulates[37] and two particular hypotheses. The postulates involve recognition (1) that ordinary mechanics is an effective tool for dealing with the dynamical equilibrium of systems in stationary states but not for the transitions of a system between any two states, and (2) that each of these transitions is accompanied by the emission of homogeneous radiation for which Planck's ratio between energy and frequency holds. The hypotheses are concerned with the possible extension of Planck's ideas. This possibility had obliged Bohr on the one hand to recognize that to each state corresponds the emission of a different number of quanta, and on the other to resort, as we have seen, to an unusual relation between the frequency of the radiation and that of the electron.

However, after drawing the reader's attention to assumptions capable, to say the least, of arousing serious misgivings as to the logical consistency of his argument, Bohr defers any comment to a later section, preferring to show immediately 'how, by the help of the above principal assumptions and of the expression [2.6] for the stationary states, we can account for the line-spectrum of hydrogen'. The briefest reflection on the nature and implications of those hypotheses is enough to make one aware that this last statement of Bohr's as to the theory's interpretative effectiveness is excessively optimistic, if not downright false, precisely because the assumptions required in order to derive the expressions (2.6) flatly contradict the content of the postulates. This may have been the reason that led Bohr to postpone an awkward discussion. One might also suspect that by presenting a positive result he was seeking to win the reader's immediate acceptance of a standpoint whose foundations were, in fact, such as to justify all manner of reservations.

In justifying the introduction of the '1/2 hypothesis', Bohr made the following observation: 'If we assume that the radiation emitted is homogeneous, the second assumption concerning the frequency of the radiation suggests itself, since the frequency of revolution of the electron at the beginning of the emission is 0'[38]. By this he can only have meant that the well-known dependence of the optical frequency on the frequency of the oscillator was to be replaced by a new relation in which the frequency of radiation would prove equal to the average of the frequencies of motion of the electron in the initial ($\omega = 0$) and final ($\omega = \omega_n$) states of the process of recombination. There is, however, clearly nothing evident or natural in the fact that such a hypothesis is supposed to follow from the homogeneous nature of the radiation involved, certainly not in the light of the quantum conceptions of the time. Bohr's choice can thus be accounted for only as an *ad hoc* solution regarding the determination both of the atom's energy levels and of the frequencies of the radiation emitted. Nor could it have been otherwise, given that the sole motivation behind it lay in the quantitative agreement it enabled Bohr to find between mathematical formulas and experimental results. In this sense, the suspicion may also arise that he corrected the initial formula by a factor of 1/2 upon ascertaining that his calculations did not agree with the experimental values, and then justified his action by resorting to the average of the frequencies[39]. However, in this connection it is also possible to raise a more serious objection: even if one accepted without reservation Bohr's view of the self-evidence of the hypothesis, it would still be necessary to recognize that it is at variance with the fundamental postulates, which would require a generalization of the said hypothesis that nothing appears to justify. In these postulates Bohr, dropping any reference to processes of ionization, speaks of generic transitions between stationary states associated with the emission of homogeneous radiation. Thus, for the hypothesis to retain its validity it would be necessary to suppose, against all the evidence and even contrary to the very reasons presented by Bohr, that the averaging procedure remains valid even when the initial frequency is not zero. In any case, the abandonment of the hypothesis regarding the atom's ionization is not without consequences for the consistency of Bohr's argument, since the extension of the condition (2.5) to the determination of the stationary states is possible only if it is admitted that the energy of radiation appearing in it is exactly equal to the mechanical energy of a state. And this can be true only if the energy required to remove the electron from that state to an infinitely great distance from the nucleus is found in the form of a field of radiation. Speaking instead of emission *via* transitions between any stationary states does not mean a banal generalization of that condition but rather a conceptual leap entailing the disappearance of the physical and theoretical conditions required by the procedure of quantization with which Bohr intended to take up Planck's ideas.

Leaving aside both this point and the more or less arbitrary content of the '1/2 hypothesis', it might however appear that the analogy with Planck's quantum ideas had proved particularly effective. Bohr had succeeded in deriving from the traditional procedure of energy quantization the physical condition enabling him to get round the obstacles of classical electrodynamics and to determine in quantitatively rigorous fashion the permitted energy levels of any atomic element. There remained, true enough, the problem of the internal consistency of a theory employing classical means of description in a phenomenal context at variance with the assumptions of the classical theories, but this was a price that Bohr had regarded as inevitable from the outset. However, the briefest examination of the meaning of the second particular hypothesis suffices for the emergence of problems entailing the drastic revision of any such judgement. It is enough to develop in the light of the second postulate the obvious consequences of an idea according to which to each stationary state there corresponds the emission of a different number of quanta of energy.

In order to derive Balmer's formula for the hydrogen spectrum from (2.6a) it is sufficient to calculate the difference between the energies of the two states (n_1 and n_2) and divide it by Planck's constant

$$v_n = \frac{W_{n_1} - W_{n_2}}{h} = \frac{2\pi^2 m e^4}{h^2}\left(\frac{1}{n_1^2} - \frac{1}{n_2^2}\right); \qquad (2.8)$$

if it is posited that $n_1 = 2$, the result is an expression similar to that derived empirically by Balmer:

$$v = R\left(\frac{1}{4} - \frac{1}{n_2}\right), \qquad (2.9)$$

and it is easily shown that the values of the constants of proportionality appearing in the two expressions are equal, within the range of experimental error. However, though formally devoid of difficulties, this step contains, as Heilbron and Kuhn have shown, a conceptual trap[40]. It is not possible for Bohr to obtain Balmer's formula in this way without the use of an implicit hypothesis contradicting the previous application of Planck's hypothesis to the problem of the atom's constitution. As we have seen, according to the formulation taken up and utilized by Bohr, this says that the energy released in radiation by an atomic system of frequency ω is $nh\omega$, and that this emission of energy is the result of distinct and separate elementary processes. Now, maintaining a close analogy with that process, the energy of each stationary state of the atom should be regarded as composed of n indivisible quanta each possessing $h\omega_n/2$ energy, and it should be claimed that in each process of radiation this energy is emitted through n distinct and separate successive processes, each of which brings one quantum of energy into play. For this reason, as Bohr's hypothesis states, to each stationary state of the atom is associated a different number of quanta, which therefore represents the essential condition for a direct application of Planck's ideas to the case of the states of the atom.

As we have seen, in derivation (2.8) of Balmer's formula it must be supposed that

$$hv = W_{n_1} - W_{n_2}, \qquad (2.10)$$

where v is the frequency of the radiation emitted when the electron passes from orbit n_1 to orbit n_2, respectively of energies W_{n_1} and W_{n_2}, with $W_{n_1} > W_{n_2}$. However, as is shown by experience and laid down by Bohr's second postulate, since the line observed at frequency $v(n_1, n_2)$ corresponds to a homogeneous radiation, it can only be produced by the emission of a single quantum hv. Hypothesis (2.10) therefore indicates that, according to the mechanism underlying the atom–radiation interaction, independently of the quantity of energy involved in the process, the energy itself is always released in the form of a single elementary quantum. However, this clearly contradicts Planck's hypothesis and therefore also Bohr's.

If therefore, as one might reasonably have expected, Bohr had chosen to discuss the two hypotheses before proceeding upon his derivation of Balmer's formula, he would, after a few pages, have been obliged at the least to scale down the objectives of his programme and to say that the attribution of a general physical meaning to the concept of quantum discontinuity and its application to Rutherford's model permitted the construction of a theory of the constitution of the atom making it possible to illustrate the mechanism binding the electrons and providing a nearly rigorous derivation of Balmer's formula in the case of hydrogen. However, for Bohr the fact of having found a theoretical value comparable with Rydberg's constant, the explanation of the differences between the spectra of an element observed in laboratory conditions and those observed in the celestial bodies, and the attribution of some lines of the spectrum of the star ζ-Puppis to ionized atoms of helium[41] were evidently results far outweighing the evident logical and conceptual shortcomings and significant confirmation of the validity of his programme.

4

'We have assumed that the different stationary states correspond to an emission of a different number of energy-quanta. Considering systems in which the frequency is a function of the energy, this assumption, however, may be regarded as improbable; for as soon as one quantum is sent out the frequency is altered. We shall now see that we can leave the assumption used and still retain the equation [2.5] and thereby the formal analogy with Planck's theory'[42]. These words, which express in the clearest and most unequivocal terms the untenable nature of some of the hypotheses introduced in the preceding derivation of Balmer's formula, introduce the second version of the quantum theory of the atom contained in the trilogy. Bohr's judgement leaves little room for doubt as to the disappearance of his original confidence that a solution would be found permitting a direct grafting of Planck's ideas onto Rutherford's atomic model. The analogy between the two theories can be maintained, but only on a formal level: if there exists no evident and immediate relation between optical and mechanical frequencies then the objections to which the previous procedure is open can be avoided by abandoning the physical analogy with Planck's oscillators, which entails the establishment of a quantitatively rigid relationship between the energy of the radiation and the frequency of oscillation of an electron. By instead retaining the analogy on a purely formal level, it is possible to establish between the two a simple proportional relation of the type:

$$W_n = f(n) \, h\omega_n, \qquad (2.11)$$

where $f(n)$ is a certain function of the whole variable n to be determined (in the first version, $f(n)$ assumed the value 1/2); relations analogous to (2.6) are thus obtained:

$$W_n = \frac{\pi^2 m e^4}{2h^2 f^2(n)} \qquad \omega_n = \frac{\pi^2 m e^4}{2h^3 f^3(n)} \qquad (2.12)$$

By utilizing the hypothesis implicit in (2.10), simple substitution gives:

$$\nu = \frac{\pi^2 m e^4}{2h^3} \left(\frac{1}{f^2(n_2)} - \frac{1}{f^2(n_1)} \right). \qquad (2.13)$$

Although it implies a drastic reduction of the theory's potential, the next step is described by Bohr in just two lines: 'We see that in order to get an expression of the same form as the Balmer series we must put $f(n) = cn$' with c as the constant to be determined[43]. Evidently, since (2.13) and

$$\nu = R \left(\frac{1}{n_2^2} - \frac{1}{n_1^2} \right) \qquad (2.14)$$

are formally analogous, the unknown f must be a linear function of the discrete variable n. However, in this way the theory abandons all claim to deduce Balmer's formula and to give it a physical interpretation in terms of the mechanism of radiation. On the contrary, the formula is assumed as true since it makes it possible to correlate with great precision the numerical data relative to the frequencies of the lines and therefore, once the impossibility of obtaining the conditions of state of the atomic system through a Planck-type quantization procedure has been established, is the only tool remaining to determine properties of formal type.

The problem thus comes down to the determination of the value of the constant c, for which Bohr considers a transition of the electron between two contiguous stationary states characterized respectively by the whole numbers N and $N - 1$. From (2.13) it follows that this transition involves the emission of radiation of frequency

$$\nu = \frac{\pi^2 m e^4}{2c^2 h^3} \frac{2N - 1}{N_2 (N - 1)^2}.$$
(2.15)

For these two states it is also possible to determine the values of the electron's frequencies of revolution before and after the emission of radiation:

$$\omega_N = \frac{\pi^2 m e^4}{2c^3 h^3 N^3} \quad \text{and} \quad \omega_{N-1} = \frac{\pi^2 m e^4}{2c^3 h^3 (N - 1)^3},$$
(2.16)

whose ratio is given by

$$\frac{\omega_N}{\omega_{N-1}} = \frac{(N - 1)^3}{N^3}.$$
(2.17)

In the case in which N is great – i.e. when the states considered are characterized by low frequencies – this ratio is equal to 1, and therefore there are states in which the motions of the electrons differ little from one another. In these conditions, Bohr observes, we must expect, according to classical electrodynamics, the frequency of the radiation to be equal to the frequency of revolution; for great N

$$\frac{\nu_n}{\omega_n} \to 1,$$
(2.18)

or rather

$$\frac{\nu_n}{\omega_n} = \frac{cN(2N - 1)}{(N - 1)^2} \to 1,$$
(2.19)

which is verified on the growth of N if $c = 1/2$. From (2.11) it thus follows that the quantum condition for the permitted levels of the hydrogen atom is $W_n = nh\,(\omega_n/2)$, which is exactly the same as the (2.5) already obtained by Bohr with the '1/2 hypothesis' and the 'rigorous' application of Planck's hypothesis to Rutherford's model.

As we have seen, to arrive at this conclusion Bohr makes use of a new procedure passed off in the trilogy with a couple of words as though it were quite obvious. This involves considerations developed in the region of high quantum numbers and made possible solely by acknowledgement that in the presence of transitions between states characterized by a high value of ν the correspondence between optical and mechanical frequencies not found in other areas of the spectrum is re-established. The claim is, in itself, anything but obvious, if it is true that Bohr had previously ruled out the possibility of the orbiting electron behaving like a Planckian oscillator. What he was actually doing was extending to this case the well-known theoretical result obtained in the study of heat radiation with regard to the agreement of classical electrodynamics with experimental data in the low-frequency region of the black-body spectrum. Here Planck's formula became equivalent to the classical Rayleigh–Jeans law and the quantized oscillator returned to rigorously classical behaviour[44]. It is evident that the analogy employed by Bohr in this case could not be stretched to this point. The argument of the limiting region gave no grounds for assuming – as Bohr himself later clarified – that the typical discontinuous pattern underlying the mechanism of atomic radiation would disappear in the region of large n. On the contrary, in Bohr's view the quantum character of the process remains intact here too, but when the electron in two contiguous stationary orbits is subjected to motions differing very little one from the other ($\omega_N \approx \omega_{N-1}$), then classical predictions are identical to quantum-theoretical predictions from the numerical point of view. Analogy with the classical theory of heat radiation is used to assert that optical frequencies tend to assume the same value as mechanical frequencies. A few years later (1918) Bohr was to formalize and generalize considerations of this type in the principle of correspondence[45].

In point of fact, in the trilogy Bohr already effects a generalization of what can be formally obtained in the limiting region, and once again draws conclusions – a new hypothesis – of a surprising nature, to say the least, which he saw as finally unveiling the physical significance of the '1/2 hypothesis' – a hypothesis untenable from the theoretical point of view but extraordinarily effective in its empirical consequences. Again in the limiting region and with the same approximations, for a transition between the states N and $N - n$, with $n \ll N$, we obtain

$$v = n\omega. \qquad (2.20)$$

In the light of this relation, Bohr saw the evident possibility of abandoning the previous viewpoint, according to which (2.5) was to be understood in the sense 'that the different stationary states correspond to an emission of different numbers of energy-quanta'. This was instead to be seen as indicating that 'the frequency of the energy emitted during the passing of the system from a state in which no energy is yet radiated out to one of the different stationary states, is equal to different multiples of $\omega/2$, where ω is the frequency of revolution of the electron in the state considered'[46]. This amendment was sufficient to restore consistency and simplicity to the theory, ridding it of a redundant and contradictory system of particular hypotheses, and to maintain intact the previous derivation of Balmer's formula on the basis of the quantum postulates. This, however, may well be the most arbitrary step taken by Bohr in the whole trilogy, where he had in any case furnished a brilliant demonstration of how all the rules of logic and methodology might be violated in the interests of a cavalier type of theoretical approach. There are no grounds, either formal or conceptual, whereby the discovery that in highly particular circumstances the simple relation (2.20) that exists between v and ω might lead to Bohr's hypothesis without making an assumption as to the mechanism of radiation, the sole purpose of which is to save at all costs some reference to Planck's ideas. When the condition that the states between which transition takes place should have approximately the same energy and the same frequency is abandoned, and when moreover the energy of the radiation emitted depends on the variation of the internal energy of the atom in the transition between states differing greatly one from the other, Bohr's suggestion that the nature of the radiation depends upon the mechanical frequency possessed by the electron in the initial state of the process is a claim bearing more resemblance to an act of faith than to a scientific hypothesis. This could seem an unduly harsh judgement were it not for the remark made by Bohr himself a few months later: 'The radiation of light corresponding to a particular spectral line is [...] emitted by a transition between two stationary states, corresponding to two different frequencies of revolution, and we are not justified in expecting any simple relation between these frequencies of revolution of the electron and the frequency of the emitted radiation'[47]. In any case, at that time the hypothesis was essential for Bohr's theory, since without it it would not have been possible to state that the value of c was always 1/2 for all states, including those outside the limiting region. All that Bohr could offer in defence of his choices was a series of results obtained along the way which confirmed one of his initial methodological assumptions, i.e. which showed how far we now were from ordinary electrodynamics.

5

The invitation to read a paper at the official session of the Danish Physical Society was one of the first acknowledgements obtained by Bohr from the scientific community, but also a precious opportunity to draw up the balance sheet of a year of intense work and to initiate a period of more detached reflection on the complex of theoretical conceptions that had marked the birth of his research programme. The picture presented of the physics of the time affords a glimpse of a level of reality so complex as to require a radical transformation of interpretative apparatus. Bohr regards this as a phase of transition, where new discoveries seem to cast doubt upon consolidated scientific ideas and research cannot grow peacefully in the shade of tradition. His judgements are therefore very prudent. Some of them in particular help us to a better understanding of the main reasons for his change of attitude with regard to the Planckian approach and the reasons, methodological and otherwise, that led him to present on that occasion a new version of the quantum theory of the atom. 'The discovery of these beautiful and simple laws concerning the line spectra of the elements has naturally resulted in many attempts at a theoretical explanation.' However, 'not one of the theories so far proposed appears to offer a satisfactory or even a plausible way of explaining the laws of the line spectra. Considering our deficient knowledge of the laws which determine the processes inside atoms it is scarcely possible to give an explanation of the kind attempted in these theories. The inadequacy of our ordinary theoretical conceptions has become especially apparent from the important results which have been obtained [with the theory] of temperature radiation. You will therefore understand that I shall not attempt to propose an explanation of the spectral laws; on the contrary I shall try to indicate a way in which it appears possible to bring the spectral laws into close connection with other properties of the elements, which appear to be equally inexplicable on the basis of the present state of the science'[48].

The choice implicitly taken in the second part of the trilogy to eliminate the explanation of the spectra from the theory's objectives – or rather to renounce for the time being the derivation of the spectroscopic laws from the mechanism of radiation – is here stated openly. And the reasons for this choice have a structural character in the framework of the new theory. As Bohr explicitly states, they regard the inadequacy of our ordinary theoretical conceptions with regard to a new phenomenal situation. Shortly afterwards, having run over the stages of the theoretical and experimental research leading up to black-body theory, Bohr takes the opportunity to clarify what positive contribution had come from the physics of Planck and Einstein: 'We are therefore compelled to assume, that the classical electrodynamics does not agree with reality, or expressed more carefully, that it can not be employed in calculating the absorption and emission of radiation by atoms.' With an obvious reference to the discontinuous process underlying the process of radiation, he adds: 'Fortunately, the law of temperature radiation has also successfully indicated the direction in which the necessary changes in the electrodynamics are to be sought'[49]. However, after acknowledging Planck's merits in having pointed to a fruitful area of research, Bohr's judgement becomes more critical: 'In formal respects Planck's theory leaves much to be desired; in certain calculations the ordinary electrodynamics is used, while in others assumptions distinctly at variance with it are introduced without any attempt being made to show that it is possible to give a consistent explanation of the procedure used'[50]. In the space of a few months Bohr had therefore lost his initial enthusiasm for a theoretical conception which he had seen, in the introduction to the trilogy, as a way of solving all the difficulties of Rutherford's model. The reason for this change of mind involved no questions of theoretical nature but rather the logical and epistemological weakness that seemed to mark the previous quantum theories, which Bohr viewed as incapable of encompassing all the consequences of the change in conceptual framework required by the new discoveries. Atomic physics was, in any case, seen as part of the theoretical mainstream stemming from Planck's work since the acknowledged 'fact that we can not immediately apply Planck's theory to our problem is not as serious as it might seem to be'. As Bohr went on to observe: 'in assuming Planck's theory we have manifestly acknowledged the inadequacy of the ordinary electrodynamics and have definitely parted with the coherent group of ideas on which the latter theory is based. In fact in taking such a step we can not expect that all cases of disagreement between the theoretical conceptions hitherto employed and experiment will be removed by the use of Planck's assumption regarding the quantum of the energy momentarily present in an oscillating system'[51]. Nevertheless, 'the discovery of energy quanta must be considered as one of the most important results arrived at in physics'; in fact, the demonstration that the constant h makes it possible 'at least approximately to account for a great number of phenomena about which nothing could be said previously' implies much more than the validity of 'the qualitative assumption of a discontinuous transformation of energy'. It must, that is, have a deeper theoretical significance which cannot as yet be deciphered[52]. For this reason, 'We stand here almost entirely on virgin ground, and upon introducing new assumptions we need only take care not to get into contradiction with experiment. Time, he concluded, will have to show to what extent this can be avoided; but the safest way is, of course, to make as few assumptions as possible'[53]. In concrete terms, consistency between theoretical assertions and experimental data and opposition to the uncontrolled proliferation of hypotheses are the criteria guiding the definitive reformulation of the theory presented by Bohr at the end of 1913.

On the one hand we have the renunciation of any hypothesis as to the behaviour of the systems responsible for emitting radiation, also in view of the fact that we know nothing about an atomic oscillator and the only observable quantity is the frequency of radiation. On the other, the only hypothesis we really need, and which derives from a generalization of Planck's ideas, is that in each process the energy emitted by the atom is a quantity $h\nu$, where ν is the observable frequency of radiation. In support of this assertion Bohr referred to the work of Peter Debye who, in suggesting a new derivation of Planck's law of temperature radiation, had demonstrated that it was not necessary to make any hypotheses as to the nature of the emitting systems. The theory could be founded solely on the basis of two postulates, i.e. of two assertions as to the nature of atomic systems that for the moment remain inexplicable in the light of acquired knowledge. The first states that the electron is found in a stable state, i.e. without radiating, on an orbit characterized by a certain quantum number both before and after each process of radiation. The second connects each emission and absorption of radiation with a complete transition of the electron from one stationary state to another: if the energies of these states are respectively E_1 and E_2, the frequency of the radiation ν emitted or absorbed is given by the relation

$$h\nu = E_1 - E_2. \tag{2.21}$$

Together with recognition of the validity of the empirical laws of the spectral lines and Bohr's considerations regarding the limiting region, these postulates are sufficient for the foundation of the quantum theory of the atom. Balmer's formula for the hydrogen spectrum may be written

$$\frac{1}{\lambda} = \frac{R}{n_1^2} - \frac{R}{n_2^2}, \tag{2.22}$$

where R is Rydberg's constant. Since, as is known, frequency is given by $\nu = c/\lambda$, where c is the velocity of light,

$$\nu = \frac{cR}{n_1^2} - \frac{cR}{n_2^2}. \tag{2.23}$$

Comparing this with (2.21), the energy W of each stationary state is given by

$$W = \frac{Rhc}{n^2}, \tag{2.24}$$

which, in turn, substituted in (2.3) gives

$$\omega_n^2 = \frac{2}{\pi^2} \frac{R^3 h^3 c^3}{e^4 m n^6}. \tag{2.25}$$

As we have already seen, the frequency of revolution decreases rapidly as n increases and the ratio (ω_n/ω_{n+1}) tends towards 1 as n increases. In correspondence with a transition between two stationary states n and $n + 1$, the frequency of the radiation emitted is

$$\nu = Rc \left[\frac{1}{n^2} - \frac{1}{(n + 1)^2} \right] \tag{2.26}$$

which for great n is approximately equal to

$$\nu = \frac{2Rc}{n^3}. \tag{2.27}$$

In the light of the above considerations, in this region the optical frequency (2.27) can be posited as equal to the mechanical frequency, i.e.

$$\omega_n = \frac{2Rc}{n^2}, \tag{2.28}$$

which, substituted in (2.25), supplies the expression of Rydberg's constant

$$R = \frac{2\pi^2 e^4 m}{ch^3},$$ (2.29)

whose value agrees, within the range of error, to the experimental value. However, at this point such considerations remain confined to the limiting region and no procedure of generalization is attempted since 'we cannot expect to obtain an analogous relation [i.e. analogous to 2.28] for the values of the other stationary states'. The note of self-criticism contained in these words of Bohr's regarding the hypothesized possibility of establishing some analogy between the Planckian expression of the energy of the resonator and that of the energy of the state of the atom was to become quite explicit when, in correcting earlier approaches, he observed: 'This analogy suggests another manner of presenting the theory, and it was just in this way that I was originally led into these considerations. When we consider how differently the equation is employed here and in Planck's theory it appears to me misleading to use this analogy as a foundation, and in the account I have given I have tried to free myself as much as possible from it'[54].

There would thus appear to be absolutely no historical grounds for the assertion that Bohr's theory of the atom originated in the application of Planck's quantum theoretical ideas to Rutherford's model of the atom. Or rather, such assertions now appear to give at best a very limited view of the case. Within Planck's paradigm Bohr was, in fact, unable to find such conceptual tools as would legitimize in physical terms the mechanism seen as underlying the atom's radiative behaviour. Not even in a weak version – i.e. in the context of a formal analogy – can Planck's hypothesis be used to derive the quantum condition making it possible to select the stationary states of the atom, i.e. the physically permitted electronic orbits. Bohr arrived at this drastic conclusion after his two attempts to develop an analogy between harmonic oscillator and electron rotating on an atomic orbit; attempts which had forced him to burden the theory increasingly with hypotheses that he himself recognized as largely arbitrary.

As regards the derivation of the quantum condition, at the end of 1913 the only proposal Bohr was able to make was a semi-empirical procedure for the determination of the physically possible states of the atom. All the information we can derive from this condition is that it represents a practical rule of selection for the atom's energy levels. It is capable of providing no other information, especially with regard to how energy is emitted or absorbed by the atom or the value of the frequency of the radiation that the atom exchanges with the external world. Unlike Planck, Bohr saw the quantity of energy involved in each process of radiation, and hence its characteristics, as capable of determination not in relation to the state of an electron in its orbit, but on the basis of comparison of the initial and final states of the transition accompanying the radiative process. It was therefore not the energy of a state – i.e. the energy possessed by an electron in a stable orbit – but rather the variation in energy in the passage of an electron from one state to another that was equal, minus the constant h, to the frequency of radiation. What then remains of the original quantum conceptions in Bohr's atomic theory? The assertion that the emission of energy by an atom is associated with a process of discontinuous type in which the system passes from one stable stationary state to another; which discontinuity manifests itself in the emission of a finite quantity of energy establishing a relation between the modifications within the atom and the properties of the radiation.

The theory is incapable of saying anything about the nature of this discontinuous process or about the causes of the atom's radiative behaviour. Atoms are unobservable objects when in a definite, stable state. In observing them, we have to interact with them through another physical object – the radiation – and thus irreversibly modify their state. The theory is incapable of saying what happens at the moment in which we disturb an atom with radiation. We only know that both before and after interaction with the observer the atom is in a stable state, which is however as such unobservable. In actual fact, the theory does say something more: we can obtain a spatio-temporal description of the state of the system, i.e. the motion of the electron in the nth orbit, with the tools of classical analysis. However, this is possible only on condition that the electrons do not obey Maxwell's laws of electrodynamics and only when the atom is in a stationary state, i.e. as long as it remains an unobservable object and does not interact with the observer. When this happens, we have no way of following the evolution of the system and describing the interaction in space and time: we must confine ourselves to stating that a discontinuous transition from one energy level to another is taking place. The concept of discontinuity is thus introduced into atomic theory as a first step taken with great prudence. With regard to it and to the general theoretical consequences it entailed, Bohr was stubbornly to repeat in all his writings subsequent to 1913 that until a precise idea was obtained of the process of radiation it would be quite arbitrary to assert the existence of an incompatibility in principle between quantum and classical physics, between quantum discontinuity and the theories of Newton and Maxwell.

With rare exceptions, Bohr's theory was accepted in official scientific circles, above all because some of his predictions were in fact confirmed experimentally within a few weeks of the trilogy's publication[55]. The scientific community chose to adopt a theory of practically no explanatory or descriptive content, marked by deep logical contradictions and considerable conceptual limitations[56]. For Bohr, the choice was in a certain sense inevitable: the objective of saving the model of the atom, which had been made possible by discovering in the quantum of action the missing element, had proved anything but easy. Above all, it entailed recognition that radiation provided no direct information as to the motions of the atomic particles and, as we have seen, that no causal relation could be established between the state of the atom and the processes making it observable. Although the prospect of reconciling this split within the classical models of explanation and description was not abandoned, work had begun on a revision of the conceptual foundations of physics that, as early as 1913, already foreshadowed subsequent results.

Rutherford's model of the atom had proved, in Bohr's view, a tool of great heuristic utility and the theory had been able to go on expressing itself in the language of orbits and electron motion. However, the discontinuous nature of the atomic processes had required the introduction of the new theoretical terms 'stationary state' and 'transition between states' which could not be reduced to the model's intuitive and figurative content. This immediately posed problems which were to necessitate a new theory and also a new way of thinking about the real world.

Notes

1 N. Bohr, 'On the Constitution of Atoms and Molecules', *Philosophical Magazine* **26** (1913), 1–25, 476–502, 857–75; *CW2*, 161–85, 188–214, 215–33.

2 T. S. Kuhn, *Black-Body Theory and the Quantum Discontinuity, 1894–1912*, New York: Oxford University Press, 1978, esp. ch. IX.

3 'Even when Einstein's reputation grew, as it quickly did, his views on the necessity of the quantum discontinuity remained suspect because they were repeatedly coupled with the generally rejected light-quantum hypothesis. If the physics profession was to recognize the challenge of Planck's law, better established figures would need to be persuaded that it demanded a break with classical physics. In the event, several of them quickly were. During

1908 Lorentz produced a new and especially convincing derivation of the Rayleigh–Jeans law. Shortly thereafter he was persuaded that his results required his embracing Planck's theory, including discontinuity or some equivalent departure from tradition. Wien and Planck quickly adopted similar positions, the former probably and the latter surely under Lorentz's influence. [...] These are the central events through which the energy quantum and discontinuity came to challenge the physics profession'. (T. S. Kuhn, *Black-Body Theory...* cit. n. 2, 189.) We cite these comments by Kuhn being fully aware that his interpretation – constructed though it is upon a wealth of documentation and a painstaking analysis of texts – has been the object of criticism. In particular, Martin Klein ('Paradigm Lost? A Review Symposium', *Isis* **70** (1979), 429–34) has challenged the historiographical accuracy of one of the main theses of Kuhn's work, i.e. that Planck's original derivation of the law of distribution of radiation is firmly anchored within the classical tradition and that the notion of discontinuity plays no role therein. It is, for that matter, known that Kuhn himself describes the work as a historiographical heresy.

4 This is the standard interpretation to be found in manuals of atomic physics; cf., for example, F. K. Richtmyer, E. H. Kennard and T. Lauritsen, *Introduction to Modern Physics*, New York: McGraw-Hill, 1969 (6th edn.): 'His theory constituted an extension of Planck's theory of quanta to Rutherford's nuclear atom, in an attempt both to remove the difficulties of the nuclear model and to explain the origin of the characteristic spectra of the elements'. In their view, moreover, after trying various alternative hypotheses, Bohr 'finally adopted the same assumption that Planck had made for his oscillators'. Since the classic work by J. L. Heilbron and T. S. Kuhn ('The Genesis of the Bohr Atom', *Historical Studies in the Physical Sciences* **1** (1969), 211–90), which marked the first attempt at reconstructing Bohr's theory on the basis of ample documentation, the crucial role played in this context by the Planckian paradigm has come to be regarded as more problematic.

5 The memorandum presented to Rutherford between June and July 1912 is published in *CW2*, 136–58; the quotation is taken from the note on p. A2 of the ms.

6 One of the main attempts at the quantization of the model of the atom was carried out by Arthur Erich Haas in 1910. Taking Thomson's model as his starting point (cf. below), he applied a Planck-type quantum hypothesis to the energy of an electron moving on a circumference of radius r, concentric with a sphere in which a positive charge is uniformly distributed. On its presentation at a meeting of the Vienna Society of Physical Chemistry, the theory was ridiculed by the physicists present and regarded as a joke. Cf., also for the bibliography of Haas's writings, M. Jammer, *The Conceptual Development of Quantum Mechanics*, New York: McGraw-Hill, 1966, 39–41; also J. L. Heilbron, 'Bohr's First Theories of the Atom', in A. P. French and P. J. Kennedy, eds., *Niels Bohr. A Centenary Volume*, Cambridge (Mass.): Harvard University Press, 1985, 33–49: 38. The different procedures of quantization were, however, the subject of discussion at the first Solvay Conference in 1911, during which Sommerfeld, referring explicitly to Haas's hypothesis, had stressed the general importance, beyond the model itself, of the existence of some connection between the constant h and the atom's dimensions (*La théorie du rayonnement et les quanta. Rapports et discussions de la réunion tenue à*

Bruxelles, du 30 Octobre au 3 Novembre 1911, Paris: Gauthier-Villars, 1912, 124). Of great interest in this connection are the reflections contained in Planck's paper ('La loi du rayonnement noir et l'hypothèse des quantités élémentaires d'action', *ibid.*, 93–114) and Lorentz's remarks during the discussion (ibid., 115–32). Cf. also J. Mehra, *The Solvay Conferences...* cit. ch. 1, n. 6, ch. II.

7 N. Bohr, *Studier Over Matallernes Elektrontheori*, Copenhagen, 1911; *CW1*, 167–290; English trans. *CW1*, 294–392. Bohr officially presented his doctorate thesis on 13 May 1911 and discussed it with mathematician P. Heegaard and physicist C. Christiansen; cf. J. Rud Nielsen, 'Introduction to Part II', *CW1*, 93–123, section 2.

8 Cf. L. Rosenfeld, 'Introduction', in N. Bohr, *On the Constitution of Atoms and Molecules*, Copenhagen: Munksgaard, 1963, XI–LIII; 'Biographical Sketch', *CW1*, XVII–XLVIII: XIX; and, also for an examination of the main themes dealt with by Bohr in the thesis, cf. J. L. Heilbron and T. S. Kuhn, 'The Genesis...' cit. n. 4, 213–23; J. L. Heilbron, 'Bohr's...' cit. n. 6, 34 ff.

9 In a long letter to his brother Harald dated 23 October 1911, Bohr spoke of the difficulties he had encountered in interesting Thomson in his work: 'In fact, Thomson has not so far been as easy to deal with as I thought the first day. He is an excellent man, incredibly clever and full of imagination (you should hear one of his elementary lectures) and extremely friendly; but he is so immensely busy with so many things, and he is so absorbed in his work, that it is very difficult to get to talk to him. He has not yet had time to read my paper, and I do not know if he will accept my criticism'. Nevertheless, from their brief conversations Bohr got the impression that Thomson did not agree with the conclusions of his work: '... he thinks that a mechanical model can be found which will explain the law of heat radiation on the basis of the ordinary laws of electromagnetism, something that obviously is impossible, as I have shown indirectly ...'. Finally, with regard to the problems encountered in publishing his doctorate thesis, Bohr informed his brother that he had had discouraging news from Larmor about the prospects of his request to the Royal Society: '... he thinks it will be impossible, not because it has been published in Danish, but because it contains criticism of the work of others, and the Royal Society considers it an inviolable rule not to accept criticism that does not originate in its own publications'. (*CW2*, 527–32) Bohr had been officially informed by Larmor, then Secretary of the Royal Society, of the possibility of publishing in the *Proceedings* an abstract of five or six pages purged of all aspects of exposition and of any controversial question (Larmor to Bohr, 16 October 1911, *CW2*, 104). His attempts to get the thesis published in the *Transactions of the Cambridge Philosophical Society* were to meet with similar success. Cf. also on this point, J. Rud Nielsen, 'Introduction...' cit. n. 7, section 4.

10 N. Bohr, 'On the Theory of the Decrease of Velocity of Moving Electrified Particles on Passing through Matter', *Philosophical Magazine* **25** (1913), 10–31; *CW2*, 18–39. The publication is dated August 12th Manchester but appeared only early in the following year as Bohr was waiting for the results of some experiments carried out by Rutherford. This study, as he wrote to his brother Harald (12 June 1912, *CW2*, 4–5), had been inspired by an article by C. G. Darwin ('A Theory of Absorption and Scattering of the α-Rays', *Philosophical Magazine* **23** (1912), 901–20). The latter, taking as his

starting point the hypotheses that a-particles would lose energy on collision with matter only if they managed to penetrate the atom and that electrons could be regarded as free, obtained values for the dimensions of the atom contradicting those already known. Bohr judged it as impossible that the study of this subject could be carried out without a detailed examination of electron binding. He maintained rather that it was necessary to take into consideration the nature of the collisions between particles in relation to the period of the motion of the electrons under the action of the binding forces, and hence that the losses of energy of the incident particles were correlated with the different periods of the electrons themselves. Cf. L. Rosenfeld, 'Introduction' cit. n. 8, XIX–XX; J. L. Heilbron and T. S. Kuhn, 'The Genesis ...' cit. n. 4, 239–41; U. Hoyer, 'Introduction to Part I', *CW2*, 3–10, especially sections 3–4.

11 For an overview of these themes and for references to the primary and secondary bibliography, the reader is referred to J. Mehra and H. Rechenberg, *The Historical Development of Quantum Theory*, 5 vols., New York: Springer-Verlag, 1982–87, vol. I, Part 1, 168–81.

12 J. J. Thomson, 'On the Structure of the Atom – An Investigation of the Stability and Periods of Oscillation of a Number of Corpuscles Arranged at Equal Intervals around the Circumference of a Circle; With Application of the Results to the Theory of Atomic Structure', *Philosophical Magazine* 7 (1904), 237–65: 237.

13 E. Rutherford, 'The Scattering of α and β Particles by Matter and the Structure of the Atom', *Proceedings of the Manchester Literary and Philosophical Society* 55 (1911), 18–20; 'The Scattering of α and β Particles by Matter and the Structure of the Atom', *Proceedings of the Manchester Literary and Philosophical Society* 21 (1911), 669–88; the articles are also found in *The Collected Papers of Lord Rutherford of Nelson*, 3 vols., New York: Interscience, 1962, vol. II, 212–13 and 238–54 respectively.

14 Present in Rutherford's laboratory were some of the leading experimental physicists of the day, including H. Geiger, W. McKower, E. Marsden, E. J. Evans, A. S. Russell, K. Fajans, H. G. J. Mosely, G. von Hevesy and J. Chadwick. Cf. L. Rosenfeld and E. Rüdinger, 'The Decisive Years 1911– 1918', in S. Rozental, ed., *Niels Bohr. His Life and Work as Seen by His Friends and Colleagues*, Amsterdam: North-Holland, 1967, 38–73; and for the research carried out by Bohr during his stay in Manchester, L. Rosenfeld, 'Biographical Sketch' cit. n. 8, XXI–XXV.

15 With reference to this point, Heilbron and Kuhn ('The Genesis...' cit. n. 4, p. 241 n. 81) have stressed the error often found in the literature and manuals arising from the attribution of a crucial role in the development of the first theory of the atom to radiative instability. Against such views (e.g. L. Rosenfeld, 'Introduction' cit. n. 8) they object that 'radiative, unlike mechanical, instability does not distinguish Rutherford's atom from Thomson's' and that 'the problem of radiative instability was well known and seems to have caused little concern'. In their view, reasons of theoretical nature but also related to the context of the debate at the time would suffice to dispose of the commonplace concerning the initial difficulties encountered by the nuclear model and the problems that stimulated Bohr's first studies in atomic physics.

16 This is the view expressed by Bohr himself at the end of 1913; cf. below.

17 Rosenfeld arrives at this conclusion ('Introduction' cit. n. 8, XXIX ff.) on the basis of the relations contained in the memorandum. He also advances

the hypothesis that a page has been lost, which would explain why there is no trace of Bohr's views as regards the relation that should exist between Planck's constant and the coefficient K. Cf. also J. L. Heilbron and T. S. Kuhn, 'The Genesis...' cit. n. 4, 248–51.

18 Niels to Harald Bohr, 19 June 1912, *CW2*, 103.

19 Bohr to Rutherford, 6 March 1913, *CW2*, 581–83.

20 Bohr to Rutherford, 4 November 1912, *CW2*, 577–78. On his return to Copenhagen, Bohr had become assistant to Martin Knudsen and had in that semester held lectures on the mechanical foundations of thermodynamics; cf. U. Hoyer, 'Introduction to Part II', *CW2*, 103–34, section 2.

21 Bohr to Rutherford, cit. n. 19.

22 Rutherford to Bohr, 20 March 1913, *CW2*, 583–84.

23 For a historical overview of spectroscopic research, cf. J. Mehra and H. Rechenberg, *The Historical Development...* cit. n. 11, vol. I, Part 1, 156–68, and M. Jammer, *The Conceptual Development...* cit. n. 6, 62–69. A more exhaustive and fuller study of 19th century spectroscopy is to be found in W. McGucken, *Nineteenth-Century Spectroscopy: Development of the Understanding of Spectra 1802–1897*, Baltimore: The John Hopkins University Press, 1969. For attempts to interpret the spectroscopic laws and the role they played in the first atomic theories at the beginning of the 20th century, the reader is referred particularly to N. Robotti, 'The Spectrum of ζ-Puppis and the Historical Evolution of Empirical Data', *Historical Studies in the Physical Sciences* **14** (1983), 123–45; 'The Hydrogen Spectroscopy and the Old Quantum Theory', *Rivista di Storia della Scienza* **3** (1986), 45–102; H. Kragh, 'The Fine Structure of Hydrogen and the Gross Structure of the Physics Community, 1916–26', *Historical Studies in the Physical Sciences* **15** (1985), 67–125.

24 Rutherford would actually have liked Bohr to cut his texts drastically. As he wrote in a letter dated 20 March (*CW2*, cit. n. 22): 'I think in your endeavour to be clear you have a tendency to make your papers much too long, and a tendency to repeat your statements in different parts of the paper. I think that your paper really ought to be cut down, and I think this could be done without sacrificing anything to clearness'. A few days later, 25 March, discouraged by Bohr's resistance he wrote: 'As you know, it is the custom in England to put things very shortly and tersely in contrast to the Germanic method, where it appears to be a virtue to be as long-winded as possible'. (*CW2*, 585).

25 Contrary to the views held by Rutherford, who wrote to him on 11 November 1912: 'I do not think you need feel pressed to publish in a hurry your second paper on the constitution of the atom, for I do not think anyone is likely to be working on that subject'.(*CW2*, 578.)

26 Bohr to Rutherford, 31 January 1913, *CW2*, 579–80.

27 Returning to previous models of the atom due to H. Nagaoka and J. Perrin, Nicholson had tried to interpret the lines of the stellar spectra on the hypothesis that they were caused by the transversal oscillations of the electrons occupying a determined ring of an element. On this basis, he had succeeded in establishing that the ratio between the potential energy of the orbiting electrons and the frequency of rotation was a whole multiple of Planck's constant: $[mnr^2 (2\pi\omega)^2]/\omega = ph$, where n is the number of electrons, r the radius of the ring and p an integer. Nicholson interpreted this relation as a quantization of the angular moment and, although his theory completely ignored the problem of stability, was able to calculate the

frequencies of a certain number of spectral lines in close agreement with the observational data (J. W. Nicholson, 'The Spectrum of Nebulium', *Monthly Notices of the Royal Astronomical Society* **72** (1912), 49–64; 'The Constitution of the Solar Corona', ibid., 139–50, 677–93, 729–39). However, L. Rosenfeld ('Introduction' cit. n. 8, XII) remarks on this point: 'From the mathematical point of view Nicholson's discussion of the stability conditions for the ring configurations and of their modes of oscillation is an able and painstaking piece of work; but the way in which he tries to apply the model to the analysis of physical situations must strike one as very reckless and dilettantish, and one can only regard as unfortunate accidents the cases in which he actually obtained agreement between some of his calculated frequencies and those of observed spectral lines'. Cf. also J. L. Heilbron and T. S. Kuhn, 'The Genesis...' cit. n. 4, 72 ff.; R. McCormmach, 'The Atomic Theory of John William Nicholson', *Archive for the History of Exact Sciences* **3** (1966), 160–84.

28 Bohr to Rutherford, cit. n. 26.

29 N. Bohr, 'Om Brintspektret', *Fysisk Tidsskrift* **12** (1914), 97–114; English trans., 'On the Hydrogen Spectrum', in N. Bohr, *The Theory of Spectra and the Atomic Constitution*, Cambridge: Cambridge University Press, 1922, 1–19; *CW2*, 283–301.

30 J. L. Heilbron and T. S. Kuhn, 'The Genesis...' cit. n. 4, 262–63.

31 L. Rosenfeld and E. Rüdinger, 'The Decisive Years...' cit. n. 14, 52.

32 N. Bohr, 'On the Constitution...' cit. n. 1, 1–2; *CW2*, 161–62.

33 See above, n. 6.

34 N. Bohr, 'On the Constitution...' cit. n. 1, 1–2; *CW2*, 161–62.

35 Ibid., 2–3; *CW2*, 162–63.

36 Ibid., 4; *CW2*, 164.

37 Actually, in the 1913 article, Bohr introduced the two postulates upon which he was to found his quantum theory of atomic structure and the process of radiation as 'principal assumptions'. He explicitly recognized them as postulates from 1921 onwards (N. Bohr, 'Zur Frage der Polarization der Strahlung in der Quantentheorie', *Zeitschrift fr Physik* **6** (1921), 1–9). Furthermore, the content of these postulates underwent continual modifications and conceptual improvements as a result of development of his theory, and especially on the basis of the principle of correspondence (see below, chs. 3 and 4). Having clarified this point necessary for historical rigour, I think it is logically correct to use from now on the term 'postulates'.

38 N. Bohr, 'On the Constitution...' cit. n. 1, 5; *CW2*, 165.

39 The critical literature has been variously occupied with this problem and formulated a number of different hypothesis: cf., for example, T. Hirosige and S. Nisio, 'Formation of Bohr's Theory of Atomic Constitution', *Japanese Studies in the History of Science* **3** (1964), 6–28, which sees this procedure as having been suggested by the operation of averaging the energies of the oscillators introduced by Planck in the last formulations of his theory. This interpretation is criticized by Heilbron and Kuhn ('The Genesis...' cit. n. 4, 272, n. 147), who take up Rosenfeld's view and maintain that the idea derives in some way from the fact that in his memorandum Bohr had already obtained a value very close to this; which does not prevent it from looking like 'an *ad hoc* rationalization, designed to preserve the parallelism between Bohr's radiator and Planck's' (ibid., 271–72).

40 J. L. Heilbron and T. S. Kuhn, 'The Genesis...' cit. n. 4, 270.
41 See below, n. 55.
42 N. Bohr, 'On the Constitution...' cit. n. 1, 12; *CW2*, 172.
43 Ibid., 13; *CW2*, 173.
44 It is known that the Rayleigh–Jeans law for the density of energy of temperature radiation as a function of wavelength – derived in accordance with classical procedures – agrees with experimental data only in the region of very low frequencies and that it leads to errors if used for high frequencies, where the so-called ultraviolet catastrophe takes place.
45 Many authors, starting with Heilbron and Kuhn but including also Rosenfeld, tend to see in this procedure the anticipation or embryo of the principle of correspondence. Certainly, the limiting considerations upon which the correspondence relation is based are already present in Bohr's earliest work. However, as we shall see later (ch. 3), the consistent formulation of this principle implies a logical relation not to be found in the procedure followed in 1913.
46 N. Bohr, 'On the Constitution...' cit. n. 1, 14; *CW2*, 124.
47 N. Bohr, 'On the Hydrogen Spectrum' cit. n. 29, 12; *CW2*, 294.
48 Ibid., 3–4; *CW2*, 285–86.
49 Ibid., 6; *CW2*, 288.
50 Ibid.
51 Ibid., 10; *CW2*, 292.
52 Ibid., 7; *CW2*, 289.
53 Ibid., 10; *CW2*, 292.
54 Ibid., 14; *CW2*, 296.
55 In particular, Bohr's theory succeeded in explaining evident discrepancies between Balmer's formula and the frequencies of some lines which had been observed by E. C. Pickering in the spectrum of the star ζ-Puppis (1897) and by Fowler under laboratory conditions in vacuum tubes containing a mixture of hydrogen and helium (1912). Bohr found that the anomalies could be eliminated if the lines were attributed not to hydrogen but to ionized helium and suggested to Rutherford that more careful experiments should be carried out in this direction (Bohr to Rutherford, 6 March 1913, *CW2*, 581–83). Evans was given the task of testing Bohr's hypothesis and in the summer of that year obtained results agreeing fully with the theoretical prediction (E. J. Evans, 'The Spectra of Helium and Hydrogen', *Nature* **92** (1913), 5). Cf. M. Jammer, *The Conceptual Development...* cit. n. 6, 82 ff.
56 In general, Bohr's work aroused immediate interest in all scientific circles and, apart from some understandable prudence, the theory was regarded as a highly ingenious and stimulating solution. George von Hevesy informed Bohr in a letter dated 23 October 1913 of the favourable impression made on Einstein, who he had met in Vienna on the occasion of the 85th Versammlung deutschen Naturforscher und Aertze: '... then I asked him about his view of your theory. He told me, it is a very interesting one, important one if it is right and so on and he had very similar ideas many years ago but had no pluck to develop it. I told him then that is established now with certainty that the Pickering–Fowler spectrum belongs to He. When he heard this he was extremely astonished and told me: 'Then the frequency of the light does not depend at all on the frequency of the electron – (I understood him so??) And this is an *enormous achievement*. The theory of Bohr must be then right". (*CW2*, 532) Sommerfeld also

showed interest, above all since Bohr had managed to solve the 'problem of expressing the Rydberg–Ritz constant by Planck's *h* [which] has for a long time been on my mind'. He concluded: 'Though for the present I am still rather sceptical about atomic models in general, calculating this constant is undoubtedly a great feat'. (Sommerfeld to Bohr, 4 September 1913, *CW2*, 603; English trans. 123.) Unfavourable reactions were instead to come from the physicists and mathematicians of Göttingen. As Bohr's brother Harald wrote to him in the autumn of that year: 'I have the impression that most of them – except Hilbert, however – and in particular, among the youngest, Born, Madelung, etc., [...] find the assumptions too 'bold' and 'fantastic'. If the question of the hydrogen–helium spectrum could be definitively settled, it would have quite an overwhelming effect: all your opponents cling to the statement that, in their opinion, there is no ground whatsoever for believing that they are not hydrogen lines' (*CW1*, 567).

CHAPTER 3

The principle of correspondence

1

At the beginning of the paper presented at Como in 1927 Bohr stated: 'On the one hand, the definition of the state of a physical system, as ordinarily understood, claims the elimination of all external disturbances. But in that case, according to the quantum postulate, any observation will be impossible, and, above all, the concepts of space and time lose their immediate sense. On the other hand, if in order to make observation possible we permit certain interactions with suitable agencies of measurement, not belonging to the system, an unambiguous definition of the state of the system is naturally no longer possible, and there can be no question of causality in the ordinary sense of the word. The very nature of the quantum theory thus forces us to regard the space-time co-ordination and the classical theories, as complementary but exclusive features of the description, symbolizing the idealization of observation and definition respectively'[1].

The contrast effectively illustrated between possibilities of definition and conditions of observation thus expresses the cognitive scope of quantum theory and summarizes the complementary and irreducible aspects of the description of objects belonging to the microworld. In Bohr's view, this contrast is the direct consequence of two general assumptions: the postulate regarding the discontinuity or individual nature of atomic processes, symbolically represented by the quantum of action, and an epistemologically binding judgement on the system of concepts whereby such processes may be described. In this judgement, Bohr stressed the conviction, maintained years before in dispute with Pauli, of the inevitable failure of any attempt to free the theory from classical concepts and replace them with new concepts operationally defined in the sphere of quantum phenomena, regarding as he did the language of classical physics as the only suitable tool to express the results of experiment[2]. The problem to which Bohr sought a consistent solution with his idea of complementarity thus arose on the one hand from recognition that 'all classical concepts [have been] defined through space-time pictures'[3] and are inherited from a scientific tradition that regarded causal description in space and time as an unrelinquishable ideal; and on the other from the realization from 1925 on that the concepts of classical physics are subject to a fundamental limitation when applied to atomic phenomena. In Bohr's view, once a linguistic restriction of this type is imposed on the describability of a physical reality where each process is discontinuous and consequently where each observation of a phenomenon 'involve[s] an interaction with the agency of observation not to be neglected', the quantum postulate necessarily implies 'a renunciation as regards the causal space-time co-ordination of atomic processes', and hence complementarity[4].

However, the argument with which Bohr illustrated the co-existence of concepts of observation and description only within a relation of mutual exclusion is not very different from the theoretical consequences of the two general assumptions that had made it possible to formulate the theory of the hydrogen atom at the end of 1913. In fact, it is not difficult to reread the conclusions reached then in terms analogous to those used in the passage cited and to see in them an elaboration of the relationship between definition and observation. If we wish to define the state of an atomic system – in 1913 this was still seen within a classical mechanical description of electron motion – it is necessary to consider the atom as a closed, isolated system and to eliminate any external disturbance (Bohr 1927). In other words, it must be postulated both that an atom in a stationary state enjoys radiative stability, and that emission or absorption of radiation takes place only during transition between stationary states (Bohr 1913). As we have seen, this is tantamount to eliminating all the conditions that make the atom observable. In any case, when the atomic system is subjected to observation, it is not possible to furnish an unambiguous definition of the state of the system (Bohr 1927). In fact, as Bohr was already aware in 1913, the theory is not able to establish the nature of the relationship existing between the stationary state – from which the electron effects a transition associated with interaction with radiation – and the radiation itself. In other words, it must be stated that there is no causal nexus between the two, as is demonstrated by the fact that, in general, optical frequencies cannot be reduced to mechanical ones.

The question spontaneously arises of whether Bohr really used one and the same argument to justify the launching of a consistent research programme in 1913 and to establish definitively the interpretative basis of quantum mechanics in 1927 with his principle of complementarity. Were this really so, it could even be claimed that the research programme ended with the – possibly premature – recognition of the theoretical impossibility of solving its initial problem and that the new concept was excogitated with the sole aim of reconciling contradictory and irreducible aspects of the description of the physical world by means of a logical expedient. A conclusion of this type – repeated in more or less the same terms in all the criticisms that have been levelled against the orthodox interpretation of quantum mechanics over the years[5] – is however in contrast with the judgement expressed by Bohr in some preparatory notes for the Como paper, where he summarized schematically the main phases of the development of the research programme leading to the idea of complementarity[6]. In this context, the idea is presented as the only solution Bohr thought it possible to give in quantum terms to the general problem of scientific knowledge based upon space-time pictures.

In these notes, Bohr recalls that atomic theory had, from the outset, been able to utilize such images only within precise limits and with great caution. On the one hand, full validity was attributed to the classical theory of radiation, thereby reducing the hypothesis of light quanta to a mere formal device for the interpretation of certain phenomena. On the other, the mechanical description of electron orbits was admitted despite the fact that this implied the violation of ordinary electrodynamics. However, the pictures associated with such descriptions encountered an insurmountable obstacle in the 'mechanism' responsible for the radiative behaviour of the atom, which the hypothesis of quantization made incompatible with any traditional model of description. Between the two images of the radiation field and the motion of the orbiting electron, it was possible to establish only a formal type of relation with the quantum law of frequencies which, while guaranteeing the validity of the principles of conservation, made it clear that the element connecting the two images was represented by a process of essentially discontinuous and static nature. The first attempts to develop the theory had thus been concerned with the possibility of connecting the statistical laws with the properties of the pictures, i.e. with ascertaining the degree to which classical conceptions were applicable to quantum phenomena. It was in this context that the principle of correspondence was formulated on the basis of recognition that in the limiting region of high quantum numbers, where the element of discontinuity may be overlooked in statistical applications, classical predictions are in quantitative agreement with experimental data. Bohr assigned to this principle a central function in the construction of his theory precisely because it had made it possible for the first time to establish a connection between statistical laws and the characteristics of the pictures. And this, in his view, had served to launch a new research programme, whose objective was the elaboration of a consistent 'quantitative description [of quantum processes, by] looking for analogous features in the classical theory'. This programme had come to an end upon demonstrating the impossibility of expressing those descriptions through space-time pictures, i.e. when the correspondence principle had required the hypothesis of the statistical validity of the laws of conservation. The immediate empirical falsification of this hypothesis and the important theoretical and experimental successes achieved in the following months were, in Bohr's view, to make inevitable the thesis that experience presents complementary aspects when described by means of classical concepts[7]. Acceptance of the standpoint thus summarized by Bohr would entail the conclusion that the renunciation of a mode of description involving causality, time and space was not a methodological *fiat* but an obligatory theoretical choice whose necessity was to emerge very slowly and, in fact, to be demonstrated in the context of a consistent research programme. The principle of correspondence is thus seen as having tested the possibility of applying space-time pictures to the description of quantum processes up to the point at which unequivocal indications were finally obtained.

2

The first statement of the principle of correspondence is contained in a long paper published in 1918 in the *Proceedings of the Royal Danish Academy of Science and Letters*, in which Bohr went over and generalized the considerations regarding the limiting region introduced in the trilogy[8]. However, the idea that this was a new principle of physics was made explicit only in a lecture delivered by Bohr in 1920, where he also made his first use of the term 'correspondence'[9]. The correspondence programme was finally to assume definitive shape in the paper that, on Lorentz's invitation, Bohr presented at the third Solvay Conference in April 1921[10]. Bohr did not attend the Brussels meeting in person and entrusted Ehrenfest with the task of illustrating the paper's main points and representing his views during the discussion, which concentrated almost exclusively on the meaning and the applicational consequences of the new principle[11]. Bohr's absence was due to poor health. In the previous months he had been active in setting up a new physics institute in Copenhagen and had, in particular, been deeply involved with his own studies. As he confessed in a letter to Richardson, '...my life from the scientific point of view passes of[f] in periods of overhappiness and despair, of feeling vigorous and overworked, of starting papers and not getting them published, because all the time I am gradually changing my views about this terrible riddle which the quantum theory is'[12]. Above all, in that period Bohr had had to defend himself against objections to his theory advanced from a number of quarters and not always in a constructive spirit. There were, for example, those who remarked with regard to the fundamental law of frequencies that 'the electron would need an information office to calculate the frequencies to emit'[13]. The decision not to attend the Solvay Conference had been a painful one to take and had been put off till the very last minute. While Bohr did have serious problems of health, his greatest source of affliction at the time was certainly the difficulty of finding a satisfactory formulation of his theory. It was, among other things, also for this reason that he failed to deliver the complete text of his paper, which was published in the proceedings in a form that he still regarded as provisional and without the planned second part on the theory's applications to the problem of atomic structure[14].

The paper dealt with two subjects: the determination of the conditions of state for the selection of permitted energy levels on the basis of the properties of motion possessed by an atomic system in a given stationary state; and the examination of the problem of interaction between radiation and matter from the quantum theoretical viewpoint. It was in the latter context that Bohr introduced the principle of correspondence. The whole discussion was developed within the framework of reference defined by the fundamental postulates, which Bohr reformulated in the following terms: 'An atomic system which emits a spectrum consisting of sharp lines possesses a number of separate distinguished states, the so-called *stationary states*, in which the system may exist at any rate for a time without emission of radiation, such an emission taking place only by a process of complete transition between two stationary states [...]. In the theory, the frequency of radiation emitted during a process of this kind is not directly determined by the motion of the particles within the atom in a way corresponding to the ideas of the classical theory of electromagnetism, but is simply related to the total amount of energy, emitted during the transition [...]'[15]. At this point he introduced the general relation of frequencies

$$h\nu = E' - E'', \qquad (3.1)$$

which he regarded as the formal basis of quantum theory.

Once the existence of an irreparable break with the customary ideas of physics had been recognized, the general objective of the theory became for Bohr the systematic exploration of the possibility of successfully developing a formal analogy with those ideas. The first step in this direction consisted in asking how far the quantum postulates made it possible to describe motion in stationary states with the concepts used classically to describe the behaviour of a system of charged particles. In other words, Bohr intended to ascertain with what degrees of approximation it was still possible 'to describe the motion of the particles in the stationary states of an atomic system as that of mass points moving under influence of their mutual repulsion and attraction due to their electric charges'[16]. That this was, in any case, not permitted in examining the external disturbances of particle motion was a consequence of the quantum problem of the stability of the stationary states. The theoretical conditions for their selection among the possible mechanical motions of the system referred in fact to properties dependent on the periodicity of the orbits and not on the velocities and configurations of the particles. In the case of an atomic system subjected to variable external conditions, the theory was therefore obliged to abandon the approach of ordinary mechanics, which would entail the study of the effects of the forces acting on the particles at a given instant. The theory would rather be required to determine how such conditions modified the properties of periodicity of a state and thus to arrive at the orbital motion of particles that would be compatible with them.

An example of the behaviour of atoms under the action of variable external conditions – but also of the failure of the descriptive possibilities of mechanics – was given by the phenomena of light absorption and emission, which provided further confirmation that 'the interaction of the atom with the incident electromagnetic waves can by no means be described on the basis of the classical electronic theory'[17]. In fact, these phenomena are also connected with variations in energy between stationary states. At the time Bohr saw in the 'unknown mechanism' responsible for the process of radiation the principal reason for the existence of an insuperable limit to the descriptive possibilities of the classical concepts. Although the theory provided no explanation on this point, the phenomena examined did make it possible to clarify why a rigorously classical treatment of the processes of interaction was forbidden: in such phenomena the external forces undergo significant alterations within periods of time that cannot be compared with the periods characteristic of the motion of atomic particles. In Bohr's view, this made it legitimate to suppose that the problem would present itself in very different terms if, in times of the same order of magnitude as those periods, the variations in the external forces were negligible with respect to the total force to which the particles were subjected within the atom. Or rather, Bohr added, one should not rule out, in full agreement with what was laid down by the theory's postulates, 'the possibility that the alteration in the motion of the system due to such a slow transformation of the external conditions may be deduced by means of the laws of ordinary mechanics'[18]. This was a radical revision of the procedure followed in 1913 in the study of the mechanical stability of atomic orbits. Then, as we have seen, a sharp distinction was made between the mechanical analysis of electron motion and processes of interaction. Now the intention was to ascertain whether analysis of such a type would produce significant results even when one gave up the idea of regarding the atom as an isolated system, and to try to determine how far a mechanical description of the model was still admissible. The rational tools employed by Bohr for this purpose were Ehrenfest's adiabatic principle, Sommerfeld's formal rules for the determination of stationary states (quantization of the integral of action)[19], and the Epstein–Schwarzschild theory, which made it possible to extend the conditions of state to the so-called multiperiodical motions, i.e. to a set of systems more complex than those considered at first, such as the hydrogen atom, but for which the equations of motion could still be solved with the method of separation of variables[20].

He found that, within the range of approximations required by a rigorous mechanical treatment of the motion of atomic particles, the theory's interpretative effectiveness was, in any case, somewhat reduced, since most of the phenomena examined implied the existence of physical conditions contrasting with such approximations. However, Bohr defended his mechanical/model-based approach, stressing that there was at the time no other tool capable of providing an unambiguous definition of the energies of the states appearing in the general relation of frequencies: 'at the present state of the theory we do not possess any means of describing in detail the process of direct transition between two stationary states [...]'[21].

The shortcoming that Bohr saw in the theory assumed still greater importance when one went on to examine the process of radiation, in which the initial assumptions made it necessary to renounce any attempt to establish a direct connection between particle motion and radiation and to go no further than the hypothesis that the individual components of the spectrum were due to the occurrence of a certain number of independent processes within the atom. This was decidedly meagre information, especially if one believed, as Bohr then maintained, that the full understanding of such processes had to be subordinated to the construction of 'a detailed picture of production and propagation of radiation'[22]. In any case, he ruled out the possibility that such a picture could be derived from Einstein's hypothesis of light quanta. Bohr was, of course, well aware that the study of certain phenomena appeared to demonstrate that electromagnetic radiation was not released by the atom in the form of a system of spherical waves but was propagated in discrete elements each containing a quantity of energy $h\nu$. Einstein's conception of radiation had the advantage of rigorously verifying the laws of conservation without getting bound up with the problem of the mechanism of radiation. However, in Bohr's view, Einstein's idea had the serious defect of encountering hitherto insoluble difficulties in the phenomenon of interference and hence in the determination of the frequencies and the state of polarization of the harmonic components of radiation of any type.

After over 20 years of studies and of undeniable success, the problem facing quantum theory was still the same: the absence of a real understanding of the interaction between radiation and matter. And it was with regard to this point that Bohr, called for the first time to take his place in the most prestigious group of physicists of the day, maintained that the strategy to pursue was still the search for a unified picture for the mechanism of emission and absorption and for the propagation of radiation through space. Immediately afterwards however, almost as though to tone down the pessimistic conclusions drawn by his analysis, he stated: 'We shall see, however, how it is possible to trace a connection between the motion of an atomic system and the spectrum which, even if it must be essentially different from that which would follow from the classical electromagnetic theory, still preserves such features that it gives us hope of attaining a picture which includes the interpretation of the experimental evidence regarding atomic processes as well as the phenomena of interference of light waves [...]'[23]. This hope was certainly not such as to make him change his drastic judgement as regards the break with classical theory brought about by quantum theoretical conceptions. As he put it, the mechanism underlying the new picture would most probably entail a revision of the fundamental concepts of physics themselves. In other words, Bohr's intention was not to save some fragment of theory, even if his words made it clear that the general viewpoint was still that of a field conception of electromagnetic phenomena. He was concerned rather with demonstrating the existence of sufficient evidence to relate quantum processes to the classical model of description.

Once again, in the absence of suitable tools to tackle the problem of the transition mechanism directly, he found in the limiting region the formal conditions enabling him to identify 'a certain suggestive connection between the transitions and the motion of the system'[24]. In this region, thanks to the methods of analytical mechanics, a quantitative convergence was found between spectrum and motion even more general than that discovered in 1913. It could, in fact, be demonstrated rigorously that for multiperiodic systems there exists a simple relation between the frequency of a line and the frequency of a harmonic component of motion in all transitions between states for which the values of the respective principal quantum numbers, n' and n'', are large with respect to their difference[25]. This made it possible to connect the occurrence of a transition with the properties characteristic of motion even if, as Bohr again pointed out, this did not mean a progressive elimination of the differences between the quantum nature of the radiation process and classical ideas. There remained a problem of the theory's consistency; it was not, in fact, to be forgotten that the calculations carried out 'entirely based on the postulate that radiation is always emitted as single trains of harmonic waves, and that accordingly the various trains of waves which coincide in frequency with the frequencies of the constituent harmonic components of the motion are not emitted simultaneously but by a number of independent processes, consisting in transitions between various sets of stationary states'[26]. This specification, which Bohr was to stress in all his writings of those years, shows clearly how historically unfounded and theoretically reductive the traditional point of view is in its tendency to present the correspondence principle as the simple recognition that the interpretations of classical and quantum physics converge in cases in which the value of h is negligible[27].

From Bohr's point of view, this specification was necessary to justify the subsequent step in his argument. In fact, he regarded the result obtained – though only numerical and devoid of any deeper physical implications, and despite its disappearance in the region of small n, where frequencies of motion differ greatly between one state and another – as affording an intuitive glimpse of some more general relation between the occurrence of a transition and the characteristics of motion in the stationary states involved in the process. This intuitive leap was translated by Bohr into two successive generalizations. The first consisted in asserting that in the limiting region the connection found did not regard solely the values of the frequencies since the spectrum would reflect the nature of the particle motion in full. In short, it was to be expected that the analogy would be respected in general. As in classical theory the intensity and polarization of the components of the radiation emitted by a system depend on the amplitudes and spatial orientations of the vibrations of the oscillating charges, in the same way the probability associated with each spontaneous transition between stationary states and the polarization of the radiation emitted would be in some kind of relation with the characteristics of the harmonic components of the stationary motions. Bohr called these components of motion connected with individual processes of transition 'corresponding' and defined the relation, e.g. between the probability of a transition and the amplitude of a harmonic of motion, as a 'relation of correspondence', which he saw as enabling the spectrum to reflect 'the motion in the atom in exactly the same way as in classical theory'[28].

With the second generalization, the validity of the relation of correspondence was extended also to cases in which there was no longer any numerical identity to be found between optical and mechanical frequencies and where it proved impossible 'to obtain a simple quantitative direct connection between the probabilities of the various transitions and the motion'[29]. Here, Bohr was left with his intuition alone, which was however sufficient for him to assert that 'we are led to consider the possibility of the occurrence of a transition between two given stationary states as conditioned by the appearance in the motion of the corresponding harmonic vibration'[30]. Bohr was not, of course, able to say in which motion of the system this harmonic should appear to influence the occurrence or otherwise of a process of transition. Nevertheless, he declared his conviction that the examination of atomic problems – tackled in his paper on the basis of the theory of multiperiodic systems – 'has given unrestricted and convincing support'[31] for the viewpoint that he summarized under the name of the principle of correspondence.

In actual fact, Bohr was to attempt in later writings to solve the obvious difficulty arising from the fact that outside the limiting region the 'corresponding' amplitudes may be quite different in the two stationary states involved in the transition. He was to go so far as to suggest that the frequency sought was the average value of the corresponding vibrations calculated on a continuous series of hypothetical 'intermediate states' in terms of the expression

$$v = \int_0^1 (n' - n'') \, \omega(\lambda)d\lambda, \tag{3.2}$$

where for the extreme values of λ we obtain the frequencies of the harmonic vibrations in the two states n' and n''. This was the same expedient Ehrenfest had resorted to in order to make the idea of correspondence in some way comprehensible to the participants at the Solvay Conference, despite the fact that this simple averaging operation required the hypothesis of a continuous variation of the states of the atomic system, which was clearly untenable in the light of the postulates[32]. In any case, the solution did not fully express the real heuristic importance that Bohr intended to assign to his new principle. Within the idea of a correspondence between processes of transition and components of motion lay a logical relation which Bohr regarded as capable of establishing a dependence between spectrum and motion similar in all respects to that whereby in classical theory the intensity of the radiation emitted by a particle in the course of a harmonic oscillation depends upon its amplitude. This was an unusual and indecipherable logical relation, a final attempt to disguise the enigmas of the theory by resorting to obscure linguistic formulas and concepts totally lacking in traditional scientific rigour. And yet, the same principle did produce consequences which were to have a significant effect upon the subsequent developments of Bohr's theoretical ideas. In the course of a lecture delivered in September 1923 at the British Association Meeting in Liverpool, Bohr reformulated the second postulate of his theory in the light of his new principle and, whereas it had hitherto asserted the impossibility of deriving the frequencies of the radiation emitted from the motion of the particles, it now stated that 'a process of transition between two stationary states can be accompanied by the emission of electromagnetic radiation, which will have the same properties as that which would be sent out according to the classical theory from an electrified particle executing a harmonic vibration with constant frequency'[33]. This was no marginal amendment seeing that, before the arrival in Copenhagen of the young American physicist John Slater, Bohr had already arrived, thanks to his correspondence principle, at the idea underlying the theory of virtual oscillators, the final bid to save the classical model of description.

3

In a recent essay on Bohr's philosophy, Henry Folse maintains that his approach to the problem of the superseding of the classical model of description of physical systems implicit in the notion of quantum discontinuity reveals one of the distinctive traits of his epistemology: his constant concern with the problem of the applicability of individual concepts to the description of phenomena and his deep conviction that one of the principal tasks of science was to develop as it went along 'a conceptual framework adequate for such a description'[34].

Bohr unquestionably found the first confirmation of the validity of this approach both in his initial research into the electronic theory of metals and in the revolutionary consequences of Planck's theory of heat radiation. It may, in fact, be possible to glimpse here the greatest debt owed by Bohr and his idea of complementarity to philosophy. The debt was contracted early on when, in the course of the periodical meetings of the Ekliptika circle, the young Bohr discussed with other students of Harald Høffding the philosophical problems connected with the description of psychological processes and reflected on the ambiguities of language that arise whenever one attempts to describe the activities of the subject of experience as an object[35]. In Folse's opinion, it was precisely in this context that Bohr arrived at a thesis destined to exercise a decisive influence upon his later work, i.e. that the terms appearing in scientific language are endowed with different descriptive functions, each of which depends on 'what one regards as the "object" of the description'. There would thus exist different levels of objectivity to which our descriptions may refer, and since the context of a description is not immediately given, especially when one ventures into unfamiliar areas of experience, any scientific discourse wishing to avoid dangerous ambiguities of language is required to state explicitly the level of objectivity it intends to refer to.

In the light of this thesis, Bohr is seen as always having possessed a clear awareness of the characteristic aspects of the system of conceptual reference of classical physics and of the criteria of description compatible with it. In the first place, the description employing the spatio-temporal co-ordinates and symbolizing the ideal proper to each observation of furnishing a spatio-temporal picture of the motion of bodies; in the second place, the requisite of causality, which makes it possible, through the application of the principles of conservation to the interacting bodies, to define the state of an unobserved system; in the third place, the assumption – essential for the unambiguous definition of the state of a system – that all physical systems change their state in continuity with the passage of time. Folse claims – and his analysis does provide a convincing demonstration – that the whole of Bohr's research from 1913 on was aimed at discovering what new system of conceptual reference, and hence what new mode of description, would be compatible with the notion of quantum discontinuity, a notion he regarded always as a fundamental fact of nature, not accessible to analysis in classical terms and hence to be assumed as a postulate of the new theory. The path towards complementarity would thus have an early origin and, as Folse states, was 'essentially conditioned by his attempts to understand how these three themes were interrelated so that he could determine how the first two [space-time description and causality] would be altered when the third [assumption on the continuous variation in the state of a system] was denied'[36].

As Bohr wrote in April 1927: 'The difficulties of quantum theory are connected with the concepts, or rather with the words that are used in the customary description of nature, and which all have their origin in the classical theories. These concepts leave us only with the choice between Charybdis and Scylla, according to whether we direct our attention towards the continuous or discontinuous aspect of the description'[37]. The remarks are contained in a letter to Einstein accompanying the draft of Heisenberg's famous work on indeterminacy relations. Bohr announced the discovery of his young pupil with enthusiasm since, in his view, it was precisely these relations that now pointed the right direction to take in order to overcome the dualism of the nature of light and of material particles. This dilemma – considered insuperable in the system of conceptual reference of classical physics – became apparent upon closer analysis of the applicability of the fundamental concepts of physics in the description of atomic phenomena.

Bohr drew Einstein's attention, albeit with little success, to an epistemological requisite that, though familiar to him, had found new theoretical justification at precisely that moment. With Heisenberg's discovery, the primary objective of research became that of studying in depth the conceptual aspects connected with such phases of the growth of knowledge as entail profound changes in theoretical frameworks. This was not a departure brought about by an unexpected consequence of the formalism of quantum mechanics. Since his early work Bohr had always associated the construction of the new theory with the need for a more or less radical refoundation of scientific language, and did not rule out the possibility that the end result might be a different way of describing facts. This explains, among other things, why he felt the need to insist that his contributions lacked the logical and conceptual requisites of a scientific theory and preferred to speak of a provisional formal schema[38]. However, this attitude did not stem solely from a prior philosophical choice: he could continue to work within that schema only because of his willingness to make systematic use of new theoretical terms, which were left for a long time without any non-tautological definition, and his acceptance even of considerable variations of meaning in the concepts inherited from earlier theories.

In any case, only by studying in depth the conceptual and linguistic aspects referred to by Bohr is it possible to understand the role played in those years by the atomic model in constructing the theory. As we shall see, 'electrons' and 'elliptic orbits' served to make explicit the content of a metaphorical expression that Bohr applied to the new quantum theoretical concept of 'stationary state', which had enabled the theory to explain the spectroscopic laws and the radiative behaviour of atoms. Moreover, this initial metaphor carried out a precise heuristic function in originating a research programme that made it possible to 'utilize every aspect of the classical theories in the systematic construction of quantum theory'. In other words, it made it possible to explore the classical model of description in the light of the new system of conceptual reference being formed and gradually to derive useful suggestions and indications upon which to base a new system of concepts.

4

Radically subverting some assumptions of the anti-metaphysical programme of neo-positivism, some sectors of philosophy have recently arrived at a re-evaluation of the role of metaphor in science. They regard metaphorical expressions as an irreplaceable component of the linguistic mechanism of scientific theories and recognize, above all, that they

provide essential tools in each process of more or less profound transformation of theoretical and conceptual frameworks. These philosophical studies have given rise to a rigorous and systematic epistemological
analysis of metaphor. It is known that the neo-positivist philosophers
regarded the construction of formal languages as the most effective
strategy to eliminate the ambiguities of ordinary discourse, confine the
role of intuition solely to the discovery of new hypotheses and theories,
and emphasize the cognitive function of their rational justification. Such
an epistemological standpoint would thus oblige us to locate metaphor
outside the logic of science since 'metaphorical predication is not univocal
but analogical: it induces vagueness and imprecision into language and
associates with the subject systems of implications that extend its content
and anticipate empirical data'[39].

However, from the classic works by Max Black in the early 1960s to the
studies of Mary Hesse and on up to the discussions between Richard
Boyd and Thomas Kuhn, there has gradually emerged the awareness that
it is precisely in this failing with respect to an abstract ideal of rigour that
we find the most suitable means to express the problematic nature of
science. In other words, it has been recognized that science cannot do
without metaphors because it needs to introduce terms even without
defining them. It was Black who pointed out the interactive effect that
every metaphorical statement produces on the two subjects – principal
and secondary – between which metaphor suggests similarities and
analogies. It may therefore be stated that 'metaphor works by applying to
the principal (literal) subject of the metaphor a system of 'associated
implications' characteristic of the metaphorical secondary subject'. Thus,
to look at the primary subject through a metaphorical expression – e.g. to
look at 'the evolution of the species' through 'natural selection' and the
'struggle for survival' – is equivalent to projecting it conceptually onto the
space of the meanings and implications belonging to the secondary
subject[40].

Boyd takes up Black's interactive conception in the specific context of
the analysis of scientific language and denies that the function of metaphor is to be limited to the pre-theoretical phases in the development of a
discipline or, in disciplines of greater maturity and formalization,
assigned a marginal and primarily pedagogical role. On the contrary, in
Boyd's view 'there exists an important class of metaphors which play a
role in the development and articulation of theories. [...] Their function is
[...] to introduce theoretical terminology where none previously existed',
and he thus speaks of 'theory-constitutive metaphors'[41]. Boyd's analysis

ranges over a broader area than studies in the philosophy of science. In particular, the views he puts forward take a critical look at Saul Kripke's causal theory of reference and his notion of the 'dubbing' ceremonies. Metaphors are thus seen as going beyond the limitations of Kripke's conception – pointed out also by Kuhn – to represent a way of providing a non-definitional mode of reference of a term[42].

In the context of the present analysis, however, discussion will have to be confined to the results achieved by epistemological analyses of metaphors in science. We shall therefore limit ourselves to summarizing the main points of the views put forward by Richard Boyd in this regard, despite the inevitable risk of impoverishing his arguments.

(a) Theory-constitutive metaphors represent an irreplaceable linguistic element of theory in that they 'provide a way to introduce terminology for features of the world whose existence seems probable', i.e. even though many of their properties are not yet understood. In other words, they are able to overcome an apparent paradox regarding precisely the dynamic nature of knowledge and deriving from the fact that the science must determine the object of the investigation, and at the same time it cannot determine it fully and exhaustively without losing in problematic nature.

(b) For a metaphor to be introduced, there must be good reasons to believe that there exist 'theoretically important respects of similarity or analogy' between the primary (literal) and secondary subjects of the metaphor.

(c) These possess the unusual property of not generating contradictions when it is recognized that certain implications of the secondary subject are not applicable to the primary.

(d) They are endowed with what Boyd calls inductive open-endedness, i.e. they possess an intrinsic programmatic component. The adoption of a metaphor means the immediate acceptance of the invitation it contains 'to explore the similarities and analogies between features of the primary and secondary subjects'. In this connection, there is also an interesting corollary: each metaphor suggests strategies for future investigations aimed to discover 'additional, or, perhaps, entirely different important respects of similarity and analogy'. This means that – at least for a certain period – it is not known exactly what the most important aspects of the similarities and analogies suggested by the metaphor are. Their task is not actually that of enabling us to discover new facts, but merely of suggesting a different way of looking at facts.

(e) Finally, the explanation – and consequent exhaustion – of a metaphor are an automatic consequence of the success of the research programme from which they spring[43].

As Thomas Kuhn remarks in a comment upon Boyd's essay: 'Bohr's atom model was intended to be taken only more-or-less literally; electrons and nuclei were not thought to be exactly like small billiard or Ping-Pong balls; only some of the laws of mechanics and electromagnetic theory were thought to apply to them; finding out which ones did apply and where the similarities to billiard balls lay was a central task in the development of the quantum theory'[44]. Kuhn thus suggests that the interactive process characteristic of the functioning of metaphor is also of use in explaining the role of models in science. In particular, the search for similarities and the possibility of extending the classical laws to new phenomenal contexts are the main strands in the development of quantum theory, upon which this tool is seen as having made it possible to operate systematically.

Kuhn's brief reference to the case of Bohr's theory is intended as a call for greater attention to theoretical models on the part of philosophers of science. It is, however, also worth taking up his suggestion in the field of historical analysis if it can be demonstrated that such tools may even prove decisive in deciphering the logic underlying the research programme of the quantum theory of the atom and to elucidate finally the heuristic significance of certain elements of the theory (atomic model, correspondence principle) that operate creatively and selectively within the programme. This claim is supported by subjective and objective considerations regarding both the concrete conditions in which it became necessary to make systematic use of what Boyd calls the theory-constitutive metaphors, and especially the conscious use that Bohr made of logical procedures identifiable with this tool. Though this is obviously quite a claim to make, it will be seen that the hypothesis appears to be the only one capable of solving the puzzle of the correspondence principle which, despite the abundance of books devoted to the history of quantum mechanics, still remains shrouded in the deepest obscurity.

By following the list of the aspects that Boyd regards as among the most important in the application of metaphor to theory construction, it is possible to gather together all the objective reasons legitimizing the claim that the model of orbiting electrons was, from 1913 on, the consequence

of a metaphorical expression regarding the introduction of new undefined concepts.

In the improved version of the theory presented at the end of 1913,
Bohr had made the following remark with regard to stationary states:
'During the emission of the radiation the system may be regarded as
passing from one state to another; in order to introduce a name for these
states, we shall call them 'stationary' states, simply indicating thereby
that they form some kind of waiting places between which occurs the
emission of the energy corresponding to the various spectral lines'[45]. In
his view, the possibility of providing a model upon which to base this
concept depended on the fact that the hypothesis, that the classical
expression of electron frequency might be used in an attempt to obtain a
clear concept of stationary states, 'is quite natural [...] since, in trying to
form a reasonable conception of the stationary states, there is, for the
present at least, no other means available besides the ordinary
mechanics'[46]. Therefore, once it was ascertained that Planck's ideas
could be transferred to Rutherford's model only through analogical
extension of the formal type, it became necessary to introduce the new
concepts of stationary state and transition between states. For the
moment, the theory was able to give them no definition (they were 'a kind
of waiting place') and Bohr regarded them as requiring more thorough
formulation. The mechanical treatment of stationary state in terms of
electron motion was a plausible and provisional hypothesis useful only to
give an idea of the sense of the name, which could not be understood as a
mere synonym for 'orbiting electron'.

The introduction of new theoretical terms had been suggested by
comparison of the Ritz combination principle and the quantum expression for the variation of the atom's internal energy. Such comparison
made it, in fact, highly likely that the terms of the Ritz formula and the
various terms of the empirical laws of spectroscopy corresponded to
discrete states of energy of the atom endowed with a particular stability
inexplicable in terms of classical theory, and that the atom's radiative
behaviour was manifested only in transition from one to another of these
states. These highly probable clues as to the physical nature of atoms
were assumed as postulates of the theory. 'Stationary state' thus forms
part of a new scientific terminology required in order to express 'features
of the world whose existence seems probable, but many of whose
fundamental properties have yet to be discovered'. For example, we are
not able, in the light of available knowledge, to explain what it is that can
guarantee the stability of an object endowed with electromagnetic

properties, or of forming an idea of the nature of the mechanism whereby exchanges of energy take place between the continuous electromagnetic radiation and the discrete transitions between states. Nevertheless, there are good reasons for making use of this metaphor, i.e. for treating stationary states as though there were some relation of similarity or analogy with the orbiting motion of electrons, as demonstrated by the existence of significant asymptotic agreement between spectrum and motion in the area of high quantum numbers.

The study of the atom's constitution, the determination of the rules of selection of states, the explanation of the Stark and Zeeman effects, the reconstruction of the periodic table of elements on the basis of the configurations of the various electronic orbits, all of these were results made possible – and with significant success – by a theory whose mathematical apparatus was based on the notion of the electronic orbit[47]. It follows from this that there was no reason to regard as a source of confusion the recognition that the use of that model entailed the abandonment of one of the most significant implications of the concept of the electron, i.e. the fact that the term referred to – and above all served to identify – an object satisfying by virtue of its intrinsic physical nature the laws of the classical theory of electrodynamics.

To illustrate the programmatic component of the electron model of the atom, it is sufficient to recall the developments in quantum theory subsequent to Bohr's work of 1913: Sommerfeld's generalization of the rules of quantization and his relativistic corrections to the expression of the energy levels of states; recourse to the methods of analytical mechanics in order to examine the multiperiodic motions to be applied to more complex systems than that of hydrogen or to the case of the influence of external electrical and magnetic fields upon hydrogen spectrum, and so on. The direction of the programme's development, based on a approach through mechanical modelling to the investigation of the atom's constitution, was the result of a conscious attempt to see how far the concepts and laws of classical physics could still be used when dealing with discontinuous processes and when reality itself brought to the surface what physicists of the time saw as an element of irrationality with regard to traditional conceptual frameworks[48].

Thus far we may state that the mechanical model of stationary states possesses all of the requisites Boyd lays down for the theory-constitutive metaphors. However, far different conclusions would have to be drawn were it discovered that Bohr was actually applying precisely this linguistic tool when he associated stationary states with orbiting electrons, and that this was precisely the sense of the recurrent use of terms like 'symbolic', 'formal' and 'correspondence' to be found in very many of his writings between 1913 and 1927.

5

On 17 April 1920 Bohr was invited to deliver a lecture at the Deutschen Physikalischen Gesellschaft. The occasion was particularly well suited to recalling how much atomic theory owed to Planck's ideas but also offered Bohr a stimulating opportunity to specify in front of Einstein himself, who he met here for the first time, the lines of his research programme. Though Bohr stated that he did not wish to examine the problem of the nature of radiation, this in itself enabled him to underline implicitly his scepticism as to the heuristic fruitfulness of the hypothesis of light quanta[49].

The bones of the argument developed by Bohr in the first part of his paper may be reconstructed as follows. Planck's theory of radiation tells us that, at least as regards statistical equilibrium, only certain states of the oscillator emitting and absorbing energy are to be taken into consideration. The energy of each of these states is a whole multiple of a quantum of energy

$$E_n = nh\omega. \tag{3.3}$$

This hypothesis is inapplicable to the case of atomic particles and to the interpretation of spectra since the model used in this case involves a type of particle motion that cannot be assimilated to that of a Planckian oscillator. The theory has therefore, from the beginning, set itself the problem of generalizing Planck's conceptions. In Bohr's view, this could come about in two directions: (i) one might take (3.3) as representing – albeit in approximate fashion and for the simpler cases – the properties characteristic of the motions proper to an atomic system and thus embark upon the search for a general quantum formula valid for all types of motion; (ii) one might instead take the formula as regarding a property of the radiation process, i.e. the unknown process whereby matter and radiation exchange energy[50]. In the latter case, the generalization of Planck's hypothesis may be expressed also in formal terms in that by replacing in (3.3) the frequency ω of the oscillator with the frequency ν of radiation we obtain in banal fashion the expression

$$\Delta E = h\nu. \tag{3.4}$$

This means that 'Planck's result may be interpreted to mean, that the oscillator can emit and absorb radiation only in "radiation quanta"'[51]. In this case, too, a process of generalization is involved since it must be recalled that (3.3) contains a conceptual difficulty that emerges as soon as one attempts to apply it to the case of the atom or of any molecule of matter. In this generalization it is, in fact, necessary to remove the limitation implicit in the derivation of (3.4) from (3.3) that energy exchanges in quanta always lead to a variation of the system between two contiguous states, for which the difference in quantum numbers is always equal to unity. As the laws of spectroscopy show, this is obviously not true in the case of the atom.

It was precisely this second way of interpreting the hypothesis introduced by Planck into the study of the statistical equilibrium of a system of oscillators with a field of radiation that enabled Einstein to formulate his theory of the photoelectric effect. In Bohr's view, this contribution by Einstein represented a fundamental stage in the development of quantum conceptions in that it was 'the first instance in which the quantum theory was applied to a phenomenon of non-statistical character'[52]. While Einstein saw the success of this theory as clear evidence that the generalization of Planck's ideas should move in the direction of the quantization of radiation, the so-called quanta of light, Bohr continued to regard this solution as totally sterile. It has been claimed, on the basis of his own specific statements, that the reason for his rejection of light quanta lay in the difficulty of jettisoning classical electromagnetic theory since, among other things, Einstein's hypothesis said nothing about typically undulatory phenomena[53]. This is true, though there are also grounds for claiming that the deeper reasons for this rejection are to be sought precisely in the two ways Bohr had glimpsed of generalizing Planck's result and in the fact that there was, at the time, no theoretical reason to opt for one rather than the other, especially bearing in mind the problems opened up by the theory of the constitution of the atom. On the contrary, the hypothesis of light quanta represented a drastic choice compromising the theory with a solution to the problem of exchanges of energy between radiation and matter that precluded any further investigation of the mechanism of interaction and, above all, that impoverished the contribution that Planck's ideas could make to the development of atomic theory.

The task Bohr set himself was instead 'to show how it has been possible in a purely formal manner to develop a spectral theory, the essential

elements of which may be considered as a simultaneous rational development of the two ways of interpreting Planck's result'[54]. He returned to
this conception shortly after to state that, when applied to the atomic
system, Planck's condition for the oscillator 'breaks up into two parts,
one concerning the fixation of the stationary states, and the other relating
to the frequency of the radiation emitted by a transition between these
states'[55].

The expression (3.4) has an immediate application that makes it
possible to provide a very simple explanation of the laws of spectroscopy.
It is sufficient to postulate that during emission radiation always has the
same frequency v and that it is connected with the energy of the system
before and after emission by the relation (3.1). This hypothesis has two
important consequences. In the first place, we could never obtain –
contrary to what is laid down by the ordinary theory of radiation – any
information as to the motion of the atom's particles from the nature of the
radiation. In the second place, and also for this reason, it is necessary to
introduce the new concept of stationary state to characterize the states
corresponding to the values of energy before and after each process of
radiation. It is not in fact possible to interpret the magnitudes E' and E''
appearing in (3.1) as energies associated to particular states of oscillation
of the system. As Bohr again stresses, it is rather the spectra and the
formal structure of the empirical laws representing them that reveal 'the
existence of certain definite energy values corresponding to certain
distinctive states of the atoms'[56].

Together with (3.1), the notions of stationary state and quantum
transition point to a new conceptual framework. That is to say, they point
to it but do not define it, in the sense that they make it possible to identify
those restrictions of descriptive character – inevitable and insuperable
and hence constituting the logical and epistemological presupposition of
his research programme – according to which ordinary mechanics cannot
be used for the description of transitions between stationary states and
the process of radiation cannot be described on the basis of ordinary
electrodynamics. These prohibitions made it possible to illustrate the
deep rift between the new conceptual framework and the ordinary
conceptions of classical physics and suggest a key with which to interpret
Bohr's subsequent claim that in any case the conditions existed to provide
a rational interpretation of the empirical data within a consistent formal
framework. The tool that was supposed to permit such an interpretation
was precisely the principle of correspondence. To take up an apparently

obscure expression frequently used by Bohr, this principle established a connection between the two conceptual systems, classical and quantum-theoretical, such as to make the theory of atomic spectra appear a rational generalization of the ordinary theory of radiation.

6

Five years after the Berlin conference, Bohr was invited to speak at the Congress of Scandinavian Mathematicians held in Copenhagen in August 1925. In the meantime, the state of quantum theory had changed deeply and Bohr's personal fortunes seemed to be clearly waning. The previous spring had, in fact, seen the result of the Bothe–Geiger experiment, which decreed the failure of the theory of virtual oscillators and supported Einstein's theory of light quanta. A few weeks earlier the *Zeitschrift für Physik* had published Heisenberg's brilliant work of matrix mechanics, which was based on the systematic elimination from the theory of all unobservable magnitudes and its liberation from any model-based restrictions. In no way deterred by these results, Bohr took the opportunity to draw up a balance sheet of his own research programme and to advance some very interesting considerations as to the significance of and the role played by the mechanical model in the construction of atomic theory[57].

His reconstruction of the historical evolution of mechanics and electromagnetic theory associates the birth of quantum theory with the emergence of a completely new contradiction affecting the use of scientific language and hence making it extremely difficult to achieve a more precise formulation of the content of quantum theory. The contradiction Bohr speaks of is that between the element of discontinuity introduced by Planck into the description of microscopic processes and the origin of the concepts of our scientific language, which had been inherited from previous theories based on images requiring the possibility of continuous variation. Such concepts have a meaning and are defined in the context of theories assuming that the objects to which their descriptions apply satisfy in all cases the condition that the state of a system varies with continuity in time. In Bohr's view, the nature of the contradictions deriving from the split between old and new conceptual framework is well illustrated by the difference existing between an atom and an electrodynamical model with regard to the composition of radiation. It is impossible, he claims, to find any similarity between the line spectra of the elements and the frequency of the radiation, which must, from the classical viewpoint, always vary in continuous fashion as a consequence of the property of the frequencies characteristic of motion to vary continuously with variation in energy.

The disappearance of the condition of the continuous variation of the states of a system thus necessitates a far-reaching and demanding research programme consisting of the search for a more precise formulation of the concepts of quantum theory, the first result of which being the introduction of the two postulates underlying all further development. It is worth noting how in the successive formulations of these postulates Bohr progressively eliminates all reference to elements belonging to a model-type representation of the atom to the point where he no longer speaks of electrons or orbital movement. Such terms and expressions as 'stationary state', 'discrete succession of energy values', 'peculiar stability' and 'transitions between stationary states' appear without being provided with any definitional content by the postulates themselves. Bohr's postulates also contain approximate expressions, as when it is stated that 'the possibility of an atom's emission or absorption of radiation depends on the possibility of variation of the atom's energy'. However, these aspects of linguistic vagueness and imprecision cannot be eliminated for the moment if it is true that the postulates cannot be interpreted in classical terms and are part of a theoretical framework still under formation, one of whose objectives is the precision of concepts and the rigorous definition of new terms introduced to identify, albeit in problematic fashion, hitherto unknown aspects of reality.

By the summer of 1925, Bohr had collected sufficiently reliable evidence to be able to claim that 'in the general problem of the quantum theory, one is faced not with a modification of the mechanical and electrodynamical theories describable in terms of the usual physical concepts, but with an essential failure of the pictures in space and time on which the description of natural phenomena has hitherto been based'[58]. As explicitly stated, this conclusion derives from certain consequences of the theory of virtual oscillators, which had made it possible to demonstrate that the only theoretical solution compatible with a model of spatio-temporal description of processes of a discontinuous type dependent on the laws of probability consisted in abandoning the principles of conservation in individual processes and in the renunciation of causality. This result was to have important consequences for the subsequent development of Bohr's ideas and represented a crucial step towards the formulation of the complementarity principle[59].

These questions will be analysed and considered in greater depth in the following chapter. What concerns us here is to trace and to try to elucidate a part of Bohr's reasoning that looks back on the process of the construction of the quantum theory of the atom. Despite the recognition from the outset of an unbridgeable conceptual gulf between atom and model, and although recent developments of the theory by now speak openly of the substantial failure of models, 'it has been possible to construct mechanical pictures of the stationary states which rest on the concept of the nuclear atom'[60]. But what value and what significance can be attributed to these hypothetical intuitive representations of the internal constitution of atoms when such models are embedded in a theory obliging us to admit that their characteristic elements – e.g. the frequencies of revolution and the shape of electronic orbits – must in principle be regarded as unobservable and not even 'susceptible of comparison with direct observation'? And how can we ignore, or regard as irrelevant for the theory, the fact that every mechanical model contradicts the very reality of atoms by denying that they can be stable objects even if endowed with the property of interacting with electromagnetic radiation? All of these were convincing arguments which, for Pauli and Heisenberg, suggested the advisability of ditching any model-based approach in favour of a phenomenological approach, for want of anything better, at least until it might be possible to construct a new assemblage of concepts defined on an operational basis[61]. Bohr of course resisted his pupils' prompting since he did not regard their arguments, though legitimate, as sufficient to shake his confidence in the function of intuitive representation and in the ideal of visualization. In any case, it could also be added that another answer is possible to the above questions: the arguments upon which they are based are neither convincing nor legitimate when the model is regarded as a mere articulation of the principle of correspondence.

Naturally Bohr recognized the force of the objections encountered by any attempt to deal with stationary states in terms of models of electronic orbits; warnings of the limitations of such an approach run through all his writings. Neither did he believe, or ever claim, that the model should be considered the conceptual instrument around which to elaborate an explanation of the atom's physical nature. The effectiveness of the model was not basically to be sought in its capacity to suggest a 'visualization of the stationary states through mechanical images' but rather in its having made it possible to bring 'to light a far-reaching analogy between the quantum theory and the mechanical theory'[62]. Without the model it would have been impossible either to demonstrate the existence of an asymptotic agreement between spectrum and motion or to formulate the principle of correspondence.

The discovery that in the region of high quantum numbers the values of the frequencies of radiation coincide with the frequencies of the harmonic components of motion, or that the amplitudes of the harmonic oscillations provide a 'measure' of the probability of the processes of transition, meant only having identified important elements of similarity and analogy between the quantum-theoretical concepts of stationary state and transition between states and the classical concept of oscillating charge. That this is the meaning to be attributed to the so-called asymptotic agreement is demonstrated by the fact that even in the limiting region the two terms between which similarities and analogies are discovered maintain a precise conceptual distinction. As Bohr reminds us, even in this region states are stable, transitions are discontinuous, and the process of radiation does not lead to the simultaneous emission of all the frequencies corresponding to the various harmonic components of motion. In other words, even here it is not possible to give a literal meaning to the content of the model and to say that in the limiting case stationary states become electronic orbits once again.

As we saw at the beginning, the correspondence principle was born from the recognition of the general validity of the analogy between quantum theory and classical mechanics brought to light by the asymptotic agreement between spectrum and motion, and was expressed in linguistic formulas of highly ambiguous content. The possibility of each process of transition associated with the emission of radiation was supposed to be conditioned by the existence of a harmonic component corresponding to the internal motion of the atom. In order to decipher the meaning of the analogy implicit in the idea of correspondence it is necessary to rid this formulation of any reference – however spontaneous – to the intuitive model of the atom and to render explicit the two logical steps that Bohr left implicit by recourse to terms like 'conditioned' and 'corresponding'. The analogical relationship must be such that, on the one hand, it can be stated that a transition occurs on condition that in the corresponding classical representation of the system via mechanical models there is a harmonic component of motion of frequency equal to that of the observed radiation, and on the other it remains understood that that representation is constructed within a system of conceptual reference in which the new terms 'stationary state' and 'transition between states' are indefinable and untranslatable. We must therefore recognize that in the correspondence principle and the model connected with it a linguistic tool is at work that (i) makes possible to establish a particular logical relation between terms devoid of definition and terms belonging to pre-existing theoretical contexts; (ii) permits the systematic exploration of the similarities and analogies existing between the former and the systems of implication associated with the latter, i.e. the laws and physical properties that these satisfy; and (iii) is capable of exploiting the heuristic potential of the analogy without any contradiction arising from the impossibility of applying some implications of the secondary terms to the primary, i.e. that legitimizes the continuation of work on the model.

It is clear that metaphor is the logical and linguistic tool operating in the principle of correspondence and ensuring, to Bohr's mind, the fruitfulness of a model-based approach, or at least that this tool displays all the characteristic aspects brought out by Boyd in his epistemological analysis of the theory-constitutive metaphors. What significance could there otherwise be in Bohr's emphasis on the model's symbolic character? What other interpretation could be given to his statement that 'the correspondence principle expresses the tendency to utilize in the systematic development of the quantum theory every feature of the classical theories in a rational transcription appropriate to the fundamental contrast between the postulates and the classical theories'[63]? The phrase is otherwise obscure, and perhaps for this reason hardly ever quoted in the literature, but does fully express Bohr's view of the central importance that the principle was to assume in the search for a more precise formulation of the concepts of quantum theory. The idea of a rational transcription also brings us back to one of the distinctive traits of Bohr's epistemology: his debt to philosophy, his constant attention, as Folse reminds us, to the problem of the applicability of individual concepts to the description of phenomena, and his recognition that the descriptive function of the terms appearing in scientific language varies with theoretical context and depends on what is regarded as the object of the description. As we shall see, the metaphorical use of the orbital motion of electrons to define the concept of stationary state ended in 1927 with the petering out of the programme to which it had given rise and with the definitive foundation of the same concept on the basis of the oscillations proper to Schrödinger's equation. The idea of complementarity between observation would, finally, make it possible to solve the riddle of the relationship between the stability of the states and the individual processes of transition.

Notes

1 N. Bohr, 'The Quantum Postulate...' cit. ch. 1 n. 1, 580; *CW6*, 148.
2 J. Hendry, *The Creation...* cit. ch 1 n. 49, *passim*.
3 The explicit statement to this effect is contained in the preliminary draft notes of the Como paper (ms. held in the Bohr Archive), cf. below, n. 6.
4 N. Bohr, 'The Quantum Postulate...' cit. ch. 1 n. 1, 580; *CW6*, 148.
5 This view is held in common by all the historians and philosophers of science who have seen complementarity as the expression of a primarily philosophical departure and by those physicists who, for various reasons, have maintained (and still do) the incompleteness of the description of quantum mechanics and urge its reformulation in realistic terms. See above, Introduction, *passim*.
6 This is a document of three handwritten pages contained in the folder 'Como Lecture II (1927)'. The text (in Danish) was written by Bohr and contains a final addition of two lines probably written by Oskar Klein. Though two of the three sheets are dated, Rüdinger and Kalckar claim (*CW6*, 58) that the date (10.7.1926) is wrong in that certain references contained in the document show it to date from July 1927. An anastatic copy of the three pages, transcription and English translation are to be found in *CW6*, 59–65.
7 The text of the translation of the first page of the document (*CW6*, 61) is as follows:

I 10-7-1926 [1927]

———————

All information about atoms expressed in classical concepts

———————

All classical concepts defined through space-time pictures

———————

Therefore beginning of quantum [theory?] piecewise use of space-time pictures formally connected by relations containing Planck's constant. and on conservation of energy and momentum.

———————

The connection of essentially discontinuous and statistical kind. The endeavours at connecting the statistical laws with the properties of pictures thus implied that they appeared as generalization of the classical theory, and in particular converge to the demands of this theory in the limit [where] in statistical applications one may disregard the discontinuous element. led to the recognition of a far-reaching correspondence between the quantum theory and the classical theory and to the programme of developing a [consistent?] quantitative description [by] looking for analogous features in the classical theory. However it proved impossible to express this quantitatively by space-time pictures. [Indeed?], the theory exhibited a duality when one considered on the one hand the superposition principle and on the other hand the conservation of energy and momentum.

———————

Complementarity aspects of experience that cannot be united into a space-time picture based on the classical theories.
8 N. Bohr, 'On the Quantum Theory of the Light Spectra', *Det Kongelige Danske Viedenskabernes Salskab. Skrifter, Naturvidenskabelig og matematisk Afdeling*, 8 Rœkke, IV. I (1918, 1922); *CW3*, 67–184. The

history of this paper, in English, is particularly complex (cf. J. Rud Nielsen, 'Introduction to Part I', *CW3*, 3–46, sections 4–6). The same volume contains various provisional drafts of the IV part, which was never completed (*CW3*, 186–200). In the first section, 'General Principles', Bohr claimed that from the fact that the values of the quantum frequencies coincide with those 'to be expected on the ordinary theory of radiation from the motion of the system in the stationary states' it is possible to derive 'certain general considerations about the connection between the probability of a transition between any two stationary states and the motion of the system in these states, which will be shown to throw light on the question of the polarization and intensity of the different lines of the spectrum of a given system' (ibid., 8; *CW3*, 74).

9   N. Bohr, 'Über die Serienspektra der Elemente', *Zeitschrift für Physik* **2** (1920), 423–69, which appeared in an English translation by A. D. Udden, 'On the Series Spectra of the Elements', in N. Bohr, *The Theory of Spectra and Atomic Constitution*, Cambridge: Cambridge University Press, 1922, 20–60; *CW3*, 242–82.

10   N. Bohr, 'L'application de la théorie des quanta aux problèmes atomiques', in *Atomes et électrons, Rapports et discussions du Conseil de Physique tenu à Bruxelles du 1er au 6 Avril 1921*, Paris: Gauthier-Villars, 1923, 228–47; *CW3*, 364–80, reproduces the original English ('On the Application of the Quantum Theory to Atomic Problems') from which the French translation – which shows two slight variations in the concluding section – was made. Quotations hereafter are taken from the English text. The conference was chaired by Lorentz and participants included: C. G. Barkla (Edinburgh), W. L. Bragg (Manchester), M. and L. Brillouin (Paris), M. de Broglie (Paris), M. Curie (Paris), P. Ehrenfest (Leyden), W. J. de Haas (Delft), H. Kammerlingh Onnes (Leyden), M. Knudsen (Copenhagen), P. Langevin (Paris), J. Larmor (Cambridge), R. A. Millikan (Chicago), J. Perrin (Paris), O. W. Richardson (London), E. Rutherford (Cambridge), M. Siegban (Lund), E. van Aubel (Ghent), P. Weiss (Strasburg) and P. Zeeman (Amsterdam). A. A. Michelson (Chicago), then in Europe, was also invited. Besides Bohr, others unable to attend were W. H. Bragg (London), A. Einstein (Berlin) and J. H. Jeans (Dorking). Cf. J. Mehra, *The Solvay Conferences...* cit. ch. 1 n. 6, ch. 4.

11   P. Ehrenfest, *Le principe de correspondance*, in *Atomes et électrons...* cit. n. 10, 348–54; *CW3*, 381–87. Lorentz, Bragg, Langevin, Rutherford, Zeeman and Maurice de Broglie took part in the discussion (ibid., 255–62; *CW3*, 388–95); cf. J. Mehra, *The Solvay Conferences...* cit. ch. 1 n. 6.

12   Bohr to Richardson, 15 August 1918, *CW3*, 14–15. Bohr announced his inability to attend the Solvay Conference in a letter to Ehrenfest dated 23 March 1921, *CW3*, 614; English trans. 30–31.

13   Remarks of this kind had been noted by Kramers in his meetings with Swedish physicists during a trip to Stockholm. As a comment on such criticism he added in a letter to Bohr dated 12 March 1917: 'fortunately, the formula is only formal, and one cannot deduce anything about the mechanism of the radiation'. (*CW3*, 652–53; English trans. 654–55.)

14   It was thanks to Ehrenfest's intervention, 17 July 1921, that Bohr decided to publish the text in this form, having found in any case great difficulty in cutting it as Lorentz had asked: 'The Solvay book must finally appear; that there be a piece of Bohr in it is necessary, that the entire Bohr is found in it is not necessary. That you not only become entirely well, but also happy

and free from cares is much more important for the development of physics than whether or not one of your publications remains a fragment or is a little wrong. For, I assure you that St. Peter at the gate of Heaven will not blame you for that. And a hundred years from now no one will worry about it if some article of yours was a little wrong but rather over the fact that you, at the age of 36 years, were nearly threatened with a breakdown (and then they will not blame you but those who harassed you!!!!!)' (*CW3*, 623–24). Similar encouragement was given by Ehrenfest also in a subsequent letter dated 7 August, where he reminded Bohr that 'the Congress was planned around you!' (*CW3*, 625–26).

15 N. Bohr, 'On the Application...' cit. n. 10, 365–66.

16 Ibid., 367.

17 Ibid., 368.

18 Ibid.

19 For a discussion of Sommerfeld's method of quantization and of the role of the adiabatic principle in this context, as well as for references to primary sources, see M. Jammer, *The Conceptual Development...* cit. chap. 2 n. 6, section 3.1.

20 Bohr was to develop these arguments rigorously in the article of November 1922, 'Über die Anwendung der Quantentheorie auf den Atombau', *Zeitschrift für Physik* **13** (1923), 117–65. As was pointed out in a note, the article, which dealt with the fundamental postulates of the theory, was to have constituted the first of a series of papers under the same title in which Bohr intended to deal systematically with the problems connected with the study of atomic structure. The article was translated into English by the American physicist L. F. Curtis: 'On the Application of the Quantum Theory to Atomic Structure', *Proceedings of the Cambridge Philosophical Society (Supplement)* (1924), 1–42; *CW3*, 458–99. Quotations hereafter will be taken from the English version as it is to this that Bohr refers in subsequent writings. For a modern treatment of the solution of partial differential equations with the method of variable separation and the methods of quantization, cf. C. Lanczos, *The Variational Principles of Mechanics*, Toronto: University of Toronto Press, 1970 (4th edn.), ch. VIII.

21 N. Bohr, 'On the Application...' cit. n. 10, 372.

22 Ibid., 374.

23 Ibid.

24 Ibid., 375.

25 For a formal derivation of this relation, cf. ibid.

26 Ibid., 376.

27 This way of interpreting the correspondence principle has been adopted by, among others, W. Krajewski (*Correspondence Principle and Growth of Science*, Dordrecht: Reidel, 1977, 1): 'The Correspondence Principle (CP) appeared for the first time in the old quantum theory of the atom created by Niels Bohr. According to this principle, the quantum theory of the atom and of its radiation passes asymptotically into the classical theory when the quantum numbers increase or, in other words, when we may neglect Planck's constant h'. Krajewski makes this the basis for his own epistemological reflections and, among the various philosophers of science who have taken up this principle, more or less critically, in the epistemological sphere, cites Karl Popper who, after stressing its fertility, defines it in general terms as the 'demand that a new theory should contain the old one approximately, for appropriate values of the parameters of the

new theory' (*Objective Knowledge*, Oxford: Clarendon Press, 1972, 202).
However, even the manuals of physics take the same view. See, for
example, the classic text by A. Messiah (*Mécanique quantique*, Paris:
Dunod, 1964, 25): 'It may therefore be regarded as an established fact that
the classical theory is "macroscopically correct", i.e. that it accounts for
phenomena at the limit where quantum discontinuities may be treated as
infinitely small; in all cases, the predictions of the exact theory must
coincide with those of the classical theory. This is the very restrictive
condition imposed upon quantum theory. It is often expressed in
abbreviated form in the statement: quantum theory must tend
asymptotically towards classical theory at the limit of large quantum
numbers'.

28 N. Bohr, 'On the Application...' cit. n. 10, 376.

29 Ibid.

30 Ibid.

31 Ibid., 377.

32 'This is the simplest way that can be imagined', claimed Ehrenfest during
the discussion in reply to W. L. Bragg, who had asked how it was possible
to define for a transition the average value of the corresponding frequency
ω (*Atomes et éléctrons...* cit. n. 10, 255–56; *CW3*, 388–89). In the article of
November 1922, Bohr again took up this mathematical solution to conclude
that 'the frequency of the wave-system emitted on a transition can,
therefore, be regarded as the mean value of the frequencies of the
corresponding vibration in the series of "intermediate states"' ('On the
Application...' cit. n. 10, 24; *CW3*, 481). However, in order to clear up any
remaining doubt as to the significance of this procedure in relation to the
new principle, a note in the same article concerning the formal analogy
existing between quantum theory and classical stressed that: 'such an
expression might cause misunderstanding, since [...] the Correspondence
Principle must be regarded purely as a law of the quantum theory, which
can in no way diminish the contrast between the postulates and
electrodynamic theory' (ibid., 22; *CW3*, 479).

33 N. Bohr, 'The Correspondence Principle', in *Report of the British
Association for the Advancement of Science*, Liverpool, 1923, 428–29; *CW3*,
576–77.

34 H. Folse, *The Philosophy of Niels Bohr. The Framework of
Complementarity*, Amsterdam: North-Holland, 1985, *passim*, and especially
43–55.

35 The question of the influence of Danish existentialism on Bohr has been
widely dealt with in the literature, also in studies of a biographical nature
(e.g. R. Moore, *Niels Bohr: The Man, His Science and the World They
Changed*, New York: Alfred Knopf, 1966; and also P. Forman, 'Weimar
Culture...' cit. Introduction n. 13). Cf., in particular with regard to Bohr's
youthful philosophical experiences, D. Favrholdt, 'Niels Bohr and Danish
Philosophy', *Danish Yearbook of Philosophy* **13** (1976), 206–20; 'The
Cultural Background of the Young Niels Bohr', in *Proceedings...* cit. ch. 1
n. 12, 445–61, which asserts the impossibility of tracing Bohr's scientific
thought and idea of complementarity back to this problematic environment.

36 H. Folse, *The Philosophy...* cit. n. 34, 67.

37 Bohr to Einstein, 13 April 1927, *CW6*, 418–21; English trans. 21.

38 N. Bohr, 'On the Application...' cit. n. 10, ch. III, wholly devoted to the
formal nature of quantum theory, which for Bohr meant precisely a theory

incapable of forming a consistent picture of phenomena starting from its own fundamental principles.

39 G. Piazza, 'Metafore e scoperte nella ricerca scientifica', in F. Alberoni ed., *Il presente e i suoi simboli*, Milan: Franco Angeli, 1986, 87–119: 96.

40 M. Black, *Models and Metaphors*, Ithaca and London: Cornell University Press, 1962; M. Hesse, *Models and Analogies in Science*, Nôtre Dame: University of Nôtre Dame Press, 1966; R. Boyd, 'Metaphor and Theory Change: What is "Metaphor" a Metaphor for?', and T. S. Kuhn, 'Metaphor in Science', in A. Ortony ed., *Metaphor and Thought*, Cambridge: Cambridge University Press, 1979, 356–408 and 409–19.

41 R. Boyd, 'Metaphor...' cit. n. 40, 357.

42 Cf., for example, S. Kripke, 'Naming and Necessity', in G. Harman and D. Davidson, eds., *Semantics of Natural Language*, Dordrecht and Boston: Reidel, 1972; 'Identity and Necessity', in M. K. Munitz, ed., *Identity and Individuation*, New York: New York University Press, 1971.

43 R. Boyd, 'Metaphor...' cit. n. 40, *passim*.

44 T. S. Kuhn, 'Metaphor...' cit. n. 40, 414–15.

45 N. Bohr, 'On the Spectra...' cit. ch. 2 n. 29, 11; *CW2*, 293.

46 Ibid., 12; *CW2*, 294.

47 For these interesting developments of the theory and relative interpretations the reader is referred to the work by Jammer cited frequently above and to J. Mehra and H. Rechenberg, *The Historical Development...* cit. ch. 2 n. 11, vol. 1, Part 2; J. Rud Nielsen, 'Introduction to Part I', *CW4*, 3–42.

48 Cf. above.

49 N. Bohr, 'On the Series...' cit. n. 9; cf. J. Rud Nielsen, 'Introduction...' cit. n. 8, *CW3*, 21–23. Besides Planck and Einstein, Bohr met on this occasion other German physicists including Franck, Born, Ladenburg, Landé and Kossel. With reference to their meeting, Einstein later wrote to Bohr: 'Not often in life has a person, by his mere presence, given me such joy as you. I understand now why Ehrenfest is so fond of you. I am now studying your great papers, and in so doing – when I get stuck somewhere – I have the pleasure of seeing your youthful face before me, smiling and explaining. I have learned much from you, especially also how you approach scientific matters emotionally' (2 May 1920, *CW3*, 634; English trans. 22).

50 N. Bohr, 'On the Series...' cit. n. 9, 21–22; *CW3*, 243–44.

51 Ibid.

52 Ibid.

53 The impossibility of providing a definition of the concept of frequency, which appears in Einstein's own expression of the energy of quanta, independently of a wave conception of radiation was the main reason why Bohr assigned a purely formal significance to this hypothesis. On this point, in addition to the following remarks, cf. also below, ch. 4.

54 N. Bohr, 'On the Series...' cit. n. 9, 22; *CW3*, 244.

55 Ibid., 29; *CW3*, 251.

56 Ibid., 23; *CW3*, 245. With regard to the introduction of the concept of stationary state, also on this occasion Bohr asserted: 'These states will be called the *stationary states* of the atoms, since we shall assume that the atom can remain a finite time in each state, and can leave this state only by a process of transition to another stationary state' (ibid.).

57 N. Bohr, 'Atomic Theory and Mechanics', *Nature (Supplement)* **116** (1925), 845–52; *CW5*, 273–80. The article was then published in German

('Atomtheorie und Mechanik', *Die Naturwissenschaften* **14** (1926), 1–10) and in a Danish version. *CW5* gives not only the text of the ms. of the outline of the paper in Danish and translated into English (255–68), but also a list of the major variations found in the different editions (271). The article in *Nature* was preceded by a famous editorial note ('Atomic Structure and the Quantum Theory') drafted by R. H. Fowler. For Heisenberg's work, cf. below, ch. 5.

58 N. Bohr, 'Atomic Theory...' cit. n. 57, 848; *CW5*, 276.

59 Cf. below, ch. 4, *passim*.

60 N. Bohr, 'Atomic Theory...' cit. n. 57, 848; *CW5*, 276.

61 Objections and attitudes of this type also arose out of specific interpretive problems (anomalous Zeeman effect, spectra of elements endowed with a complex electron configuration, etc.), which had made the defence of the orbital model increasingly difficult. For this important chapter in the history of atomic theory, which will not be dealt with in the present essay, the reader is referred in particular to P. Forman, 'Alfred Landé and the Anomalous Zeeman Effect, 1919–1921', *Historical Studies in the Physical Sciences* **2** (1970), 153–261; 'The Doublet Riddle and the Atomic Physics circa 1924', *Isis* **59** (1968), 156–74; D. Serwer, '*Unmechanischer Zwang*: Pauli, Heisenberg and the Rejection of the Mechanical Atom, 1923–1925', *Historical Studies in the Physical Sciences* **8** (1977), 189–256; D. Cassidy, 'Heisenberg's First Core Model of the Atom: The Formation of a Professional Style', ibid. **10** (1979), 187–224.

62 N. Bohr, 'Atomic Theory...' cit. n. 57, 848; *CW5*, 276.

63 Ibid., 849; *CW5*, 277. Far different conclusions are reached by I. Lakatos ('Falsification...' cit. Introduction n. 11, 144) in the light of his methodology of scientific research programmes: 'From this point of view, Bohr's "correspondence principle" played an interesting double role in his programme. On the one hand it functioned as an important heuristic principle which suggested many new scientific hypotheses which, in turn, led to novel facts, especially in the field of the intensity of spectrum lines. On the other hand it functioned also as a defence mechanism, which "endeavoured to utilize to the utmost extent the concepts of the classical theories of mechanics and electrodynamics, in spite of the contrast between these theories and the quantum of action", instead of emphasizing the urgency of a unified programme. In this second role it reduced the degree of problematicality of the programme'.

CHAPTER 4
The theory of virtual oscillators

1

'At the present state of science it does not seem possible to avoid the formal character of the quantum theory which is shown by the fact that the interpretation of atomic phenomena does not involve a description of the mechanism of the discontinuous processes [...]. On the correspondence principle it seems nevertheless possible to [...] arrive at a consistent description of optical phenomena by connecting the discontinuous effects occurring in atoms with the continuous radiation field [...]'. This announced a turning point in atomic physics research; for the first time there were reasons to assert that discontinuity was not in itself incompatible with the theory's descriptive content, and rational solutions were provided that related a whole set of phenomena dependent on the radiation properties of matter to the continuous picture of the radiation field. This was the conclusion arrived at in a new paper by Bohr which took up and developed the hypothesis put forward by the American physicist John Slater that 'the atom, even before a process of transition between two stationary states takes place, is capable of communication with distant atoms through a virtual radiation field' was taken up and developed. The article, 'The Quantum Theory of Radiation', signed by Bohr, Kramers and Slater, was published in the *Philosophical Magazine* in January 1924[1].

Slater had arrived in Copenhagen at the end of the preceding year with the idea that his hypothesis might lead to very different theoretical results. Indeed, he intended to use it as a basis to resolve the 'difficulties about not knowing whether light is old fashioned waves or Mr. Einstein's light particles [...] or what. Well,' he wrote to his mother, 'this is one of the topics on which I perpetually puzzle my head'[2]. Slater was not the

111

only person to encounter such difficulties at the time. For some months the question of the nature of light had been arousing new interest and new vigour had been acquired by the hypothesis of the corpuscular constitution of radiation, which Einstein had introduced in 1905 but which for two decades most physicists had been reluctant to accept because of its obscurity of meaning. In 1922 Arthur Compton, while studying X-ray scattering, had discovered that the diffused part of radiation presented an increase in wavelength neither foreseen by nor explicable in terms of classical theory. He believed it to be a new quantum phenomena that could be explained by means of light quanta and the principles of conservation of energy and momentum[3]. Sommerfeld was the first person to tell Bohr of the effect Compton had discovered and to call his attention to the fact that it probably contained fundamental new information[4]. On a trip to the United States in the autumn of 1923, Bohr himself had witnessed the heated discussions on the theoretical implications of the discovery that were taking place among American physicists. In the course of the year new experiments had been performed which seemed to confirm Compton's point of view on the elastic collisions between light quanta and electrons and above all it appeared that the only way of salvaging the classical radiation theory would be to abandon the conservation laws in interactions between radiation and matter[5]. Despite this, Bohr held fast to the wave conception and, in referring to his encounter with Michelson at the American Physical Society meeting in Chicago, he described the attitude of the young physicists who supported Compton's ideas as 'simply horrifying for a man who spend[s] his life studying the most refined interference phenomena and for whom the wave theory is a creed'[6].

Now the framework for combining the wave and corpuscular theories had probably been found, and the result was due to none other than that John Slater whom Edwin Kemble had recommended to Bohr as 'the most promising student of physics we have had at Harvard University for many years'[7]. Slater's idea was that a classical mechanism was at work in the atom that could reconcile, in quantitative terms as well, the statistical character of quantum emission processes with the customary treatment of the electromagnetic field. He saw no valid alternative to the hypothesis of light quanta and it appeared equally evident to him that the quanta did not move solely along straight paths at the speed of light. Slater therefore imagined that on the one hand atoms continually produced electromagnetic fields not by the actual motion of electrons but by periodic motions of frequencies equal to those of the possible emission lines and, on the other, that fields of this sort determined the quanta's direction of motion. To illustrate the function of these hypothetical 'pilot waves' he said in a letter to Kramers that it was as if the light particles were drawn along by waves and for this reason followed non-rectilinear paths. In his view, this made it possible to understand how large numbers of quanta could fall on the illuminated areas that produce the fringes characteristic of interference phenomena[8]. The introduction of fields associated with the various stationary states suggested, furthermore, an entirely original probabilistic treatment of emission and transition processes. According to Slater, an atom in an excited state should be thought of in classical terms as a system that generates a spherical wave resulting from internal vibratory motions; for every oscillation frequency v therefore one could define – by means of the corresponding Poynting's vector s_v – the elementary energy flux crossing an infinitesimal surface ds in a time dt

$$(s_v \cdot ds)\, dt. \tag{4.1}$$

At this point Slater advanced the hypothesis that the ratio between (4.1) and the energy of quantum hv, integrated on a closed surface surrounding the atom, expressed the probability of emission of a quantum. This mechanism also explained the atom's passage from one stationary state to another: as long as the system is in a given state the fields determine, according to their amplitudes, the probability of a quantum being released by the atom for each of the possible frequencies of transition. Upon emission the process of radiation from the stationary state is interrupted and the atom immediately passes to another state giving birth to a new field. Between emission and absorption the quantum of energy followed a path perfectly defined at every point by the direction of the Poynting's vector of the wave associated with it. 'It should be noted that the only place where chance and discontinuity comes into the theory is in emission; once a quantum is emitted, the rest of the process is prescribed exactly as in the classical theory, and the existence of quantities describing the probabilities of certain processes is exactly similar to the existence of such quantities in the dynamic theory of gases [...] This leads to the hope that, when the dynamics of the inside of atoms are better known, chance may be eliminated there also'[9]. Bohr and Kramers were immediately interested in the scheme Slater proposed, even if what they saw in it was not only quite contrary to his intentions but something he could not even understand very clearly: 'I got started a couple of days after Christmas telling about this theory', he wrote on 2nd January, 'and that has got them decidedly excited. I think, of course, they don't agree with it all yet. But they do agree with a good deal, and have no particular arguments except their preconceived opinions against the rest of it, and seem prepared to give those up if they have to. So I think there are hopes'[10]. This was not at all the case; within a few weeks a new theory was worked out that left their differences of opinion unaltered, which can be gathered among other things from the letter Slater sent from the Copenhagen Institute for Theoretical Physics to *Nature* on 28th January. Slater did not intend it to publicize his dissent, but there is certainly nothing in his words showing acceptance of the criticisms he had received: 'The idea of the activity of the stationary states presented here suggested itself to me in the course of an attempt to combine the elements of the theories of electrodynamics and of light quanta by setting up a field to guide discrete quanta, which might move, for example, along the direction of Poynting's vector. But when the idea with that interpretation was described to Dr. Kramers, he pointed out that it scarcely suggested the definite coupling between emission and absorption processes which light quanta provided, but rather indicated a much greater independence between transition processes in distant atoms than I had perceived. The subject has been discussed at length with Prof. Bohr and Dr. Kramers, and a joint paper with them will shortly be published in the *Philosophical Magazine*, describing the picture more fully, and suggesting possible applications in the development of the quantum theory of radiation'[11]. The article appeared under the signature of the three authors, but Slater must have felt that his views were scarcely represented. Otherwise it would be difficult to understand why the introduction reiterates the fact that his hypothesis was originally intended to establish 'a harmony between the physical pictures of the electrodynamical theory of light and the theory of light quanta', or why he felt the need to specify in a letter to van Vleck that the article had been written entirely by Bohr and Kramers[12]. In any case, once Slater's idea had been reinterpreted in the light of the correspondence principle, there was very little left of the classical mechanism with which he had tried to solve the problem of the production and propagation of radiation. Slater spoke of his colleagues' preconceived opinions. In reality his scheme contained a serious logical inconsistency; and he was excessively optimistic in claiming that everything except emission took place in perfect accord with the classical point of view. Kramers' criticism concerned the presence of a theoretically unjustified asymmetry in the scheme: if the amplitudes of the fields associated with a stationary state determine the probabilities for the emission of a quantum and therefore of the transition to a different state, then something very similar should occur in transitions involving the absorption of a quantum. In any case, if the field acts on transitions solely by defining their probabilities, Kramers was right in pointing out to Slater that his proposal necessarily implied an independence of the transition processes in two distant atoms. It is in fact entirely arbitrary to affirm that the second atom must absorb the same quantum that the first atom emits. Slater had nothing to say in reply but was convinced both that further attempts should be made to re-establish harmony and that Bohr and Kramers were negatively influenced by their preconceived rejection of the corpuscular picture of radiation.

2

Michelson was one of the first Bohr informed about the progress made since his return to Copenhagen: 'It may perhaps interest you to hear that it appears to be possible for a believer in the essential reality of the quantum theory to take a view which may harmonize with the essential reality of the wave theory conception even more closely than the views I expressed during our conversation'[13]. While acknowledging Slater's merit in suggesting the fundamental idea, he was careful to point out in his letter that it was thanks to the correspondence principle that a connection had been established between the discontinuous processes occurring inside the atom and the continuous character of the radiation field. Bohr thus reiterated a concept already clearly expressed in the opening sentences of the article, and he did so on purpose. Contrary to what is often maintained in the literature, also on the basis of the views expressed by Slater at the time, and afterwards, the main cause of disagreement between the three authors was not whether light quanta existed or not but rather, the basic incompatibility between Slater's approach to the problem and Bohr's conviction that the concept of virtual field would facilitate an important generalization of the correspondence principle. While this will become clear in our analysis of the paper, there is also other evidence to justify such a claim. First, Kramer's initial criticisms were not at all directed, as we have seen, at the picture Slater had suggested for the propagation of radiation (waves drawing the light quanta along), but rather at the mechanism of radiation. Secondly, the use of the term 'virtual' to indicate the fields emitted by the oscillators associated with stationary states is not indisputably Slater's, since there is no trace of it in his writings prior to his arrival in Copenhagen. He speaks of 'virtual fields' in his letter to *Nature*, which however was written when the article was practically complete. In any case, we shall see that in light of Bohr's interpretation based on the correspondence principle, Slater's fields must be considered entirely real[14]. Thirdly, in Slater's scheme the correspondence principle plays an entirely marginal role and is taken up only to determine the amplitudes of the oscillations corresponding to the various emission frequencies. Its function, in any case, is certainly not that of linking the continuity of the field with the discontinuity of quantum processes. The reference Slater makes to statistical thermodynamics shows rather that he considered the probabilistic nature of the transitions to be a temporary characteristic of the theory due to incomplete knowledge of atomic processes and not an intrinsic element of quantum phenomena. Finally, the very brief observations contained in the article about the problem of light quanta do not seem to justify the thesis that it was the main point of disagreement between the three authors. There is nothing in it that Bohr had not already written; the question of 'pilot waves' is not even mentioned, and after the ritual recognition of the great heuristic value of Einstein's hypothesis the solution is quickly dismissed since 'the radiation "frequency" ν appearing in the theory is defined by experiments on interference phenomena which apparently demand for their interpretation a wave constitution of light'[15].

Bohr therefore presented the new quantum theory of radiation as a further development of the correspondence programme, with the purpose of establishing a continuity which was not just hypothetical: 'The present paper', it says towards the end of the introduction, 'may in various respects be considered as a supplement to the first part of a recent treatise by Bohr, dealing with the principles of the quantum theory, in which several of the problems dealt with here are treated more fully'[16]. The text respected this requirement even in its form; the discussion deals only with certain problems and lacks the completeness that Bohr usually gave to each new formulation of the theory. In any case, the new conceptions neither modified the substance of the results already attained, nor altered the theory's claim to a purely formal validity. Above all, they did not dispel doubts as to whether it would in fact ever be possible to provide a 'detailed interpretation of the interaction between matter and radiation [...] in terms of a causal description in space and time of the kind hitherto used for the interpretation of natural phenomena'[17]. In fact, the authors themselves stressed that the modifications the theory had made had achieved no real advance in the study of the properties of spectra: the relationship between the structure of the atom and the frequency, intensity and polarization of each line was still represented by the fundamental law of frequencies and by the considerations of correspondence regarding the periodic motions of stationary orbits. The importance of the new theory lay elsewhere: the hypotheses on which it rested led, though the interpretative content of its theoretical framework was still unsatisfactory, to the formation of 'a picture as regards the time-spatial occurrence of the various transition processes on which the observations of the optical phenomena ultimately depend'[18]. With respect to previous work, only limited progress had been made in the interpretation of observed radiation phenomena 'by connecting these phenomena with the stationary states and the transitions between them in a way somewhat different from that hitherto followed'. This had been possible, the article states, because 'the correspondence principle has led to comparing the reaction of an atom on a field of radiation with the reaction on such a field which, according to the classical theory of electrodynamics, should be expected from a set of "virtual" harmonic oscillators with frequencies equal to those for the various possible transitions between stationary states'[19]. The modes of comparison are defined by two new hypotheses suggested by a more general application of the principle: (1) 'a given atom in a certain stationary state will communicate continually with other atoms through a time-spatial mechanism which is virtually equivalent with the field of radiation which on the classical theory would originate from the virtual harmonic oscillators corresponding to the various possible transitions to other stationary states'; (2) 'the occurrence of transition processes for the given atom itself, as well as for the other atoms with which it is in mutual communication, is connected with this mechanism by probability laws which are analogous to those which in Einstein's theory hold for the induced transitions between stationary states when illuminated by radiation'[20]. These words sum up a decisive chapter in the history of atomic physics. Not so much because, as is generally recognized, the idea of associating a set of classical oscillators to the stationary states created, with Kramers' dispersion theory, the conditions that allowed Heisenberg to construct the mathematical formalism of the new mechanics[21]; but rather because the decided obscurity of the first hypothesis can represent a point of divergence for historical interpretations of Bohr's work, of the evolution of the Copenhagen school of thought, and of the debates that have followed in its wake. There is a tendency to consider this logical device as a desperate attempt of Bohr's to salvage a research programme he had built to defend the mechanical model of the atom and the classical conception of radiation[22]. If this were the case, the immediate empirical falsification of some of the theory's consequences would obviously force historians to reappraise the real impact that Bohr's programme had on the final elaboration of quantum mechanics and to be extremely wary of his tendency to present complementarity as the goal of the programme[23]. A reading of the text – the only reading that does not oblige us to accept gross paradoxes and gratuitous claims – proves, as we shall see, that the theory's main objective, the hypothesis Bohr wanted to test, has nothing whatever to do with the orbit model or with Maxwell waves. Interpretation of the paper will be facilitated if we first clearly distinguish its two levels of discourse, that concerning the description of the virtual model and that referring to the real physical situation of quantum systems, and then try to explain the 'virtual equivalence' Bohr established between them by means of the correspondence principle. The second hypothesis referred explicitly to the probabilistic considerations Einstein had used in 1917 to arrive at a new derivation of Planck's formula of heat radiation starting from the notion of quantum transition. Einstein's approach was based on the definition of the probability dW that in a time dt a transition would take place between the quantum states Z_m and Z_n of a molecule with energies ε_m and ε_n, with $\varepsilon_m > \varepsilon_n$. Using constants A and B, characteristic of the states in question, he introduced three different probabilities: the first pertained to the process of emission of radiation ($dW = A_m^n \, dt$); the second, to the absorption of a quantity of energy under the influence of a radiation field with density ρ and frequency v ($dW = B_n^m \, \rho \, dt$); the third regarded the probability that, in the presence of the same field, the atom would release a quantity of energy corresponding to the transition $m \to n$ ($dW = B_m^n \, \rho \, dt$). According to Einstein, therefore, there were two distinct emission processes, one which took place spontaneously when the system was in an excited state, and another which was induced by the presence of a radiation field of the suitable frequency[24]. Bohr simplified Slater's hypothesis by eliminating every reference to electromagnetic energy fluxes and light quanta, and took advantage of the analogy with Einstein's theory to give it a more general formulation: the probability of every transition process is determined by fields produced by the virtual oscillators. This also had immediate consequences for Einstein's hypotheses, since it appeared evident from Bohr's point of view that so-called spontaneous emissions, like all the others, were also transitions induced by virtual radiation fields. But the implications of this assumption were much more far-reaching: they undermined the rational foundations of the understanding of nature. In the virtual oscillator model, the interaction of radiation and matter is described on the basis of the activity of the virtual fields which establish communication between one atomic system and another. One has to imagine that in the model the quantum stationary states are replaced, on the basis of correspondence, by a system of charges oscillating at the transition frequencies allowed by the state, and that in general every field – generated according to classical laws by the oscillators – acts probabilistically in Einsteinian fashion on the transitions between states. It obviously follows that a process of transition will depend both on the virtual fields of its own oscillators which correspond to the initial state of the transition and on all the communicating fields of atoms. Furthermore, the occurrence of one transition does not influence the transitions taking place in the other atoms; in fact, during the entire process the atom does not emit any virtual fields. If this is true, we are forced to abandon 'any attempt at a causal connection between the transitions in distant atoms, and especially a direct application of the principles of conservation of energy and momentum, so characteristic for the classical theories'[25]. By means of its own virtual fields atom A can contribute to the occurrence of a transition in atom B, and then undergo an entirely different transition. This implies not only that the events are independent of each other, i.e. devoid of any causal connection, but above all the quantities of energy involved in the various transitions of the atoms are not in any case such as to satisfy the principle of the conservation of energy (analogous considerations can be applied to momentum). The observed validity of the conservation principles, the article concluded, cannot be anything but the result of a statistical average over a great number of individual events, for which these principles are not rigorously satisfied[26].

The model also described the interaction of radiation with matter as the result of the interference between virtual fields and incident electromagnetic waves. If the latter possess a frequency close to that of a virtual harmonic oscillator, depending on whether the real incident waves and the secondary waves produced by the oscillator are in phase or not, the electromagnetic radiation causes either an increase or a decrease in the intensity of the virtual radiation field and can therefore affect the probability that a transition corresponding to that oscillator will occur. This leads to a different explanation of absorption spectra: there is no reason to affirm that the line observed is the result of a transition process induced by incident radiation of the same frequency as that of the line. Its appearance on the spectroscope is due to a diminution in the intensity of the incident radiation resulting from the [classical] interaction with waves generated by a virtual oscillator, whereas 'the induced transitions appear only as an accompanying effect [of the process] by which a statistical conservation of energy is ensured'[27]. The model therefore implied a violation of the conservation laws and challenged the concept of causality. But, the article concluded, this seems to be 'the only consistent way of describing the interaction between radiation and atoms by a theory involving probability considerations'[28]. If for the time being we set aside certain not immediately intelligible questions, such as the presumed interaction of virtual and real objects, few rational arguments remain for rejecting such a statement. The virtual model is based on the hypothesis that transition or, to use language more appropriate to the model itself, the passage from one system of oscillators to another is a probabilistic process, and furthermore that it is the fields generated by the oscillators that determine the probabilities. Thus, given these premises, there is no doubt that the model does, in fact, provide a space-time description of the interaction of radiation with matter. The argument, however, plunges into the depths of obscurity if the model is viewed as the result of an attempt to represent the real physical situation of atomic processes and systems coherently. In this case, not only do all the logical anomalies connected with virtual entities emerge, but we must do violence to our imagination, since we are forced for each particular problem considered to associate the stationary states either with periodic systems of orbiting electrons or with hypothetical systems of oscillating charges. Fortunately this is not the task Bohr intended to assign to the virtual model through the principle of correspondence. What in fact exists between atom and model is a virtual equivalence and not a real correspondence. The theoretical terms appearing in the description of the model do not identify elements of reality. The latter can be defined solely within the conceptual framework of stationary states and transitions. There is an abyss between this and Slater's position. Slater holds that the fields produced by oscillators are real objects that draw energy particles through space. For Bohr, the model is a purely logical tool, a theoretical fiction which, though constructed within a conceptual framework irreducible to the quantum-theoretical, can nevertheless enable us to explore certain aspects of the reality of atoms. In particular, Bohr asks himself in this paper what the general physical and theoretical consequences would be if a real space-time mechanism existed that enabled atoms to communicate with one another. The fact that Bohr uses a vague and undefined term such as 'communication' – instead of simply saying that the mechanism is precisely an electromagnetic field of the classical type – is not accidental, and shows the superficiality of interpretations that reduce the whole history of those years to a conflict between the wave and corpuscular theories. The choice is a perfectly consistent one and is even entailed for Bohr by his having admitted the existence of two distinct and incompatible levels of interpretation. On the one hand, there is quantum theory, which tackles the problem of the constitution of atoms and of radiation processes with a language suggested by acquired empirical knowledge, whose vocabulary is, however, extremely poor and still only approximate (e.g. it includes the undefined terms 'stationary state', 'transition', and 'communication mechanisms'). On the other hand, there is classical theory, which possesses a vast store of knowledge expressed in a rigorous and highly formalized language but which cannot account for the world of micro-objects. The only thing to do, according to Bohr, is to use this second level systematically in order to gain as much information from it as possible and thereby endow quantum theory with new interpretative and conceptual tools.

The only elements in the theory of virtual oscillators to imply the correspondence relation are the probabilistic character of all processes that imply discontinuous variations and the existence of a continuous mechanism of space-time type ensuring the transfer of information between spatially separate physical systems. These are the conceptual constants that make the analogy between atom and model possible. In Bohr's scheme of thought, for the model to fulfil its heuristic function it has no importance whether the stationary states can be described as virtual oscillators or not, or whether virtual fields exist or not in reality. This is explicitly stated in his paper when stress is laid on the formal character of the analogy between quantum theory and classical theory, which Bohr believes to be most clearly illustrated 'by the fact that on the quantum theory the absorption and emission of radiation are coupled to different processes of transition, and thereby to different virtual oscillators'[29]. In other words, only by renouncing a literal interpretation of the model, can one understand why quantum transitions do not appear in it; only in this way does it come as no surprise that virtual fields can interact with real ones. In order for the model to fulfil the logical and analogical function for which it was constructed it is, on the contrary, necessary to assume that some implications of its classical treatment be also true for terms corresponding to the concepts of virtual oscillator and virtual field and that these may therefore be transferred to the first term of the analogy, that is, that they hold for quantum theory. Only in this way can one conclude that, if a mechanism existed in reality corresponding to an electromagnetic field – if it were possible, that is, to provide a space-time description of the interaction between matter and radiation – then the virtual oscillator model and the correspondence principle would prove, even in the absence of any knowledge of the mechanism, that the laws of conservation must be violated and that it is necessary to impose severe restrictions on the use of the category of causality. And this is a scientific assertion that Bohr maintains has a precise falsifiable content[30].

In September 1922 the Danish philosopher Harald Høffding had written to Bohr asking him to clarify the meaning of the various expressions he had often used in his writings to indicate an analogy between the constitution of atoms and physical and chemical data. 'The situation which you emphasize concerning the role of analogy in scientific investigations', Bohr replied, 'is no doubt an essential feature of all studies in the natural sciences, although it does not always manifest itself clearly. It is probably often possible to apply a picture of a geometrical or arithmetical nature which covers the problem dealt with, to the extent discussed in a manner so clear that the consideration just about obtains a logical character. However, one must in general and especially in new fields of work incessantly keep in mind the apparent or possible inadequacy of the picture and be satisfied so long as the analogy is so manifest that the utility or rather fertility of the picture to the extent that it is used, is beyond doubt. This is the kind of situation that we are in, especially at the present stage of the atomic theory. We are here in the peculiar situation that we have fought our way to certain pieces of information concerning the structure of the atom, which must be considered as just as valid as any other facts in natural sciences. On the other hand we meet with difficulties of such a deep-set nature that we have no idea how to solve them; my personal viewpoint is that these difficulties are of a kind that probably do not permit us to hope to accomplish a spatial and temporal description of a kind corresponding to our usual sense-impressions. Under these circumstances one must of course continuously have in mind that we employ analogies, and the caution with which the fields of application of these analogies are demarcated in each single case is of decisive importance for progress'[31]. An eye alert to the possible inadequacy of pictures, a scrupulous control of the productivity of analogies, and constant care in circumscribing their field of application are therefore methodological precepts to which Bohr assigned a dominant role in the progress of knowledge, especially when entirely new fields of research are being charted. He had rigorously abided by them in the construction of the virtual oscillator model. But this is not enough. In the letter – written about a year before the discovery of the new theory of radiation processes – he explicitly set down the conviction he had drawn from his search for a consistent framework of interpretation and especially from the repeated failure of his efforts, upon which he based the hypothesis that the difficulties he was encountering derived from the incompatibility of quantum phenomena with the classical model of description. And this was the hypothesis he tried to test as soon as he saw in Slater's idea the theoretical tool that would enable him to do so. Thanks to the theory of virtual oscillators, the correspondence programme fully achieved its objective of relating the statistical laws of quantum processes to a space-time description. But, as Bohr emphasized in 1927, the programme ineluctably led to the violation of the conservation principles. The concepts of virtual oscillator and virtual field, furthermore, showed that the true meaning of correspondence was that which Bohr would give it on the eve of the Como conference: a relation capable of correlating statistical laws and space-time pictures.

3

The first to read the article was Pauli. On 16th February Bohr informed his young pupil that he was sending him the German translation of the new work, and asked him for suggestions to improve the exposition. However, he urged Pauli to 'look with favour if at all possible upon the words "communicate" and "virtual", for, after lengthy consideration, we have agreed here on these basic pillars of the exposition'[32]. Even before reading the article, Pauli replied: 'I laughed a little (you will certainly forgive me for that) about your warm recommendation of the words "communicate" and "virtual". [...] On the basis of [my] knowledge of these two words [...] I have tried to guess what your paper may deal with. But I have not succeeded'[33]. Pauli did not imagine that in addition to the linguistic details, which Bohr had always said made him feel somewhat awkward, those words concealed theoretical conceptions he would dissent with entirely. In the following months he would be far more critical of Bohr than Heisenberg, who had also initially expressed serious doubts as to whether any essential progress had been made[34]. As might have been foreseen, the sharpest reaction came from Einstein, who had been told by Haber of a discussion he had had with Bohr in Copenhagen during which Bohr had expressed himself 'with a mixture of admiration for and disapproval of your theory of light quanta'. Haber's impression was that Bohr 'strives with all fibres back to the classical world [...]; he no longer believes that radiation accompanies the transition, but that the transition merely terminates the period of radiation that begins with the excitation of the atom'[35]. As soon as he found out what the article contained, Einstein wrote to Max Born: 'Bohr's opinion about radiation is of great interest. But I should not want to be forced into abandoning strict causality without defending it more strongly than I have so far. I find the idea quite intolerable that an electron exposed to radiation should choose of *its own free will*, not only its moment to jump off, but also its direction. In that case, I would rather be a cobbler or even an employee in a gaming-house, than a physicist'[36]. On 31st May, while telling Ehrenfest of the lecture in which he had publicly discussed the theory of Bohr, Kramers and Slater, he expressed the reasons for his disagreement in more measured terms, saying that he could not understand why – if *Nature* seemed to adhere strictly to the conservation laws (as had been shown, for example, by Franck and Hertz's experiment) – atoms acting upon each other at a distance should be an exception. Furthermore, for aesthetic reasons he could not agree with the hypothesis that one virtual radiation field does not result in another virtual radiation but rather in the probability of a transition[37]. Some points must have appeared insuffi-ciently clear even to the minority of physicists who expressed appreci-ation and in some cases enthusiasm for the new theory. Oskar Klein, who had worked in Bohr's Institute in 1922, informed Bohr of the reaction of the American physicists and asked for confirmation that he had properly understood the notion of virtual radiation, which he saw as being closely tied up with problems of observability: 'I suggested that you use this expression because such a radiation field can only be investigated with the aid of transition processes governed by probability laws, so that one cannot at all define such concepts as force and energy for the field'[38]. The idea must have appeared just as obscure to Schrödinger, for after having declared his appreciation of Bohr's work as an important return to classical theory, he admitted that he was unable to understand the reference to radiation as 'virtual'. 'Which is then the "real" radiation', he added, 'if not that which "causes" the transitions, *i.e.*, creates the transition probabilities?' According to Schrödinger, only from a philo-sophical point of view was it possible to satisfy his own curiosity to know 'which of the two electron systems has the greater reality – the "real" which describes the stationary orbits or the "virtual" which emits the virtual radiation and scatters the incident virtual radiation'[39]. However, not even on the scientifically less compromising terrain of philosophy was Schrödinger's curiosity legitimate. In fact, within the idea of correspondence, the very system of electrons describing stationary orbits would have to be, for Bohr, only a virtual one. Perhaps the only person who managed to follow what Bohr had in mind was Born who, after having heard Heisenberg give a brief description of the work, immediately wrote to him: 'I am quite convinced that your new theory hits the truth, also that it is in a certain sense the last word that can be said about these questions: it is the rational extension of the classical conceptions about radiation to discontinuous elementary processes'[40]. Pauli remained instead a steadfast opponent of the theory, even though – in the absence of sufficient experimental results for expressing a definitive judgement – he confessed to basing himself 'only on intuitive arguments': 'At that time we discussed at length [with other physicists] many physical problems and especially the interpretation of radiation phenomena presented in the paper by you, Kramers and Slater. By your arguments you succeed for now in silencing my scientific conscience, which revolts strongly against this interpretation'; but in the end he recognized that 'if you should ask me what I believe about statistical dependence or independence of quantum processes in spatially distant atoms, I would honestly have to answer: I don't know'[41]. Bohr soothed Pauli's qualms of conscience and strenuously defended the validity of his programme: 'I ought perhaps also to have a bad conscience with respect to the radiation problems; but even if, from a logical point of view, it is perhaps a crime, I must confess that I am nevertheless convinced that the swindle of mixing the classical theory and the quantum theory will in many ways still show itself to be fruitful in tracking the secrets of nature'[42].

4

'I was recently in Berlin; everyone there spoke of the result of the Geiger–Bothe experiment which has apparently turned out in favour of light quanta. Einstein was triumphant'[43], wrote Born to Bohr at the beginning of 1925. The experimental falsification of the independence of transition processes in separate atoms interacting through radiation was interpreted in scientific circles at the time as a corroboration of the 'photon' hypothesis, as it still is today in most historical reconstructions. The reaffirmed validity of the conservation principles was thus seen as having crushed Bohr's programme under indisputable experimental proof. Bohr himself, for that matter, could only admit defeat, and in the postscript to a letter dated 21st April 1925, he declared to Fowler: 'At this very moment I have received a letter from Geiger, in which he says, that his experiment has given strong evidence for the existence of a coupling in the case of the Compton-effect. It seems therefore, that there is nothing else to do than to give our revolutionary efforts as honorable a funeral as possible'[44]. But immediately afterwards he hastened to reply to Geiger, making surprising remarks on the consequences of his experiment, and displaying an attitude that was hardly that of an impotent witness to the failure of years of research: 'I was quite prepared to learn that our proposed point of view about the independence of the quantum process in separated atoms would turn out to be wrong. The whole matter was more an expression of an endeavour to attain the greatest possible applicability of the classical concepts than a completed theory'[45]. Though experimental evidence had refuted the results of the correspondence programme, it nevertheless merited the greatest respect because by then it had already positively and constructively achieved its purpose. Despite, or rather because of, its falsification, the Bohr–Kramers–Slater theory provided clear signposts for the future construction of quantum theory. The conclusions reached contained, in Bohr's eyes, far more than a mere pronouncement in support of the reality of quanta. 'In general', Bohr concluded in his letter to Geiger, 'I believe that these difficulties exclude the retention of the ordinary space-time description of phenomena to such an extent that, in spite of the existence of coupling, conclusions about a possible corpuscular nature of radiation lack a sufficient basis'[46]. Bohr was probably the only one to interpret the results of these experiments in such a light. Evidently, in his view, the falsifiable content of the theory of virtual oscillators involved precisely the classical model of description. In any case, if further proof is needed, one has only to read what Bohr wrote to Heisenberg three days prior to his letter to Geiger when news of the result was already spreading and coupling was beginning to be seen as the answer to other questions (such as the explanation of collision phenomena): 'In spite of all obscurity, at the moment things are probably relatively much better with the secrets of the atoms than with the general description of the space-time occurrence of quantum processes. Stimulated especially by talks with Pauli, I am forcing myself these days with all my strength to familiarize myself with the mysticism of nature and I am attempting to prepare myself for all eventualities, indeed even for the assumption of a coupling of quantum processes in separated atoms. However, the costs of this assumption are so great that they cannot be estimated within the ordinary space-time description'[47]. The article by Bohr, Kramers and Slater was an attempt, the most consistent and successful one in the context of the correspondence principle, to 'develop a description of optical phenomena in line with the quantum theory of spectra'[48]. The abandonment of both the coupling of individual transition processes (violation of causality) and the rigorous validity of the conservation laws was the direct result of the last-ditch attempt to give a visualizable representation of quantum processes. It was only from a limited theoretical viewpoint that the experimental test to ascertain either the coupling or the independence of observable atomic processes could be reduced to nature's verdict on the conflict between two conceptions of light propagation in empty space[49]. The test concerned a far more general and much more crucial problem for the future of quantum theory and would have been positive in any case, independently of the specific answer it provided. The problem, in fact, concerned the extent to which 'the space-time pictures, by means of which the description of natural phenomena has hitherto been attempted, are applicable to atomic processes'[50]. According to Bohr, the result of the experiment ruled out 'the possibility of a simple description of the physical events in terms of intuitive pictures'. 'Of course', he added in a letter to Born, 'this is in the first place a purely negative statement, but I feel, especially if the coupling should really be a fact, that we must take recourse to symbolic analogies to a still higher degree than before. Just lately I have been racking my brains trying to imagine such analogies'[51]. The correspondence principle made it possible to ask nature a precise question and to receive a precise answer regarding the limits the classical model of description encountered when trying to explain the physical behaviour of micro-objects. And the answer meant that 'one must be prepared to find that the generalization of the classical electrodynamic theory [i.e. the future quantum theory] that we are striving for will require a fundamental revolution in the concepts upon which the description of nature has been based until now'[52]. This is what Bohr wrote in 1925, even before Heisenberg published his matrix mechanics.

Notes

1 N. Bohr, H. A. Kramers and J. C. Slater, 'The Quantum Theory of Radiation', *Philosophical Magazine* **47** (1924), 785–802: 785–86; *CW5*, 101–18: 101–2; also in B. L. van der Waerden, ed., *Sources of Quantum Mechanics*, Amsterdam: North-Holland, 1967, 159–76; the German version of the article, 'Über die Quantentheorie der Strahlung', appeared in *Zeitschrift für Physik* **24** (1924), 69–87.
2 Slater to his mother, 8 November 1923, cit. in K. Stolzenburg, 'Introduction to Part I', *CW5*, 1–96:7.

3 The first results of Compton's research were reported in the 13 December 1922, article, 'A Quantum Theory of the Scattering of X-Rays by Light Elements', *Physical Review* **21** (1923), 483–502. Compton's explicit declaration in favour of the light quanta as a means of interpreting his discovery is in A. H. Compton, 'The Scattering of X-Rays', *Journal of the Franklin Institute* **198** (1924), 54–72, which is based on the text of the lecture he gave at the American Physical Society meeting in Cincinnati. See K. Stolzenburg, 'Introduction...' cit. n. 2, 3–6. For the secondary literature, see R. H. Stuewer, *The Compton Effect. Turning Point in Physics*, New York: Science History Publications, 1975, especially chs. 6–7.

4 Sommerfeld visited the United States in the winter of 1923, and on the 21st of January he wrote to Bohr saying that 'the most scientifically interesting thing I discovered in America is a paper by Arthur Compton from St. Louis' (*CW5*, 502–4).

5 In this regard, the following works should be mentioned: W. Bothe, 'Über eine neue Sekundärstrahlung der Röntgenstrahlen, I Mitteilung', *Zeitschrift für Physik* **16** (1923), 319–20; 'II Mitteilung', *Zeitschrift für Physik* **20** (1923), 237–55; and C. T. R. Wilson, 'Investigations on X-Rays and β-Rays, *Proceedings of the Royal Society of London* **A104** (1923), 1–24; 192–212.

6 Bohr to Rutherford, 9 January 1924, *CW5*, 486–87.

7 Kemble to Bohr, 21 March 1923, *CW5*, 381.

8 Slater to Kramers, 8 December 1923, *CW5*, 492–93. Slater's position can be reconstructed not only from the text of this letter, but also from other, unpublished documents dated 1st and 4th November, which are available at the Niels Bohr Library of the American Institute of Physics, cit. in K. Stolzenburg, 'Introduction...' cit. n. 2, 7–8. Analogous attempts to utilize the conceptions of wave theory to explain certain properties of light quanta were being made at the time by other physicists, and especially by Louis de Broglie ('Ondes et quanta', *Comptes Rendus de l'Académie des Sciences* **127** (1923), 507–10; 'A Tentative Theory of Light Quanta', *Philosophical Magazine* **47** (1924), 446–58). On several occasions, however, Slater denied having heard about de Broglie's work during his stay in Cambridge, from Fowler; see J. Hendry, 'Bohr–Kramers–Slater: A Virtual Theory of Virtual Oscillators and Its Role in the History of Quantum Mechanics', *Centaurus* **25** (1981), 189–221.

9 Ms. of 4 November, cit. n. 8.

10 Slater to his parents, 2 January 1924, cit. in K. Stolzenburg, 'Introduction...' cit. n. 2, 9.

11 J. C. Slater, 'Radiation and Atoms', *Nature* **113** (1924), 307.

12 Slater to van Vleck, 27 July 1924, cit. in K. Stolzenburg, 'Introduction...' cit. n. 2, 20. Various autobiographical writings – in particular Slater's interview (3 and 8 October 1963) in *SHQP* – contain some interesting details on the subject: for example, the letter published in *Nature* was the third version of a text he had rewritten at Bohr and Kramers' repeated insistence; the inclusion of his name among the signatories of the article was a courtesy done to him as a foreign guest; and Slater left Copenhagen sooner than had been originally planned. See also J. C. Slater, *The Development of Quantum Mechanics in the Period 1924–26*, Report No. 297 (28 July 1972) Quantum Theory Project for Research in Atomic, Molecular and Solid-State Chemistry and Physics, University of Florida, Gainesville,

Florida; *Solid-State and Molecular Theory: A Scientific Biography*, New York: John Wiley and Sons, 1975.

13 Bohr to Michelson, 7 February 1924, *CW5*, 404–5.
14 For this reason especially one can trust Slater when he recalled many years later that 'as soon as I discussed [my ideas] with Bohr and Kramers, I found that they were enthusiastic about the idea of electromagnetic waves being emitted by the oscillators whilst in the stationary states – they immediately came up with the name 'virtual oscillator''; he had immediately added, however: 'but to my surprise I discovered that they entirely refused to admit that photons really existed. It had not occurred to me that they might have objected to what seemed such an obvious deduction from many kinds of experiment' (J. C. Slater, *Solid-State* ... cit. n. 12).
15 N. Bohr, H. A. Kramers and J. C. Slater, 'The Quantum Theory...' cit. n. 1, 787; *CW5*, 103.
16 Ibid., 786; *CW5*, 103. The reference is to the November, 1922, article, 'On the Application of the Quantum Theory to Atomic Structure', see above, ch. 3 n. 20. The initials 'P.Q.T.' were used nine times to refer to various parts of the treatise.
17 N. Bohr, H. A. Kramers and J. C. Slater, 'The Quantum Theory...' cit. n. 1, 790; *CW5*, 106.
18 Ibid., 791; *CW5*, 107.
19 Ibid., 789–90; *CW5*, 105–6. The article at this point mentions that 'such a picture has been used by Ladenburg in an attempt to connect the experimental results on dispersion quantitatively with considerations on the probability of transitions between stationary states'; and, almost as if to qualify Slater's contribution, direct reference is made to section 3 of Bohr's 1922 paper: 'Thus it seems necessary, in order to account for the phenomena of reflection and dispersion, to assume that an atom reacts on the field of radiation just as a system of electrified particles in the classical theory – in other words, that the atom forms the starting point for a secondary wave-train which stands in a coherent phase-relation with the original field of radiation'. It is basically the same hypothesis which, thanks to the correspondence principle, had enabled Bohr to reformulate the second postulate of quantum theory at the conference held in Liverpool in September, 1923 (see above, ch. 3, section 2). Bohr arrived at this conclusion, however, in a different way, in light of the 'paradoxical contrast [existing] between the classical theory of dispersion and the postulates of the quantum theory [...]. On the one hand, as is well known, the phenomena of dispersion in gases show that the process of dispersion can be described on the basis of a comparison with a system of harmonic oscillators, according to the classical electron theory, with very close approximation if the characteristic frequencies of these oscillators are just equal to the frequencies of the lines of the observed absorption spectrum of the corresponding gas. On the other hand, the frequencies of these absorption lines, according to the postulates of the quantum theory, are not connected in any simple way with the motion of the electrons in the normal state of the atom [...]. According to the form of the quantum theory presented in this work, the phenomena of dispersion must thus be so conceived that the reaction of the atom on being subjected to radiation is closely connected with the unknown mechanism which is answerable for the emission of the radiation on the transition between stationary states' ('On

the Application...' cit. ch. 3 n. 10, 38–39; *CW3*, 495–96). The problem of the interpretation of the phenomenon of dispersion will be analysed in ch. 5; it is worth emphasizing, however – and many authors in fact do – that the formulation of the virtual oscillator model was undoubtedly affected by the perspectives that had been opened by the study of this phenomenon, as is also evidenced by the explicit reference made to it in the article and by the fact that Kramers was actively involved with the problem at the time.

20 N. Bohr, H. A. Kramers and J. C. Slater, 'The Quantum Theory...' cit. n. 1, 780–91; *CW5*, 106–7.

21 See below, ch. 5.

22 A. I. Miller ('Visualization Lost ...' cit. ch. I n. 12, 83–84), for example, states: 'Thus, in order to maintain the wave concept of radiation Bohr was willing to pay a high price – namely, relinquishing the picture of an electron as a localized quantity. This was a desperate time for Bohr because he could very well have believed that the hypothesis of the virtual oscillators was the last gasp of his programme for a description of the interaction of light with matter that was macroscopically continuous. He as much as admits that this is a physics of desperation [...]'.

23 The impression that this report is obscure and represents Bohr's last attempt to salvage a model representation of the atom is expressed, with varying degrees of emphasis, in most of the history and philosophy of science papers which mention it; I. Lakatos ('Falsification...' cit. Introduction n. 11, section 3.c.2, 140–54), in particular, sees in the results of this report also the beginning of the regressive phase of Bohr's programme.

24 A. Einstein, 'Zur Quantentheorie der Strahlung', *Physikalische Zeitschrift* **18** (1917), 121–28; also in B. L. van der Waerden, ed., *Sources...* cit. n. 1, 63–77; the article is dated 3 March 1917.

25 N. Bohr, H. A. Kramers and J. C. Slater, 'The Quantum Theory...' cit. n. 1, 791; *CW5*, 107.

26 'Besides Slater's conception of a virtual radiation field, the paper by Bohr, Kramers and Slater assumed that the laws of conservation of energy and momentum have only statistical validity. This assumption was probably introduced by Bohr, while the abolition of a causal connection between emission and absorption processes in distant atoms may have been due to Kramers'. This opinion, contained in Stolzenburg's very well-documented and rigorous introduction to *CW5* (cit. n. 2, 13) is, in my opinion, highly ambiguous, and might even be misleading in the interpretation of the paper. Aside from the restated attribution to Slater of the idea of 'virtual field' (see above), Stolzenburg leads one to believe that the abandoning of the principles of conservation and of causality in the theory are hypotheses on the same level as Slater's. As we have seen, the latter are instead necessary consequences of the virtual oscillator model and of the existence of discontinuous processes governed by probabilistic laws. On the other hand, in support of his interpretation, in section 3 ('Doubts About the Validity of the Law of Conservation of Energy', ibid., 13–19) Stolzenburg reconstructs a parallel history of those years in which it appears that the problem of the validity of the law of conservation of energy had been on Bohr's mind at least since 1919. The documents reproduced are of very great interest, especially because they prove that some of the results attained in the winter of 1924 were working hypotheses which had been entertained for some time as elements of possible solutions to the problems encountered in the construction of quantum theory. In a manuscript from

those years, for example, Bohr notes that: 'It would seem that any theory capable of an explanation of the photoelectric effect as well as the interference phenomena must involve a departure from the ordinary theorem of conservation of energy as regards the interaction between radiation and matter' (ibid., 15). He was prompted to take up the problem again by a paper ('A Critique of the Foundation of Physics') in which the English physicist Charles Galton Darwin came to the same conclusions (Darwin's 1919 ms. and Bohr's comments are in ibid., 13–16). Ideas of the sort, however, had not only been expressed in private conversations and correspondence; Bohr had mentioned this possible viewpoint in the paper he sent to the Solvay Conference in 1921, which states: '[...] at the present state of the theory we do not possess any means of describing in detail the process of direct transition between two stationary states accompanied by an emission or absorption of radiation and cannot be sure beforehand that such a description will be possible at all by means of laws consistent with the application of the principle of conservation of energy' ('On the Application...' cit. ch. 3 n. 10, 372). The fact that there were doubts on the matter does not imply, however, that the 1924 quantum theory of radiation was the direct result of a conviction that ripened over the years and was finally assumed as the foundation of a new interpretative scheme.

27 N. Bohr, H. A. Kramers and J. C. Slater, 'The Quantum Theory...' cit. n. 1, 798; *CW5*, 114.

28 Ibid., 792–93; *CW5*, 108–9.

29 Ibid., 797; *CW5*, 113.

30 Hendry's and Miller's studies, for all their considerable differences, come to conclusions which illustrate in equally meaningful ways the interpretation that has been commonly given by historians of science, which tends to emphasize above all the arbitrariness of the project on which the theory of virtual oscillators was based, and the obscurity of the model through which the project expressed itself. Hendry maintains that the origins of Bohr's theory should be sought mainly in the positions he developed at the start of the 1920s: on the one hand, 'although he had been the first to suggest that quantum phenomena would entail a radical revision of the classical conceptions, Bohr was convinced that these conceptions were the only ones through which an intuitive picture of physical processes could be attained'; on the other, 'his pessimism as to the possibility of an intuitive description in any new conceptual framework led him to concentrate on the attainment of such a description, albeit necessarily incomplete, in the old framework'. He thus came to believe that 'both causality and conservation could be seen as restrictions on the classical theory, the removal of which might well widen the scope for the provision of an intuitive description'. In Hendry's opinion, 'the virtual oscillator theory entailed no more than a very slight, but crucial, development of Bohr's position. Departing from his somewhat ambivalent attitude to the problem of an intuitive picture he decided that such a picture was essential, and that it would be possible if and only if causality and conservation were abandoned and the oscillator representation of the atom, previously no more than a heuristic device, were reinterpreted as a physically meaningful model'. The result of such a choice was always, according to Hendry, implicitly vague; 'he described the oscillators as having a "virtual" existence – a characteristic that was at best ambiguous and at worst quite meaningless – and he did not commit himself as to the relationship between the new oscillator model and the old orbital

one, the validity of which he appeared to uphold. Even the rejection of causality, for which the paper is perhaps most famous, was left open to interpretation as a temporary measure. [...] But there can be little doubt, especially in view of his later reaction to its refutation, that Bohr took the new model of interpretation seriously, and that he saw his decision to concentrate on an intuitive description in terms of the classical wave conceptions as both fundamental and necessary' (J. Hendry, 'Bohr–Kramers–Slater...' cit. n. 8, 196 ff.). In regard to the virtual oscillator model, Miller ('Visualization Lost...' cit. ch. 1 n. 12, 83) emphasizes another contradiction resulting from the use of the new model, the fact, that is, that in speaking of pictures (*Bild*) Bohr radically modified the meaning he had given the notion in his previous writings, in which 'it was meant as visualization. Indeed', Miller notes, 'one cannot visualize the planetary electron in a stationary state in the hydrogen atom represented by as many oscillators as there are transitions from this state. The set of virtual oscillators replacing the image of the planetary electron in a stationary state continually emits a virtual radiation field transporting only the probability for an electron to make a transition': it was, as we said, the physics of despair of a physicist who meant to save the visualizable content of the theory. Having established the external motivations leading to such a bizarre solution, and how – to use one of Hendry's expressions – 'a master of caution, Bohr, [could] come to adopt such an ill-fated conceit', Hendry and Miller, together with many other historians of science, do not even attempt any reconstruction of the contents of the theory.

31 Høffding to Bohr, 20 September 1922, and Bohr's reply, 22 September 1922, are cited in D. Favrholdt, 'Niels Bohr...' cit. ch. 3 n. 35, 212–13.

32 Bohr to Pauli, 16 February 1924, *CW5*, 408–9; English trans., 409–10; *WB*, 146.

33 Pauli to Bohr, 21 February 1924, *CW5*, 410–12; English trans., 412–14; *WB*, 147–49.

34 See Heisenberg's letter to Pauli, 4 March 1924, cit. in K. Stolzenburg, 'Introduction...' cit. n. 2, 26.

35 Haber to Einstein, no date, probably from the beginning of 1924, cit. in K. Stolzenburg, 'Introduction...' cit. n. 2, 23.

36 Einstein to Born, 29 April 1924, in M. Born, ed., *The Born–Einstein...* cit Introduction n. 1.

37 Einstein to Ehrenfest, 31 May 1924, cit. in K. Stolzenburg, 'Introduction...' cit. n. 2, 26–27.

38 Klein to Bohr, 30 May 1924, *CW5*, 386–87 (in Danish); English trans., 388–89.

39 Schrödinger to Bohr, 24 May 1924, *CW5*, 490–92; English trans., 29–30.

40 Born to Bohr, 16 April 1924, *CW5*, 299; English trans., 24.

41 Pauli to Bohr, 2 October 1924, *CW5*, 414–18; English trans., 418–21; *WB*, 163–66. In this letter from Hamburg, Pauli told Bohr of his conversations with Einstein, whom he had met in September in Innsbruck, where the 88. Versammlung der Gesellschaft Deutscher Naturforscher und Ärzte had been held. Pauli summed up Einstein's main objections to the article in four points.

42 Bohr to Pauli, 11 December 1924, *CW5*, 421–22; English trans., 34–35; *WB*, 184–85.

43 Born to Bohr, 15 January 1925, *CW5*, 302–4; English trans. of passages from the letter, 76. Attempts to verify the predictions of the Bohr–

Kramers–Slater theory experimentally were begun immediately after the article appeared, and already by June Bothe and Geiger had published a note ('Ein Weg zur experimentellen Nachprüfung der Theorie von Bohr, Kramers und Slater', *Zeitschrift für Physik* **26** (1924), 44) in which their project was explained. It consisted in performing more accurate measurements of the Compton effect and seeing whether a quantum of diffused radiation appeared simultaneously with the corresponding recoil electron, as foreseen by the corpuscular theory. If this did not occur the hypothesis of the violation of conservation laws in individual processes would be confirmed. Despite the great interest with which this attempt was followed, they managed to obtain some results only in the spring of the following year. Though they were not altogether favourable to quanta, the results clearly disagreed with the interpretation of the Compton effect via the virtual oscillator model (W. Bothe and H. Geiger, 'Experimentelles zur Theorie von Bohr, Kramers und Slater', *Die Naturwissenschaften* **13** (1925), 440–41; 'Über das Wesen des Comptoneffekts; ein experimentelles Beitrag zur Theorie der Strahlung', *Zeitschrift für Physik* **32** (1925), 639–63). In the same period Compton and Alfred Simon obtained analogous results while studying the 'kinematics' of the Compton effect in a cloud chamber: A. H. Compton, 'On the Mechanism of X-Ray Scattering', *Proceedings of the National Academy of Science USA* **11** (1925), 303–6; A. H. Compton and A. W. Simon, 'Directed Quanta of Scattered X-Rays', *Physical Review* **26** (1925), 289–99. For an in-depth discussion of the measurement methods and characteristics of the experimental devices that were utilized, see also: R. H. Stuewer, *The Compton Effect...* cit. n. 3, especially p. 237 ff.

44 Bohr to Fowler, 21 April 1925, cit. in K. Stolzenburg, 'Introduction...' cit. n. 2, 81–83.

45 Bohr to Geiger, 21 April 1925, *CW5*, 353–54; English trans., 79.

46 Ibid.

47 Bohr to Heisenberg, 18 April 1925, *CW5*, 360; English trans., 361.

48 'Addendum' of July 1925 added to the proofs of an article sent to the review *Zeitschrift für Physik* on 30 March. Though the article on the behaviour of atoms during collisions contained a viewpoint which was by then obsolete in light of the new results, Bohr decided to publish it anyway; he added a note, however, in which, for the first time, he took an official stance on the meaning of the falsification of the virtual oscillators ('Über die Wirkung von Atomen bei Stössen', *Zeitschrift für Physik* **34** (1925), 178–90; 'Nachschrift '(Juli 1925), 190–93: 190; text and English trans. in *CW5*, 178–93; 194–206).

49 'The renunciation of the strict validity of the conservation laws, and consequently of a coupling between the individual transition processes, was occasioned by the fact that no space-time mechanism seemed conceivable that permitted such a coupling and at the same time achieved a sufficient connection with classical electrodynamics [...]. In this connection it must be emphasized that the question of a coupling or an independence of the individual observable atomic processes cannot be looked at as simply distinguishing between two well-defined conceptions of the propagation of light in empty space corresponding to either a corpuscular theory or a wave theory of light' (ibid., 154; *CW5*, 190).

50 Ibid.

51 Bohr to Born, 1 May 1925, *CW5*, 310–11; English trans., 85.

52 N. Bohr, 'Nachschrift' cit. n. 48, 155; *CW5*, 191.

CHAPTER 5

The conceptual foundation of quantum mechanics

1

'Sprache und Wirklichkeit in der modernen Physik' is the title of a lecture Heisenberg gave in 1960 at the Bayerische Akademie der Schönen Künste[1]. The polemics that had accompanied the establishment of quantum mechanics were over by then and the so-called problems of its foundations had lost much of their initial interest. Einstein had been dead for some years. Right up to the end he had expressed his profound dissatisfaction with a theory which, in his opinion, had something unreasonable about it. With the volume dedicated to him by the community of physicists and philosophers, the long debate between Bohr and Einstein had come to an end. It had been a disappointing conclusion, marked by the reaffirmation of the respective viewpoints of two scientists who by now found great difficulty even in defining a common code of communication[2]. As though seeking to narrow the gap between them, Heisenberg took the opportunity to underline the existence of a common feature in their contributions to 20th century physics. Their discoveries had in fact made it possible to recognize that 'even the fundamental and most elementary concepts of science, such as space, time, place, velocity, have become problematic and must be re-examined'[3]. The conceptual and cognitive implications of relativity and of quantum mechanics were obviously different but Heisenberg maintained that both theories asked the same question: 'Does the language we use when we speak of experiments correspond to the artificial language of mathematics which, as we know, describes real relationships correctly; or has it become separated from it so that we must be content with imprecise linguistic formulations and only return to the artificial language of mathematics when we are forced to express ourselves with precision?'[4]. A similar dilemma had arisen and had become crucial when science had been faced with aspects of physical reality which ran counter to the intuitive character of some of its concepts.

Through their revision of the foundations of physics, Einstein and Bohr had demonstrated the existence of a new epistemological dimension obliging scientists to question established interpretative models and criteria. Thus the great problem of what language to use when describing relationships between natural objects had been raised, and doubt had been cast on the idea that, if one made the right changes and additions, the expressive potential of the language of classical physics could be extended indefinitely. In the investigation of certain types of phenomena it was in fact impossible 'to introduce new artificial words into the language to mean previously unknown objects or relationships'[5]. This discovery undoubtedly meant that careful thought would have to be given to questions which had previously been of secondary importance in scientific development. According to Heisenberg, however, it was to some extent an inevitable consequence of the fact that natural language – from which science had gradually drawn its theoretical terminology – is formed on the basis of man's sense experience. When sophisticated experimental equipment made it possible to penetrate regions of the world inaccessible to the senses, the scientist was thus faced with unusual tasks. It was no longer sufficient to devote oneself to the search for relationships between objects; one also had to ask oneself in what language these might be described. On this view, the ground for the majority of this century's scientific discoveries was prepared by a critical awareness of the process which has enabled science to equip itself with increasingly precise linguistic tools as a result of the systematic application of the laws of logic and mathematical abstraction.

According to Heisenberg, the increase of scientific rigour had depended on a two-fold interaction between formal languages and natural language. Since Newton's *Principia* physics had found in mathematics the most efficient means of eliminating the ambiguities of the terms of everyday language and of providing these terms with a rigorous definitional content. It had linked the fundamental concepts in the different fields of experience to mathematical symbols. In other words, by means of the systems of definitions and axioms forming the basis of every theory, it had laid down the rules of correspondence between the symbols and the concepts they represented. The establishment of the unambiguous and rigorous meaning of the symbols had thus created the conditions for the systematic application of deductive reasoning and for the consequent reduction of the complexity of natural phenomena to a limited number of elementary laws. Since the results of our observations are always expressed in terms of ordinary language, it is clear that a theory's formal apparatus relates to the facts only in the light of univocal rules of this sort. Heisenberg was very far, however, from attributing a purely instrumental function to mathematics. In his opinion, one of the most important consequences of the increase in rigour was that 'the symbols are connected by means of mathematical equations, which represent a valid and exact expression of the so-called laws of nature'[6]. A theory's cognitive content is thus immediately given by its formal relations. It is to a large degree independent, in other words, of the concrete possibilities of description of the real physical objects and events which employ the elements of intersubjective communication.

Significant confirmation of this thesis would be provided by the fact that the introduction of new symbols, resulting from the autonomous development of mathematical language leads to the problem of the reinsertion of a part of this language into everyday language; requiring among other things that new names be invented for new symbols. This presents an inverse problem of translation, for which there are no criteria of linguistic or conceptual rigour. A correspondence has to be established between a symbol, whose richness and complexity can be adequately expressed only in the conceptual framework and in the formal relations of the theory, and a term which is always imprecise and ambiguous, belonging to natural language. Although the modes applied case by case to assimilate these names into the vocabulary of a given discipline follow no rules, according to Heisenberg, names have generally been chosen which seem adequate in representing, within certain limits, the intuitive content of the phenomena. The acquisition of such theoretical terms as 'impulse', 'entropy' and 'electric field' has progressively enriched ordinary language, and this has created the feeling that there should be no objective limitations to our possibilities of describing and understanding processes taking place in nature. However, Heisenberg suggests, developments in physics in this century have shaken this belief and revealed the deficiencies of our language: 'Its concepts', he observes, 'seem like somewhat blunted tools, no longer suited for use in the new fields of experience, no longer capable of being efficient'[7].

The constructive interaction of concepts, names and mathematical symbols which regulates science's linguistic universe first reached a crisis point – according to Heisenberg – with Einstein's theories of relativity. The reason why the effects of the crisis were not immediately felt in all of their epistemological force lies in the local character of our experiences. It is this characteristic which enables us to go on using terms such as 'space', 'time', 'simultaneity' and organizing experimental data in a Euclidean space even though, as far as the theory is concerned, 'the real geometrical relations of the world can only be correctly described in a non-Euclidean geometry of the Riemannian type, that is, in a non-intuitive geometry'[8].

The crisis did however explode, with what Heisenberg describes as terrible results, when the problem arose of which language to use when speaking of atoms and elementary particles. In this case it was no longer possible to make language conform with mathematics. In order to describe the objects of microphysics, scientists started to develop, not so much a language, but 'ways of speaking, in which various intuitive and mutually contradictory images alternate', and to employ concepts apparently endowed with meaning chosen to meet contingent needs and 'according to what seemed most appropriate to certain experiments'. In Heisenberg's view, physicists speak indiscriminately of waves and particles, electron orbits and stationary states, and this is possible because they know, or should know, that 'these images are imprecise analogies, that in a certain sense they are figures of speech with which we try to approach real phenomena'[9].

Even if scientists like Einstein did not resign themselves to this situation, as far as quantum phenomena were concerned, the new mechanics showed that it was impossible to compile a dictionary permitting unambiguous translation between symbols and the terms of natural language or concepts of classical physics. These then were the irreversible consequences of the revision of the foundations of physics that had begun in the first decades of the century. However, if we adopt Heisenberg's point of view, we should conclude that the premises for this shift had been created long before when the question of rigour arose and a start was made on the formalization of scientific languages. It was only in the study of atoms and of a new dimension of physical reality that these aspects emerged in all their epistemological force. Traditional modes of representation and description were so undermined that physicists who wanted to speak of quantum objects had to make do with an imprecise and symbolic language. To make the sense of this passage still clearer, Heisenberg made use of comparisons such as would disconcert any champion of scientific rationality and objectivity: physicists today are more and more like poets seeking 'to elicit with images and comparisons certain impressions in the mind of the listener which lead in the desired direction without forcing him through unambiguous formulation to follow precisely any specific reasoning'. But, he concluded, their 'way of speaking becomes clear only when they use mathematical language'[10].

2

'Über quantentheoretische Umdeutung kinematischer und mechanischer Beziehungen' is not only the title of the article Heisenberg sent in July 1925 to the *Zeitschrift für Physik*, but also summarizes a theoretical programme which was to contribute decisively to the construction of the formalism of quantum mechanics[1]. Heisenberg's aim was to reformulate all the quantities and relations appearing in kinematics and classical mechanics in terms acceptable to quantum theory, on the condition that what was then considered the fundamental law of quantum theory, the so-called Einstein–Bohr frequency condition, would be implicitly satisfied by the new symbols and equations. Heisenberg's project was not one of immediately solving particular problems of interpretation, but rather of considering the theory's structural aspects with the aim of providing quantum physics with a formal language able to express and represent processes of a discontinuous nature. This was, in his view, the only avenue open to research, since the objections which had been raised for some time regarding the validity of a model-based approach had by then become conclusive[12]. Heisenberg did not adduce reasons of a philosophical or epistemological nature against the method characterizing the first phase in the construction of the atomic theory. For him the problem was theoretical and arose from the fact that Bohr and Sommerfeld's formal rules, with which it had been possible to calculate observable quantities such as the energies of the hydrogen atom, were expressed in terms of the motion properties of the orbiting electron – in other words, on the basis of quantities in principle unobservable according to quantum theory. For Heisenberg, these rules could therefore have no physical basis, unless there was sufficient evidence to allow for hope in an eventual experimental determination of the position and mechanical frequency of an atomic electron. However, neither from the point of view of the theory's internal consistency nor, still less, from that of the interpretative efficacy of these rules, which were rigorously valid only for the hydrogen atom and the Stark effect, were there any rational grounds to sustain such a hope.

Heisenberg furthermore identified an obvious bending of logic and theory in the arguments usually used to defend the heuristic validity of the model and the choice to proceed with a programme based on it. Without specifically referring to it, he rejected the argument by means of which Bohr had transformed the inconsistency between quantum postulates and the concepts and laws of classical physics into an element in support of the programme's fertility. Bohr had long maintained that the failure of the quantization rules should not be considered a particularly serious problem seeing that, since they derived from classical mechanics, their limits indicated how far removed atomic phenomena were from ordinary physical conceptions. He hoped in this way that the mechanical model itself would suggest the best strategies for arriving at a correct theory; and the correspondence principle actually did represent a particularly brilliant confirmation of his approach. For Heisenberg, on the other hand, these arguments had no meaning at all and were rendered useless by the fact that the law of frequencies – which had proved to be valid in all the problems dealt with – not only already marked an irreparable break with classical mechanics, but actually proved that such mechanics could not even be applied to the simplest of quantum problems. The only thing to do was to consider the partial agreement of quantum rules with certain aspects of experience as more or less coincidental and to try 'to establish a quantum-theoretical mechanics, analogous to classical mechanics, but in which only relations between observable quantities occur'[13].

Heisenberg's declaration was a demanding one and marked a turning point in the theoretical debate. However, his comments touched upon many of the themes that had been at the centre of discussion in the Copenhagen School in those years and over which in particular there had been marked disagreement between Bohr and Pauli. While Bohr was still engaged upon the defence of the virtual oscillator theory and the model of space-time description, Pauli had been the first to raise the problem of a physics utilizing only directly observable quantities. In December 1924, he wrote to Bohr that he was so convinced of the need to modify the kinematic concept of motion that he had avoided using the term 'orbit' in his writing. 'Since this concept of motion', Pauli added, 'also underlies the correspondence principle, its clarification must be the foremost effort of the theoreticians. I believe that the energy and momentum values of the stationary states are something much more real than "orbits". The aim (not yet achieved) must be to deduce these and all other physically real, observable properties of the stationary states from the (integral) quantum numbers and the quantum-theoretical laws. We must not, however, put the atoms in the shackles of our prejudices (of which in my opinion the assumption of the existence of electron orbits in the sense of the ordinary kinematics is an example); on the contrary, we must adapt our concepts to experience'[14]. Bohr's thesis, in which the validity of the correspondence principle depended on the electrons' properties of motion, was therefore considered by Pauli as too weak a defence of the mechanical model, which he dismissed, along with the orbits, as a sort of conceptual crutch for the intellectually feeble[15].

Thus, Heisenberg seems to have agreed entirely with Pauli's point of view, and was perhaps also influenced by his hypothesis that it was necessary to make concepts conform to experience or rather develop a new conceptual apparatus in which the meaning of every term was operationally defined[16]. It is difficult to evaluate the extent to which this epistemological attitude may have helped to orientate the choices that overturned the methods and aims of research in atomic physics. Instead it is clear that in the summer of 1925 Heisenberg's decision was far less arbitrary and far less influenced by personal inclinations than the idea of a physics of observable quantities had probably seemed to Bohr only a few months before. Heisenberg's work was made possible precisely by the perspectives opened by the Bohr–Kramers–Slater theory, which had marked the collapse of the last rational argument making it difficult or at least inadvisable to abandon the mechanical model. The results of that theory, and nothing else, had shown once and for all that it was no longer possible to appeal to a hypothetical hidden mechanism to try to link discontinuous quantum processes with the classical mode of description. In the final analysis, Bohr's theoretical programme had for years been based on this hypothesis alone. In any case, thanks to the notion of the virtual oscillator, a rigorous treatment of the phenomenon of dispersion had been achieved; and it was not by chance that in the introduction to his article Heisenberg judged this result the most important step taken so far towards a theory of quantum mechanics.

3

Great interest had been shown in dispersion from the first formulation of the quantum theory of the atom, above all for its unique capacity of creating problems which were the opposite of those connected with the interpretation of the spectroscopic laws. The stationary state postulate and the orbiting electron model had in fact removed any physical foundation for the formulas of the classical electron theory, which in this case achieved a good approximation to experimental results. According to the theory of Lorentz and Drude, the study of dispersion could be reduced to the determination of the interaction between an electric field with frequency v and a system of particles with mass m and charge $-e$, which oscillate with their own frequencies v_0 in the absence of external forces. The framework outlined was obviously incompatible with the new ideas regarding the constitution of atoms. The attempts Debye, Sommerfeld and Davisson had made in the context of the atomic model, on the other hand, had not yielded significant results. They had tried in vain to obtain dispersion formulas by applying the methods of classical perturbation theory to the orbiting motion of electrons[17].

It was only in 1921 that a first quantum treatment of the phenomenon was achieved when Ladenburg, abandoning any attempt to employ models and developing only Einstein's probability considerations, obtained the expression

$$A = \frac{c^3 E}{32\pi^4} \sum_k \frac{A_i^k}{v_{ik}^2 \, (v_{ik}^2 - v^2)} \tag{5.1}$$

for the amplitude of the variable electric moment of the atom under the action of an electric field E oscillating with a frequency v – in (5.1) the v_{ik} are the quantum frequencies relative to the pairs of states i and k, the A_i^k are Einstein's coefficients of probability, and the value of v differs from the frequencies of absorption and emission of the element under consideration[18]. Ladenburg's work was to be taken up and generalized a few years later by Kramers who, shortly before the publication of the paper on virtual oscillators, had written a letter to *Nature* which contained an interesting application of the new theory of radiation[19]. It was the only case in this context to be analysed also in quantitative terms which, as we shall see, in addition to confirming the heuristic function of the analogical procedure underlying the idea of a virtual model, also made it possible to explicate what was potentially contained in the correspondence principle.

Kramers faithfully applied the interpretative framework of the virtual oscillator theory. In this instance, however, the problems that had arisen when dealing with the processes of emission and absorption no longer existed. Suffice it to point out that the basic hypothesis of the theory – the atom in a stationary state reacts to radiation in an analogous way to that foreseen by the ordinary laws for a system of virtual oscillators associated with such a state – succeeded in explaining why the phenomena of dispersion, reflection and diffusion were consistently described by classical electromagnetic theory. Some authors have maintained that it was precisely the classical nature of these phenomena and the impossibility of interpreting them in terms of the quantum theory of the atom that were the real reasons leading Bohr to take up Slater's idea and to replace for the stationary states the image of the electron's orbiting motion with that of a system of oscillating charges[20]. However, what we wish to emphasize is another aspect of the apparent identity between the hypotheses underlying the classical dispersion theory and the Bohr–Kramers–Slater theory. While for the spectra it was a question of developing a space-time model of description of the process of interaction between radiation and matter compatible with quantum formulas – the only ones capable of representing the empirical laws of emission and absorption correctly – now the opposite problem had arisen: how to generalize the corrected classical formulas for dispersion in quantum terms, assuming that the phenomenon is describable in space and time according to ordinary models. Once the virtual equivalence between atom and model had been admitted, the quantum treatment of dispersion amounted – in concrete terms – to the determination of what the formal modifications were that needed to be applied to the classical expression for the electric moment of an atom containinng an electron with its own oscillation frequency v_i

$$P = E \frac{e^2}{m} \frac{1}{4\pi^2(v_i^2 - v^2)}, \qquad (5.2)$$

or, in the more general case, to the expression

$$P = E \sum_i f_i \frac{e^2}{m} \frac{1}{4\pi^2(v_i^2 - v^2)}, \qquad (5.3)$$

in which the f_i represent the number of dispersion electrons for each frequency v_i. One had merely to make proper use of the hypotheses on the nature and properties of the oscillators. Thus, even though dispersion did not depend on processes of transition between stationary states, the conditions required by the virtual equivalence of the Bohr–Kramers–Slater theory implied: first, that in (5.3) the v_i were replaced with the frequencies of the virtual oscillators, or rather with the quantum frequencies associated with transitions; and secondly, that account should be taken of the probabilistic mechanism by means of which the incident fields, interacting with the virtual fields, determined the transitions from one system of oscillators to another[21]. If in the virtual model, therefore, a generic stationary state was associated to two sets of oscillators with frequencies v_i^a and v_j^e, corresponding respectively to the absorption and the emission processes then, according to Kramers, (5.3) had to be rewritten in the following way

$$P = E \sum_i A_i^a \, \tau_i^a \frac{e^2}{m} \frac{1}{4\pi^2 \, (v_i^{a2} - v^2)} -$$

$$E \sum_j A_j^e \, \tau_j^e \frac{e^2}{m} \frac{1}{4\pi^2 \, (v_j^{e2} - v^2)}, \qquad (5.4)$$

where A_i^a and A_j^e were Einstein's coefficients and the τ_i^a $[\tau_j^e]$ were given by $3mc^2/8\pi^2 e^2 v_i^{a2}$ $[3mc^2/8\pi^2 e^2 v_j^{e2}]$. This was the correct result according to Kramers, both because it became asymptotically equivalent to the classical expression and especially because it showed the approximate nature of Ladenburg's formula which, since it lacked the term of emission, could only refer to atomic systems in the fundamental state. He added nothing else with regard to the procedure he had used to obtain the formula, but did note that 'the reaction of the atom against the incident radiation can thus formally be compared with the action of a set of virtual harmonic oscillators inside the atom, conjugated with the different possible transitions to other stationary states'[22].

Kramers expressed himself in the same obscure and apparently ambiguous language as Bohr. However, his claim pointed to a new aspect of the relation existing between the concrete physical situation of the atoms and their virtual image. Equation (5.4) was not a demonstration of the compatibility of quantum notions with classical interpretative schemes – it was simply a law of quantum theory. It contained no reference to the properties of the model and along with observable quantities such as E, v, e and m, included only symbols with two indices (the exponents a and e stand for pairs of quantum numbers n_1 and n_2) representing processes of a discontinuous nature. The idea that from a formal point of view the real phenomenon of dispersion could be treated on the basis of its virtual representation, or rather that such a relation could be derived from a quantitative analysis of the model, indicated that the quantum symbols correspond to symbols that are associated to rigorously defined classical concepts in the system of reference of the Maxwell–Lorentz theory. Only in this sense would it be possible to say simply that in (5.4) the v_i^a and the v_j^e are the frequencies of the oscillators. Kramers himself suggested that this was the correct way of interpreting the physical meaning of the quantum formula for dispersion when he tackled the problem of naming the τ symbols which, in his view, 'represent the time in which on the classical theory the energy of a particle of charge e and mass m is reduced to $1/e$ of its original value, where e is the base of the natural logarithms'[23]. In the quantum theory τ is instead always a two-index symbol which for the time being cannot be associated to any defined physical concept. In any case, Kramers emphasized the need to keep the treatment on the level of pure symbolic correspondence, and showed the paradoxes one could fall into if one tried to eliminate the virtual equivalence in order to assign an immediate physical significance to the model. The comparison of (5.2) and (5.4) might in fact lead one to think that the new formula for dispersion is the result of the classical treatment of the interaction process in which electrons are replaced by virtual oscillators with a charge e^* and a mass m^*, such that $e^{*2}/m^* = A\tau e^2/m$; but, in so doing, we would have to admit that for the 'emission oscillators' this ratio is a negative number.

In attempting to illustrate the descriptive content of the quantum formula, Kramers instead exploited its formal analogy with (5.3) and, after pointing out that the product $A\tau$ was dimensionless, suggested that 'one might introduce the following terminology: in a final state of the transition the atom acts as a "positive virtual oscillator" of relative strength $+f$; in the initial state it acts as a "negative virtual oscillator" of strength $-f$'. There was, according to Kramers, sufficient theoretical justification to adopt such an unintuitive expression. 'However unfamiliar this "negative dispersion" might appear from the point of view of the classical theory, it may be noted that it exhibits a close analogy with the "negative absorption" [the so-called induced emission] which was introduced by Einstein, in order to account for the law of temperature radiation on the basis of the quantum theory'[24].

A few months later, in another letter to *Nature*, Kramers returned to his quantum theory of dispersion to clarify the procedure enabling him to obtain (5.4). The letter dropped all reference to the virtual oscillator model and again took up Bohr's theory of multiperiodical systems[25]. According to this theory, in a non-perturbed system the electrical moment in any given direction is:

$$M = \Sigma\, C \cos (2\pi\omega t + \gamma), \tag{5.5}$$

where ω is a linear combination of the fundamental frequencies ω_i, and the amplitudes C depend on the action variables I, which in the quantum conditions for the stationary states are expressed as integral multiples of h. The electrical moment of the system's forced vibrations produced by the action of the external electric field $E \cos 2\pi vt$ is therefore equal to

$$P = \frac{E}{2} \sum \frac{\partial}{\partial I} \left(\frac{C^2 \omega}{\omega^2 - v^2} \right) \cos 2\pi vt. \tag{5.6}$$

Bearing in mind that in the limits of high quantum numbers the frequencies of the spectral lines associated with possible transitions coincide asymptotically with the frequencies ω_i of the harmonic components of motion, Kramers assumed that in this limiting region (5.6) yielded the asymptotically correct expression for dispersion. The correspondence principle was still the logical tool with which to try to generalize the formula. According to Kramers, however, the analogy between atom and mechanical model was not confined to the hypothesis of the existence of harmonic components of motion corresponding to the quantum frequencies of the transitions, but also regarded the symbols of the two formalisms. He noted that whereas in classical terms the fundamental frequencies of motion depend on the energy according to

$$\omega = \frac{\partial H}{\partial I}, \tag{5.7}$$

in general for any quantum number the exact expression of the frequencies of the spectra is given by

$$v_q = \frac{\Delta E}{h}, \tag{5.8}$$

or rather is expressed as a function of the finite difference between the energies of two stationary states. In his opinion it was therefore natural to assume that generalizing (5.6) was equivalent to replacing the differential symbol $\partial/\partial I$ with the corresponding symbol for difference Δ, divided by Planck's constant. 'This is just what has been done in establishing formula [5.4]. In fact, this formula is obtained from [5.6] by replacing the differential coefficient multiplied by h, by the difference between the quantities

$$\frac{3c^2 A^a h}{(2\pi)^4 \nu^{a2}(\nu^{a2} - \nu^2)} \quad \text{and} \quad \frac{3c^2 A^e h}{(2\pi)^4 \nu^{e2}(\nu^{e2} - \nu^2)} \qquad [5.9]$$

referring to the two transitions coupled respectively with the absorption and emission of the spectral line which corresponds with the harmonic component under consideration'. One thereby obtains, Kramers concluded, a formula which 'contains only such quantities as allow of a direct physical interpretation on the basis of the fundamental postulates of the quantum theory of spectra and atomic constitution, and exhibits no further reminiscence of the mathematical theory of multiple periodic system'[26].

However, Kramers was not prudently abandoning the virtual oscillator model in order to adopt a different technique which would enable him to obtain the same result. In fact, as we have seen, not only is the final formula in both cases independent of the properties of the original model, but the virtual oscillator hypothesis in particular, as Kramers understood it, retained the same validity: 'The notation "virtual oscillators"', the note concluded, 'used in my former letter does not mean the introduction of any hypothetical mechanism, but is meant only as a terminology suitable to characterize certain main features of the connection between the description of optical phenomena and the theoretical interpretation of spectra'[27]. In other words, the model established a correspondence between symbols belonging to different theoretical and conceptual contexts, and was thus the only tool making it possible to associate a descriptive content with a quantum formalism. Kramers thus made it clear that in any case the success of the quantum theory of dispersion would not give new strength and credibility to the severely compromised hypothesis of a model-based approach to the study of atoms. His two brief papers contained something far more fundamental for the future of quantum theory. By virtue of the specific theoretical nature of the dispersion phenomenon it had been possible to demonstrate that the correspondence principle did not confine itself to suggesting a heuristic criterion to ascertain the compatibility of classical concepts and quantum processes. In this restricted sense it had exhausted its potential with the Bohr–Kramers–Slater theory, i.e. with the superseding of the classical model of space-time description. In reality, correspondence expressed a relation between symbols belonging to different formal languages. This is precisely the aspect Heisenberg was referring to when he said that Kramers' work represented the most important step toward a new mechanics taken in those years.

4

The reinterpretation of the symbols and relations of classical kinematics and mechanics necessarily led to the recognition that the technique of formal manipulation Kramers had applied to a specific case was valid in general – as a correct reformulation of the correspondence principle might, for that matter, have suggested. Heisenberg's interest in Kramers' theory was obvious. For the first time there were two mathematical formulas, one classical and one quantum, which described the same phenomenal situation equally well even though the quantities associated to analogous mathematical symbols in the two formulas differed completely[28]. Though this was apparently not much of a clue to go on, Heisenberg glimpsed in it a tool of great methodological efficacy. The clue in fact said that it was possible to pass from the classical to the quantum formula for dispersion, i.e. from one formal language to the other, by applying rules of a simple nature and such as would not compromise the theory over conceptual questions. The rules required that quantities which were functions of a continuous variable should be replaced with symbols dependent on two discrete variables, and that all the differential operators be replaced with finite differences between quantities. These linguistic rules thus contained the key to decipher the correspondence principle and translate it into a rigorous technical tool and it was now possible to give a meaning to the otherwise obscure procedure of rational transcription. Its real meaning was the literal one: rational transcription is a translation of mathematical symbols and relations leading to the construction of a new formal language; a translation guided by rules making it possible case by case to discover the corresponding term in quantum-theoretical language of each symbol or relation between symbols appearing in classical mechanics[29].

It has been said with regard to this paper that Heisenberg's theoretical choice was based primarily on a deep conviction that there had to be a typically discontinuous element in the domain of atomic phenomena, irreducible to visualizable models, i.e. ones based on space-time pictures. For this reason he had supported the programme of Born and the Göttingen School in their attempt at replacing the continuous mode of explanation of physics with a discrete descriptive approach[30]. There is no need to bring in the emerging philosophies of the time and their influence on scientific thought in order to trace the origins of this conviction: discontinuity was a theoretical result consolidated by more than two decades of research and it clearly expressed the split that had formed between microphysics and classical conceptions. Neither is it at all surprising that physicists such as Born and Heisenberg should agree with Bohr to view the results of the virtual oscillator theory as definitively superseding all space-time pictures rather than as mere confirmation of the light-quanta hypothesis.

This does not explain, however, what ground Heisenberg thought there was for the idea upon which the entire procedure of the reinterpretation of classical symbols and relations implicitly rested. In other words, where did he get the far more fundamental conviction, not so much that such a translation was possible, but that the resulting language would actually speak of something and not boil down to a set of empty symbols connected by bizarre syntactic rules? The question is not only legitimate but becomes crucial to the reconstruction of the origins of quantum mechanics when one notes that at the time his article was published, Heisenberg was not aware of the nature of the new symbols and could in no way have been certain that they belonged to a rigorous mathematical structure. In the summer of 1925 he was so far from guessing where the work of symbolic rewriting would lead him that he told Pauli of his doubts as to the validity of the results he had obtained: 'My opinion about what I have written ['das Geschreibsel'], and about which I am not happy at all, is this: that I am firmly convinced about the negative critical part, but that the positive part is fairly formal and meagre: however, perhaps people who know more can turn it into something reasonable'; and he asked Pauli to let him know promptly what he thought of it, because 'I do wish either to complete it in the last days of my presence here [in Göttingen] or to burn it'[31].

Aside from the epistemological aspects connected with the question of observable quantities, the need to develop a quantum kinematics resulted above all from a new approach to the problem of radiation. Heisenberg did not confine himself to eliminating all residue of the model-based approach and putting the oscillators technique to intelligent use, but also carried out a critical revision of the assumptions of the research programme Bohr had formulated in 1913. In reality, the outcome of that programme had been determined from the very start by its judgement on the failure of classical electrodynamics. While this judgement had made possible the defence of the mechanical picture of the atom, it had above all acted as a powerful filter to select theoretically relevant problems. The impossibility of deriving the properties of radiation from the motion of the electrons in atoms had been considered the weakest conceptual point of the classical theories and a clear demonstration of the limits of the laws of ordinary electrodynamics. For this reason, the irreducibility of optical frequencies to mechanical ones had been assumed among the postulates of quantum theory. Analytical instruments had been developed to deal separately with the orbiting motion of electrons and the radiation process and, finally, the generalization of the laws of classical electrodynamics had come to be considered one of the programme's main objectives.

Heisenberg now showed how arbitrary that judgement had been. The problem, he said, 'has nothing to do with electrodynamics but rather – and this seems to be particularly important – is of a purely kinematic nature'[32]. He maintained that the classical formulas should be salvaged in order to establish a new connection between radiation and kinematics, and in this way he refounded the quantum theory programme, which was now to be based on a different judgement. On the one hand, all attempts in the domain of atomic physics to reach a definition of the space-time co-ordination of electrons through observable quantities had been unsuccessful; or rather, as Heisenberg observed, 'it has not been possible to associate the electron with a point in space, considered as a function of time'[33]. On the other, one of the fundamental ideas of classical electrodynamics, namely that the electron is the cause of the emission of radiation, still resisted even from the quantum viewpoint. However, the idea resisted only in a weak form, because in the world of atoms that cause could no longer be identified with the kinematic behaviour of electrons, for which there are in fact no spatial and temporal co-ordinates. As far as the interaction of radiation with matter was concerned, the theory only stated that there was a formal, empirically well-founded relation between the frequency of emitted radiation and the energy difference between two discontinuous states of the electron.

On the basis of this judgement, it therefore had to be admitted that to associate the electron's position, velocity and acceleration to the symbols $x(t)$, $\dot{x}(t)$ and $\ddot{x}(t)$ which appear in the classical formulas made no sense whatsoever. Those symbols had instead to be replaced by the corresponding quantum quantities which would implicitly define what Heisenberg, in order to stress the formal equivalence between the old and new set of symbols, called 'quantum kinematics'. In order to concretely carry out the reinterpretation or translation of the formalism, however, another step was necessary which entailed making a weighty epistemological assumption. It had to be assumed that the theory's formal apparatus retained an autonomy of its own despite the disappearance of the conditions leading us to associate certain names to certain symbols, i.e.

despite the loss of all validity on the part of the system of axioms and definitions establishing a correspondence between symbols and fundamental concepts. In the final analysis, this amounted to admitting that only in formal language can we speak about reality with precision, independently of the possible intuitive images that may be derived from it. On the other hand, only in the light of this assumption would it have made sense to carry out a series of transformations on the formalism of classical mechanics; to take, for example, the mathematical expression of the Fourier expansion of electron motion and to find the quantum analogues of the symbols and relations in it, having however freed the symbols from the names 'position', 'amplitude', 'phase', 'frequency' or, rather, knowing that for the time being these names are meaningless as far as quantum theory is concerned[34].

The result of the translation was a new system of symbols whose physical or geometric meaning was, in many cases, unclear. Heisenberg also discovered that the new symbols were peculiar objects for which the commutative property of multiplication was not in general valid. When he sent his paper to the printers he did not know that these objects were matrices and that his multiplication law of quantum-theoretical quantities was none other than the well-known mathematical rule of matrix multiplication. He only knew, or rather he had the feeling, that this strange, barely outlined mathematical formalism must refer to some reality; not so much because it contained symbols corresponding to actually observable quantities such as the frequency and amplitude of radiation, but above all because there was a theorem of conservation in it analogous to the law of energy in classical mechanics and because the fundamental law of frequencies was automatically satisfied.

Bohr welcomed Heisenberg's paper as a fundamental step forward, especially because the new mathematical apparatus could be 'regarded as a precise formulation of the tendencies embodied in the correspondence principle'[35]. Heisenberg preferred to confine himself to indicating his method's need of further investigation: 'Whether a method to determine quantum-theoretical data [...] such as that proposed here, can be regarded as satisfactory in principle, or whether this method after all represents far too rough an approach to the physical problem of constructing a theoretical quantum mechanics [...] can be decided only by a more intensive mathematical investigation of the method which has been very superficially employed here'[36]. Heisenberg's words had a truly surprising effect on the mathematical physicists of the University of Göttingen, who not only immediately recognized in his paper the formalism of matrix algebra, but also had the mathematical knowledge necessary to put his suggestion quickly into effect. In the space of a few weeks Born and Pascual Jordan, with the collaboration of Heisenberg himself, perfected the mathematical apparatus of quantum mechanics, working solely on the assumption that the matrices represented the physical quantities given as functions of time in classical theory, and that the use of a matrix analysis should replace that of numerical analysis[37].

Their work laid the mathematical foundations of the modern theory of the atom and particles. Above all, confirmation was obtained of the hypothesis that had inspired their formal approach, i.e. 'the conviction that the difficulties which have been encountered at every step in quantum theory in the last few years could be surmounted only by establishing a mathematical system for the mechanics of atomic and electronic motions, which would have a unity and simplicity comparable with the system of classical mechanics'[38]. It must have seemed an important result from this viewpoint 'that the basic postulates of quantum theory form an inherent organic constituent of this [new] mechanics, e.g., that the existence of discrete stationary states is just as natural a feature of the new theory as, say, the existence of discrete vibration frequencies in classical theory'[39]. They were obviously well aware that this did not restore to the theory a consistent conceptual basis; it was still a question of symbols which were not 'directly amenable to a geometrically visualizable interpretation, since the motion of electrons cannot be described in terms of the familiar concepts of space and time'[40]. While this was a predictable result, seeing that the new formalism had sprung precisely from the need for a symbolic rewriting of classical kinematics, with the idea of visualization Born, Heisenberg and Jordan specifically posed the problem of the conceptual content and descriptive modes of the new mechanics. In their view, this was to be regarded as an exact formulation of Bohr's correspondence principle understood as the expression of a relation between symbols belonging to different formal languages. Investigating the nature of this relation and describing 'the manner in which symbolic quantum geometry goes over into visualizable classical geometry' was thus the way they indicated to re-establish a link between old concepts and new symbols[41].

Dirac was among the first to grasp the profound theoretical innovation that Heisenberg's work represented. In the introduction to an article published in November 1925 he lucidly reconstructed the transition from Bohr's old programme to the new mechanics without even mentioning the question of observable quantities[42]. He observed that in quantum theory the contrast between experimental facts and classical electrodynamics had been encompassed within the new concept of stationary state, which was attributed with physical properties incompatible with the ordinary conceptions. The inexact and approximate classical laws appeared only in the description of the motion of the stationary states and in the hypothesis of an asymptotic correlation between spectrum and motion. According to Dirac, the shift in perspective Heisenberg introduced consisted in having understood 'that it is not the equations of classical mechanics that are in any way at fault, but that the mathematical operations by which physical results are deduced from them require modification'; it was the operations, he explained further on, which allowed definite physical concepts to be associated to mathematical symbols. '*All* the information supplied by the classical theory', he concluded, 'can thus be made use of in the new theory'[43].

Dirac accentuated the symbolic character of quantum mechanics, inventing the term '*q*-numbers' for the variables the theory used to describe a dynamical system. 'At present', he stated, 'one can form no picture of what a *q*-number is like [...] One knows nothing of the processes by which the numbers are formed except that they [unlike the *c*-numbers, *i.e.* those of classical mathematics] satisfy all the ordinary laws of algebra, excluding the commutative law of multiplication'[44]. In the same way as Born, Heisenberg and Jordan, but using a different language, Dirac posed a problem of translation: 'In order to be able to get results comparable with experiment from our theory, we must have some way of representing *q*-numbers by means of *c*-numbers, so that we can compare these *c*-numbers with experimental values'[45].

Bohr had not come out defeated. His was the greatest contribution to the superseding of the 1913 programme, to the abandonment of the space-time model of description, and therefore in the reformulation of the concepts of kinematics. He was right therefore to claim the heuristic importance of the mechanical model of the atom. In January 1926, he wrote to Oseen: 'We are gradually progressing, I hope, but in every result lurks the temptation to stray from the right path. This is so true in atomic theory that at the present stage of the development of the quantum theory we can hardly say whether it was good or bad luck that the properties of the Kepler motion could be brought into such a simple connection with the hydrogen spectrum, as was believed possible at one time. If this connection had merely had that asymptotic character which one might expect from the correspondence principle, then we should not have been tempted to apply mechanics as crudely as we believed possible for some time. On the other hand, it was just these mechanical considerations that were helpful in building up the analysis of the optical phenomena which gradually led to quantum mechanics'[46].

5

'I tried to say what space meant and what velocity meant and so on. I just tried to turn the question around according to the example of Einstein. You know Einstein just reversed the question by saying, "We do not ask how we can describe nature by mathematical schemes, but we say that nature always works so that mathematical schemes can be fitted to it". [...] Therefore, I just suggested for myself, "Well, is it not so that I can only find in nature situations which can be described by quantum mechanics?" Then I asked, "Well what are these situations which you can define?" Then I found very soon that these are situations in which there was this Uncertainty Relation'[47]. It was thus, in the course of a long interview given many years later, that Heisenberg reconstructed the process that had led him in February 1927 to the discovery of what was to become known as the principle of indeterminacy. This way of reasoning was certainly not greeted favourably by Bohr, who at the time considered the dualism of waves and corpuscles as the central point of the problem and, according to Heisenberg, did not seem very willing to subscribe to the thesis that nature imitates a mathematical scheme or rather that in nature there is nothing that cannot be described by the scheme of quantum mechanics. But Heisenberg insisted: 'Waves and corpuscles are, certainly, a way in which we talk [...], but since classical physics is not true there, why should we stick so much to these concepts? Why not say just that we cannot use these concepts with a high degree of precision? [...] When we get beyond this range of the classical theory we must realize that our words don't fit. They don't really get a hold in the physical reality and therefore a new mathematical scheme is just as good as anything because the new mathematical scheme then tells you what may be there and what may not be there'[48]. Whether this sort of consideration really underlay Heisenberg's discovery and inspired the article 'Über den anschaulichen Inhalt der quantentheoretischen Kinematik und Mechanik'[49] is a question that will probably remain unanswered, and may even be a futile one. These a posteriori considerations can serve, if anything, to orientate our reading of the article, with all due caution, and to identify the basic problem that he was trying to solve.

Heisenberg had arrived in Copenhagen in the spring of 1926 after having accepted Bohr's invitation to hold an annual course of lectures. Since then, great progress had been made in atomic physics: Schrödinger had formulated wave mechanics and demonstrated its mathematical equivalence to matrix mechanics; Jordan and Dirac had published their papers on the theory of transformations; and Born had suggested the probabilistic interpretation of Schrödinger's wave function[50]. All this had not helped solve the paradoxes deriving from the apparently dual nature of radiation and matter. Bohr and Heisenberg were seriously engaged in the search for a consistent physical interpretation of the new formalism, but approached the problem from very different theoretical viewpoints. Where they differed was above all in their evaluation of the implications of the notion of discontinuity and in their attitude to Schrödinger's contribution.

Heisenberg maintained[51] that the specific problem of atomic physics – and hence the content of all reflection on the foundations of quantum mechanics – concerned on the one hand the typically discontinuous element arising when one examines events occurring in very restricted times and spaces, and on the other the kind of reality to ascribe to atoms and electrons. This was consistent with his way of viewing the process which had led to the new mechanics and which he reduced essentially to a conflict between the discontinuity of elementary physical processes and our forms of visualization, i.e. our tendency to represent these processes by means of the usual concepts of space and time. In his opinion, nature had expressed herself unambiguously on the matter: it was impossible to ascribe to atomic objects the degree of immediate reality that one did to the objects of everyday experience. Furthermore, the explanation of a broad range of phenomena required that only discrete states of matter be taken into consideration. The discovery of light corpuscles had only rendered this conflict more acute in that it became immediately evident that if they were attributed with the same properties of localization in space and time as particles of matter, unacceptable contradictions would arise with the laws of classical optics.

It was therefore necessary, according to Heisenberg, to break with Bohr's methodological approach, which involved the systematic use of the concepts and images of classical physics wherever it was logically admissible. A true epistemological turning point had been reached: the programme of quantum mechanics came into being when it was understood that the cause of all the interpretative difficulties was the fact that the problem of the constitution of the atom was marked by 'a strange transferal of classical concepts and representations to the fundamental postulates of quantum theory', i.e. the fact that one had relied 'on merely intuitive models and images to interpret physical regularities whose intuitive content was not, in reality, at all recognizable'[52]. One therefore abandoned a theory which 'combined the advantage of an immediate visualizability and of the use of accepted physical principles with the disadvantage of calculating, generally speaking, by means of relations not, in principle, verifiable, and which could therefore lead to internal contradictions', and adopted a theory which, while relinquishing any demand for visualization, contained however 'only concrete relations, susceptible of direct experimental control and therefore unlikely to be subject to internal contradictions'[53]. Everything gained by the new formalism in terms of logical consistency was lost in terms of descriptive content. The clearest demonstration of this was given precisely by the reformulation of kinematics, which Heisenberg linked to the question of the reality of electrons. It was by no means impossible to keep a corpuscular representation for the latter; it would suffice – perhaps by appealing to the fact that they are not directly observable – to abandon the assignation of a specific point in space to an electron as a function of time. Quantum mechanics had expressed this drastic limitation of the reality of corpuscles, replacing the 'position of the electron' with a quantity completely defined from the physical point of view and, at the same time, mathematically equivalent to such a term. The result had been that 'in place of the classical "co-ordinates of the electron", in quantum mechanics there is a two-dimensional "table" with the quantities of radiation'. The new formalism did not seem capable, in any case, of contributing anything to the understanding of the reality of the atomic world: 'for microscopic events', Heisenberg concluded, 'so far we have only relations between experimentally obtained observable quantities, and for the moment we cannot give an immediate intuitive interpretation of the physical events on which they rest'[54]. Once again, discontinuity represented the obstacle to the understanding of the theory's intuitive content, as demonstrated by the impossibility of translating the matrix tables into terms suitable for a description of those events.

However, once it was acknowledged that – as Einstein's reasoning had suggested to Heisenberg – it was not a question of identifying the descriptive content of the mathematical frameworks, but rather of assuming that the frameworks adequately represented situations actually occurring in nature, the problem took on a new appearance from the elimination of the characteristics of abstract generality which had prevented any solution. An understanding of the theory's contents depended, in other words, not on whether the formalism was compatible with a model based on our customary modes of space-time description but, as Heisenberg stated in the opening lines of his paper, on the possibility of thinking in qualitative terms about the experimental consequences of the theory in all of the simplest cases. One therefore had to ask which experimental situations could be defined on the basis of the formalism, and then ascertain case by case whether they could be described consistently. In any case, the fact that the quantum theory did possess an immediate intuitive significance was evident not only from the existence within it of antinomies, but above all from the fact that 'quantum mechanics arose exactly out of the attempt to break with all the concepts of ordinary kinematics and replace them with relations between concrete, experimentally determinable numbers'[55]. It is not surprising therefore that these concepts offer no hold on reality when we are dealing with typically quantum processes; and we would perhaps do well to prepare to abandon them and replace them with new concepts if a revision of the concepts of kinematics and mechanics were not demanded, according to Heisenberg, by the fundamental equations of quantum mechanics themselves.

In the physics of macro-objects we have no difficulty in understanding the meaning of terms such as 'position' or 'velocity' when speaking of a body of a certain mass m. In quantum mechanics, on the contrary, if between mass, position and velocity there is a relation of the type

$$pq - qp = -ih/2\pi, \tag{5.10}$$

i.e. if we decide to assign these names to p and q, it is not clear what use we will be able to make of them. 'We have good reason to become suspicious', Heisenberg maintained, 'every time uncritical use is made of the words "position" and "velocity"'[56], i.e., when one tries to retain the same meaning for the words as they have in the descriptive language of classical physics.

In other words, the problem Heisenberg was seeking to draw attention to when he spoke of the acritical use of certain words concerned translation from one language to another and the correspondence between symbols of formal language and the terms of ordinary language. There is no *a priori* guarantee that once the symbols of the formal language of classical physics have been translated into those of the new mechanics it will still be possible to associate the same names to analogous symbols in the two languages. We cannot ignore the fact that the system of axioms and definitions ensuring the unambiguous character of this correspondence in the original language has been completely replaced in the new theory. Carrying out a more precise analysis of these concepts thus means ascertaining the conditions whereby, starting from the new system of axioms of quantum mechanics, it is possible to give definitions of the concepts of 'position', 'velocity', 'energy' and 'time' compatible with the nature of the new formalism. And this, according to Heisenberg, meant laying down the conditions under which what remained of those concepts could be associated to the new mathematical symbols.

In principle, according to Heisenberg, we could even confine ourselves to recognizing that the form ('Gestalt') of a quantum object is completely exhausted as soon as we know (in a non-relativistic approximation of the theory) the mass of the object and the way it interacts with all fields and other objects. These are, in fact, the data required to write the Hamiltonian of any quantum-mechanical system. However, this is not enough because if we want to express the results of our observations we are forced to use expressions such as 'position of the electron'. For this reason, and not for any abstract philosophical requirement, it is necessary to establish what meaning a term such as 'position' can have for quantum theory, or rather to what degree mathematical symbols are translatable into the terms of ordinary language and the concepts of classical physics. Since natural language is indispensable to the theory only as a tool for describing experimental apparatus and the data collected thereby, the only possible quantistically acceptable definition of these terms and concepts is that which can be derived from the concrete experimental procedures by means of which it is possible to determine the position or the velocity of an electron. Consequently, only in experiments in which we try to measure the 'position of an electron' can we speak of the position of an electron. Otherwise, according to Heisenberg the term has no meaning and in no way helps to suggest a mental image of the intuitive content of the theory.

In the analysis of the concrete conditions for measurement of position and velocity, energy and time interval, he finally discovered the key to resolve the obvious contradictions one falls into when trying to attain an intuitive understanding of the formulas of quantum mechanics. The discontinuity of microscopic processes has physical consequences such as to prevent the use of these words – it correctly referred always and only to defined experimental situations – from coming into contradiction with the computation rules (5.10) holding for the symbols they may be associated with. In the classical example of the measurement of an electron's position, the experimental procedure involves observations by microscope under electron illumination. As is known, the classically foreseen diffraction effects are such that the wavelength of the light used for this purpose limits the accuracy of the measurement. This, according to Heisenberg, is not a problem since by choosing the right wavelength – he mentions a γ-ray microscope – we can, in principle, measure an electron's position as accurately as we desire. It must, however, be borne in mind that on the basis of the quantum laws, when the measurement is carried out the photon-electron scattering causes through the Compton effect a discontinuous variation in the momentum of the particle observed, which is the greater the shorter the wavelength of the light is, i.e. the more precise the measurement of the position. Quantum discontinuity, therefore, entails that 'the more precisely the position is determined, the less precisely the momentum is known, and conversely'[57]. In other words, in situations in which one can correctly speak of position, as a result of the discontinuous character of the processes caused by the experimental device's disturbance of the physical system, knowledge of part of the system is irreversibly precluded. In the example chosen, this makes it quite improper to use the term 'momentum'.

The conclusions Heisenberg drew from his analysis are therefore clear: the γ-ray microscope and other thought experiments discussed in the paper were aimed exclusively at the search for conditions making possible an unambiguous definition of the concepts of classical physics. He thus found that *'all the concepts used in classical theory for the description of a mechanical system can also be defined exactly for atomic processes in analogy to the classical concepts'*[58]. It is, in fact, a simple analogy that is involved, because the experiments that provide these definitions always entail a discontinuous interaction and hence an unavoidable uncertainty whenever we wish them to determine two canonically conjugated quantities simultaneously. In quantum formalism, the term 'co-ordinate of a particle', or rather its corresponding symbol, has been replaced with a two-dimensional table: an electron can no longer be represented as a corpuscle describing a trajectory and therefore susceptible of precise space-time co-ordination. We can nevertheless still speak of the 'position' or 'velocity' of the electron, using words inadequate to the task of describing physical reality, only because the conditions for the object's observability do not involve any ambiguity with respect to the original meaning of these terms. In this sense, according to Heisenberg, the necessary conditions for thinking that one had achieved an understanding of the intuitive content of the theory were fully satisfied.

We might also add that from the mathematical point of view Heisenberg did not make any particularly important discovery. The uncertainty relations, which Heisenberg expressed in the form

$$pq \approx h, \tag{5.11}$$

are nothing but a direct consequence of the quantum multiplication rule (5.10) and may be obtained, as he remarked in the paper, from a very simple generalization of Dirac and Jordan's formulation of the theory. He identified in these relations rather a general rule of translation between the symbols of the formal language of quantum mechanics and the terms of classical theory, and discovered – here the word is appropriate – that the restrictions imposed on their use derive from relations necessarily present in 'all experiments that we can use for the definition of these terms'[59]. In his view, a significant analogy existed between quantum mechanics and Einstein's theory of relativity. On the one hand, the definition of the concept of simultaneity is based on experiments in which it is assumed that the velocity of light is constant: finding a broader definition of the concept, e.g. with signals propagating themselves instantaneously, would mean showing that the theory was unfounded. On the other, an experiment allowing a broader simultaneous definition of the terms 'position' and 'velocity' than that contemplated by (5.11) would falsify quantum mechanics. It is no coincidence that Einstein himself tried to come up with ideal situations of this type in his first attempts to refute the Copenhagen interpretation[60].

According to Heisenberg, 'the applicability of the concepts of classical kinematics and mechanics can be justified neither from our laws of thought nor from experiment', i.e. it is not justifiable either logically or empirically. It was a consequence of formal relations which expressed the indeterminacy of certain symbols as a function of Planck's constant. The fact that these relations only lent themselves to qualitative predictions, while the concepts of momentum, position, energy and so on were precisely defined concepts for classical theory, should not be the cause of too much regret. He pointed out to those who might have criticized the abstract and symbolic character of quantum mechanics that to say 'the velocity in X direction is "in reality" not a number but the diagonal term of the matrix, is perhaps no more abstract and anti-intuitive than the statement that the electric field strengths are "in reality" the time part of an antisymmetric tensor located in space-time. The expression "in reality" here is as much and as little justified as it is in any mathematical description of natural processes'[61].

6

'Heisenberg['s] view was based on the following consideration: On one hand, the co-ordinates of a particle can be measured with any desired degree of accuracy by using, for example, an optical instrument, provided radiation of sufficiently short wave-length is used for illumination. According to the quantum theory, however, the scattering of radiation from the object is always connected with a finite change in momentum, which is the larger the smaller the wave-length of the radiation used. [...] The essence of this consideration is the inevitability of the quantum postulate in the estimation of the possibilities of measurement. A closer investigation of the possibilities of definition would still seem necessary in order to bring out the general complementary character of the description. Indeed, a discontinuous change of energy and momentum during observation could not prevent us from ascribing accurate values to the space-time co-ordinates, as well as to the momentum–energy components before and after the process. The reciprocal uncertainty which always affects the values of these quantities is [...] essentially an outcome of the limited accuracy with which changes in energy and momentum can be defined, when the wave-fields used for the determination of the space-time co-ordinates of the particle are sufficiently small'[62]. In this manner Bohr raised a crucial objection to Heisenberg's argument challenging its theoretical and epistemological assumption: the idea that the reality of atoms and electrons cannot be likened to that of the objects of our ordinary experience. Furthermore, he located the origin of the uncertainty relations in a different problem regarding the precision of the classical concepts, which he saw as making the complementary character of description in quantum mechanics quite clear.

By showing the compatibility of the formalism with the description of individual experimental situations, Heisenberg's interpretation had undoubtedly contributed to making the theory more consistent. Bohr himself was the first to recognize that 'this very circumstance that the limitations of our concepts coincide so closely with the limitations in our possibilities of observation, permits us – as Heisenberg emphasizes – to avoid contradictions'[63]. This did not prevent the theory, however, from being open to fundamental criticism, the first charge being directed at its presumed completeness. Heisenberg had assigned the task of providing a definition of individual concepts to the physical conditions of measurement and, furthermore, he had made the indeterminacy of some of the quantities of the system dependent on its discontinuous interaction with the experimental device. As a consequence of this, he had no argument against those who maintained that all quantities had been defined rigorously both before and after the interaction, and could therefore speak, for example, of the 'trajectory of an unobserved electron'. At best, therefore, quantum mechanics could thus be considered a phenomenologically well-constructed theory that was sufficiently protected from empirical falsification; of course, it could not be said to have great explanatory content. Heisenberg's viewpoint in fact admitted an entirely different conclusion from Bohr's as regards the question of physical reality: electrons are corpuscles of the classical type which, in principle, could be imagined as having exact space-time co-ordinates; quantum discontinuity rules out experimental determination of their state at a given instant and justifies the probabilistic nature of theoretical predictions. It is certainly no coincidence that this sort of argument was to serve as a basis for regarding quantum mechanics as incomplete. As early as the end of 1927, Einstein remarked that 'it might be a correct theory of statistical laws, but an insufficient conception of the individual elementary processes'[64].

Heisenberg had found the uncertainty relations and written his paper in a very few days, while Bohr was in Norway for a holiday. Without waiting for him to return to Copenhagen, he informed him about his new results by letter and, after having submitted the content of the theory to Pauli[65], sent the article to *Zeitschrift für Physik*. Bohr who had probably succeeded in defining his notion of complementarity in those weeks, greeted the discovery with enthusiasm but disagreed with the interpretation Heisenberg had given it. A deeper analysis of the possibilities of definition was to lead him to derive of the same uncertainty relations by other means and to carry out the final synthesis of the parallel theoretical paths that had contributed to the founding of quantum mechanics.

First of all, Bohr corrected a conceptual error Heisenberg had made in his discussion of the thought experiment of the γ-ray microscope – as we shall see, it was in reality a rather marginal element compared to the substance of his criticisms. The error Bohr noticed involved no modification of the conclusions Heisenberg had reached; it remained true that the precise determination of the position of the electron entailed an unavoidable indeterminacy in the value of the momentum. It was, however, incorrect to trace the cause of this result to the discontinuous variation in momentum, associated in quantum terms with the interaction between the system observed and the light quantum used to locate the electron. Even the most recent experiments on the Compton effect showed that if the direction of the reflected light quantum were established exactly it would be possible to deduce the discontinuous variation in momentum. In the discussion of the experiment, however, it was necessary to take into account the fact that the finite value of the angular aperture of the microscope places a limit on its resolving power; which, for a radiation of wavelength λ, entailed an uncertainty

$$2\varepsilon h/\lambda \qquad (5.12)$$

in the knowledge of the component of momentum of the light quantum parallel to the focal plane (in (5.12) ε is the sine of the semiangle of convergence). It could be easily demonstrated that the relation between this value and the minimum imprecision in the measurement of the electron's position was such that their product would always agree with (5.11)[66].

This was the point of departure for a more general discussion between Bohr and Heisenberg aimed at clarifying the extent to which the uncertainty relations were a consequence of the wave or of the discontinuous aspects of quantum theory. In those days Heisenberg wrote to Pauli: 'Bohr emphasizes that, *e.g.*, in the γ-ray microscope the diffraction of the waves is essential; I emphasize that the theory of light quanta and even the Geiger–Bothe experiment are essential. By exaggerating to one side as well as to the other one may argue at length without saying anything new'[67]. Heisenberg ended up accepting Bohr's amendments but very reluctantly, and perhaps because analogous objections had been voiced to him by Dirac[68], and was willing to admit that 'certain points could be better expressed and discussed in every detail, if only one begins a quantitative discussion directly with the waves'. But he stuck to his view that 'in the q[uantum] th[eory] only the discontinuities are interesting and that one can never emphasize them enough. For this reason I am also now, as previously, very happy with this latest work – in spite of the error mentioned – all the results of the paper are correct after all, and I am also in agreement with Bohr concerning these. Otherwise, there is a considerable difference of taste between Bohr and me regarding the word "visualizable"'[69]. The direct intervention of Pauli – who had gone to Copenhagen at the beginning of June – proved decisive in resolving the contrast between Bohr and Heisenberg with a compromise solution. The paper, which had been held up for two months, would be published without any corrections, but Heisenberg would add to the proofs a note of about 30 lines in which Bohr's name appeared five times and, more importantly, Heisenberg recognized that 'the uncertainty in our observation does not arise exclusively from the occurrence of discontinuities, but is tied directly to the demand that we ascribe equal validity to the quite different experiments which show up in the corpuscular theory on one hand, and in the wave theory on the other'. This was an enormous concession for Heisenberg. He concluded by thanking Bohr for having given him the opportunity to discuss the results of his most recent investigations, which will 'appear soon in a paper on the conceptual structure of quantum theory'[70].

Heisenberg had emphasized the discontinuity of quantum processes and mentioned their different ways of understanding the problem of intuition. Some historians have instead chosen to attribute their disagreement to Bohr's desire to place his pupil's discovery within the conceptual framework of complementarity[71]. Once again, however, the nature of the controversy was at bottom more theoretical than epistemological and concerned, in this instance, the contribution of wave mechanics to the definition of the interpretative basis of quantum mechanics.

The analysis of Bohr's scientific development and the reconstruction of the theoretical assumptions of complementarity have led to a drastic selection of the topics discussed and now to the omission of an important aspect of the history of quantum mechanics: the research programme which resulted from de Broglie and Einstein's wave approach to the study of the motion of atomic particles, and which culminated in Schrödinger's theory of 1926. This is not to say that we wish to reproduce here the by now traditional interpretative scheme tending to lend credence to the image of a sharp juxtaposition between two traditions of research within quantum physics: on the one side the advocates of a physics of the continuum; on the other the defenders of a discontinuous and acausal conception of the atomic world. In fact, as we shall see, the thesis which regards the official interpretation of quantum mechanics as the end result of this conflict, with the views of the physicists of Copenhagen and Göttingen prevailing, is approximative and reductive, or rather in at least one case historically untenable because it is incapable of adequately accommodating Bohr's 1927 paper. The theoretical roots of complementarity are largely embedded in the idea underlying wave mechanics: the wave representation of matter, or rather the utilization of wave fields to determine a particle's space-time co-ordinates.

Bohr had invited Schrödinger to Copenhagen in October 1926 to discuss the problems of quantum mechanics face to face and clarify their respective viewpoints. As Heisenberg was later to recall, those were days of extremely intense work and of discussions that went on for hours without ever reaching agreement[72]. Bohr defended the physical significance of wave theory and saw it as an equally essential component of Heisenberg and Born's mechanics; but he considered the epistemological goals of their programme naïve, and disagreed with Schrödinger, who sought to give a literal interpretation to the concept 'waves of matter' in order to expel the discontinuities of elementary quantum processes from atomic physics. To sustain his theses Bohr used his opponents' strong points and claimed that without the concept of transition one would have to drop the Einsteinian derivation of Planck's formula for radiation. Schrödinger believed that by representing the discrete states of the atom as stationary waves of matter he could describe the transitions as a resonance effect leading in a continuous process from one vibration to another; but then faced with Bohr's insistence, he limited himself to stating: 'If one has to stick to this damned quantum jumping, then I regret having ever been involved in this thing'[73].

They had the chance to restate the points of disagreement that had emerged from their discussions in two letters exchanged after the meeting. Schrödinger, though aware of the many cases in which his theory could not account for the experimental results, was unwilling to accept Bohr's viewpoint, which suggested attributing a merely symbolic character to all the apparently visualizable images. In his opinion, one contradiction was still unresolved: to use the language of waves, 'when a light wave strikes a large number of atoms (like a gas), then every single atom must after all emit a weak secondary wave, otherwise one cannot understand the attenuation and dispersion of the light wave. On the other hand, if the light wave has the resonance frequency [i.e. the frequency of a transition], then only a few single atoms may in fact suffer a considerable change ("being raised to a higher state")'. And in reply to Bohr's idea that the contradiction could be overcome by saying that 'the words and concepts used until now no longer suffice', he stated 'I do not feel satisfied with this ascertainment ['Konstatierung'], and from it I cannot deduce that I am justified in continuing to operate with contradictory statements. One may weaken the statements, by saying, e.g., that the collection of atoms "in certain respects behaves as if ..." and "in certain respects so as if ...", but this is so to speak merely a juridical expedient that cannot be converted into clear reasoning'. Schrödinger confessed to not knowing how one might free oneself from the contradiction; 'What I vaguely see before my eyes is only the thesis: Even if a hundred attempts have failed, one ought not to give up hope of arriving at the goal, I don't say through classical pictures, but through logically consistent conceptions of the true nature of the space-time events. It is extremely likely that this is possible'[74].

In his reply Bohr once again took the opportunity to express his own positive evaluation of a theory which, in his view, enabled one to understand many aspects of the discontinuous atomic processes, and to reaffirm that 'the concept of wave or corpuscle presents itself as the more suitable concept, according to the point in the description where the assumption of the discontinuities explicitly appears. In my opinion this is easily understood, since the definition of every concept or rather every word presupposes the continuity of the phenomena and hence becomes ambiguous as soon as this presupposition cannot be upheld'. But then he too yielded to the bitterness of the polemics: 'This is merely the abomination of the subterranean that you find disgusting, and I need hardly stress with what great interest I follow your endeavours to realize your brighter hopes. If you are not able completely to kill the ghosts in ordinary space and time, then perhaps a settlement may be reached in the future in a five-dimensional world'[75].

In a letter to Fowler, Bohr gave a more detached account of Schrödinger's visit: 'The discussions centred themselves gradually on the problem of the physical reality of the postulates of the atomic theory. We all agreed that a continuity theory in the form indicated in his last paper at a number of points leads to expectations fundamentally different from those of the usual discontinuity theory. Schrödinger himself continued in his hope that the idea of stationary states and transitions was altogether avoidable, but I think that we succeeded at least in convincing him that for the fulfilment of this hope he must be prepared to pay a cost, as regards reformation of fundamental concepts, formidable in comparison with that hitherto contemplated by the supporters of the idea of a continuity theory of atomic phenomena. I understood that Schrödinger had been working under the impression that the essential characteristics of the matrix mechanics was the final recognition of the impossibility of ascribing a physical reality to a single stationary state, but I think that this is a confounding of the means and aims of Heisenberg's theory. Just in the wave mechanics we possess now the means of picturing a single stationary state which suits all purposes consistent with the postulates of the quantum theory. In fact, this is the very reason for the advantage which the wave-mechanics in certain respects exhibits when compared with the matrix method'[76].

Where Bohr and Schrödinger did agree, Heisenberg dissented entirely. He did not even think the conditions existed for a comparison of the two programmes: 'Just as nice as Schrödinger is as a person, just as strange I find his physics. When you hear him, you believe yourself 26 years younger. In fact, Schrödinger throws overboard everything [that tastes] "quantum theoretical": Photo-electric effect, Franck collisions, Stern–Gerlach effect etc. Then it is not difficult to make a theory. But it just does not agree with experience'[77].

Bohr certainly did not defend Schrödinger's wave approach because it offered support for his own philosophical point of view or confirmed the ideas he had derived from Høffding's teaching and from his reading of James's psychological writings. He required no intellectual prompting enabling him to proclaim a priori the insuperability of dualism and the inseparability of subject and object. Wave mechanics was sufficient for him to solve definitively the problem he had been faced with in all its complexity from the time that he had sent Rutherford his memorandum on the atom's constitution. He could finally understand the physical and theoretical significance of Planck's hypothesis, of the universal constant that had long forced physicists to attribute nature with irrational behaviour. He therefore went back to the simple formulas of quantum theory,

$$E = h\nu \quad \text{and} \quad p = h\sigma \qquad (5.13)$$

whose real content he was now able to recognize clearly. They expressed nothing other than the fundamental contrast between the quantum of action and the classical concepts, precisely by virtue of the power the universal constant h has to establish a linear dependence between the energy E and the number of vibrations per unit of time ν, or between the momentum p and the number of waves per unit of length σ. Bohr would never have been able to arrive at such a conclusion, however, if the absolute generality of the formulas had not been demonstrated, that is without the contributions of de Broglie and of Schrödinger. Thanks to the light-quantum theory, they had initially been considered expressions of the so-called dual character of radiation; but after the wave theory of material particles and its significant experimental confirmations they appeared as the expression of a dualism intrinsic to the reality of microphysics. Although numerous experiments on the atomic nature of electricity unequivocally demonstrated the individual character of electrons, in certain cases one had to ascribe a typically wave-like behaviour to them. As is generally known, it is impossible to explain the results of the experiments of C. J. Davisson and L. H. Germer on electron diffraction unless the wave superposition principle is applied to the electrons[78]. For matter, therefore, the same anomalous experimental situation occurred whereby different phenomena alternately brought out unequivocally wave-like and corpuscular properties. Bohr could now show that this dualism was the result of the limits imposed by the quantum of action on the definition of certain classical concepts, in other words, the direct consequence of the hypothesis Planck had formulated at the start of the century.

The formulas, according to Bohr, symbolically summed up the opposition between the two conceptions, wave and corpuscular, of light and of matter. On the one hand, energy and momentum are quantities 'associated with the concept of particles, and hence may be characterized according to the classical point of view by definite space-time coordinates'; on the other, wavelength and period are quantities that 'refer to a plane harmonic wave train of unlimited extent in space and time'[79]. Bohr thus intended to emphasize in the first case that if we want the laws of conservation of energy and momentum to be satisfied in interaction between radiation and matter we cannot avoid referring to the corpuscular concept of the light quantum; and in the second case, that the wavelength and period serve to define the properties of a physical object which by its very nature lacks any location in space-time.

The doubts expressed in previous years about the validity of the superposition principle or the conservation principles arose precisely from the possibility of reading the formulas in such a way as to accentuate either the corpuscular or the wave aspects connected with the meaning of the symbols appearing there. The quantum postulate had been a theoretically acceptable translation of the content of the Planck–Einstein relations. However, it implied on the one hand that acceptance of the ordinary laws of the space-time propagation of light meant limiting oneself to statistical considerations (e.g., through Einstein's hypothesis of transition probability coefficients); and on the other that the requirement of causality for radiation processes could be satisfied only by accepting the notion of light quanta, and thereby renouncing all space-time description. This was at the heart of the disagreement between Bohr and Einstein. In the first case, the hypothesis of the quantization of radiation was rejected by means of rational arguments (the definition of the concept of frequency) which in the final analysis implied the defence of the principle of wave superposition, but one went no further than a probabilistic treatment of the radiation process. In the second, the rigorous verification of the conservation principles was demanded and a causal description of the interaction of matter and radiation was provided; but despite the attempts made (e.g. pilot waves), one gave up the possibility of describing the motion of the light quanta.

One could obviously not think of applying the notions of space-time and causality separately. In Bohr's opinion, the problem of dualism had to be tackled from a new perspective: the terms 'radiation in empty space' and 'isolated material particle', deriving from the association of the symbols of the quantum formulas with concepts defined in classical theory, were 'abstractions' as far as quantum theory was concerned. This was an effective way of saying that the names identified no object possessing physical reality and established no reference since the propositions necessary to explicate their meaning can apparently not be formulated in the language of quantum physics. On the contrary, it had to be borne in mind that the properties of the real physical objects abstractly referred to by the terms 'wave' and 'particle' are definable and observable only through processes of interaction with other systems and that, according to the fundamental quantum hypothesis, the physical quantity action exchanged between two systems is quantized, i.e. can never have a value less than h. Given these limitations, the verification of the concepts' conditions of definition would make it possible to identify the causes of the difficulties encountered in quantum theory by a causal space-time description, which were the source of the problem of dualism.

Bohr noted, however, that despite the contrast existing between the two conceptions, it was possible, on the basis of the wave representation of light and of matter, to re-establish the conditions for the validity of the ordinary modes of description. The superposition principle, in fact, allows us to regard a limitation of the extent of the wave fields in space and time as resulting from the interference of a group of elementary harmonic waves. Sufficiently localized wave fields then make it possible to determine the space-time co-ordinates of a particle. We can thus describe the individual elements of light and of matter in the language of waves, identifying for example, as de Broglie had demonstrated, the velocity of an electron with the so-called group velocity. It is, however, precisely these conditions which limit the field of applicability of space-time pictures in quantum theory, since the results of this localization are in some respects catastrophic. As shown by Rayleigh's theory on the resolving power of spectroscopes, if Δt and Δx represent the extension of the wave field in time and space, then the equations

$$\Delta t \, \Delta \nu \approx 1 \quad \text{and} \quad \Delta x \, \Delta \sigma_x \approx 1, \qquad (5.14)$$

which express the condition that the wave trains extinguish each other by interference at the space-time boundary of the wave field, must be satisfied. The localization of the wave field therefore entails a loss of precision in the definition of the period and the wavelength and, as is quite obvious on the basis of the simple formulas (5.13) of quantum theory, the constant h carries this loss of precision over into the definition of the corresponding energy and momentum. Therefore, any rigorous definition of the energy and momentum, and hence of the frequency and wavelength associated with a particle in its wave representation, shatters the notion of space-time localization. Vice versa, any definition of exact space-time co-ordination entails a loss of meaning of the concepts of energy and momentum and, in the final analysis, the inapplicability of the conservation laws. The theoretical role of the quantum of action, therefore, is to connect the superposition principle to the conservation principles, and this is precisely why it clashes with the classical concepts. In this manner one arrives at a conclusion that dissolves the basis of the dualism, in that it overturns the relationship between the fundamental physical principles and the theory's conceptual apparatus. Ultimately, the dualism arose from the fact that in order to save the classical concepts one ended up admitting that the quantum of action created a breach between the superposition principle and the laws of conservation. The exact definition of the concepts of time and space is now found in a relation of mutual exclusion with that of the concepts of energy and momentum. For this reason, Bohr concludes that in general 'the very nature of the quantum theory thus forces us to regard the space-time co-ordination and the claim of causality, the union of which characterizes the classical theories, as complementary but exclusive forms of the description'[80]. The conditions of definition of the concepts show, therefore, that though 'waves' and 'particles' remain in any case abstractions, the descriptions linked to those names can be assimilated into the language of quantum physics provided that a new logical relation of mutual exclusion is set up between them, to which Bohr gives the name complementarity. In other words, precisely because 'waves' and 'particles' are abstractions in the sense specified above, quantum mechanics is a theory of complementarity.

The passage to the uncertainty relations is, at this point, quite obvious from the formal point of view. Mathematically speaking one has only to compare the (5.14) relations with those of (5.13) to obtain Heisenberg's famous laws:

$$\Delta t \Delta E \approx h, \quad \Delta x \Delta p_x \approx h, \tag{5.15}$$

which set a maximum limit to the accuracy with which energy and time or momentum and position can be simultaneously determined.

The word 'determined' used in this statement is deliberately ambiguous because the meaning of these uncertainties can be interpreted in at least two different ways. We can claim, as Heisenberg did, that they are simply the consequence of the discontinuous variation in energy and momentum during an interaction of radiation and matter in the measurement of the space-time co-ordinates of particles. In his view, this is equivalent to admitting that quantum discontinuity imposes a restriction on our observations since with 'our observations of the position of an electron, we completely disturb its mechanical behaviour'; we must therefore resign ourselves 'to being unable to know, in principle, the present in all of its details'. However, once we have accepted the restrictions imposed by the uncertainty relations on the meaning of words such as 'position', 'velocity', etc. through the concrete procedures of measurement, we can also claim, as Heisenberg does, that a coherent intuitive content has been restored to quantum mechanics. To avoid any accusation of incompleteness, it is sufficient to impose on our model of description clauses like: 'the trajectory of an electron comes into existence only when we observe it'[81]. According to Heisenberg, there exists an identity or essential compatibility between observation and definition so that all of the restrictions imposed on our observations by discontinuity are directly reflected, through the theory's mathematical structure, in the limited use of the concepts: the impossibility of theoretically specifying velocity and position simultaneously therefore corresponds to the operative problem of their simultaneous observability. The question 'What is meant by the words "position [or velocity] of the electron"?' must therefore be replaced with the more correct formulation: 'How can we determine the position [or the velocity] of the electron?' And Heisenberg maintains that consistency with the uncertainty relations entails the reply that 'one can measure the position exactly, given that with the intervention of the measuring instrument we are confounding our knowledge of its velocity; vice versa, a more precise measurement of the velocity confounds our knowledge of the position'. It can thus be understood, Heisenberg reiterates, 'that the incomplete knowledge of a system is an essential component of any formulation of quantum theory'[82]; and in this Heisenberg is closer to Einstein than he is to Bohr.

Bohr's interpretation is diametrically opposed to this. In his view, there is a fundamental contradiction between conditions of observation and possibilities of definition, or rather that these stand in a relation of complementarity to each other. The question should therefore be answered in this way: if I measure the position of the electron precisely, the chosen conditions of observation preclude any definition of its velocity, and vice versa. In other words, emphasis should not be laid on the operational content of the definition of the concept of position when carrying out measurements of position, but rather the fact that the classical concepts employed in the space-time description of the phenomenon in quantum theory can only be defined if the classical concepts that allow us to give a causal description of the same phenomenon remain indeterminate, devoid of unambiguous definition. It is in this sense that we should interpret Bohr's statement to the effect that 'any measurement which aims at the ordering of the elementary particles in time and space requires us to forego a strict account of the exchange of energy and momentum between the particles and the measuring rods and clocks used as a reference system. Similarly, any determination of the energy and momentum of the particles demands that we renounce their exact co-ordination in time and space'[83].

From this we can deduce the arguments Bohr probably used in trying to convince Heisenberg to modify the substance of his article; 'the measurement of the positional co-ordinates of a particle is accompanied not only by a finite change in the dynamical variables, but also the fixation of its position means a complete rupture in the causal description of its dynamical behaviour, while the determination of its momentum always implies a gap in the knowledge of its spatial propagation'[84]. But Bohr did not even agree with Heisenberg on the theory's intuitive or visualizable content. In the letter he sent Einstein with the proofs of Heisenberg's article, he expressed all his doubts regarding this concept, preferring instead to emphasize the need to appeal precisely to those continuous aspects of the field theory that guaranteed, in his view, a coherent representation of quantum processes. 'As long as we only talk about particles and quantum jumps, it is difficult to find a simple presentation of the theory [...] This is because the uncertainty mentioned is not only connected to the presence of discontinuities but also to the very impossibility of a detailed description in accordance with those properties of material particles and light that find expression in the wave theory'[85].

7

'By amending the error running through the Heisenberg paper, [Bohr] has pushed the uncertainty relations into the foreground, but at the same time in a marvellously simple manner provided them with a quite marvellous universality. Something like this: Consider first solely the questions of LIGHT. Then immediately from pure WAVE KINEMATICS the following uncertainties (for example) $\Delta t \, \Delta \nu \approx 1$. The shorter the time duration of the wave signal, the greater the uncertainty in the definition of its frequency [...]. Further, from this result, on account of the Planck–Einstein relation $\varepsilon = h\nu, p = h/\lambda$ (momentum), the "reciprocal uncertainty relations"

$$\delta t \delta \varepsilon \approx h, \, \delta x \delta p \approx h.$$

Thus, the reciprocal uncertainty of the space-time data as opposed to the dynamical data emerge in general FIRST OF ALL IN THE DOMAIN OF LIGHT

$$xyzt \text{ contra } pqr$$

(in the exponent of the wave function they appear just in the combination

$$(2\pi i/h)(x_1 p_1 + x_2 p_2 + x_3 p_3 + x_4 p_4).)$$

So much for light. Now, however, such effects like the Compton effect in particular prove that the *CONSERVATION LAW* for the energy-momentum vector is valid in the interaction between light and movable matter. THUS, it follows for every such interaction that thanks to the conservation laws (!!!!!!!!!!!!) the above reciprocal uncertainty relations are transferred from light to matter (!!!!!!! BRAVO BOHR !!!!!!). This might cause you complete despair (witness indeed the desperate attempt of Slater Kramers Bohr) if it were not for the fact that just de Broglie–Schrödinger with the wave calculus and Born–Heisenberg–Dirac with the non-permutative matrix calculus were also "coming up with uncertainties" just from the matter aspect'[86].

This is how Ehrenfest summed up the arguments Bohr used in his discussions with Einstein at the 1927 Solvay Conference to defend his own interpretation of quantum mechanics and to illustrate the general content of Heisenberg's relations. Ehrenfest was exultant, and with his brief mention of the Bohr–Kramers–Slater theory he seemed to grasp the contribution that came from their attempt to defend the classical descriptive model. Only now did one understand what Bohr had clearly stated as soon as the empirical falsification of the virtual oscillator theory was confirmed: the model and the conservation laws were incompatible with one another. The uncertainty principle was the theoretical instrument which indicated how to go beyond the classical model of description and to reconcile within quantum physics the apparent conflict between the superposition principle and the conservation principles implicit in the dualism of light or radiation. The possibilities of definition of the concepts used in the description of experience clearly brought out a split in that model giving rise to a relation of complementarity between space-time description and causal description.

The whole of the reasoning behind Bohr's derivation of the uncertainty relations not only expresses the distance separating him from Heisenberg, but above all shows that the dualism is not its fundamental logical premise. The idea of complementarity stems from the contradiction between the concept of the quantum of action and the classical model of description, whereas dualism is simply the result of the attempt to describe microscopic phenomena in terms of this model and of an acritical application of the concepts and categories of classical physics. Logical or linguistic expedients would be of no avail in solving his problems. From the spring of 1925 on, his objective was to find the model of description of quantum physics. By then he had already understood that the dualism was a false or apparent problem, and this explains why, in spite of everything, he refused to accept experiments on the Compton effect as evidence in favour of the light-quanta hypothesis. The reality of atoms clearly showed that the space-time description conflicted with causality and the principles of conservation, and vice versa. In any case, with the idea of complementarity and a deeper analysis of the conditions of definition, dualism – understood as the existence of two opposing conceptions of physical reality – disappeared: electrons are neither waves nor particles but objects that accept modes of description which, when referred to classical criteria, force us to conclude that the world of atoms rests on the systematic violation of the law of causality and on the probabilistic course of all processes[87]. This cast no shadow on the completeness of the theory, it only showed the approximate character of our concepts and interpretative categories[88].

Notes

1 W. Heisenberg, 'Sprache und Wirklichkeit in der modernen Physik', in W. Heisenberg, *Schritte über Grenzen*, Munich: Piper Verlag, 1971, 160–81.

2 P. A. Schilpp, ed., *Albert Einstein...* cit. ch. 1 n. 7.

3 W. Heisenberg, 'Sprache...', cit. n. 1, 167.

4 Ibid., 169.

5 Ibid., 160.

6 Ibid., 165.

7 Ibid., 166.

8 Ibid., 170.

9 Ibid., 172–73.

10 Ibid., 173.

11 W. Heisenberg, 'Über quantentheoretische Umdeutung kinematischer und mechanischer Beziehungen', *Zeitschrift für Physik* **33** (1925), 879–93; *GW*, 382–96; English trans. in B. L. van der Waerden, ed., *Sources...* cit. ch. 4 n. 1, 261–76.

12 See, for example, D. Serwer, '*Unmechanischer Zwang...*' cit. ch. 3 n. 61; D. C. Cassidy, 'Heisenberg's First Core Model...', cit. ibid.

13 W. Heisenberg, 'Über quantentheoretische...' cit. n. 11, 880; *GW*, 383.

14 Pauli to Bohr, 12 December 1924, *CW5*, 422–26; English trans., 426–30; *WB*, 186–89.

15 See Pauli to Bohr, 31 December 1924, *CW5*, 433–35; English trans., 435–37; *WB*, 197–99.

16 This is Hendry's interpretation in particular: 'In preparing this paper, he adopted both Pauli's phenomenological approach and, after talking out the interpretation of the scheme with him during a short visit to Hamburg, his operational ideas as well. In its final form, Heisenberg's new presentation was based on a restriction to quantities that were in principle observable, and on a complete revision of kinematics. The electron orbits were finally abandoned, and the electrons themselves were replaced, as Pauli had earlier suggested, by systems of complex oscillators. Pauli himself could write, following the completion of this paper, that he and Heisenberg were as much in agreement as any two individuals could be. Bohr, meanwhile, turned away from the world of publication to that of contemplation' (*The Creation...* cit. ch. 1 n. 49, 66).

17 For a treatment of Lorentz and Drude's theory, see E. Whittaker, *A History of the Theories of Aether and Electricity*, Edinburgh–London: Nelson and Sons, 1953; for a discussion of the attempts of Debye, Sommerfeld and Davisson, see M. Jammer, *The Conceptual Development...* cit. ch. 2 n. 6, 189, which also contains a primary bibliography.

18 R. Ladenburg, 'Die quantentheoretische Deutung der Zahl der Dispersionelektronen', *Zeitschrift für Physik* **4** (1921), 451–71; English trans. in B. L. van der Waerden, ed., *Sources...* cit. ch. 4 n. 1, 139–57. For a discussion of Ladenburg's work and of subsequent developments of the

quantum theory of dispersion, see J. Mehra and H. Rechenberg, *The Historical Development...* cit. ch. 2 n. 11 , vol. II, section 3.5.

19 H. A. Kramers, 'The Law of Dispersion and Bohr's Theory of Spectra', *Nature* **113** (1924), 673–74; *CW5*, 44–45. The letter was sent on 25 March from the Copenhagen Institute for Theoretical Physics. In reality (as attested in Slater's letter to van Vleck of 27 July 1924, cit. in K. Stolzenburg, 'Introduction to Part I' cit. ch. 4 n. 2, 43), Kramers had derived the correct formula for dispersion directly from the correspondence principle, before Slater's arrival in Copenhagen; but it was only on the basis of the notion of virtual oscillators that he was able to interpret it physically by analogy with the classical process of dispersion.

20 This is what is maintained, for example, by J. Hendry ('Bohr–Kramers– Slater: A Virtual Theory...' cit. ch. 4 n. 8), who claims that the Bohr– Kramers–Slater theory 'was not a new theory, but rather the combination of a new interpretation with the existing technique of the quantum theory of dispersion' (190).

21 See above, ch. 4, *passim*.

22 H. A. Kramers, 'The Law of Dispersion...', cit. n. 19.

23 Ibid.

24 Ibid.

25 H. A. Kramers, 'The Quantum Theory of Dispersion', *Nature* **114** (1924), 310–311, mailed on 22 July. The letter is a reply to some critical observations by the American physicist Gregory Breit (ibid.), who found Kramers' second negative term unsatisfactory from the point of view of an oscillator model; Breit suggested a new approach, based on the correspondence principle, in which the virtual oscillators would be replaced by 'virtual orbits'.

26 Ibid. The method followed here by Kramers had been used also by Born in an article which appeared on 13 June ('Über Quantenmechanik', *Zeitschrift für Physik* **26** (1924), 379–95; English trans. in B. L. van der Waerden, ed., *Sources...* cit. ch. 4 n. 1, 181–98), in which he used the same form to repropose Kramers' theory of dispersion. It is interesting to note that Born, though he admitted to making ample use of 'the intuitive ideas, introduced by Bohr, Kramers and Slater [...] about the connection between frequencies and quantum jumps', claimed that 'our line of reasoning will be independent of the critically important and still disputed conceptual framework of that theory, such as the statistical interpretation of energy and momentum transfer' (ibid., 386).

27 H. A. Kramers, 'The Quantum...' cit. n. 25.

28 It might be useful to recall that Heisenberg collaborated with Kramers in the formal development and generalization of the theory of dispersion, and published with him a long paper, 'Über die Streuung von Strahlen durch Atome', *Zeitschrift für Physik* **31** (1925), 681–708; *GW*, 354–81; English trans. in B. L. van der Waerden, ed., *Sources...* cit. ch. 4 n. 1, 223–51.

29 E. Rüdinger, 'The Correspondence Principle as a Guiding Principle', in *Proceedings...* cit. ch. 1 n. 12, 357–67, takes up Heisenberg's claim to the effect that his work was the result of a 'sharpening of the correspondence principle', and reconstructs the formal developments which turned the correspondence principle into a rigorous mathematical tool.

30 This argument constitutes, for example, the interpretative presupposition of the work of Mara Beller ('Matrix Theory before Schrödinger: Philosophy, Problems, Consequences', *Isis* **74** (1983), 469–91: 471–72) on the

developments of the mechanics of matrices: 'Born had made a pivotal contribution towards a "truly discontinuous" theory by inventing a method (used in Heisenberg's 1925 paper) of replacing all differential coefficients by the corresponding difference quotients. This replacement reflected Born's belief that in the new quantum theory each physical quantity should depend on two discrete stationary states, and not on one continuous orbit, as in classical mechanics'. Beller's essay views this programme as part of the reconstruction of the origins of quantum philosophy, which was the result of 'a hybrid of the original radical matrix program, concepts revived from Bohr's work, and statistical compromises necessitated by the acceptance of Schrödinger's continuous theory'. According to the author, even sociological aspects should not be brushed aside as irrelevant to the theory: 'The Göttingen–Copenhagen physicists, however, presented a united front. They cooperated intimately, each contributing extensively to the emergence of the new philosophy. The distribution of talents in the Göttingen–Copenhagen group could not have been better. [...] Young physicists, who streamed into these centers from all over the world, were exposed automatically to the new philosophy' (ibid., 490–91). For a reconstruction which tends to emphasize especially the theoretical aspects underlying Heisenberg's method, see E. MacKinnon, 'Heisenberg, Models and the Rise of Matrix Mechanics', *Historical Studies in the Physical Sciences* **8** (1977), 137–88.

31 Heisenberg to Pauli, 9 July 1925, *WB*, 231–32.
32 W. Heisenberg, 'Über quantentheoretische...' cit. n. 11, 881; *GW*, 384.
33 Ibid.
34 'As characteristic of the comparison between classical and quantum theory with respect to frequency, one can write down the combination relations:

Classical:

$$v(n, \alpha) + v(n, \beta) = v(n, \alpha + \beta)$$

Quantum-theoretical:

$$v(n, n - \alpha) + v(n - \alpha, n - \alpha - \beta) = v(n, n - \alpha - \beta)$$

or

$$v(n - \beta, n - \alpha - \beta) + v(n, n - \beta) = v(n, n - \alpha - \beta).$$

In order to complete the description of radiation it is necessary to have not only the frequencies but also the amplitudes. [...]

Quantum-theoretical:

$$\mathrm{Re}\{A(n, n - \alpha)\, e^{i\omega(n, n - \alpha)t}\}$$

Classical:

$$\mathrm{Re}\{A_\alpha(n)\, e^{i\omega(n)\alpha t}\}.$$

[...] If we now consider a given quantity $x(t)$ in classical theory, this can be regarded as represented by a set of quantities of the form

$$A_\alpha(n)\, e^{i\omega(n)\alpha t}.$$

He also remarked that Fourier classical theory describes the orbital electron motion with a function

$$x(n, t) = \Sigma_\alpha A_\alpha(n)e^{i\omega(n)\alpha t}$$

'[but] a similar combination of the corresponding quantum-theoretical quantities seems to be impossible in a unique manner and therefore not meaningful, in view of the equal weight of the variables n and $n - \alpha$. However, one may readily regard the ensemble of quantities

$$A(n, n - \alpha)e^{i\omega(n, n - \alpha)t}$$

as a representation of the quantity $x(t)$ and then attempt to answer the above question: how is the quantity $x(t)^2$ to be represented?' In the representation of the product $x(t)y(t)$, based on the same procedure, Heisenberg found the commutative property for the corresponding quantum quantities. Ibid., 881–84; *GW*, 384–87.

35 N. Bohr, 'Atomic Theory...' cit. ch. 3 n. 57, 852; *CW5*, 280. Furthermore, Bohr saw the abandoning of all attempts at a space-time description as the major contrast between the new mechanics and classical mechanics: 'In contrast to ordinary mechanics, the new quantum mechanics does not deal with a space-time description of the motion of atomic particles. It operates with manifolds of quantities, which replace the harmonic oscillating components of the motion and symbolize the possibilities of transitions between stationary states in conformity with the correspondence principle. These quantities satisfy certain relations which take the place of the mechanical equations of motion and the quantization rules' (ibid.).

36 W. Heisenberg, 'Über quantentheoretische...' cit. n. 11, 893; *GW*, 396.

37 M. Born and P. Jordan, 'Zur Quantenmechanik', *Zeitschrift für Physik* **34** (1925), 858–88; English trans. in B. L. van der Waerden, ed., *Sources...* cit. ch. 4 n. 1, 277–306. In their application of matrix calculus to the foundation of the new mechanics, the authors refereed to R. Courant and D. Hilbert, *Methoden der mathematischen Physik I*, Berlin: Springer Verlag, 1924, ch. I. and to M. Born, W. Heisenberg and P. Jordan, 'Zur Quantenmechanik II', *Zeitschrift für Physik* **35** (1925), 557–615; *GW*, 397–455; English trans. in B. L. van der Waerden, ed., *Sources...* cit. ch. 4 n. 1, 321–85.

38 M. Born, W. Heisenberg and P. Jordan, cit. n. 37, 557–58; *GW*, 397–98.

39 Ibid., 558; *GW*, 398.

40 Ibid.

41 Ibid.

42 P. A. M. Dirac, 'The Fundamental Equations of Quantum Mechanics', *Proceedings of the Royal Society of London* **A109** (1925), 642–53; also in B. L. van der Waerden, ed., *Sources...* cit. ch. 4 n. 1, 307–20.

43 Ibid., 642.

44 P. A. M. Dirac, 'Quantum Mechanics and a Preliminary Investigation of the Hydrogen Atom', *Proceedings of the Royal Society of London* **A110** (1926), 561–79: 562; also in B. L. van der Waerden, ed., *Sources...* cit. ch. 4 n. 1, 417–27. The article is dated 22 January 1926.

45 Ibid., 563.

46 Bohr to Oseen, 26 January 1926, *CW5*, 405–8 (in Danish); English trans., 238–40

47 *SHQP*, Interview with W. Heisenberg, conducted by T. S. Kuhn (Munich 25 February 1963), Tape 52a, Transcript 16–17.

48 Ibid.
49 W. Heisenberg, 'Über den anschaulichen Inhalt der quantentheoretische Kinematik und Mechanik', *Zeitschrift für Physik* **43** (1927), 172–98; *GW*, 478–504; *CW5*, 160–86. The English translation of the article is in J. A. Wheeler and W. H. Zureck, eds., *Quantum Theory and Measurement*, Princeton: Princeton University Press, 1983, 62–84. In this regard, attention should be drawn to what we regard as the excessively free character of the translation made by the editors of the volume, who, for example, translate the title of the paper as 'The Physical Content of Quantum Kinematics and Mechanics'.
50 For the secondary literature as well, see the already cited general histories of quantum mechanics by Jammer, Mehra and Rechenberg. See also E. MacKinnon, *Scientific Explanation and Atomic Physics*, Chicago and London: The University of Chicago Press, 1982; 'The Rise and Fall of Schrödinger's Interpretation', in P. Suppes, ed., *Foundation of Quantum Mechanics: The 1976 Stanford Seminar*, Mich.: Lansing, 1979, 1–57; L. Wessels, 'Schrödinger's Route to Wave Mechanics', *Studies in History and Philosophy of Science* **10** (1979), 311–40.
51 The text used here is that of the 'Quantenmechanik' lecture presented at the 89 Versammlung Deutscher Naturforscher und Aertze in Düsseldorf in the autumn of 1926 and published in *Die Naturwissenschaften* **45** (1926), 989–94. In it, Heisenberg expressed his own point of view on the most controversial theoretical and epistemological problems of quantum theory; it is therefore a fundamental point of reference for reconstructing the presuppositions of his 1927 paper.
52 Ibid., 990.
53 Ibid.
54 Ibid., 991.
55 W. Heisenberg, 'Über den anschaulichen Inhalt...' cit. n. 49, 172; *GW*, 478; *CW6*, 160.
56 Ibid., 173; *GW*, 479; *CW6*, 161.
57 Ibid., 175; *GW*, 481; *CW6*, 163.
58 Ibid., 179; *GW*, 485; *CW6*, 167.
59 Ibid.
60 See above, ch. 1 n. 7.
61 W. Heisenberg, 'Über den anschaulichen Inhalt...' cit. n. 49, 196; *GW*, 502; *CW6*, 184. Heisenberg recalled the intellectual experience of those months in the following manner: '[...] just by these discussions with Bohr I learned that the thing which I in some way attempted could not be done. That is one cannot go entirely away from the old words because one has to talk about something. [...] So I could realize that I could not avoid using these weak terms which we always have used for many years in order to describe what I see. So I saw that in order to describe phenomena one needs a language. [...] Well we do have a language and that is the situation in which we are. [...] we actually do use these precise terms and then we actually learn by quantum theory that we have used them in too precise a manner. The terms don't get hold of the phenomena, but still, to some extent, they do. I realized, in the process of these discussions with Bohr, how desperate the situation is. On the one hand we knew that our concepts don't work, and on the other hand we have nothing except the concepts with which we could talk about what we see. [...] I think this tension you just have to take; you can't avoid it. That was perhaps the strongest experience of these months'

(*SHQP*, Interview with W. Heisenberg, conducted by T. S. Kuhn (Munich 27 February 1963), Tape 52b, Transcript 26).

62 N. Bohr, 'The Quantum Postulate...' cit. ch. 1 n. 1, 582–83; *CW6*, 150–51.

63 Bohr to Einstein, 13 April 1927, *CW6*, 418–21, English trans., 21–24.

64 Einstein to Sommerfeld, 6 November 1927, cit. in J. Kalckar, 'Introduction to Part I' cit. ch. 1 n. 1, 41. See below, ch. 6.

65 Heisenberg had written a long letter to Pauli in which he reported at length on the contents of his paper (27 February 1927, *WB*, 376–81). What Pauli's response was is not known, but from a letter of Heisenberg's of 9 March (*WB*, 383–84) it is possible to deduce that Pauli, though accepting the substance of the argument, had offered certain criticisms and suggestions, for which Heisenberg thanked him.

66 N. Bohr, 'The Quantum Postulate...' cit. ch. 1 n. 1, 583; *CW5*, 151.

67 Heisenberg to Pauli, 4 April 1927, *WB*, 390–91.

68 See Heisenberg's letter to Dirac of 27 April, cit. in J. Kalckar, 'Introduction to Part I' cit. ch. 1 n. 1, 17–18.

69 Heisenberg to Pauli, 16 May 1927, *WB*, 394–96.

70 W. Heisenberg, 'Über den anschaulichen Inhalt...' cit. n. 49, 197–98; *GW*, 503–4; *CW5*, 185–86.

71 For example, Jammer corrects the historico-conceptual error in the interpretation according to which the notion of complementarity was derived from Heisenberg's relations. In his view, the contrast between the two physicists was, on the contrary, the result of the position whereby Bohr 'rejected [Heisenberg's] more formal approach and regarded the wave–particle duality as the ultimate point of departure for an interpretation of the theory'. 'Heisenberg's work prompted Bohr to give his thoughts on complementarity a consistent and final formulation'; 'in Heisenberg's reciprocal uncertainty relations', however, 'he saw a mathematical expression which defines the extent to which complementary notions may overlap, that is, may be applied simultaneously but, of course, not rigorously' (M. Jammer, *The Conceptual Development...* cit. ch. 2 n. 6, 345 ff.).

72 'The discussions between Bohr and Schrödinger began already at the railway station in Copenhagen and were continued each day from early morning until late at night. Schrödinger stayed in Bohr's house and so for this reason alone there could hardly be an interruption in the conversations. And although Bohr was otherwise most considerate and amiable in his dealings with people, he now appeared to me almost an unrelenting fanatic, who was not prepared to make a single concession to his discussion partner or to tolerate the slightest obscurity. It will hardly be possible to convey the intensity of passion with which the discussions were conducted on both sides, or the deep-rooted convictions which one could perceive equally with Bohr and with Schrödinger in every spoken sentence. [...] So the discussion continued for many hours throughout day and night without a consensus being reached. After a couple of days, Schrödinger fell ill, perhaps as a result of the enormous strain. He had to stay in bed with a feverish cold. Mrs. Bohr nursed him and brought tea and cakes, but Niels Bohr sat on the bedside and spoke earnestly to Schrödinger: 'But surely you must realize that ...'" (*SHQP*, Interview with W. Heisenberg, conducted by T. S. Kuhn (Munich 25 February 1963), Tape 52a, Transcript 11–12).

73 Ibid.

74 Schrödinger to Bohr, 23 October 1926, *CW6*, 459–61; English trans., 12–13.

75 Bohr to Schrödinger, 2 December 1926, *CW6*, 462–63; English trans., 14.
76 Bohr to Fowler, 26 October 1926, *CW6*, 23–24.
77 Heisenberg to Pauli, 28 July 1926, *WB*, 337–38.
78 For a reconstruction of the investigations which led to Davisson and Germer's discovery, and for references to the primary literature, see M. Jammer, *The Conceptual Development...* cit. ch. 2 n. 6, 149 ff.; A. Russo, 'Fundamental Research at Bell Laboratories: The Discovery of Electron Diffraction', *Historical Studies in the Physical Sciences* **21** (1981), 117–60.
79 N. Bohr, 'The Quantum Postulate...' cit. ch. 1 n. 1, 581; *CW6*, 149.
80 Ibid., 5 80; *CW6*, 148.
81 Heisenberg to Pauli, cit. n. 65.
82 W. Heisenberg, 'Atomforschung...' cit. ch 1 n. 48.
83 N. Bohr, 'Die Atomtheorie...' cit. ch. 1 n. 19, 76–77.
84 N. Bohr, 'The Quantum Postulate...' cit. ch. 1 n. 1, 584; *CW6*, 152.
85 Bohr to Einstein, 13 April 1927, *CW6*, 418–21; English trans., 21–24.
86 Ehrenfest to Goudsmit, 3 November 1927, in J. Kalckar, 'Introduction to Part I' cit. ch. 1 n. 1, 37–41.
87 D. Murdoch (*Niels Bohr's Philosophy of Physics*, Cambridge: Cambridge University Press, 1987, 56 ff.) gives a different interpretation, tracing the origin of the notion of complementarity and Bohr's interpretation of the uncertainty relations directly to the problem of dualism. In his view, Bohr, who had had always manifested his scepticism in regard to the question of dualism, 'towards the end of 1926 [...] changed [his attitude] somewhat: he came to hold that in any situation in which one of the two classical models fails, it is not only appropriate to employ the other but also desirable. He had hit upon one of the two main points in his thesis of complementarity, viz. that the two models are indispensable; it was the uncertainty principle that gave him the idea of the other point, viz. that the two models are applicable only in mutually exclusive experimental circumstances'. The notion of complementarity was therefore, according to Murdoch, born from the conviction Bohr had arrived at in 1927 'that quantum mechanics required in a sense the generalization of the two classical models of particle and wave. In classical physics these two models generally pertain to different theories, the particle model to the mechanical theory of matter, the wave model to the electromagnetic theory of radiation. In quantum physics, however, the two models pertain to one theory, quantum mechanics, and each is applicable to matter and radiation'. Given his point of view, however, Murdoch is forced to claim that the quantum postulate, according to Bohr, gives rise to two distinct types of complementarity: the wave–corpuscle complementarity, and the complementarity between space-time descriptions and the energy-momentum descriptions.
88 Complementarity, inasmuch as it rendered plain the meaning of Planck's idea, marked the end of Bohr's 15-year programme of research. The new theory, among other things, provided him with the tools with which to solve the many problems raised by the introduction of the notion of stationary state and the formulation of the correspondence principle. In reality, only one question needed answering: how could it be that concepts so disparate from, and defined – what is more – in theoretical contexts incompatible with, one another, such as the notion of stationary state and that of orbiting electron, in certain cases were endowed with the same interpretative efficacy; why did terms which could be given diverging descriptions have the singular property of fixing the same reference? In quantum mechanics, the

rigorous definition of the concept of stationary state had been obtained by applying Schrödinger's theory to the case of bound electrons: the stationary states are adequately represented by the oscillations of the wave function – in this way the notion of quantum number could be related very simply to the number of nodes in an oscillation. But Schrödinger had also shown, on the one hand, that one could 'associate with the solutions of the wave equation a continuous distribution of charge and current, which, if applied to a characteristic vibration, represents the electrostatic and magnetic properties of an atom in the corresponding stationary state'; and, on the other, that 'the superposition of two characteristic solutions corresponds to a continuous vibrating distribution of electrical charge, which on classical electrodynamics would give rise to an emission of radiation' (N. Bohr, 'The Quantum Postulate...' cit. ch. 1 n. 1, 586; *CW6*, 154). It is precisely on the basis of these results that Schrödinger came to believe that the developments of his theory would lead to the elimination of the irrational element present in the quantum postulate and to a complete description of quantum phenomena in the spirit of the classical theories. Once again, such a hope seemed to Bohr entirely unfounded because he thought it was evident that the theory of stationary states referred to closed systems which, by definition, exclude all processes of interaction; on the other hand, it was precisely this that made it possible to understand how the quantum theory of the atom could have developed on the basis of the mechanical model, despite the inadequacy of the concept of orbit. The formalism of Schrödinger's theory unravelled, in the first place, the enigma of the limit region, where the stationary states can be described using the laws of the motion of electrons. The wave representation of the stationary states enables us to determine the values of their energies; in accordance with Heisenberg's relations, this implies that, generally speaking, one has to give up all space-time description of hypothetical particles associated with those states. The fact that the general solution of the wave equation is obtained by means of superpositions of proper vibrations, however, showed that in certain cases a description of this type was allowed, and that one could therefore speak of the motion of an electron in a stationary state. In the states with large quantum numbers, in fact, it is possible to construct, by superimposing separate oscillations, a wave group which is sufficiently localized – which is small, in other words, compared to the size of the atom – whose propagation approximates the image of a material particle in motion. To express a judgement on the reality of the stationary states and on their representation in terms of the motion of electrons, one had to reconsider, however, in light of the complementary way of describing a particle, the quantistically defined properties of such a concept: the stationary state entails the complete renunciation of all temporal descriptions, and excludes all interactions with physical entities not part of the system. These were the hypotheses required in order to apply the quantum postulate to all problems concerning the structure of the atom. The fact of having assumed that the system always had a well-established energy value associated to it, in any case, amounted to implicitly admitting that the causal connection requirement expressed by the conservation laws was always satisfied. Now, the autonomy of the concept of stationary state and its irreducibility to a coherent mechanical picture were proven precisely in the limit region where, according to wave theory, the conditions exist that allow one to speak in terms of the motion of particles. To identify a stationary state one must assume that the system interacts, for example, with radiation, that it has a sufficiently well-defined energy level for the conservation laws to be applied. In this case, however, the uncertainty relations entail a loss of temporal definition, which forces us to assume that the interaction lasts longer than the period of oscillation given by (5.3) – of the oscillation, that is, associated with the transition process. In the region of large quantum numbers where there exists, to use the old language of the mechanical model, a coincidence between mechanical frequencies and optical frequencies, this period of oscillation can be interpreted as the period of the electron's revolution. Hence one deduces that to establish the energy level of a stationary state entails a loss of definition in the concept of time, and therefore an uncertainty in the localization of the electron which is at least equal to the electron's motion along an entire orbit. Both the possibilities of definition and the conditions of observation required for the determination of a stationary state rule out any possibility of its representation in terms of electronic orbits; it is in fact impossible to establish a causal connection between observations which tend to determine a stationary state and preceding observations from which one could have derived information on the behaviour of the individual particles. According to Bohr, however, one must conclude that 'the concepts of stationary states and individual transition processes within their proper field of application possess just as much or as little "reality" as the very idea of individual particles. In both cases we are concerned with a demand of causality complementary to the space-time description, the adequate application of which is limited only by the restricted possibilities of definition and of observation' (ibid., 589; *CW6*, 157). If the correspondence relation expressed the impossibility of translating those concepts into the properties of the orbiting electron model, thereby protecting the theory from the limitations deriving from the application of the laws of mechanics and electromagnetism, the relation of complementarity showed that the reality of atoms can never be assimilated to any form of model-based representation.

CHAPTER 6

The Bohr–Einstein confrontation: phenomena and physical reality

1

As Quine wrote in 1961, what strikes us in a paradox is its initial air of absurdity, which develops into a sort of psychological discomfort when we compare the conclusions of the reasoning with the apparently irrefutable arguments on which it is based. However, as he went on to observe, 'More than once in history the discovery of paradox has been the occasion for major reconstruction at the foundations of thought'. Catastrophe may therefore lurk even in the most innocent-seeming of paradoxes and force us to recognize the arbitrary nature 'of a buried premise or of some preconception previously reckoned as central to physical theory, to mathematics or to the thinking process'[1]. More recently, ideas of this kind have been used to assert in general that the role of paradox in the growth of knowledge is to generate category switches and to construct new universes of discourse[2]. It could also be argued that paradoxes constitute elements of the logic of discovery capable of amplifying and thus making intelligible the still obscure phases accompanying paradigm shifts. Paradoxes would thus represent points of accumulation for the tension created between a given system of conceptual representation and a theory or empirical discovery that violates it.

Historians of science have tried different interpretative approaches in their attempts to unravel the thought process that was to lead Einstein in 1905 to the formulation of special relativity and the simultaneous demolition of the classical conception of space and time. However, the only definite clue discovered remains the identification at the very basis of Einstein's arguments of a paradox supposedly written directly into Maxwell's equations or, to be more precise, of a paradoxical consequence arising from the attempt to fit the description of electromagnetic phenomena into the world-view of Newtonian mechanics. This is the well-known paradox, which Einstein first encountered at the age of 16, of the observer following a light ray at the speed of light. The paradox arises from the fact that if we assume the classical condition on co-ordinate transformations for inertial systems, and hence admit the validity of Galileo's composition of velocity, the observer should see the ray as an electromagnetic field oscillating in space in a state of rest. We would thus be obliged to conclude that, at least for that particular observer, the laws of physics are not the same laws as those experienced by any other inertial observer[3].

It was probably either ignorance of this paradox or underestimation of its logical force that prevented Lorentz and Poincaré from anticipating Einstein's discovery by a few years and obliged them to use artful expedients to solve the problem of the formal invariance of Maxwell's equations. Given the failure of experimental attempts to detect effects caused by the existence of a hypothetical aether wind – which would have made it possible, among other things, to determine the absolute velocity of the Earth – they tinkered with the system of hypotheses of electrodynamic theory in such a way as to reconcile the validity of the general principles of physics with the impossibility of observing certain empirical consequences of the theory[4]. However, the paradox was one of exceptional heuristic power if it is true, as Einstein claims, that it already contained the germ of special relativity. In fact, it could never have been satisfactorily clarified 'as long as the axiom of the absolute character of time, viz., of simultaneity, unrecognizably was anchored in the unconscious'[5]. However, if identification of this axiom and recognition of its arbitrary character were necessary conditions for what we may call the technical solution to the paradox, this entailed a whole series of philosophical choices of a decidedly arduous character in the light of the modern tradition of science. This explains why, again in his 'Autobiographical Notes', Einstein felt the need to recall the intellectual debt his theory owed to the writings of David Hume and Ernst Mach. Bringing to light the archetype of absolute time to then reveal its arbitrary nature as an implicit axiom of a particular theoretical system involved some general theses in the methodological sphere. For example, that our modes of apprehension have an intrinsic variability and historical character marked by the various attempts made to equip our languages for the description of the objects of knowledge. Furthermore, that there exist no modes of thought or languages, however formalized, reflecting some structure of reality that we can be said to have grasped once and for all from an absolute viewpoint. The acceptance of such theses was, at the time, anything but an obvious step since it actually meant calling into question one of the ideals long pursued by modern science, i.e. the identification of a finite nucleus of laws of nature valid on all spatial and temporal scales. It also meant abandoning the idea that such a nucleus represented the limit towards which our knowledge would converge[6].

The 'constancy of the light velocity' and the 'independence of the laws of the choice of the inertial system' are thus contradictory assertions for the classical picture of the world. However, it can be demonstrated that their incompatibility is only apparent on the following conditions. First, we adopt a new universal principle asserting that the laws of physics are invariant with respect to the Lorentz transformations. Secondly, we construct a new universe of discourse which renounces the customary separation of the ideas of space and time. Finally, we accept a new physical picture of reality calling into question the absolute character of phenomena.

The history of quantum mechanics is also a history of paradoxes, of attempts made either to remove the theoretical and epistemological obstacles arising from the impossibility of analysing quantum effects by reference to the normal frameworks of physics, or to identify limiting-case experimental situations such as would justify the search for theoretical solutions better capable of expressing the cognitive aims of science. The fact that, as in the case of Einstein's relativity theory, the interpretative problems involved in the discovery of quantum mechanics have often assumed this concise and highly expressive form is no coincidence. In this case, too, it was a matter of bringing to light certain preconceptions and recognizing both that they have acted as axioms for particular theoretical representations of nature and that it is arbitrary to defend their absolute validity once new elements of knowledge have led to paradoxical consequences within such representations. Again it was recognized that the contradictions could be eliminated by adopting a new general physical principle together with a new and more abstract picture of reality. Above all, with the solution of the paradoxes produced by the indivisibility of the quantum of action, the subjective character of all physical phenomena became more evident and the description of objects still more closely and necessarily dependent upon the positions of the observer and the observed.

Thus, one of the strongest and least vulnerable arguments used above all by Bohr and Pauli to defend the idea of complementarity and the probabilistic interpretation of the wave function claimed that these were the only conceptual tools capable of unravelling the paradox of wave–

corpuscle dualism. For that matter, neither is it any coincidence that at the origin of Einstein's rejection of the theory and call for a redefinition of the foundations of microphysics lay an apparently paradoxical implication of quantum mechanics.

2

'What would you say of the following situation? Suppose two particles are set in motion towards each other with the same, very large, momentum, and that they interact with each other for a very short time when they pass at known positions. Consider now an observer who gets hold of one of the particles, far away from the region of interaction, and measures its momentum; then, from the conditions of the experiment, he will obviously be able to deduce the momentum of the other particle. If, however, he chooses to measure the position of the first particle, he will be able to tell where the other particle is. This is a perfectly correct and straightforward deduction from the principles of quantum mechanics; but is it not very paradoxical? How can the final state of the second particle be influenced by a measurement performed on the first, after all physical interaction has ceased between them?'[7]. This was how, in 1933, Einstein explained to Rosenfeld the reasons for his firm opposition to the official interpretation of quantum mechanics. The same problem was taken up in the paper he wrote in the spring of 1935 together with Boris Podolski and Nathan Rosen[8], which was to become known as the Einstein–Podolski–Rosen paradox although the term is not quite appropriate in this case. In fact, not only is the paradox not the object of their analysis, but above all, as we shall see, no reason is given why, within the framework of quantum mechanics, it would be possible to conclude that the act of measurement on one system transfers information to another system – at a distance and instantaneously – enabling it to modify its own state. This is true in the sense that no logical contradiction is demonstrated or arbitrary premise identified in the argument that makes it possible to derive such absurd conclusions from general physical principles. This had, in actual fact, been precisely the aim of Einstein's initial attempts at refutation, when he had sought in vain to demonstrate the inconsistency of the theory by means of thought experiments not subject to the restrictions imposed by the indeterminacy relations[9]. The Einstein–Podolski–Rosen paradox is actually a demonstration making it possible to infer from a final contradiction the falsity of the premise and hence to regard the theory as incomplete. However, the premises of the demonstration are various and not all so evident. 'Any serious consideration of a physical theory must take into account the distinction between the objective reality, which is independent of any theory, and the physical concepts with which the theory operates. These concepts are intended to correspond with the objective reality, and by means of these concepts we picture this reality to ourselves'[10]. The paper opens with this philosophical demand, which binds science with regard to the cognitive scope of its conceptual frameworks, lays down criteria for assessing the success of a theory, and establishes definitive criteria for its acceptance. It is not sufficient that its calculations as regards the facts of nature should agree closely with observation and measurement. This may tell us something about its correctness, but the three authors themselves regard quantum mechanics as a correct theory. What is required in their view is that the theory should fulfil the so-called condition of completeness: *'every element of the physical reality must have a counterpart in the physical theory'*[11]. Given the premises, this was an obvious epistemological requirement. If we assume the existence of a reality corresponding to our modes of representation only on condition that the concepts defined within our theoretical framework have fixed unambiguous reference and that, conversely, each element of reality possesses a corresponding theoretical term, we can then believe that the pictures described by these concepts are capable of reflecting the structure of the external world. The problem was not new. The interpretative objectives proposed were, as we have seen, the same as had characterized and influenced the initial development of the quantum theory of the atom. However, as Podolski was to stress, the authors saw a demand for realism of this type as implicit in the very nature of scientific knowledge: 'Physicists believe that there exist real material things independent of our minds and our theories. We construct theories and invent words (such as electron, positron, etc.) in an attempt to explain to ourselves what we know about our external world and to help us to obtain further knowledge of it'. In his view, asking a theory to supply a good picture of objective reality was equivalent to subjecting it to severe controls to make sure that it 'contain[s] a counterpart for every element of the physical world'[12].

It is, however, obvious that any attempt to translate this general criterion into a concrete tool to analyse the structure of a theory immediately gives rise to a difficulty threatening to compromise the basis on which the whole argument rests. The completeness condition would, in fact, appear to depend upon a priori philosophical assumptions making it possible first to determine what are to count as the elements of reality and then to establish rules for correspondence between them and the system of concepts. This difficulty is referred to explicitly by the authors of the paper, who do not, however, consider an exhaustive definition of reality necessary for their purposes and maintain that the question can be confined to simple considerations regarding the results of measurement and experimental procedures: 'We shall be satisfied with the following criterion, which we regard as reasonable. *If, without in any way disturbing a system, we can predict with certainty (i.e. with probability equal to unity) the value of a physical quantity, then there exists an element of physical reality corresponding to this physical quantity.* It seems to us that this criterion, while far from exhausting all possible ways of recognizing a physical reality, at least provides us with one such way, whenever the conditions set down in it occur. Regarded not as a necessary, but merely as a sufficient, condition of reality, this criterion is in agreement with classical as well as quantum-mechanical ideas of reality'[13].

The assessment of how much there is that is trivial and how much that is reasonable in this assumption and in the whole epistemological preamble to the paper would require a great deal of analysis and inevitably involve key chapters in the history of philosophy and philosophy of science. In the discussions following the paper it has very often been preferred simply to point out the cautious nature of this formulation, which would appear to imply no judgement as to the nature of physical reality: the quantities appearing in our interpretative frameworks are not real but merely correspond to elements of reality[14]. It is not our intention to tackle such questions here, also because for our purposes it is sufficient to draw attention to an aspect concerning the logical structure of Einstein, Podolski and Rosen's argument, an aspect moreover upon which both critics and supporters of their views agree: the criterion of reality is so essentially tied up with the argument that were it to be proven untenable the whole demonstration would collapse. In any case, the purpose of the paper is clear. The authors intend to test the completeness of quantum mechanics or, to be more precise, to ascertain whether the type of description of physical reality admitted by its formalism fulfils the requisites that, according to their assumptions, any complete description must meet. The demonstration is divided into two parts reflecting the structure of the programme. The first attempts to characterize the theory's modes of description in the light of the completeness condition and defines the degree of reality attributable to the quantities determining the state of a quantum system. The second establishes the existence of experimental situations requiring broader description than that permitted by quantum mechanics. It is at this point that the criterion of reality comes into play and that an implicit assumption becomes necessary which, as we shall see, involves a singular solution to the paradox of 1933.

To illustrate the descriptive potential of quantum mechanics, the authors discuss the example of a particle with only one degree of freedom. The quantum state of the system is completely characterized, for the theory, by the wave function Ψ, which describes its physical quantities. In general, to each physical quantity α of the system there corresponds an operator A such that, if the wave function Ψ that determines its state is an autofunction of A then

$$A\Psi = a\Psi, \tag{6.1}$$

where a is a number. This means that for any particle in state Ψ, the theory lays down that the physical quantity α certainly possesses the value a, and this is also the result that would be obtained by measuring α. On the basis of the criterion of reality, we can therefore state that there exists an element of reality that corresponds to the quantity α. If, for example, the wave function is given by

$$\Psi = e^{(2\pi i/h)p_o x}, \tag{6.2}$$

where p_o is a constant and x an independent variable, since the operator associated with the momentum is

$$p = (h/2\pi i)\frac{\partial}{\partial x}, \tag{6.3}$$

(6.1) becomes

$$p\Psi = (h/2\pi i)\frac{\partial}{\partial x} e^{(2\pi i/h)p_o x} = p_o\Psi. \tag{6.4}$$

Therefore, if the state of the particle is represented by (6.2), the momentum will certainly have the value p_o, and for Einstein, Podolski and Rosen: 'It thus has meaning to say that the momentum of the particle in [this] state is real'[15]. We could not, however, in this case assign a

definite value to the position of the particle since there corresponds to it
an operator which for state [6.2] does not satisfy equation [6.1]. Quantum
mechanics says, for example, that if one measures position there is a
certain probability that the result will lie within a certain interval of
values. However, as the authors observe, 'Such a measurement however
disturbs the particle and thus alters its state. After the coordinate is
determined, the particle will no longer be in the state given by [6.2]. The
usual conclusion from this in quantum mechanics is that *when the
momentum of a particle is known, its coordinate has no physical reality*'[16].
On the one hand, when the state of a particle is described by a wave
function that permits us to predict the value of its momentum with
certainty, the value of its position remains indeterminate and we can only
make probabilistic predictions as to the result of its measurement. On the
other hand, the authors claim that each measurement carried out to
determine position disturbs the particle, alters its state and therefore
modifies the initial wave function.

If knowing a physical quantity with precision and making an element of
reality correspond to it is equivalent to the condition that the system be
described by a wave function satisfying (6.1) – i.e. that the wave function
be an autofunction of the operator associated with that quantity – then
the criterion of reality gives us the following assertion: the wave function
describes the state of the particle only if when its momentum is known the
co-ordinate has no physical reality. However, this is true in general for
any pair of physical quantities associated with operators that do not
commute. Hence, 'the precise knowledge of one of them precludes such a
knowledge of the other. Furthermore, any attempt to determine the
latter experimentally will alter the state of the system in such a way as to
destroy the knowledge of the first'[17]. This means that any operation of
measurement or attempt to determine experimentally the value of a
quantity as to which the theory is unable to make precise predictions and
to which it cannot therefore immediately assign physical reality has the
effect of destroying the reality content of the second quantity characterizing the state of the system. Quantum mechanics would therefore be left
with this rigid alternative: '*either* (1) *the quantum-mechanical description
of reality given by the wave function is not complete or* (2) *when the
operators corresponding to two physical quantities do not commute the two
quantities cannot have simultaneous reality*'[18]. If the state of a quantum
system were represented accurately and exhaustively by the wave function – i.e. if every element of reality had a counterpart in the theory – the
impossibility of predicting with precision both quantities would simply

mean that they corresponded to incompatible elements of reality. Otherwise one would have to regard the theory as incomplete and assert that the restrictions imposed by the formalism on the prediction of physical quantities derive not from shortcomings in reality but from the limitations of the descriptive content of wave functions.

Despite the stringent logic of the argument, conclusions of this type may in fact be regarded as not strictly necessary. The observation that 'the information obtainable from a wave function seems to correspond exactly to what can be measured without altering the state of the system' itself suffices to defend – with arguments that are reasonable at first sight – the view that 'the wave function does contain a complete description of the physical reality of the system in the state to which it corresponds'[19]. Evidently the authors themselves would see no problem of completeness for a theory capable of predicting exactly the quantities that can be measured without the disturbance of the system bringing about an alteration of its state and hence a change in the wave function. And this is, in fact, what happens in quantum mechanics. However, for Einstein, Podolski and Rosen such an argument is untenable as it is demonstrated that, by taking as true the hypothesis of the theory's completeness, the criterion of reality leads in at least one case to a contradiction with the possibilities of description admitted by the wave function. The second part of the paper is devoted to discussion of the well-known thought experiment of the system composed of two particles which, after interacting for some time, may be considered and studied as two independent subsystems. It is demonstrated, under suitable conditions but in full agreement with the formalism of the theory, that by means of measurements performed on the first particle it is possible to predict with certainty, and without in any way disturbing the second system, either the value of the momentum P or the value of the position Q of the other particle[20]. In consistent agreement with the criterion of reality defined by the authors, it thus makes sense to regard the quantities P and Q as elements of reality. As in classical physics, these quantities thus define the state of the particle. The conclusion of the demonstration is as follows: 'Previously we proved that either (1) the quantum-mechanical description of reality given by the wave function is not complete or (2) when the operators corresponding to two physical quantities do not commute the two quantities cannot have simultaneous reality. Starting then with the assumption that the wave function does give a complete description of the physical reality, we arrived at the conclusion that two physical qualities, with noncommuting operators, can have simultaneous reality. Thus the negation of (1) leads to the negation of the only other alternative (2). We are thus forced to conclude that the quantum-mechanical description of physical reality given by wave functions is not complete'[21].

Even before the paper appeared in the *Physical Review*, a comprehensive account of the views it contained was splashed over the pages of the *New York Times* in an article headlined 'Einstein Attacks Quantum Theory'[22]. Although the episode aroused the irritation of Einstein – who did not regard a newspaper as a suitable place for the serious discussion of scientific matters – the prominence given the event was fully justified. Above all, its importance was to be confirmed both by the immediate reactions of the community of physicists and by the vast interest that the Einstein–Podolski–Rosen paradox has aroused in half a century of theoretical and philosophical discussion of the foundations of quantum mechanics[23]. However, while the article did raise serious questions as to the cognitive value of science, this must not lead us to lose sight of its real significance, i.e. the thesis it demonstrated: if we assume the principle according to which the completeness of a scientific theory is defined by a strict relation of correspondence between concepts and elements of reality, and if we agree to consider real those elements which are defined by means of the criterion of reality formulated by the authors, then quantum mechanics is an incomplete theory. But a further assumption is required for the demonstration of this thesis: it must be assumed that the so-called locality hypothesis holds also for microscopic objects: 'since at the time of measurement the two systems can no longer interact, no real change can take place in the second system in consequence of anything that may be done to the first system'[24]. For the authors, this was a point so obvious as to require no particular comment. They regarded it as expressing in different terms one of the conditions required by the two-particle experiment, i.e. the absence of any interaction between the two subsystems from a given instant on. The intuitive character of this assumption can hardly be called into question. Among other things, its violation would also appear to imply, in contrast with the special theory of relativity, the possibility of transmitting a signal at a speed greater than the velocity of light. This does not, however, alter the fact that the demonstration of incompleteness thus needed to assume as a hypothesis the negation of the paradox that Einstein saw as implicit in the interpretative framework of quantum mechanics. As we have seen, the argument put forward by Einstein, Podolski and Rosen instead fails to offer any explanation of why this paradox arises or to demonstrate its apparent character. In other words, it shows us neither the shortcomings of the theory nor the assumptions giving rise to consequences violating common sense. Or rather, their argument could even be regarded as a solution to the paradox. In this case, however, it would have to be recognized that it can only be solved by arbitrary negation, and that the only way to prevent such an awkward situation from arising is to regard the theory as incomplete, i.e. as incompatible with a model of description of reality presupposed by the theory itself and justifiable in general philosophical terms. To eliminate the paradox, we are thus obliged to jettison the theory[25]. This explains why quantum mechanics in fact emerged unscathed from the severe test to which Einstein, Podolski and Rosen had subjected it. The latter had pointed out neither a formal contradiction nor a conceptual lacuna but rather the violation of an abstract ideal of explanation and representation of the physical world. It is precisely for this reason that, despite declaring themselves totally convinced as to the existence of a description of physical reality also for micro-objects, they were unable to say whether such a description was to be sought by modifying the theory or whether a complete theory was incompatible with the very foundations of quantum mechanics. Their paper contained no indications of any use for a future research programme.

3

Two months after the publication of Einstein, Podolski and Rosen's article, the same American review published a long paper by Bohr under the same title. This opened with a denial of the supposed incompleteness of quantum mechanics or, to be more precise, by challenging the premises from which this was thought to derive: 'The trend of their argumentation [...] does not seem to me adequately to meet the actual situation with which we are faced in atomic physics'[26]. The question contained in the title common to both papers – 'Can Quantum-Mechanical Description of Physical Reality Be Considered Complete?' – cannot be answered yes or no for the simple reason that if the words 'description', 'physical reality' and 'complete' are assigned the meanings desired by Einstein then the question itself is wrongly phrased. Bohr thus counters with the 1927 interpretation, which he sees as showing clearly that, in its specific field of validity, quantum mechanics 'would appear as a completely rational description of physical phenomena, such as we meet in atomic processes'[27]. The nature of phenomena involving micro-objects is such that the contradictions and paradoxes are only apparent: they are not evidence of the theory's alleged incompleteness but demonstrate 'only an essential inadequacy of the customary viewpoint of natural philosophy for a rational account of physical phenomena of the type with which we are concerned in quantum mechanics'[28].

Bohr thus seeks to turn upside-down an approach claiming, as Podolski seems to suggest, to measure the interpretative validity of a theory with the rod of an idealization of reality consistent with a particular phenomenal situation – that characterizing macroscopic physics – and compatible with the forms of description admitted by classical theory. In other words, an approach requiring every theory to contain an adequate picture of objective reality and, in any case, to provide a visualizable model of it. According to Bohr, on the contrary, the problem was to assess the nature of the phenomena with which the theory is concerned through an analysis of the conditions in which the quantum phenomenon may be observed and investigated experimentally and of the possibility of defining the words we invent, the physical concepts characterizing the state of a system. Only in this way is it possible to obtain a model of description capable of accounting for the reality of quantum objects.

Bohr and Einstein could not even come to any agreement on a general description of the cognitive goals of their discipline. For Einstein, 'Physics is an attempt conceptually to grasp reality as it is thought independently of its being observed. In this sense one speaks of "physical reality"'[29]. Bohr rejected the very presuppositions underlying the charges of incompleteness levelled at quantum mechanics since, in his view, the adoption of a different methodological approach made it easy to discover that Einstein's criterion of reality 'contains – however cautious its formulation may appear – an essential ambiguity when it is applied to the actual problems', especially as regards the meaning to be given to the expression 'without in any way disturbing a system'[30]. This was the central problem of quantum physics: the existence of an indeterminate interaction in any process of measurement entails a redefinition of the concept of phenomenon entering into conflict with Einstein's ideal of a conceptualization of reality in no way influenced by our observation and therefore requires, in Bohr's view, 'a radical revision of our attitude towards the problem of physical reality'[31].

The substance of Bohr's reply, the element of greatest theoretical weakness that he detected in his opponents' argument, was indicated clearly in his short letter to *Nature* dated 29 June announcing the publication of his article in the *Physical Review*[32]. After referring to Einstein, Podolski and Rosen's criterion of reality and summarizing in a few lines the essential passages of their demonstration, the letter ended as follows: 'I should like to point out, however, that the named criterion contains an essential ambiguity when it is applied to problems of quantum mechanics. It is true that in the measurements under consideration any direct mechanical interaction of the system and the measuring agencies is excluded, but a closer examination reveals that the procedure of measurements has an essential influence on the conditions on which the very definition of the physical quantities in question rests. Since these conditions must be considered as an inherent element of any phenomenon to which the term "physical reality" can be unambiguously applied, the conclusion of the above-mentioned authors would not appear to be justified'[33]. The strategy adopted by Bohr in his reply is therefore aimed at demolishing the assumptions on which the demonstration rests rather than at challenging its logical consistency. This did not, however, require him to embark on a dispute as to the ontological implications of the new physics. His arguments were theoretical and concerned the nature of the quantum phenomenon, the relationship between conditions of observation and possibility of definition, the problem of the disturbance of the system in the course of measurement, and the distinction between physical object and experimental apparatus. Bohr also discussed some thought experiments even though, as he pointed out, this meant merely repeating well-known points analysed on previous occasions. The premise of the argument, the logical and theoretical presupposition of any examination of the problem of description in quantum mechanics, was for Bohr a judgement as to the significance of Planck's hypothesis – a judgement which, as we have seen, had been formed slowly over decades of research: in the study of phenomena connected with the microscopic world, an element of individuality is present that is completely foreign to classical physics. In the light of this postulate, the impossibility of carrying out more detailed analysis of the interaction between particle and instrument of measurement – i.e. the fact that any observation of a microobject always gives rise to what Einstein called a loss of knowledge of a part of the system – is not a characteristic of a particular experimental procedure but an essential property of any device serving to investigate a phenomenon of this type. Leaving aside their different philosophical leanings, the theoretical point upon which Bohr and Einstein clashed was this. Einstein did not accept the quantum postulate as an essential premise of the theory. In point of fact, they had taken opposite standpoints on the problem of the conceptual and physical implications of Planck's hypothesis ever since discussion began on the nature of radiation. The selfsame problem now led them to speak different languages, to fail to agree even on the choice of scientifically relevant questions, and to go each his own way as regards interpretative perspectives and research programmes. If quantum mechanics were not founded upon the postulate of the individual nature of atomic processes and if the mathematical structure simply reflected through Heisenberg's relations the cognitive limitations required by particular procedures of measurement, Einstein's thought experiment would really have demonstrated that the impossibility of an exhaustive analysis of the properties of a system depended on an inadequate theoretical representation of physical reality. In this case the individual nature of the phenomenon in quantum mechanics, which Bohr saw as deriving from the indeterminate interaction implicit in the idea of the quantum of action, would boil down to 'an incomplete description characterized by the arbitrary picking out of different elements of physical reality at the cost of sacrificing other such elements'[34]. Changing experimental apparatus would mean no more than selecting from case to case conditions of observation making it possible to ascertain only some aspects of the physical system.

The conclusions to be drawn from the postulate are, however, very different. Quantum-mechanical individuality expresses a fundamental epistemological aspect of the new physics that cannot be ignored by any definition of reality whatsoever: the very nature of quantum phenomena imposes upon us 'a rational discrimination between essentially different experimental arrangements and procedures which are suited either for an unambiguous use of the idea of space location, or for a legitimate application of the conservation theorem of momentum'[35]. From this point of view, the theory certainly takes into account an element of arbitrary nature in our freedom to choose the conditions of observation. However, the fact the one is forced to renounce one of the two aspects of description that together defined the classical model is a fact regarding physical reality itself and the conceptual constraints it imposes. In fact, this renunciation 'depends essentially on the impossibility, in the field of quantum theory, of accurately controlling the reaction of the object on the measuring instruments, i.e. the transfer of momentum in case of position measurements, and the displacement in case of momentum measurements'[36]. The problematic aspect of the loss of control over a part of the interaction does not, in any case, consist of the impossibility of knowing the value of a given physical quantity when studying a quantum phenomenon, but rather concerns the impossibility of defining such quantities. Paradoxes thus arise from the contrast between conditions of observation and possibility of definition, from an indiscriminate and acritical use of the concepts of position and momentum, from failure to take into account that in particular experimental situations, either concretely realized or simply imagined, these concepts are not always definable or meaningful for quantum theory.

In Bohr's view, the argument of Einstein, Podolski and Rosen rests upon non-existent foundations. Their definition of reality is unacceptable for quantum theory since the problem to which they refer in the expression 'without in any way disturbing a system' misses the real nature of interaction between object and instrument. In all the examples discussed, Bohr observes, there is in fact 'no question of a mechanical disturbance of the system under investigation during the last critical stage of the measuring procedure. But even at this stage there is essentially the question of an *influence on the very conditions which define the possible types of predictions regarding the future behaviour of the system*'[37]. The intervention of the observer neither leads to alteration of the real state of the system, nor conceals knowledge of one of the physical quantities, nor cancels out its reality. It only determines the conditions under which it is possible to give an unambiguous definition of the concepts which are used in the description of the phenomenon and which enable us to make predictions as to the system's evolution. Since in Bohr's view the expression 'physical reality' can only refer to the phenomenon, it makes no sense to speak of an incomplete description of physical reality.

For that matter, in his reply Bohr made no use of the argument attributed by Einstein, Podolski and Rosen to those maintaining the completeness of quantum mechanics. He would never have defended his views by claiming that the theory was complete because it was capable of predicting with certainty the quantities that may be measured without in any way disturbing the system, disturbance here being again of mechanical type. This would have meant utilizing what had been criticized in his opponents' viewpoint so as to replace their demand for reality with a reduction of the theory's cognitive scope in phenomenological terms, i.e. countering one philosophical conception of science with another. The defence of his interpretative standpoint required no steps of this kind since, as he saw it, quantum mechanics could in no case have been evaluated on Einstein's criterion but was rather to be 'characterized as a rational utilization of all possibilities of unambiguous interpretation of measurements, compatible with the finite and uncontrollable interaction between the objects and the measuring instruments in the field of quantum theory'[38]. It can hardly be claimed that Bohr countered the intuitive self-evidence of Einstein's argument with simple, easily comprehensible solutions. In the above definition he in fact returned to the interpretative scheme summarized in his idea of complementarity. In his view, the problem of the description of phenomena could not be posed in general, abstract terms since it was closely tied up with the possibility of considering the description of physical reality independently of the particular conditions of observation. With the idea of finite and uncontrollable interaction, the quantum postulate had called this possibility into question for the first time and marked a sharp departure from classical physics. Einstein did not acknowledge the need for a quantum postulate and thus, logically enough, demanded that the theory should contain an objective description of the physical world, i.e. one independent of our observations. According to Bohr, the problem of description needed, on the contrary, to be tackled in the light of a completely new situation. It required a rational solution capable of reconciling the element of individuality peculiar to the reality of quantum processes with the need to use classical concepts in the interpretation of experimental results, i.e. to utilize instruments of description not only defined in theoretical contexts by now superseded but also presupposing the independence of the event from its observability. In his view, the only rational solution capable of overcoming this conflict was the following: the symbols of quantum mechanics may be interpreted without ambiguity only in cases in which its mathematical apparatus 'allow us to predict the results to be obtained by a given experimental arrangement described in a totally classical way'[39]. In other words, the existence of linguistic constraints obliging us to speak of 'position' or 'momentum' in order to express the results of measurement has no important consequences on the way in which the formalism of quantum mechanics represents the state of a system and describes its evolution. This is because it is correct to associate the terms 'position' or 'momentum' with the symbols x or p appearing in the wave function only when the theory is able to predict the exact result of measurement under given conditions of observation. For quantum theory, as we have seen, these conditions delimit the possibilities of definition of the classical concepts and hence ensure that an unambiguous interpretation may be given to the measurement and establish a correspondence between defined concepts and mathematical symbols.

Einstein, Podolski and Rosen's claim that if, for a state represented by the wave function (6.2), we seek to ascertain the position of the particle experimentally, the disturbance of the system alters this state and thus deprives it of physical reality by leaving the value of the momentum indeterminate, should thus be reformulated in Bohr's language as follows. It is possible to interpret without ambiguity the symbol p_0 of (6.2) and to associate it with the concept of momentum since (6.4) enables us to assert that when a measurement is carried out with an appropriate device described in classical terms, the momentum found will have precisely the value p_0. The correspondence between the symbol 'p' and the term 'momentum' is valid only for these particular conditions of observation. If we change experimental apparatus so as to determine, for instance, the position of the particle, we cannot employ this term, not even to say that when position is measured momentum is indeterminate. As Bohr puts it: 'it is only the mutual exclusion of any two experimental procedures, permitting the unambiguous definition of complementary physical quantities, which provides room for new physical laws'[40]. In accordance with the idea of complementarity taken up again in this context, we should thus deny any validity to either the premise or the conclusion of Einstein, Podolski and Rosen's demonstration. On the one hand, it is false to make the assertion that in quantum mechanics 'when the operators corresponding to two physical quantities do not commute, the two physical quantities cannot be simultaneously real'. However, it is false not because it implicitly contains a questionable criterion of reality, but rather because it presupposes that 'the precise knowledge of one of them precludes such a knowledge of the other' and thus makes what we should call the arbitrary assumption that those physical quantities, i.e. the concepts corresponding to the symbols P and Q of

$$PQ - QP = h/2\pi i \qquad (6.5)$$

are always defined. On the other hand, equally false is the conclusion as to the simultaneous reality of these quantities that is derived from the two-particle experiment, since this conclusion fails to take into account the fact that the exact predictions as to the values P and Q of the second particle are obtained through two successive operations of measurement on the first, hence from two different conditions of observation and, obviously, from two different possibilities of definition of the concepts associated with these symbols.

Foreseeing objections of this nature, Einstein, Podolski and Rosen had written at the end of their paper: 'Indeed, one would not arrive at our conclusion if one insisted that two or more physical quantities can be regarded as simultaneous elements of reality *only when they can be simultaneously measured or predicted*. On this point of view, since either one or the other, but not both simultaneously, of the quantities *P* and *Q* can be predicted, they are not simultaneously real. This makes the reality of *P* and *Q* depend upon the process of measurement carried out on the first system, which does not disturb the second system in any way. No reasonable definition of reality could be expected to permit this'[41]. They ruled out this possibility by appealing, once again, to the paradoxical consequences that would inevitably follow. However, the problem was one regarding neither the disturbance nor reality but only our concepts[42].

With regard to his reply, Bohr was to write some years later: 'Rereading these passages, I am deeply aware of the inefficiency of expression which must have made it very difficult to appreciate the trend of the argumentation aiming to bring out the essential ambiguity involved in a reference to physical attributes of objects when dealing with phenomena where no sharp distinction can be made between the behaviour of the objects themselves and their interaction with the measuring instruments'[43]. In speaking of obscurity of exposition, Bohr may have had in mind assertions such as 'the term "physical reality" can be correctly referred only to the phenomenon', from which he had drawn the logically necessary conclusion of the arbitrary nature of the judgement that quantum-mechanical description was incomplete. He did not, however, challenge the validity of the arguments used on that occasion, but simply acknowledged that Einstein, Podolski and Rosen's criterion of reality and attempted refutation had obliged him to clarify certain aspects of his previous formulations, which probably provided the basis for objections of this type. It was no coincidence that his reply had been constructed around the concepts of indeterminate interaction and the individuality of the phenomenon. These were, in fact, points to which he would feel the need to return in subsequent writings. This time the central theme of discussion was a different paradox and the dispute no longer involved Einstein but physicists who had supported the Copenhagen interpretation from the outset.

4

'The quantum paradoxes': these words were jotted down by Bohr in his notes for the Como conference. In another manuscript he asserted: 'From the point of view of the complementary nature of observation and definition it appears possible to treat the paradoxes of the quantum theory in a uniform manner in immediate contact with the simplest experiences'[44]. The paradoxes referred to are those arising from the so-called dual nature of radiation and matter. As Pauli was to remark in illustrating the situation in physics at the end of 1926: 'the difference between the implications of the two images is as insurmountable as the analogous difference between the logical relations "either–or" and "both–and"'[45]. In the case of the classic thought experiment of the photon and the two slits, according to the corpuscular picture the photon can only pass through one slit or the other. On the other hand, if we take the wave picture we must, in order to interpret the interference produced, bear in mind that the resulting distribution of the photon obviously depends on the possible paths of the partial waves through both one and the other slit.

As we have seen, Heisenberg's uncertainty relations showed that the paradoxes were written into the simple formulas of quantum theory where Planck's constant appears. In those formulas, h determines a relation of direct proportionality between pairs of symbols to which are associated concepts utilized respectively for a wave or corpuscular representation of a physical object. The dualism was therefore implicit in the very idea of the quantum of action, and the indeterminacy relations furnished a comparatively simple technical solution to the paradox by excluding from our observations disconcerting situations such as those arising from any attempt to represent the behaviour of a photon visually. In this case 'we would, thus, meet with the difficulty: to be obliged to say, on the one hand, that the photon always chooses *one* of the two ways and, on the other hand, that it behaves as if it had passed *both* ways'[46]. Instead there should be no contradiction in the use of wave description and corpuscle description since one of the consequences of the theory is to show that the experiments to which the different descriptions may be applied are mutually incompatible. It is therefore not a matter of assigning a dual nature to a photon or an electron, but of recognizing that in the study of a quantum phenomenon the experiments describable in the language of waves and those describable in the language of corpuscles are mutually exclusive. In fact, the uncertainty relations allow for an indeterminate interaction between object and measuring apparatus whereby any measurement seeking to determine the direction of propagation of a photon makes it impossible to study the phenomenon of interference. Vice versa, an interference experiment rules out the possibility of following the photon in space and time. In the above-mentioned paper of 1949, Bohr stressed that this was a point 'of great logical consequence, since it is only the circumstance that we are presented with a choice of *either* tracing the path of the particle or observing interference effects, which allows us to escape from the paradoxical necessity of concluding that the behaviour of an electron or a photon should depend on the presence of a slit in the diaphragm through which it could be proved not to pass'[47].

However, this could only be a technical solution to the paradox: if quantum mechanics really limited itself to justifying in these terms the co-existence of contradictory conceptions as to the nature of microscopic objects it would be by no means immune to objections of the kind raised by Einstein[48]. For such paradoxes to be really eliminated it was necessary to grasp the nexus between the limitations imposed by Heisenberg's relations on the use of classical concepts and the discontinuous nature of microscopic processes. And this required, in the final analysis, that the meaning of the concept of indeterminate interaction be rendered explicit. On this front, however, the supporters of the Copenhagen interpretation were far less compact than is usually claimed.

On the occasion of his receiving the Nobel Prize in 1933, Heisenberg returned to the interpretative problems of quantum mechanics and definitively clarified his own position. In his view, while the aim of classical physics is the investigation of objective processes taking place in space and time, 'in the quantum theory [...] the situation is completely different. The very fact that the formalism of quantum mechanics cannot be interpreted as visual description of a phenomenon occurring in space and time shows that quantum mechanics is in no way concerned with the objective determination of space-time phenomena'[49]. The cause of this reversal of interpretative perspective is identified by Heisenberg in the following terms: 'Whereas in the classical theory the kind of observation has no bearing on the event, in the quantum theory the disturbance associated with each observation of the atomic phenomenon has a decisive role'[50]. The discontinuous disturbance of a system thus consti-tutes a decisive element in assessing the limits of all spatio-temporal description. The indeterminacy relations are thus interpreted as a law of the theory expressing the essence of any measurement process where a part of the disturbance remains fundamentally unknown: 'The experi-mental determination of whatever space-time events invariably necessit-ates a fixed frame – say the system of coordinates in which the observer is at rest – to which all measurements are referred. The assumption that this frame is "fixed" implies neglecting its momentum from the outset, since "fixed" implies nothing other, of course, than that any transfer of momentum to it will evoke no perceptible effect. The fundamentally necessary uncertainty at this point is then transmitted via the measuring apparatus into the atomic event'[51]. It was therefore necessary to abandon the framework of classical physics, which seeks to objectivize the results of observation by reference to spatio-temporal processes that obey laws, or rather to recognize that this framework clashes with the non-visualizable nature of events symbolized by Planck's constant. Heisenberg thus concluded with regard to the limits of the validity of classical mechanics: 'Classical physics represents that striving to learn about *Nature* in which essentially we seek to draw conclusions about objective processes from observations and so ignore the consideration of the influences which every observation has on the object to be observed; classical physics, therefore, has its limits at the point from which the influence of the observation on the event can no longer be ignored'[52].

It is thus clear that for Heisenberg indeterminate interaction concerns the consequences of a physical effect of discontinuous nature, of a disturbance occurring in every observation. In this sense he still stuck to the position he had defended against Bohr in the spring of 1927. Then however, as we have seen, Einstein's criticisms would be at least comprehensible and there would be nothing arbitrary in his conviction that there is 'something like the real state of a physical system, which exists objectively, independently of any observer or measurement, and which can be described, at least in principle, with the means of expression of physics'[53]. Heisenberg's viewpoint certainly did nothing to prevent this thesis from giving rise to an alternative programme of research; and it was no coincidence that Einstein also saw the indeterminacy relations as a loss of knowledge of a part of the system brought about by the process of measurement. In any case, how could this way of understanding the idea of indeterminate interaction furnish convincing arguments against Schrödinger's ironic comments on the evasive answers behind which, in his opinion, the supporters of the official interpretation usually took shelter? According to Schrödinger, the only merit of such answers lay in the fact that 'they appear to be unassailable, for they seem to rest on the simple and safe principle that sound and sober reality, for the purposes of science, coincides with what is (or might be) observed' and because they took for granted that 'what is, or might be, observed coincides exactly with what quantum mechanics is pleased to call observable'. Schrödinger was quite right to stress that the roots of the controversy were to be sought in the meaning attributed to the methodological principle that 'it is the theory that decides what we can observe'[54].

Heisenberg's sole counter to this type of objection was to make a stand on the cognitive limits of the theory, which is not in fact concerned with the objective determination of spatio-temporal phenomena. His argument entailed the implicit admission that the state of a system is definable independently of any process of observation: the indeterminacy relations thus accounted for the physical effect whereby, owing to finite interaction of the apparatus with the system, our observations allow us only to obtain incomplete information as to that state. In this he differed little from those physicists who, at the end of the 19th century, sought plausible hypotheses to explain why we cannot measure the absolute velocity of the Earth, as should indeed be possible assuming the classical conception of absolute space and time. In both cases an attempt was made to explain the impossibility of determining an aspect of reality experimentally. However, this meant renouncing a priori any analysis of the assumptions making such unobservable predictions necessary and renouncing any reflection on just how arbitrary these assumptions were in the light of the new laws of physics.

Bohr rejected Heisenberg's viewpoint precisely because of its use of arguments upon which Einstein's criticism was based: 'It would in particular not be out of place in this connection to warn against a misunderstanding likely to arise when one tries to express the content of Heisenberg's well known indeterminacy relations [...] by such a statement as: "the position and momentum of a particle cannot simultaneously be measured with arbitrary accuracy". According to such a formulation it would appear as though we had to do with some arbitrary renunciation of the measurement of either the one or the other of the two well-defined attributes of the object, which would not preclude the possibility of a future theory taking both attributes into account on the lines of classical physics. From the above considerations it should be clear that the whole situation in atomic physics deprives of all meaning such inherent attributes as the idealizations of classical physics would ascribe to the object. On the contrary,' Bohr points out, 'the proper role of the indeterminacy relations consists in assuring quantitatively the logical compatibility of apparently contradictory laws which appear when we use two different experimental arrangements, of which only one permits an unambiguous use of the concept of position, while only the other permits the application of the concept of momentum defined, as it is, solely by the law of conservation'[55].

The primary objective for Bohr, as for Pauli, was to make explicit the meaning and the physical and theoretical consequences of Planck's discovery of the indivisibility of the quantum of action. Neither is it by chance that both saw in this a close analogy with what had occurred in physics upon the discovery of another constant of nature, the velocity of light. In their view, there was no problem regarding the disturbance of the object observed by the instrument. The real question was another: what happens if in principle – i.e. because of the very nature of physical processes – interaction remains indeterminate in every case and cannot be controlled even by improving the instruments? Which physical concepts and interpretative categories are we called upon to modify with the advent of the idea of discontinuity?[56] It seems almost as though they were following to the letter the methodological teaching of Einstein, who had abandoned the assumptions of the physics of the aether in 1905 to ask himself which concepts and categories would have to be modified if one assumed the existence of a limit to the velocity of propagation of action, and what new picture of reality would be compatible with the new theory. It was precisely because Bohr and Pauli considered this the fundamental question that they assumed the finite nature of the quantum of action and the discontinuity or individuality of atomic processes as a postulate of the new mechanics. The ideas of discontinuity and individuality bring out aspects of reality totally foreign to classical theory, just as the postulate of the velocity of light concerns aspects of reality incomprehensible in terms of the conception of space and time of Newtonian mechanics. The indeterminate interaction associated with each process of measurement is the observational consequence of the individuality of atomic processes and of the laws of quantum mechanics, just as the dependence of the simultaneity of events on the state of the observer's motion is, for the theory of relativity, the observational consequence of the postulate of the velocity of light and of the laws of electromagnetism. And in both cases, the consequences of the postulates entail a violation of common sense.

The relation between indeterminate interaction and the individuality of the phenomenon is to be understood in the sense that whenever we attempt to investigate the interaction that remains indeterminate in the course of measurement – e.g. momentum when we measure position – we have to use a new experimental device, which in itself inevitably gives rise to new indeterminate interaction and hence to a totally new phenomenon. Each atomic process thus possesses its own intrinsic individuality in that, as Bohr said, any attempt to subdivide the phenomenon – i.e. to control the aspects left indeterminate once a certain experimental device is chosen – always produces a different phenomenon[57]. It must therefore be concluded that each phenomenon is unambiguously determined and inseparable from the experimental conditions in which it appears. In this sense, according to Bohr, quantum mechanics develops the relativistic idea of the dependence of phenomena on the frame of reference. However, the dependence of which quantum mechanics speaks expresses a still stronger condition in that it rules out any possibility of describing atomic objects unambiguously through the normal physical properties, i.e. of describing phenomena independently of the way in which they have been observed.

According to Pauli, the revision of the classical concept of the phenomenon required 'the logical possibility of a new and wider pattern of thought', which obliges us to 'take into account the observer, including the apparatus used by him, differently from the way it was done in classical physics'. The observer no longer has the detached or hidden position he is implicitly attributed with in the idealizations of the classical models of description but is, as Pauli puts it, 'an observer who by his indeterminable effects creates a new situation, theoretically described as a new state of the observed system'[58]. This model of thought takes into account the fact that each observation is the result of free choice on the part of the observer between experimental procedures each of which excludes the others. However, unlike Heisenberg, Bohr held that this choice did not imply any renunciation in cognitive terms; it was rather the consequence, implicit in the quantum postulate, of 'a recognition that [a more detailed analysis of atomic phenomena] is *in principle* excluded'[59]. And it was precisely to avoid the objections to which Heisenberg's argument was open that he advised against the use of 'phrases, often found in the physical literature, such as "disturbing of phenomena by observation" or "creating physical attributes to atomic objects by measurements". Such phrases, which may serve to remind of the apparent paradoxes in quantum theory, are at the same time apt to cause confusion, since words like "phenomenon" and "observations" just as "attributes" and "measurements", are used in a way hardly compatible with common language and practical definition'[60]. To express the new state of affairs, he suggested using 'the word *phenomenon* exclusively to refer to the observations obtained under specified circumstances, including an account of the whole experimental arrangement'[61]. The phenomenon thus has an individuality of its own which manifests itself in the conceptual impossibility of effecting a clean separation between the physical system, classically definable and describable independently of any observation, and the measuring device through which that system can be observed. By fixing the conditions under which an atomic object is observed, the observer carries out each time an intervention of indeterminate effect. That is to say, he imposes constraints on the course of the phenomenon without, however, influencing the results of measurement.

The paradox of dualism disappears technically, as we have seen, when it is recognized that each description always refers to a particular experimental situation and regards individual phenomena. In this context, paradox can only arise from a philosophical assumption: for it to exist one must, in fact, admit that the classical images of waves and corpuscles used in turn to describe single phenomena refer also to properties possessed by systems independently of any interaction with the instruments of observation. It is thus still possible to use the classical concepts of 'position', 'velocity' and 'frequency' in the description of quantum processes without falling into the abyss of dualism only if one renounces this philosophical assumption; in other words, only if one recognizes that it derives from arbitrarily bestowing absolute status on one scientific picture of the world. The paradox disappears only if it is admitted – to put it in traditional terms – that the use of classical concepts to describe the phenomenal manifestations of objects does not necessarily imply that the objects themselves possess properties corresponding to such terms when they are not observed.

The paradoxes of reality are thus transformed into paradoxes of our language and of its different descriptive functions with respect to what is regarded as the object of the description. And if we wish to translate the preceding argument onto this new plane, we are forced to conclude that the paradoxes disappear only if we renounce our belief that that language reflects a structure of reality and recognize that our descriptions are not independent of the viewpoint chosen by the observer to describe reality with the language at his disposal. This is, among other things, the consequence of the process of conceptual abstraction which accompanies the growth of knowledge and which, in microphysics, means that the formal language in which a theory is expressed is no longer capable of suggesting an intuitive and visualizable picture of reality.

In his last paper, Planck pointed out that the substantial difference between classical mechanics and quantum mechanics deriving from the introduction of the quantum of action did not regard the much debated question of causality and determinism. In his view, the really new factor to be taken into consideration was that the meaning of each symbol appearing in the theory was no longer 'immediately and directly intelligible'[62]. If it is, in fact, true that the wave function of quantum mechanics is 'completely determined for all points and all times by the initial and background conditions', then 'the principle of determinism is as rigorously valid in the quantum-mechanical picture of the world as it is in that of classical physics'. 'The difference' – he added – 'lies only in the symbols and in the mathematics'; a difference that, as rigorously expressed in Heisenberg's relations, is reflected in an 'uncertainty of translation' of the symbols from theoretical language into the language in which we describe the results of our observations. It is precisely the uncertainty of this translation that obliges us to acknowledge that 'the meaning of a certain symbol has no defined sense unless we specify the conditions of the particular measuring device' used to translate that symbol into a term of our language. The uncertainty of our predictions, Planck concluded, thus boils down to an uncertainty in translation between terms of two different languages. This uncertainty is taken into account by the laws of quantum mechanics, where the wave function 'does not give the values of the coordinates as a function of time, but merely the probability that the coordinates possess certain values at certain moments'[63].

Pauli followed the same line of reasoning as Planck in suggesting that these probabilities should be regarded as 'primary'. He thus sought to underline that, unlike the classical concept of probability, these 'cannot be reduced by means of suitable hypotheses to deterministic laws'[64]. Primary probabilities are determined by fields in multidimensional spaces, which can either describe the statistics of a series of measurements carried out under identical initial conditions or, for a single measurement, simply express possibilities. In order to clarify his meaning, Pauli asserted that the result of an individual measurement is not comprehended by laws, in the classical sense of prediction of the exact value of a quantity. It presents itself as a primary fact, not determined by causes, and for this reason he took up an expression of Bohr's and spoke of the 'irrational occurrence of an individual event'[65]. A probability field defined in a multidimensional space thus represents for Pauli a sort of 'catalogue of expectation', and the laws expressing the evolution of the field describe an abstract ordering of the possibilities of observation[66]. Unlike the fields of classical physics, these cannot in principle be measured in the same way in different points: 'The carrying out of a measurement in a given place has as its consequence the passage to a phenomenon with different initial conditions, to which corresponds a new complex of possible results to be obtained, and therefore a field everywhere entirely new'[67].

To speak of primary probabilities in this context means saying that once the conditions of observation have been chosen – i.e. once the constraints have been laid down for a certain phenomenon – the laws of the theory are not capable of making exact predictions as to the result of measurement but rather describe the different possible evolutions of the system. This generalization of the classical concept of law takes into account the fact that the phenomena in atomic physics have 'the new property of *wholeness*, in that they do not admit of subdivision into partial phenomena without the whole phenomenon changing essentially every time'[68]. The broader framework of ideas to which Pauli referred was thus supposed to allow the theory 'to include the irrational occurrence of an individual event' and therefore 'as a combination of the rational and irrational aspects of an essentially paradoxical reality, it may also be defined as a theory of becoming'[69].

As Bohr was to put it, recalling the discussions of the fifth Solvay Conference: 'The question was whether, as to the occurrence of individual events, we should adopt a terminology proposed by Dirac, that we were concerned with a choice on the part of "nature" or, as suggested by Heisenberg, we should say that we have to do with a choice on the part of the "observer" constructing the measuring instruments and reading their recording. Any such terminology would, however, appear dubious since, on the one hand, it is hardly reasonable to endow nature with volition in the ordinary sense, while, on the other hand, it is certainly not possible for the observer to influence the events which may appear under the conditions he has arranged. To my mind, there is no other alternative than to admit that, in this field of experience, we are dealing with individual phenomena and that our possibilities of handling the measuring instruments allow us only to make a choice between the different complementary types of phenomena we want to study'[70].

The basic difference between the classical and the quantum-mechanical descriptions of physical reality thus arises from a redefinition of the very concept of phenomenon and from the inevitable consequences of the distinction made in this case between measuring apparatus and object under examination. In the world of atoms and particles, the interaction produced in each measuring process forms an inseparable part of the phenomenon: this is the consequence not of the macroscopic nature of the instruments and the microscopic nature of the elementary processes, but of a new law of nature that obliges us to abandon the requisite of continuity peculiar to our forms of representation. In any case, implicit in the very concept of description is the assumption that it is in principle possible to separate the phenomenon described from the instruments by means of which we gather data for its description. The very description of the result of measurement – e.g. when we say, 'the electron is in position a' – involves a conceptual operation objectifying the meaning of this assertion, i.e. the assumption that the result is, in principle, independent of the conditions of observation: a possibility that quantum mechanics rules out in principle. On the contrary, quantum mechanics sees each process of measurement as giving rise to an individual phenomenon admitting its own modes of description, and takes account of this by establishing a rigorous relation between conditions of observation and possibilities of definition of the classical concepts used in single descriptions. The idea of complementarity thus expresses the mutually exclusive character of descriptions referring to particular conditions of observation and hence to individual phenomena. In any case, quantum mechanics can admit only complementary descriptions because each of these presupposes a conceptual operation distinguishing between object and apparatus that is incompatible with the nature of quantum phenomena[71]. In this sense, it may thus be asserted that 'the real conditions of measurement constitute an element inherent in the description of each phenomenon', so that an independent reality in the ordinary meaning of the term can be assigned neither to the phenomenon nor to the instrument of observation[72]. Stress should instead be laid, as Bohr pointed out in a letter to Dirac, on the subjective nature of the idea of observation and on the contrast existing between it and the classical idea of the isolated object[73]. Quantum mechanics thus represents a form of rational description of the phenomena of atomic physics and is the only one possible for a reality that constantly obliges us to specify the viewpoint from which we intend to describe it, i.e. to indicate the conditions in which each description is compatible with the unambiguous definition of the concepts it employs. Outside of these conditions there is no description of reality or, to put it more precisely, if experimental conditions are not taken into consideration, the concept of the physical reality of a quantum system is totally meaningless. The only correct way to use the term 'reality' is therefore by applying it to the whole constituted by the system and the experimental apparatus.

Bohr thus sees quantum mechanics as raising 'the old philosophical problem of the objective existence of phenomena independently of our observations' and enriching it with new significance: 'The discovery of the quantum of action shows us, in fact, not only the natural limitation of classical physics, but [...] confronts us with a situation hitherto unknown in natural science. As we have seen, any observation necessitates an interference with the course of the phenomena, which is of such a nature that it deprives us of the foundation underlying the causal mode of description'[74]. In criticizing those who sought to interpret quantum physics as the confirmation of some particular philosophical viewpoint – such as positivism – Pauli pointed out that 'the gnoseological situation facing modern physics had been foreseen by no philosophical system'[75].

In actual fact, however, though the situation may have been completely unknown and new as regards the implications of the abandoning of causality, this was not the case, in Bohr's view, as regards either the problem of physical reality or the independence of phenomena from their conditions of observation. He also reminded Einstein that it was relativity theory that had first drawn attention to 'the essential dependence of any physical phenomenon on the system of reference of the observer'. The same theory had, in fact, made possible 'the clarification of the paradoxes connected with the finite velocity of propagation of light and the judgment of events by observers in relative motion which first disclosed the arbitrariness contained even in the concept of simultaneity, and thereby created a freer attitude toward the question of space-time coordination'[76]. On the conceptual level, relativity theory in fact obliges us to give up our customary separation of the ideas of time and space on pain of being barred from any understanding of the laws of physics. According to Bohr, quantum mechanics does nothing more than develop the revision of our attitude to physical reality started off by Einstein's relativity theory, which had contributed 'to the fundamental modification of all ideas regarding the absolute character of physical phenomena': 'We have learned from the theory of relativity that the expediency of the sharp separation of space and time, required by our senses, depends merely on the fact that the velocities commonly occurring are small compared with the velocity of light. Similarly, we may say that Planck's discovery has led us to recognize that the adequacy of our whole customary attitude, which is characterized by the demand for causality, depends solely upon the smallness of the quantum of action in comparison with the actions with which we are concerned in ordinary phenomena'[77]. In his objections to the Copenhagen interpretation of quantum mechanics and, above all, in his paper of 1935, Einstein seemed instead to have forgotten the great lesson that relativity had taught us with regard to the problem of physical reality[78].

As Ehrenfest wrote in November 1927: 'It was delightful for me to be present during the conversations between Bohr and Einstein. Like a game of chess. Einstein all the time with new examples. [...] Bohr from out of philosophical smoke clouds constantly searching for the tools to crush one example after the other. [...] But I am almost without reservation pro Bohr and contra Einstein. His attitude to Bohr is now exactly like the attitude of the defenders of absolute simultaneity towards him'[79].

Notes

1 W. V. O. Quine, 'Paradox', *Scientific American* **206** (1962), 84–96: 84; also in W. V. O. Quine, *The Ways of Paradox and other Essays*, New York: Random House, 1966.

2 Cf., for example, M. Ceruti, *Il vincolo...* cit. ch. 1 n. 45.

3 A. Einstein, 'Autobiographical Notes', in P. A. Schilpp, ed., *Albert Einstein...* cit., ch. 1 n. 7, 3–95: 51 ff.

4 Cf., for example, R. McCormmach, 'Einstein, Lorentz and the Electron Theory', *Historical Studies in the Physical Sciences* **2** (1970), 41–87; A. I. Miller, 'A Study of Henri Poincaré's "Sur la dynamique de l'électron"', *Archive for the History of Exact Sciences* **10** (1973), 207–328; *Albert Einstein's Special Theory of Relativity – Emergence (1905) and Early Interpretation (1905–1911)*, Reading (Mass.): Addison-Wesley, 1981.

5 A. Einstein, 'Autobiographical Notes' cit. n. 3, 53.

6 Cf. M. Ceruti, *Il vincolo...* cit. ch. 1 n. 45.

7 L. Rosenfeld, 'Niels Bohr in the Thirties. Consolidation and Extension of the Conception of Complementarity', in S. Rozental, ed., *Niels Bohr...* cit. ch. 2 n. 14, 114–36: 127–28.

8 A. Einstein, B. Podolski and N. Rosen, 'Can Quantum-Mechanical Description of Physical Reality Be Considered Complete?', *Physical Review* **47** (1935), 777–80. This issue of the review was published 15 May and the article dated 25 March.

9 Cf., for example, M. Jammer, *The Philosophy of Quantum Mechanics. The Interpretation of Quantum Mechanics in Historical Perspective*, New York: John Wiley and Sons, 1974, ch. 5.

10 A. Einstein, B. Podolski and N. Rosen, 'Can Quantum-Mechanical...' cit. n. 8, 777.

11 Ibid.

12 The assertion by Podolski is reported in the *New York Times* article; cf. n. 22.

13 A. Einstein, B. Podolski and N. Rosen, 'Can Quantum-Mechanical...' cit. n. 8, 777–78.

14 Cf., for example, F. Selleri, *Die Debatte um die Quantentheorie*, Braunschweig: Vieweg, 1983; *Paradossi e realtà. Saggio sui fondamenti della microfisica*, Bari: Laterza, 1987.

15 A. Einstein, B. Podolski and N. Rosen, 'Can Quantum-Mechanical...' cit. n. 8, 778.
16 Ibid.
17 Ibid.
18 Ibid.
19 Ibid., 778–79.
20 For a discussion of the experiment and a logico-conceptual analysis of the paper, cf. C. A. Hooker, 'The Nature of Quantum Mechanical Reality: Einstein *versus* Bohr', in R. G. Colodny, ed., *Paradigms and Paradoxes*, Pittsburg: University of Pittsburg Press, 1972, 67–302. Cf. also M. Jammer, *The Philosophy...* cit. n. 9; B. d'Espagnat, *Conceptual Foundations of Quantum Mechanics*, London: Benjamin, 1976.
21 A. Einstein, B. Podolski and N. Rosen, 'Can Quantum-Mechanical...' cit. n. 8, 780.
22 The article appeared in the *New York Times* of 4 May 1935 (84, n. 28,224, 11).
23 For an ample bibliography concerning this debate, cf. C. A. Hooker, 'The Nature of Quantum Mechanical...' cit. n. 20.
24 A. Einstein, B. Podolski and N. Rosen, 'Can Quantum-Mechanical...' cit. n. 8, 779.
25 Einstein was continually to stress his opposition to quantum mechanics, which he backed up with arguments such as the following: 'On the strength of the successes of this theory they consider it proved that a theoretically complete description of a system can, in essence, involve only statistical assertions concerning the measurable quantities of this system. [...] In what follows I wish to adduce reasons which keep me from falling in line with the opinion of almost all contemporary theoretical physicists. I am, in fact, firmly convinced that the essentially statistical character of contemporary quantum theory is solely to be ascribed to the fact that this [theory] operates with an incomplete description of physical systems'. (A. Einstein, 'Reply to Criticism', in P. A. Schilpp, ed., *Albert Einstein...* cit. ch 1 n. 7, 665–88:666). Cf. also A. Pais, *'Subtle is the Lord'...* cit. ch. 1 n. 47.
26 N. Bohr, 'Can Quantum-Mechanical Description of Physical Reality Be Considered Complete?', *Physical Review* **48** (1935), 696–702: 696. The issue of the review was published 15 October, the article is dated 17 July 1935.
27 Ibid.
28 Ibid., 697.
29 A. Einstein, 'Autobiographical Notes' cit. n. 3, 81.
30 N. Bohr, 'Can Quantum-Mechanical...' cit. n. 26, 697.
31 Ibid.
32 N. Bohr, 'Quantum Mechanics and Physical Reality', *Nature* **136** (1935), 65.
33 Ibid.
34 N. Bohr, 'Can Quantum-Mechanical' cit. n. 26, 699.
35 Ibid.
36 Ibid.
37 Ibid., 700.
38 Ibid.
39 Ibid., 701.
40 Ibid., 700.
41 A. Einstein, B. Podolski and N. Rosen, 'Can Quantum-Mechanical...' cit. n. 8, 780.
42 According to Hooker ('The Nature of Quantum Mechanical...' cit. n. 20,

142 ff.), Bohr's reply to the paper by Einstein, Podolski and Rosen develops around the following two theses: '... the fact that we cut ourselves off from the unambiguous application of some classical concepts (and descriptions) by arranging for other classical concepts to be unambiguously applicable'; and that 'the proper application of classical concepts, hence the availability of classical descriptions using these concepts, requires that the appropriate physical conditions be realized'. In the light of this reading of Bohr's reply, Hooker examines the mistakes contained in the interpretations of this point put forward by Popper and Feyerabend, which he considers representative of the views contained in the literature (K. Popper, *The Logic of Scientific Discovery*, London: Hutchinson, 1959; P. K. Feyerabend, 'Problems in Microphysics', in R. G. Colodny, ed., *Frontiers of Science and Philosophy*, Pittsburg: University of Pittsburg Press, 1962; 'On a Recent Critique of Complementarity', *Philosophy of Science* Part I: **35** (1968), 309–21; Part II: **36** (1969), 82–105). In particular, Hooker stresses that the peculiar aspect of Bohr's conception of measurement in quantum physics 'is that the *physical* circumstances have *conceptual* consequences': 'Classical concepts referring to conjugate physical quantities are not simultaneously applicable to a given situation *because the quantum-mechanical interaction between system and instruments does not permit the necessary physical conditions for joint applicability to be realized*' ('The Nature of Quantum Mechanical...' cit. n. 20, 152).

43 N. Bohr, 'Discussions with Einstein...' cit. ch. 1 n. 7, 234.

44 N. Bohr, 'Fundamental Problems of the Quantum Theory', *CW6*, 75–88; this gives the transcription and anastatic copy of the ms. (in English) of eight pages, dated 13 September 1927. The second quotation is taken from the ms. 'The Quantum Postulate and the Recent Development of Quantum Theory', *CW6*, 91–98: 98 (p. 12 of the ms.).

45 W. Pauli, 'Die philosophische Bedeutung der Idee der Komplementarität', *Experientia* **6** (1950), 72–81; *CSP2*, 1149–58: 1151. Conference held at the Philosophischen Gesellschaft of Zurich in February 1949.

46 N. Bohr, 'Discussions with Einstein...' cit. ch. 1 n. 7, 222.

47 Ibid., 217–18.

48 In accordance with his interpretation of complementarity (cf. above, ch. 5 n. 87), Murdoch (*Niels Bohr's...* cit. ibid., 64–65) maintains that 'wave–particle complementarity itself resolves the paradoxes of dualism: since the wave and particle models are complementary, they are applicable only to mutually exclusive experimental situations': in any case, 'the incompatible models need never be applied to an object at the same time; they are called for only in mutually exclusive physical situations'.

49 W. Heisenberg, 'The Development of Quantum Mechanics', in *Nobel Lectures. Physics. 1922–1941*, Amsterdam: Elsevier, 1965, 290–301: 296.

50 Ibid., 297.

51 Ibid., 298.

52 Ibid., 299.

53 A. Einstein, 'Einleitende Bemerkungen ber Grundbegriffe', in *Louis de Broglie, physicien et penseur*, Paris: Albin Michel, 1953, 4–15: 6 (French trans. opposite).

54 E. Schrödinger, 'The Philosophy of Experiment', *Il nuovo cimento* series 10, vol. 1 (1955), 5–15: 15.

55 N. Bohr, 'Kausalität und Komplementarität', *Erkenntnis* **6** (1936), 293–303; English trans. 'Causality and Complementarity', *Philosophy of Science* **4**

(1937), 289–98: 292–93. On the so-called 'disturbance' problem in the context of the Copenhagen interpretation, cf. H. Folse, *The Philosophy...* cit. ch. 3 n. 34, esp. ch. IV.

56 'It was Bohr who not only developed Planck's ideas further to a theory of atomic structure and spectral lines, but who also worked out the epistemological consequences of the new quantum mechanics or wave mechanics, which since 1927 removed the logical contradictions from the theoretical explanation of the quantum phenomena. These consequences are not quite easy to understand; and the point of view called "complementarity", which was developed by Bohr and others for this purpose, though shared by the majority of physicists, did not remain without opposition. In order to understand the meaning of complementarity, you have to imagine objects, which always start to move as soon as you look at them with help of an apparatus suitable to locate their position. That would not matter if you could compute this motion and so theoretically determine the disturbance caused by the measurement. But what if this disturbance could not be kept under control in principle? And if the empirical measurement of this disturbance would introduce new measuring instruments, the interaction of which with the old ones would introduce new disturbances indeterminable and uncontrollable in principle? This is indeed the actual situation created by the finiteness of the quantum of action'. (W. Pauli, 'Matter', in *Man's Right to Knowledge, International Symposium Presented in Honor of the Two-Hundredth Anniversary of Columbia University*, 1754–1954, New York: H. Muschel, 1954, 10–18: 15; *CSP1*, 1125–33: 1130.)

57 'This crucial point [...] implies *the impossibility of any sharp separation between the behaviour of atomic objects and the interaction with the measuring instruments which serve to define the conditions under which the phenomena appear*. In fact, the individuality of the typical quantum effects finds its proper expression in the circumstance that any attempt of subdividing the phenomena will demand a change in the experimental arrangement introducing new possibilities of interaction between objects and measuring instruments which in principle cannot be controlled'. (N. Bohr, 'Discussions with Einstein...' cit. ch. 1 n. 7, 209–10.)

58 W. Pauli, 'Matter' cit. n. 56, 16; *CSP1*, 1131.

59 N. Bohr, 'Discussions with Einstein...' cit. ch. 1 n. 7, 235.

60 Ibid., 237. Cf. also N. Bohr, 'Quantum Physics and Philosophy. Causality and Complementarity', in R. Klibansky, ed., *Philosophy in Mid-Century: A Survey*, Florence: La Nuova Italia, 1958, 308–14; also in N. Bohr, *Essays, 1958–1962, on Atomic Physics and Human Knowledge*, New York: Wiley, 1963, 1–7.

61 N. Bohr, 'Discussions with Einstein...' cit. ch. 1 n. 7, 238. Henceforth we shall refer to this definition of the notion of phenomenon which, as Folse has well pointed out ('The Philosophy...' cit. ch. 3 n. 34, 158–59), took on a crucial role in Bohr's terminology and contributed to the clarification of complementarity itself: 'Adopting the word "phenomenon" to refer to "the effects observed under given experimental conditions" had a significant impact on Bohr's expression of complementarity after 1939. As we saw [...] Bohr's leading idea in formulating complementarity centred on the complementarity of two modes of description, that of space-time co-ordination and that of the claim of causality. However, because the debate with Einstein showed the tendency to regard position observations and

movement observations as determinations of the properties of the *same* observed system (i.e., the *same* "phenomenon" as Bohr used that term in the Como paper), Bohr began to emphasize that these two observational interactions are *different* phenomena [...] Thus he eventually adopted a way of speaking which referred to the complementarity of different *phenomena* or complementary *evidence* from different observations'. The problem of Bohr's redefinition of the concept of phenomenon has been analysed with great philosophical sensitivity by Catherine Chevalley in her introductory essay to N. Bohr, *Physique atomique et connaissance humaine*, Paris: Gallimard, 1991, 17–147. Chevalley shows that for Bohr 'There do not exist quantum *concepts*, that is to say concepts which have a correlation with our intuitions, and therefore the only concepts at our disposition are the concepts of classical physics. But if there are no quantum concepts, it follows that it is impossible to talk of quantum *objects*. Rejecting such an impossibility, Bohr was driven to proposing a redefinition of the term *phenomenon* and indicating what might be a new form of the nature of objectivity' (ibid., 81–82). According to Chevalley, in this process of the redefinition of the notion of phenomenon, Bohr can be seen to have moved away to a considerable extent from the Kantian concept of forms of intuition (*Anschauungsformen*).

62 M. Planck, *Il concetto di causalità in fisica*, in M. Planck, *La conoscenza del mondo fisico*, Boringhieri: Torino, 1964, 392–409: 402.

63 Ibid., 401–2.

64 W. Pauli, 'Wahrscheinlichkeit und Physik', *Dialectica* **8** (1954), 112–24: 115; *CSP2*, 1199–211: 1202. Expanded version of the lecture delivered at the Schweizerischen Naturforschenden Gesellschaft, Berne, 1952.

65 Ibid., 118; *CSP2*, 1205.

66 'The non-deterministic character of the natural laws postulated by quantum mechanics rests precisely upon these possibilities of a free choice of experimental procedures complementary one with the other. It is thus that the observation assumes the character of an *irrational individual act* with an unpredictable result. The impossibility, then, of subdividing the experimental procedure without changing the phenomenon substantially gives rise to a new characteristic of *wholeness* of physical events. To this *irrational* aspect of concrete phenomena, which are those actually observed, is juxtaposed the rational aspect, which consists in an abstract ordering of the possibilities of observation, with the help of the mathematical concept of probability and the psi function'. (W. Pauli, 'Wahrscheinlichkeit...' cit. n. 64, 116; *CSP2*, 1203.)

67 W. Pauli, 'Naturwissenschaftliche und erkenntnistheoretische Aspekte der Ideen vom Unbewussten', *Dialectica* **8** (1954), 283–301: 285; *CSP2*, 1212–30: 1214.

68 Ibid., 285–86; *CSP2*, 1214–15.

69 W. Pauli, 'Wahrscheinlichkeit...' cit. n. 64, 118; *CSP2*, 1205.

70 N. Bohr, 'Discussions with Einstein...' cit. ch. 1 n. 7, 223.

71 'In this wider sense the quantum-mechanical description of atomic phenomena is still an objective description, although the state of an object is not assumed any longer to remain independent of the way in which the possible sources of information about the object are irrevocably altered by observations. The existence of such alterations reveals a new kind of wholeness in nature, unknown in classical physics, inasmuch as an attempt to subdivide a phenomenon defined by the whole experimental arrangement

used for its observation creates an entirely new phenomenon'. (W. Pauli, 'Matter' cit. n. 56, 17; *CSP1*, 1132.) For an interesting philosophical and theoretical investigation of the relationship between natural language and physical object in this context, cf. C. Chevalley, 'Complémentarité et langage dans l'interprétation de Copenhague', *Revue d'histoire des sciences* **38** (1985), 251–92; 'Introduction', in N. Bohr. *Physique atomique...* cit. n. 61.

72 Cf. H. Folse, *The Philosophy...* cit. ch. 3 n. 34, ch 5.

73 Bohr to Dirac, 24 March 1928, *CW6*, 44–46.

74 N. Bohr, 'Die Atomtheorie...' cit. ch 1 n. 19, 77.

75 W. Pauli, 'Die philosophische Bedeutung...' cit. n. 45, 2; *CSP2*, 1150. Cf. also W. Pauli, 'Phenomen und physikalische Realität', *Dialectica* **11** (1957), 36–48; *CSP2*, 1350–61. Introduction to the International Congress of Philosophy, Zurich 1954.

76 N. Bohr, 'Causality...' cit. n. 55, 290.

77 N. Bohr, 'Die Atomtheorie...' cit. ch. 1 n. 19, 77.

78 'If in spite of the logical consistency and mathematical elegance of quantum mechanics some physicists still harbour a certain regressive hope that the above gnoseological situation will finally be demonstrated to be incorrect, this arises in my view from the power of those traditional forms of thought that may be grouped under the name of "ontologism" or "realism". And yet, even those physicists who do not side fully with the "sensists" or "empiricists" must still ask themselves the question – justified by virtue of the nature of the postulate of the traditional forms of thought and inevitable because of the existence of quantum mechanics – whether such forms are a necessary condition for the possibility of physics in general or whether they might be replaced with other, more general forms of thought. Analysis of the theoretical foundations of wave or quantum mechanics has shown that the second alternative is the correct one'. (W. Pauli, 'Wahrscheinlichkeit...' cit. n. 64, 117; *CSP2*, 1204.)

79 Ehrenfest to Goudsmit, Uhlenbeck and Dieke cit. ch. 1 n. 7.

General bibliography

In addition to the primary and secondary sources that have been used in this study, some of the more important general histories of quantum mechanics and studies of the foundations of quantum mechanics are included in the bibliography. For primary sources the original version has been given, along with any subsequent translation that may have appeared in contemporary scientific journals; additionally, where available, indication is given to any republication in any collected works. The following abbreviations have been used:

CW N. Bohr, *Collected Works*, L. Rosenfeld and E. Rüdinger, eds., Amsterdam: North-Holland – New York: American Elsevier. Vol. 1, *Early Work (1905–1911)*, 1972; vol. 2, *Work on Atomic Physics (1912–1917)*, 1976; vol. 3, *The Correspondence Principle (1918–1923)*, 1977; vol. 4, *The Periodic System (1918–1923)*, 1977; vol. 5, *The Emergence of Quantum Mechanics (Mainly 1924–1926)*, 1984; vol. 6, *Foundations of Quantum Physics I (1926–1932)*, 1985.

GW W. Heisenberg, *Gesammelte Werke – Collected Papers*, W. Blum, H.-P. Dürr and H. Rechenberg, eds., Berlin: Springer Verlag, 1985.

CSP W. Pauli, *Collected Scientific Papers*, R. Kronig and W. F. Weisskopf, eds., 2 vols., New York: Interscience, 1964.

WB W. Pauli, *Wissenschaftlicher Briefwechsel mit Bohr, Einstein, Heisenberg, u. a.*, A. Hermann, K. von Meyenn and W. F. Weisskopf, eds., vol. 1: 1919–29, New York: Springer Verlag, 1979.

SHQP *Sources for the History of Quantum Physics*.

Aaserud, F. (1990), *Redirecting Science: Niels Bohr, Philanthropy and the Rise of Nuclear Physics*, Cambridge: Cambridge University Press.

Agassi, J. (1958), 'A Hegelian View of Complementarity', *British Journal for the Philosophy of Science* **9**, 57–63.

Agazzi, E. (1988), 'Waves, Particles and Complementarity', in G. Tarozzi and A. van der Merwe, eds., *The Nature of Quantum Paradoxes*, Kluwer Academic Publisher.

Audi, M. (1974), *The Interpretation of Quantum Mechanics*, Chicago and London: The University of Chicago Press.

Balibar, F. (1985), 'Bohr entre Einstein et Dirac', *Revue d'Histoire des Sciences* **38**, 293–307.

Beller, M. (1983),'Matrix Theory before Schrödinger: Philosophy, Problems, Consequences', *Isis* **74**, 469–91.

Bellone, E. (1973), *I modelli e la concezione del mondo nella fisica moderna da Laplace a Bohr*, Milan: Feltrinelli.

Bensaude, B. (1985), 'L'évolution de la complementarité dans les textes de Bohr', *Revue d'Histoire des Sciences* **38**, 231–50.

Bergman, H. (1974), 'The Controversy Concerning the Law of Causality in Contemporary Physics', *Boston Studies in the Philosophy of Science* **13**, 392–462.

Bergstein, T. (1972), *Quantum Physics and Ordinary Language*, London: Macmillan.

Bernkopf, M. (1967), 'A History of Infinite Matrices', *Archive for the History of Exact Sciences* **4**, 308–58.

Black, M. (1962), *Models and Metaphors*, Ithaca and London: Cornell University Press.

Blaedel, N. (1988), *Harmony and Unity. The Life of Niels Bohr*, Berlin: Springer Verlag.

Block, F. (1976), 'Heisenberg and the Early Days of Quantum Mechanics', *Physics Today* **29***(12)*, 23–27.

Blokhintsev, D. I. (1968), *The Philosophy of Quantum Mechanics*, Dordrecht: Reidel.

Bohr, N. (1911), 'Studier Over Metallernes Elektrontheori', Copenhagen; *CW1*, 167–290; English trans., *CW1*, 294–392.

Bohr, N. (1913), 'On the Constitution of Atoms and Molecules', *Philosophical Magazine* **26**, 1–25; 474–502; 857–75; *CW2*, 161–85; 188–214; 215–33.

Bohr, N. (1913), 'On the Theory of the Decrease of Velocity of Moving Electrified Particles on Passing Through Matter', *Philosophical Magazine* **25**, 10–31; *CW2*, 18–39.

Bohr, N. (1914), 'Om Brintspektret', *Fysisk Tidsskrift* **12**, 97–114; English trans., 'On the Hydrogen Spectrum', in N. Bohr, *The Theory of Spectra and the Atomic Constitution*, Cambridge: Cambridge University Press, 1922, 1–19; *CW2*, 283–301.

Bohr, N. (1918–22), 'On the Quantum Theory of the Light Spectra', *Det Kongelige Danske Viedenskabernes Salskab. Skrifter, Naturvidenskabelig og mathematisk Afdeling* **8***(4)*; *CW3*, 67–184.

Bohr, N. (1920), 'Über die Serienspektra der Elemente', *Zeitschrift für Physik* **2**, 423–69; English trans. 'On the Series Spectra of the Elements', in N. Bohr, *The Theory of Spectra and Atomic Constitution*, Cambridge: Cambridge University Press, 1922; *CW3*, 242–82.

Bohr, N. (1923), 'L'application de la théorie des quanta aux problèmes atomiques', in *Atomes et électrons, Rapports et discussions du Conseil de Physique tenu à Bruxelles du 1er au 6 Avril 1921*, Paris: Gauthier-Villars, 228–47; *CW3*, 364–80.

Bohr, N. (1923), 'The Correspondence Principle', in *Report of the British Association for the Advancement of Science*, Liverpool, 428–29; *CW3*, 576–77.

Bohr, N. (1923), 'Über der Anwendung der Quantentheorie auf den Atombau', *Zeitschrift für Physik* **13**, 117–65; English trans. 'On the Application of the Quantum Theory to Atomic Structure', *Proceedings of the Cambridge Philosophical Society (Supplement)*, 1924, 1–42; *CW3*, 458–99.

Bohr, N. (1925), 'Atomic Theory and Mechanics', *Nature (Supplement)* **116**, 845–52; *CW5*, 73–80.

Bohr, N. (1925), 'Über die Wirkung von Atomen bei Stössen', *Zeitschrift für Physik* **34**, 178–90; *CW5*, 178–93; English trans., *CW5*, 194–206.

Bohr, N. (1928), 'The Quantum Postulate and the Recent Development of Atomic Theory', in *Atti del Congresso Internazionale dei Fisici*, 11–12 settembre 1927, 2 vols., Bologna: Zanichelli, vol. II, 565–88; 'Das Quantenpostulat und die neuere Entwicklung der Atomistik', *Die Naturwissenschaften* **16**, 245–57; 'Le postulat des quanta et le nouveau dévelopment de l'atomistique', in *Electrons et photons. Rapport et discussions du cinquième Conseil de physique tenu à Bruxelles du 24 au 29 Octobre 1927*, Paris: Gauthier-Villars; 'The Quantum Postulate and the Recent Development of Atomic Theory', *Nature (Supplement)* **121**, 580–90; *CW6*, 148–58.

Bohr, N. (1929), 'Atomteorien og Grunprincipperne for Naturbeskrivelsen', in *Beretning om det 18. skandinaviske Naturforkermode i Kobenhavn 26–31 August 1929*, Copenhagen: Frederiksberg Bogtrykkeri, 71–83; *CW6*, 223–35; 'Die Atomtheorie und die Prinzipien der Naturbeschreibung', *Die Naturwissenschaften* **18**, 73–78 (1930).

Bohr, N. (1929), 'Wirkungsquantum und Naturbeschreibung', *Die Naturwissenschaften* **17**, 483–86, *CW6*, 203–06.

Bohr, N. (1935), 'Can Quantum-Mechanical Description of Physical Reality Be Considered Complete?', *Physical Review* **48**, 696–702.

Bohr, N. (1936), 'Kausalität und Komplementarität', *Erkenntnis* **6**, 293–303; 'Causality and Complementarity', *Philosophy of Science* **4**, 289–98.

Bohr, N. (1948), 'On the Notions of Causality and Complementarity', *Dialectica* **2**, 312–19.

Bohr, N. (1949), 'Discussions with Einstein on Epistemological Problems in Atomic Physics', in P. A. Schilpp, ed., *Albert Einstein, Philosopher–Scientist*, New York: Harper & Row.

Bohr, N. (1958), 'Quantum Physics and Philosophy. Causality and Complementarity', in R. Klibansky, ed., *Philosophy in Mid-Century: A Survey*, Florence: La Nuova Italia.

Bohr, N., Kramers, H. A. and Slater, J. C. (1924), 'The Quantum Theory of Radiation', *Philosophical Magazine* **47**, 785–802; *CW5*, 101–18.

Born, M. (1924), 'Über Quantenmechanik', *Zeitschrift für Physik* **26**, 379–95.

Born, M., ed. (1971), *The Born–Einstein Letters*, New York: Walker.

Born, M. and Jordan, P. (1925), 'Zur Quantenmechanik', *Zeitschrift für Physik* **34**, 858–88.

Born, M., Heisenberg, W. and Jordan, P. (1925), 'Zur Quantenmechanik II', *Zeitschrift für Physik* **35**, 557–615; *GW*, 397–455.

Bothe, W. (1923), 'Über eine neue Sekundärstrahlung der Röntgenstrahlen', I Mitteilung, *Zeitschrift für Physik* **16**, 319–20; II Mitteilung, *Zeitschrift für Physik* **20**, 237–55.

Bothe, W. and Geiger, H. (1924), 'Ein Weg zur experimenteller Nachprüfung der Theorie von Bohr, Kramers und Slater', *Zeitschrift für Physik* **26**, 44.

Bothe, W. and Geiger, H. (1925), 'Experimentelles zur Theorie von Bohr, Kramers und Slater', *Die Naturwissenschaften* **13**, 440–41.

Bothe, W. and Geiger, H. (1925), 'Über das Wesen des Comptoneffekts; ein experimentelles Beitrag zur Theorie der Strahlung', *Zeitschrift für Physik* **32**, 639–63.

Boyd, R. (1979), 'Metaphor and Theory Cange: What is "Metaphor" a

Metaphor for?', in A. Ortony, ed., *Metaphor and Thought*, Cambridge: Cambridge University Press.

Breit, G. (1924), 'The Quantum Theory of Dispersion', *Nature* **114**, 310.

Bromberg, J. (1976), 'The Concept of Particle Creation Before and After Quantum Mechanics', *Historical Studies in the Physical Sciences* **7**, 161–83.

Brush, S. G. (1976), 'Irreversibility and Indeterminism: Fourier to Heisenberg', *Journal of the History of Ideas* **37**, 603–30.

Brush, S. G. (1980), 'The Chimerical Cat: Philosophy of Quantum Mechanics in Historical Perspective', *Social Studies of Science* **10**, 393–447.

Bub, J. (1974), *The Interpretation of Quantum Mechanics*, Dordrecht: Reidel.

Bunge, M. (1955), 'Strife about Complementarity', *British Journal for the Philosophy of Science* **6**, 141–54.

Bunge, M. (1963), *Causality. The Place of the Causal Principle in Modern Science*, Cambridge (Mass.): Harvard University Press (2nd edn.).

Bunge, M. (1967), *Quantum Theory and Reality*, Berlin: Springer Verlag.

Cassidy, D. C. (1979), 'Heisenberg's First Core Model of the Atom: the Formation of a Professional Style', *Historical Studies in the Physical Sciences* **10**, 187–224.

Cassirer, E. (1936), *Determinismus und Indeterminismus in der modernen Physik*, Göteborgs Högskolas Arsskrift, vol. 42; English trans., *Determinism and Indeterminism in Modern Physics: Historical and Systemic Studies of the Problem of Causality*, New Haven: Yale University Press.

Ceruti, M. (1985), 'La costruzione del soggetto e il soggetto della costruzione. Per una teoria dell'osservatore', *Intersezioni* **5**(*3*), 513–29.

Ceruti, M. (1985), 'La hybris dell'onniscienza e la sfida della complessità', in G. Bocchi and M. Ceruti, eds., *La sfida della complessità*, Milan: Feltrinelli.

Ceruti, M. (1986), *Il vincolo e la possibilità*, Milan: Feltrinelli.

Chevalley, C. (1985), 'Complementarité et language dans l'intérpretation de Copenhague', *Revue d'histoire des sciences* **38**, 251–92.

Chevalley, C. (1989), 'De Bohr et von Neumann à Kant. L'Ecole allemande de logique quantique', *L'Age de la Science* **2**, 151–79.

Chevalley, C. (1989), 'Histoire et philosophie de la mécanique quantique', *Revue de Synthèse*, 469–81.

Chevalley, C., ed. (1991), *Niels Bohr. Physique atomique et connaissance humaine*, Paris: Gallimard.

Chevalley, C. (1993), 'Complémentarité et réprésentation: Bohr et la tradition philosophique allemande', in S. Petruccioli, ed., *Lezioni della Scuola superiore di storia della scienza della Domus Galilaeana di Pisa – Sezione storico-epistemologica*, Rome: Istituto della Enciclopedia Italiana.

Cini, M. (1982), 'Cultural Traditions and Environmental Factors in the Development of Quantum Electrodynamics (1925–1933)', *Fundamenta Scientiae* **3**, 229–53.

Colodny, R. G., ed. (1972), *Paradigms and Paradoxes: The Philosophical Challenge of the Quantum Domain*, Pittsburgh: University of Pittsburgh Press.

Compton, A. H. (1923), 'A Quantum Theory of the Scattering of X-Rays by Light Elements', *Physical Review* **21**, 483–502.

Compton, A. H. (1924), 'The Scattering of X-Rays', *Journal of the Franklin Institute* **198**, 54–72.

Compton, A. H. (1925), 'On the Mechanism of X-Rays Scattering', *Proceedings of the National Academy of Science USA* **11**, 303–06.

Compton, A. H. and Simon, A. W. (1925), 'Directed Quanta of Scattered X-Rays', *Physical Review* **26**, 289–99.

Courant, R. and Hilbert, D. (1924), *Methoden der mathematischen Physik*, Berlin: Springer Verlag.

d'Abro, A. (1951), *The Rise of the New Physics*, New York: D. Van Nostrand.

D'Agostino, S. (1985), 'The Problem of the Link between Correspondence and Complementarity in Niels Bohr's Papers 1925–1927', in *Proceedings of the International Symposium on Niels Bohr, Rome 25–27 November 1985, Rivista di Storia della Scienza* **2**(*3*), 369–90.

D'Agostino, S. (1987), 'Il principio di indeterminazione e la transizione dall'ontologia della fisica classica a quella della meccanica quantistica', in M. La Forgia and S. Petruccioli, eds., *Rappresentazione e oggetto dalla fisica alle altre scienze*, Rome: Theoria.

Darrigol, O. (1985), 'La complementarité comme argument d'autorité', *Revue d'Histoire des Science* **38**, 309–23.

Darrigol, O. (1991), 'Cohérence et complétude de la mecanique quantique: l'exemple de Bohr–Rosenfed', *Revue d'Histoire des Science* **44**, 137–79.

Darrigol, O. (1992), *From c-Numbers to q-Numbers. The Classical Analogies in the History of Quantum Theory*, Berkeley and Los Angeles: University of California Press.

Darwin, C. G. (1912), 'A Theory of Absorption and Scattering of the α-Rays', *Philosophical Magazine* **23**, 901–20.

de Broglie, L. (1923), 'Ondes et quanta', *Comptes Rendus de l'Académie des Sciences* **127**, 507–10.

de Broglie, L. (1924), 'A Tentative Theory of Light Quanta', *Philosophical Magazine* **47**, 446–58.

de Broglie, L. (1924), 'Recherches sur la théorie des quanta', *American Journal of Physics* **40**, 1315–20.

de Broglie, L. (1938), *Le principe de correspondance entre la matière et le rayonnement*, Paris: Hermann.

de Broglie, L. (1941), *Continu et discontinu en physique moderne*, Paris: Albin Michel.

de Broglie, L. (1947), *Physique et microphysique*, Paris: Albin Michel.

de Broglie, L. (1948), 'Sur la complementarité des idées d'individu et de système', *Dialectica* **2**, 325–29.

de Broglie, L. (1955), *Le dualisme des ondes et des corpuscles dans l'oeuvre de Albert Einstein*, Paris.

de Broglie, L. (1973), 'The Beginnings of Wave Mechanics', in W. C. Price, S. S. Chissick and T. Ravensdale, eds., *Wave Mechanics: The First Fifty Years*, New York: John Wiley & Sons.

de Broglie, L. (1975), *Certitude et incertitude de la science*, Paris: Albin Michel.

de Broglie, L. (1982), *Les incertitudes de Heisenberg et l'interprétation probabiliste de la mécanique quantique*, Paris: Gauthier-Villars.

De Maria, M. and La Teana, F. (1982), 'I primi lavori di E. Schrödinger sulla meccanica ondulatoria e la nascita delle polemiche con la scuola di Göttingen–Copenhagen sull'interpretazione della meccanica quantistica', *Physis* **24**, 33–54.

De Maria, M. and La Teana, F. (1982), 'Schrödinger's and Dirac's Unorthodoxy in Quantum Mechanics', *Fundamenta Scientiae* **3**, 129–48.

De Maria, M. and La Teana, F. (1983), 'Dirac's "Unorthodox" Contribution to Orthodox Quantum Mechanics (1925–1927)', *Scientia* **118**, 595–611.

d'Espagnat, B. (1976), *Conceptual Foundations of Quantum Mechanics*, London: Benjamin (2nd edn.).

d'Espagnat, B. (1981), *A la recherche du réel. Le regard d'un physicien*, Paris: Bordas.

Dingles, H. (1970), 'Causality and Statistics in Modern Physics', *British Journal for the Philosophy of Science* **21**, 223–46.

Dirac, P. A. M. (1925), 'The Fundamental Equations of Quantum Mechanics', *Proceedings of the Royal Society of London* **A109**, 642–53.

Dirac, P. A. M. (1926), 'Quantum Mechanics and a Preliminary Investigation of the Hydrogen Atom', *Proceedings of the Royal Society of London* **A110**, 561–79.

Dorling, J. (1971), 'Einstein's Introduction of Photons: Argument by Analogy or Deduction from the Phenomena?', *British Journal for the Philosophy of Science* **22**, 1–8.

Einstein, A. (1917), 'Zur Quantentheorie der Strahlung', *Physikalische Zeitschrift* **18**, 121–28.

Einstein, A. (1948), 'Quantenmechanik und Wirklichkeit', *Dialectica* **2**, 320–24.

Einstein, A. (1953), 'Einleitende Bemerkungen über Grundbegriffe', in E. Whittaker, ed., *Louis de Broglie, physicien et penseur*, Paris: Albin Michel.

Einstein, A. and Besso, M. (1972), *Correspondance 1903–1955*, P. Speziali, ed., Paris: Hermann.

Einstein, A., Podolski, B. and Rosen, N. (1935), 'Can Quantum-Mechanical Description of Physical Reality Be Considered Complete?', *Physical Review* **47**, 777–80.

Enz, C. P. (1973), 'W. Pauli's Scientific Work', in J. Mehra, ed., *The Physicist's Conception of Nature*, Dordrecht: Reidel.

Enz, C. P. and Mehra, J., eds. (1974), *Physical Reality and Mathematical Description*, Dordrecht: Reidel.

Erlichson, H. (1972), 'The Einstein–Podolski–Rosen Paradox', *Philosophy of Science* **39**, 83–85.

Evans, E. J. (1913), 'The Spectra of Helium and Hydrogen', *Nature* **92**, 5.

Favrholdt, D. (1976), 'Niels Bohr and the Danish Philosophy', *Danish Yearbook of Philosophy* **13**, 206–20.

Favrholdt, D. (1985), 'The Cultural Background of the Young Niels Bohr', in *Proceedings of the International Symposium on Niels Bohr, Rome 25–27 November 1985, Rivista di Storia della Scienza* **2**, 445–61.

Favrholdt, D. (1992), *Niels Bohr's Philosophical Background*, Det Kongelige Danske Videnskabernes Selskab, Historisk-filosofiske Meddelelser **63**.

Faye, J. (1979), 'The Influence of Harald Høffding's Philosophy on Niels Bohr's Interpretation of Quantum Mechanics', *Danish Yearbook of Philosophy* **16**, 37–72.

Faye, J. (1991), *Niels Bohr: His Heritage and Legacy. An Antirealistic View of Quantum Mechanics*, Dordrecht: Kluwer.

Feyerabend, P. K. (1958), 'Complementarity', *Proceedings of the Aristotelian Society (Supplement)* **32**, 76–78.

Feyerabend, P. K. (1961), 'Niels Bohr's Interpretation of the Quantum Theory', in H. Feigl and G. Maxwell, eds., *Current Issues in the Philosophy of Science*, New York: Holt, Rinehart and Winston.

Feyerabend, P. K. (1962), 'Problems of Microphysics', in R. G. Colodny, ed., *Frontiers of Science and Philosophy*, Pittsburgh: University of Pittsburgh Press.

Feyerabend, P. K. (1968–69), 'On a Recent Critique of Complementarity: Part I', *Philosophy of Science* **35**, 1968, 309–31; 'On a Recent Critique of Complementarity: Part II', *Philosophy of Science* **36**, 1969, 82–109.

Fine, A. (1976), 'The Young Einstein and the Old Einstein', in R. S. Cohen, P. K. Feyerabend and M. Wartofsky, eds., *Essays in Memory of Imre Lakatos*, Dordrecht: Reidel.

Folse, H. (1977), 'Complementarity and the Description of Experience', *International Philosophical Quarterly* **17**, 378–92.

Folse, H. (1978), 'Kantian Aspects of Complementarity', *Kant-Studien* **69**, 58–66.

Folse, H. (1985), *The Philosophy of Niels Bohr. The Framework of Complementarity*, Amsterdam: North-Holland.

Folse, H. (1987), 'Niels Bohr: Complementarity and Realism', *Proceedings of the 1986 Biennal Meetings of the Philosophy of Science Association (1986)* **1**, 96–104.

Forman, P. (1968), 'The Doublet Riddle and the Atomic Physics circa 1924', *Isis* **59**, 156–74.

Forman, P. (1970), 'Alfred Landé and the Anomalous Zeeman Effect, 1919–1921', *Historical Studies in the Physical Sciences* **2**, 153–261.

Forman, P. (1971), 'Weimar Culture, Causality and Quantum Theory, 1918–1927: Adaptation by German Physicists and Mathematicians to a Hostile Intellectual Environment', *Historical Studies in the Physical Sciences* **3**, 1–116.

Forman, P. (1974), 'The Financial Support and Political Alignment of Physicists in Weimar Germany', *Minerva* **12**, 39–66.

Forman, P. (1980), 'The Reception of an Acausal Quantum Mechanics in Germany and Britain', in S. H. Mauskopf, ed., *The Reception of Unconventional Science*, Westview Press for the American Association for the Advancement of Science, Boulder, Colorado.

Forman, P. and Raman, V. V. (1969), 'Why was It Schrödinger who developed de Broglie's Ideas?', *Historical Studies in the Physical Sciences* **1**, 291–314.

Gamow, G. (1966), *Thirty Years that Shook Physics. The Story of Quantum Theory*, New York: Anchor Books.

Gerber, J. (1969), 'Geschichte der Wellenmechanik', *Archive for the History of Exact Sciences* **5**, 349–414.

Grünbaum, A. (1957), 'Complementarity in Quantum Physics and Its Philosophical Generalization', *Journal of Philosophy* **54**, 713–27.

Hall, R. J. (1965), 'Philosophical Basis of Bohr's Interpretation of Quantum Mechanics', *American Journal of Physics* **33**, 624–27.

Hanle, P. A. (1977), 'Erwin Schrödinger's Reaction to Louis de Broglie's Thesis on the Quantum Theory', *Isis* **68**, 606–9.

Hanle, P. A. (1977), 'The Coming of Age of Erwin Schrödinger: His Quantum Statistics of Ideal Gases', *Archive for the History of Exact Sciences* **17**, 165–92.

Hanle, P. A. (1979), 'Indeterminacy before Heisenberg: the Case of Franz Exner and Erwin Schrödinger', *Historical Studies in the Physical Sciences* **10**, 225–70.

Hanle, P. A. (1979), 'The Schrödinger–Einstein Correspondence and the Sources of Wave Mechanics', *American Journal of Physics* **47**, 644–48.

Hanson, N. R. (1959), 'The Copenhagen Interpretation of Quantum Theory', *American Journal of Physics* **27**, 1–15.

Hanson, N. R. (1959), 'Five Cautions for the Copenhagen Interpretation's Critics', *Philosophy of Science* **26**, 325–37.

Hanson, N. R. (1960), 'The Copenhagen Interpretation of Quantum Theory', *Philosophy of Science* **27**, 450–71.

Hanson, N. R. (1961), 'Are Wave Mechanics and Matrix Mechanics Equivalent Theories?', in H. Feigl and G. Maxwell, eds., *Current Issues in the Philosophy of Science*, New York: Holt, Rinehart and Winston.

Heelan, P. A. (1955), 'The Development of the Interpretation of Quantum Theory', in W. Pauli, ed., *Niels Bohr and the Development of Physics*, London: Pergamon Press.

Heelan, P. A. (1975), 'Heisenberg and the Radical Theoretic Change', *Zeitschrift für Allgemeine Wissenschaftstheorie* **6**, 113–36.

Heilbron, J. L. (1967), 'The Kossel–Sommerfeld Theory and the Ring Atom', *Isis* **58**, 451–82.

Heilbron, J. L. (1977), 'J. J. Thomson and the Bohr Atom', *Physics Today* **30**, 23–30.

Heilbron, J. L. (1981), 'Rutherford–Bohr Atom', *American Journal of Physics* **49**, 223–31.

Heilbron, J. L. (1983), 'The Origins of the Exclusion Principle', *Historical Studies in the Physical Sciences* **13**, 261–310.

Heilbron, J. L. (1985), 'Bohr's First Theories of the Atom', in A. P. French and P. J. Kennedy, eds., *Niels Bohr. A Centenary Volume*, Cambridge (Mass.): Harvard University Press.

Heilbron, J. L. (1985), 'The Earliest Missionaries of the Copenhagen Spirit', *Revue d'histoire des sciences* **38**, 195–230.

Heilbron, J. L. (1986), *The Dilemnas of an Upright Man. Max Planck as a Spokesman for German Science*, Berkeley: University of California Press.

Heilbron, J. L. and Kuhn, T. S. (1969), 'The Genesis of the Bohr Atom', *Historical Studies in the Physical Sciences* **1**, 211–90.

Heisenberg, W. (1925), 'Über quantentheoretische Umdeutung kinematischer und mechanischer Beziehungen', *Zeitschrift für Physik* **33**, 879–93; *GW*, 382–96.

Heisenberg, W. (1926), 'Quantenmechanik', *Die Naturwissenschaften* **45**, 989–94.

Heisenberg, W. (1927), 'Über den anschaulichen Inhalt der quantentheoretische Kinematik und Mechanik', *Zeitschrift für Physik* **43**, 172–98; *GW*, 478–504.

Heisenberg, W. (1955), 'The Development of the Interpretation of the Quantum Theory', in W. Pauli, ed., *Niels Bohr and the Development of Physics*, London: Pergamon Press.

Heisenberg, W. (1958), *Physics and Philosophy. The Revolution in Modern Science*, New York: Harper & Row.

Heisenberg, W. (1960), 'Erinnerungen an die Zeit der Entwicklung der Quantenmechanik', in M. Fierz and V. F. Weisskopf, eds., *Theoretical Physics in the Twentieth Century*, New York: Interscience.

Heisenberg, W. (1965), 'The Development of Quantum Mechanics', in *Nobel Lectures, Physics. 1922–1941*, Amsterdam: Elsevier.

Heisenberg, W. (1967), 'Quantum Theory and Its Interpretation', in S. Rozental, ed., *Niels Bohr: His Life and Work as Seen by His Friends and Colleagues*, Amsterdam: North-Holland and New York: John Wiley & Sons.

Heisenberg, W. (1969), *Der Teil und das Ganze. Gespräche in Umkreis der Atomphysik*, München: Ripper; English trans., *Physics and Beyond: Encounters and Conversations*, New York: G. Allen & Unwin, 1971.

Heisenberg, W. (1971), 'Atomforschung und Kausalgesetz', in W. Heisenberg, *Schritte über Grenzen*, Munich: Piper Verlag; English trans., *Across the Frontiers*, New York: Harper & Row, 1974.

Heisenberg, W. (1971), 'Sprache und Wirklichkeit in der modernen Physik', in W. Heisenberg, *Schritte über Grenzen*, Munich: Piper Verlag; English trans., *Across the Frontiers*, New York: Harper & Row, 1974.

Heisenberg, W. (1973), 'Developments of Concepts in the History of Quantum Theory', in J. Mehra, ed., *The Physicist's Conception of Nature*, Dordrecht: Reidel.

Heisenberg, W. and Kramers, H. A. (1925), 'Über die Streuung von Strahlen durch Atome', *Zeitschrift für Physik* **31**, 681–708.

Hendry, J. (1980), 'The Development of Attitudes to the Wave–Particle Duality of Light and Quantum Theory, 1900–1920', *Annals of Science* **37**, 59–79.

Hendry, J. (1980), 'Weimar Culture and Quantum Causality', *History of Science* **18**, 155–80.

Hendry, J. (1981), 'Bohr–Kramers–Slater: A Virtual Theory of Virtual Oscillators and Its Role in the History of Quantum Mechanics', *Centaurus* **25**, 189–221.

Hendry, J. (1984), *The Creation of Quantum Mechanics and the Bohr–Pauli Dialogue*, Dordrecht: Reidel.

Hendry, J. (1985), 'The History of Complementarity: Niels Bohr and the Problem of Visualization', in *Proceedings of the International Symposium on Niels Bohr, Rome 25–27 November 1985*, *Rivista di Storia della Scienza* **2**, 391–407.

Hermann, A. (1969), *Frühgeschichte der Quantentheorie (1899–1913)*, Physik, Mosbach in Baden; English trans., *The Genesis of Quantum Theory*, Cambridge (Mass.) and London: The MIT Press, 1974.

Hermann, A. and von Meyenn, K. (1976), 'Wolfgang Paulis Beitrag zur Göttinger Quantenmechanik', *Physikalische Blätter* **32**, 145–50.

Hesse, M. B. (1966), *Models and Analogies in Science*, Nôtre Dame: University of Nôtre Dame Press.

Hirosige, T. and Nisio, S. (1964), 'Formation of Bohr's Theory of Atomic Constitution', *Japanese Studies in the History of Science* **3**, 6–28.

Hirosige, T. and Nisio, S. (1970), 'The Genesis of the Bohr Atom Model and Planck's Theory of Radiation', *Japanese Studies in the History of Science* **9**, 35–47.

Holton, G. (1973), 'The Roots of Complementarity', in G. Holton, *Thematic Origins of Scientific Thought*, Cambridge (Mass.): Harvard University Press.

Holton, G. (1978), *The Scientific Imagination: Case Studies*, Cambridge: Cambridge University Press.

Honner, J. (1982), 'The Trascendental Philosophy of Niels Bohr', *Studies in History and Philosophy of Science* **13**, 1–29.

Honner, J. (1987), *The Description of Nature. Niels Bohr and the Philosophy of Quantum Physics*, New York: Oxford University Press.

Hooker, C. A. (1971), 'Sharp and the Refutation of the Einstein, Podolski, Rosen Paradox', *Philosophy of Science* **38**, 224–33.

Hooker, C. A. (1972), 'The Nature of Quantum Mechanical Reality: Einstein versus Bohr', in R. G. Colodny, ed., *Paradigms and Paradoxes*, Pittsburgh: University of Pittsburgh Press.

Hoyer, U. (1973), 'Über die Rolle der Stabilitätsbetrachtungen in der Entwicklung der Bohrschen Atomtheorie', *Archive for the History of Exact Sciences* **10**, 177–206.

Hoyer, U. (1974), *Die Geschichte der Bohrschen Atomtheorie*, Weinheim.

Hoyer, U. (1976), 'Introduction to Part I', *CW2*, 3–10.

Hund, F. (1974), *The History of Quantum Theory*, London: Harrap.

Jammer, M. (1966), *The Conceptual Development of Quantum Mechanics*, New York: MacGraw-Hill; 2nd edn. (1989), New York: American Institute of Physics.

Jammer, M. (1974), *The Philosophy of Quantum Mechanics: The Interpretations of Quantum Mechanics in Historical Perspective*, New York: John Wiley & Sons.

Jauch, J. M. (1973), *Are Quanta Real? A Galilean Dialogue*, Indiana University Press.

Jensen, C. (1985), 'Two One-Electron Anomalies in the Old Quantum Theory', *Historical Studies in the Physical Sciences* **15**, 81–106.

Jordan, P. (1926), 'Über kanonische Trasformationen in der Quantenmechanik', *Zeitschrift für Physik* **37**, 383–86.

Jordan, P. (1932), 'Die Quantenmechanik und die Grundproblem der Biologie und Psychologie', *Die Naturwissenschaften* **20**, 815–21.

Jordan, P. (1934), 'Quantenphysikalische Bemerkungen zur Biologie und Psychologie', *Erkenntnis* **4**, 215–52.

Jordan, P. (1935), 'Ergänzende Bemerkungen über Biologie und Quantenmechanik', *Erkenntnis* **5**, 348–52.

Jordan, P. (1936), *Anschauliche Quantenmechanik*, Berlin: Springer Verlag.

Jordan, P. (1947), *Verdrängung und Komplementarität*, Stromverlag Hamburg-Bergedorf.

Kalckar, J. (1985), 'Introduction to Part I', *CW6*, 7–51.

Kalckar, J. (1985), 'Introduction to Part II', *CW6*, 189–98.

Klein, M. J. (1962), 'Max Planck and the Beginnings of the Quantum Theory', *Archive for the History of Exact Sciences* **1**, 459–79.

Klein, M. J. (1964), 'Einstein and the Wave–Particle Duality', *Natural Philosopher* **3**, 1–49.

Klein, M. J. (1970), 'The First Phase of the Bohr–Einstein Dialogue', *Historical Studies in the Physical Sciences* **2**, 1–39.

Klein, M. J. (1977), 'The Beginnings of Quantum Theory', in C. Weiner, ed., *History of Twentieth Century Physics*, New York: Academic Press.

Klein, M. J. (1979), 'Einstein and the Development of Quantum Physics', in A. P. French, ed., *Einstein. A Centenary Volume*, London: Heinemann.

Klein, M. J. (1980), 'No Firm Foundation: Einstein and the Early Quantum Theory', in H. Woolf, ed., *Some Strangeness in the Proportion: A Centennial Symposium to Celebrate the Achievements of Albert Einstein*, Reading (Mass.): Addison–Wesley.

Klein, M. J. (1985), 'Great Connections Come Alive: Bohr, Ehrenfest and Einstein', in J. de Boer, E. Dal and O. Ulfbeck, eds., *The Lessons of Quantum Theory, Niels Bohr Centenary Symposium, 3–7 Octobre 1985*, Amsterdam: North-Holland.

Klein, O. (1967), 'Glimpses of Niels Bohr as Scientist and Thinker', in S. Rozental, ed., *Niels Bohr: His Life and Work as Seen by His Friends and Colleagues*, Amsterdam: North-Holland and New York: John Wiley & Sons.

Konno, H. (1983), 'Slater's Evidence of the Bohr–Kramers–Slater Theory', *Historia Scientiarum* **25**, 39–52.

Konro, H. (1978), 'The Historical Roots of Born's Probabilistic Interpretation', *Japanese Studies in the History of Science* **17**, 129–45.

Kragh, H. (1977), 'Chemical Aspects of Bohr's 1913 Theory', *Journal of Chemical Education* **54**, 208–10.

Kragh, H. (1979), 'Niels Bohr's Second Atomic Theory', *Historical Studies in the Physical Sciences* **10**, 123–86.

Kragh, H. (1982–83), 'Erwin Schrödinger and the Wave Equation: the Crucial Phase', *Centaurus* **26**, 154–97.

Kragh, H. (1985), 'Bohr's Atomic Theory and the Chemists, 1913–1925', in *Proceedings of the International Symposium on Niels Bohr, Rome 25–27 November 1985, Rivista di Storia della Scienza* **2**, 463–86.

Kragh, H. (1985), 'The Fine Structure of Hydrogen and the Gross Structure of the Physics Community, 1916–26', *Historical Studies in the Physical Sciences* **15**, 67–125.

Kragh, H. (1985), 'The Theory of Periodic System', in A. P. French and P. J. Kennedy, eds., *Niels Bohr. A Centenary Volume*, Cambridge (Mass.): Harvard University Press.

Krajewski, W. (1977), *Correspondence Principle and Growth of Science*, Dordrecht: Reidel.

Kramers, H. A. (1924), 'The Law of Dispersion and Bohr's Theory of Spectra', *Nature* **113**, 673–74; *CW5*, 44–45.

Kramers, H. A. (1924), 'The Quantum Theory of Dispersion', *Nature* **114**, 310–11.

Kripke, S. (1971), 'Identity and Necessity', in M. K. Munitz, ed., *Identity and Individuation*, New York: New York University Press.

Kripke, S. (1972), 'Naming and Necessity', in G. Harman and D. Davidson, eds., *Semantics of Natural Language*, Dordrecht and Boston: Reidel.

Kubli, F. (1970), 'Louis de Broglie und die Entdeckung der Materiewellen', *Archive for the History of Exact Sciences* **7**, 26–68.

Kuhn, T. S. (1978), *Black-Body Theory and the Quantum Discontinuity, 1894–1912*, New York: Clarendon Press and Oxford: Oxford University Press.

Kuhn, T. S. (1979), 'Metaphor in Science', in A. Ortony, ed., *Metaphor and Thought*, Cambridge: Cambridge University Press.

Kuhn, T. S. (1983–84), 'Revisiting Planck', *Historical Studies in the Physical Sciences* **14**, 231–52.

Kuhn, T. S., Heilbron, J. L., Forman, P. and Allen, L. (1967), *Sources for History of Quantum Physics. An Inventory and Report*, Philadelphia: American Philosophical Society.

La Forgia, M. (1987), 'Componenti immaginali della scoperta scientifica', *Metaxú* **3**, 69–83.

Ladenburg, R. W. (1921), 'Die quantentheoretische Deutung der Zahl der Dispersionelektronen', *Zeitschrift für Physik* **4**, 451–71.

Lakatos, I. (1970), 'Falsification and the Methodology of Scientific Research Programmes', in I. Lakatos and A. Musgrave, eds., *Criticism and the Growth of Knowledge*, Cambridge: Cambridge University Press.

Lanczos, C. (1970), *The Variational Principles of Mechanics*, Toronto: University of Toronto Press (4th edn.).

Lanczos, C. (1974), *The Einstein Decade (1905–1915)*, New York: Academic Press.

MacKinnon, E. (1977), 'Heisenberg, Models and the Rise of Matrix Mechanics', *Historical Studies in the Physical Sciences* **8**, 137–88.

MacKinnon, E. (1979), 'The Rise and Fall of Schrödinger's Interpretation', in P. Suppes, ed., *Foundations of Quantum Mechanics: The 1976 Stanford Seminar*, Lansing (Mich.): Philosophy of Science Association.

MacKinnon, E. (1982), *Scientific Explanation and Atomic Physics*, Chicago and London: The University of Chicago Press.

Margenau, H. (1950), *The Nature of Physical Reality: A Philosophy of Modern Physics*, New York: McGraw-Hill.

McCormmach, R. (1966), 'The Atomic Theory of John William Nicholson', *Archive for the History of Exact Sciences* **3**, 160–84.

McCormmach, R. (1970), 'Einstein, Lorentz and the Electron Theory', *Historical Studies in the Physical Sciences* **2**, 41–87.

McGucken, W. (1969), *Nineteenth-Century Spectroscopy: Development of the Understanding of Spectra 1802–1897*, Baltimore: The Johns Hopkins University Press.

Mehra, J. (1972), 'The Golden Age of Theoretical Physics', in A. Salam and E. Wigner, eds., *Aspects of Quantum Theory*, Cambridge: Cambridge University Press.

Mehra, J. (1973), 'The Quantum Principle: Its Interpretation and Epistemology', *Dialectica* **27**, 75–157.

Mehra, J. (1975), *The Solvay Conferences on Physics*, Dordrecht: Reidel.

Mehra, J. and Rechenberg, H. (1982–87), *The Historical Development of Quantum Theory*, 5 vols., New York: Springer Verlag.

Meyer-Abich, K. M. (1965), *Korrespondenz, Individualität und Komplementarität: Eine Studie zur Geistesgeschichte der Quantentheorie in den Beiträgen Niels Bohr*, Wiesbaden: Franz Steiner Verlag.

Miller, A. I. (1973), 'A Study of Henri Poincare's "Sur la dynamique de l'électron"', *Archive for the History of Exact Sciences* **10**, 207–328.

Miller, A. I. (1978), 'Visualization Lost and Regained: The Genesis of the Quantum Theory in the Period 1913–1927', in J. Wechsler, ed., *On Aesthetics in Science*, Cambridge (Mass.): MIT Press.

Miller, A. I. (1983), 'Redefining Anschaulichkeit', in A. Shimony and H. Fescbach, eds., *Physics as Natural Philosophy. Essays in Honour of Laszlo Tisza on his Seventy-fifth Birthday*, Cambridge (Mass.): MIT Press.

Miller, A. I. (1984), *Imagery in Scientific Thought: Creating 20th Century Physics*, Boston: Birkhäuser.

Moore, R. (1966), *Niels Bohr. The Man, His Science and the World They Changed*, New York: Alfred Knopf; 2nd edn. Cambridge (Mass.): MIT Press, 1985.

Murdoch, D. (1987), *Niels Bohr's Philosophy of Physics*, Cambridge: Cambridge University Press.

Nicholson, J. W. (1912), 'The Constitution of the Solar Corona', *Monthly Notices of the Royal Astronomical Society* **72**, 139–50.

Nicholson, J. W. (1912), 'The Spectrum of Nebulium', *Monthly Notices of the Royal Astronomical Society* **72**, 49–64.

Nisio, S. (1969), 'X-Rays and Atomic Structure in the Early Stage of the Old Quantum Theory', *Japanese Studies in the History of Science* **8**, 55–75.

Nisio, S. (1973), 'The Formation of the Sommerfeld Quantum Theory of 1916', *Japanese Studies in the History of Science* **12**, 39–78.

Pais, A. (1979), 'Einstein and the Quantum Theory', *Review of Modern Physics* **51**, 869–914.

Pais, A. (1980), 'Einstein on Particles, Fields, and Quantum Theory', in H. Woolf, ed., *Some Strangeness in the Proportion: A Centennial Symposium to Celebrate the Achievements of Albert Einstein*, Reading (Mass.): Addison–Wesley.

Pais, A. (1982), *'Subtle is the Lord...'. The Science and the Life of Albert Einstein*, Oxford: Oxford University Press.

Pais, A. (1982), 'Max Born's Statistical Interpretation of Quantum Mechanics', *Science* **218**, 1193–98.

Pais, A. (1991), *Niels Bohr's Times: in Physics, Philosophy and Polity*, Oxford: Clarendon Press.

Paty, M. (1985), 'Einstein et la complémentarité au sens de Bohr: du retrait dans le tumulte aux arguments d'incompletude', *Revue d'histoire des sciences* **38**, 325–51.

Pauli, W. (1950), 'Die philosophische Bedeutung der Idee der Komplementarität', *Experientia* **6**, 72–81; *CSP2*, 1149–58.

Pauli, W. (1954), 'Matter', in *Man's Right to Knowledge, International Symposium in Honor of the Two-Hundredth Anniversary of Columbia University, 1754–1954*, New York: H. Muschel; *CSP1*, 1125–33.

Pauli, W. (1954), 'Naturwissenschaftliche und erkenntnistheoretische Aspekte der Ideen vom Unbewussten', *Dialectica* **8**, 283–301; *CSP2*, 1212–30.

Pauli, W. (1954), 'Wahrscheinlichkeit und Physik', *Dialectica* **8**, 112–24; *CSP2*, 1199–211.

Pauli, W. (1957), 'Phänomen und physikalische Realität', *Dialectica* **11**, 36–48; *CSP2*, 1350–61.

Petersen, A. (1963), 'The Philosophy of Niels Bohr', *Bulletin of the Atomic Scientists* **19**, 8–14.

Petersen, A. (1968), *Quantum Physics and the Philosophical Tradition*, Cambridge (Mass.): MIT Press.

Petersen, A. (1968), 'Bohr and Philosophy of Science', in R. Klibansky, ed., *Contemporary Philosophy, III. Philosophy of Science*, Florence: La nuova Italia.

Petersen, A. (1969), 'On the Philosophical Significance of the Correspondence Argument', *Boston Studies in the Philosophy of Science* **5**, 242–52.

Petruccioli, S. (1981), 'Modello meccanico e regole di corrispondenza nella costruzione della teoria atomica', *Physis* **23**, 555–79.

Petruccioli, S. (1985), 'Fisica classica e concezioni quantistiche nell'opera di Niels Bohr', in C. Mangione, ed., *Scienza e filosofia. Saggi in onore di Ludovico Geymonat*, Milan: Garzanti.

Petruccioli, S. (1985), 'Quantum Discontinuity and Space-Time description in Bohr's Early Atomic Theory', in *Proceedings of the International Symposium on Niels Bohr, Rome 25–27 November 1985, Rivista di Storia della Scienza* **2**, 409–43.

Petruccioli, S. (1986), 'Ideale della visualizzazione, modelli di descrizione e discontinuità nella fisica atomica', *Intersezioni* **4**, 479–501.

Petruccioli, S. (1986), 'Modelli, immagini e metafore: un'ipotesi storiografica per la genesi della meccanica quantistica', *Rivista di Storia della Scienza* **3**, 113–42.

Petruccioli, S. (1987), 'Significato teorico e implicazioni metaforiche del principio di corrispondenza', in M. La Forgia and S. Petruccioli, eds., *Rappresentazione e oggetto dalla fisica alle altre scienze*, Rome: Theoria.

Piazza, G. (1986), 'Metafore e scoperte nella ricerca scientifica', in
    F. Alberoni, ed., *Il presente e i suoi simboli*, Milan: Franco Angeli.
Popper, K. R. (1959), *The Logic of Scientific Discovery*, London: Hutchinson.
Popper, K. R. (1972), *Objective Knowledge*, Oxford: Clarendon Press.
Popper, K. R. (1982), *Quantum Theory and the Schism in Physics. From the
    Postscript to the Logic of Scientific Discovery*, London: Hutchinson.
Prigogine, I. (1980), *From Being to Becoming*, San Francisco: Freeman.
Prigogine, I. and Stengers, I. (1979), *La nouvelle alliance. Métamorphose de la
    science*, Paris: Gallimard.
Pritzbaum, K., ed. (1963), *Schrödinger, Planck, Einstein, Lorentz: Briefe zur
    Wellenmechanik*, Wien: Springer Verlag; English trans., *Letters on Wave
    Mechanics*, New York: Philosophical Library, 1967.
Putnam, H. (1965), 'A Philosopher Looks at Quantum Mechanics', in R. G.
    Colodny, ed., *Beyond the Edge of Certainty: Essays in Contemporary
    Science and Philosophy*, New York: Prentice Hall; also in Putnam, H.
    (1975), *Philosophical Papers*, vol. I, Cambridge: Cambridge University
    Press.
Quine, W. V. O. (1966), *The Ways of Paradox and Other Essays*, New York:
    Random House.
Radder, H. (1982), 'Between Bohr's Atomic Theory and Heisenberg's Matrix
    Mechanics: A Study of the Role of the Dutch Physicist H. A. Kramers',
    Janus **69**, 223–52.
Radder, H. (1983), 'Kramers and the Forman Thesis', *History of Science* **21**,
    165–82.
Reichenbach, H. (1944), *Philosophical Foundations of Quantum Mechanics*,
    Los Angeles: University of California Press.
Robertson, P. (1979), *The Early Years. Niels Bohr Institute 1921–1930*,
    Copenhagen: Akademisk Forlag Universitetsforlaget.
Robotti, N. (1976), 'La genesi del modello di Bohr sulla costituzione
    dell'atomo: Generalizzazione teorica e base empirica', *Physis* **18**, 319–41.
Robotti, N. (1983), 'The Spectrum of ζ-Puppis and the Historical Evolution of
    Empirical Data', *Historical Studies in the Physical Sciences* **14**, 123–45.
Robotti, N. (1986), 'The Hydrogen Spectroscopy and the Old Quantum
    Theory', *Rivista di Storia della Scienza* **3**, 45–102.
Rosenfeld, L. (1936), 'La première phase de la théorie des quanta', *Osiris* **23**,
    149–96.
Rosenfeld, L. (1942), 'L'évolution de l'idée de causalité', *Mémoires de la
    Societé Royale des Sciences de Liège* **6**, 59–87.
Rosenfeld, L. (1953), 'Strife about Complementarity', *Science Progress* **163**,
    393–410.
Rosenfeld, L. (1961), 'Foundation of Quantum Theory and Complementarity',
    Nature **190**, 384–88.
Rosenfeld, L. (1961), *Niels Bohr – An Essay Dedicated to Him on the Occasion
    of His Sixtieth Birthday 1945*, Amsterdam: North-Holland (2nd edn.).
Rosenfeld, L. (1963), 'Niels Bohr's Contribution to Epistemology', *Physics
    Today* **16**, 47–54.
Rosenfeld, L. (1963), 'The Epistemological Conflict between Einstein and
    Bohr', *Zeitschrift für Physik* **171**, 242–45.
Rosenfeld, L. (1967), 'Niels Bohr in the Thirties: Consolidation and Extension
    of the Conception of Complementarity', in S. Rozental, ed., *Niels Bohr,
    His Life and Work as Seen by his Friends and Colleagues*, Amsterdam:
    North-Holland and New York: John Wiley & Sons.

Rosenfeld, L. (1971), 'Men and Ideas in the History of Atomic Theory', *Archive for the History of Exact Sciences* **7**, 69–90.
Rosenfeld, L. (1971), *Quantum Theory in 1929: Recollections from the First Copenhagen Conference*, Copenhagen: Rhodos.
Rosenfeld, L. (1972), 'Biographical Sketch', *CW1*, XVII–XLVIII.
Rosenfeld, L. (1979), *Selected Papers*, Cohen, R. S. and Stachel, J. J., eds., Dordrecht: Reidel.
Rosenfeld, L. and Rüdinger, E. (1967), 'The Decisive Years: 1911–1918', in S. Rozental, ed., *Niels Bohr, His Life and Work as Seen by His Friends and Colleagues*, Amsterdam: North-Holland and New York: John Wiley & Sons.
Rozental, S., ed., (1967), *Niels Bohr, His Life and Work as Seen by his Friends and Colleagues*, Amsterdam: North-Holland – New York: John Wiley & Sons.
Rud Nielsen, J. (1963), 'Memories of Niels Bohr', *Physics Today* **16**, 22–30.
Rud Nielsen, J. (1972), 'Introduction to Part II', *CW1*, 93–123.
Rud Nielsen, J. (1977), 'Introduction to Part I', *CW3*, 3–46.
Rud Nielsen, J. (1977), 'Introduction to Part I', *CW4*, 3–42.
Rüdinger, E. (1985), 'The Correspondence Principle as a Guiding Principle', in *Proceedings of the International Symposium on Niels Bohr, Rome 25–27 November 1985, Rivista di Storia della Scienza* **2**, 357–67.
Rüdinger, E. and Stolzenburg, K. (1984), 'Introduction to Part II', *CW5*, 219–40.
Russo, A. (1981), 'Fundamental Research at Bell Laboratories: The Discovery of Electron Diffraction', *Historical Studies in the Physical Sciences* **21**, 117–60.
Rutherford, E. (1911), 'The Scattering of α and β Particles by Matter and the Structure of the Atom', *Proceedings of the Manchester Library and Philosophical Society* **55**, 18–20.
Rutherford, E. (1911), 'The Scattering of α and β Particles by Matter and the Structure of the Atom', *Philosophical Magazine* **21**, 669–88.
Scheibe, E. (1973), *The Logical Analysis of Quantum Mechanics*, Oxford and New York: Pergamon Press.
Scheibe, E. (1989), 'Die Kopenhagener Schule', in G. Böhme and C. H. Beck, eds., *Klassiker der Naturphilosophie*, Berlin.
Schilpp, P. A., ed. (1949), *Albert Einstein: Philosopher–Scientist*, Evanston (Illinois): The Library of Living Philosophers.
Schöpf, H. G. (1983), 'Das Bohrschen Komplementaritätskonzept im historischen Kontext der physikalischen Ideen', *Abhandlungen der Sächsischen Akademie der Wissenschaften zu Leipzig, mathemathische-naturwissenschaftliche Klasse* **55**(5), in W. Buchheim, ed., *Beiträge zur Komplementarität*, Berlin: Akademie-Verlag.
Schrödinger, E. (1952), 'Are There Quantum Jumps?', *British Journal for the Philosophy of Science* **3**, 109–23; 233–42.
Schrödinger, E. (1955), 'The Philosophy of Experiment', *Il nuovo Cimento* series **10**, vol. I, 5–15.
Selleri, F. (1983), *Die Debatte um die Quantentheorie*, Braunschweig: Vieweg.
Selleri, F. (1987), *Paradossi e realtà. Saggio sui fondamenti della microfisica*, Bari: Laterza.
Serwer, D. (1977), '*Unmechanischer Zwang*: Pauli, Heisenberg and the Rejection of the Mechanical Atom, 1923–1925', *Historical Studies in the Physical Sciences* **8**, 189–256.

Shimony, A. (1983), 'Reflections on the Philosophy of Bohr, Heisenberg, and Schrödinger', in R. S. Cohen and L. Laudan., eds., *Physics, Philosophy and Psychoanalysis*, Dordrecht: Reidel.

Slater, J. C. (1924), 'Radiation and Atoms', *Nature* **113**, 307.

Stapp, H. P. (1972), 'The Copenhagen Interpretation', *American Journal of Physics* **40**, 1098–116.

Stolzenburg, K. (1977), *Die Entwicklung des Bohrschen Komplementaritätgedankens in den Jahren 1924 bis 1929*, Stuttgart: Universität Stuttgart.

Stolzenburg, K. (1985), 'Introduction to Part I', *CW5*, 1–96.

Strauss, M. (1972), 'The Logic of Complementarity and the Foundation of Quantum Theory', in M. Strauss, ed., *Modern Physics and its Philosophy*, Dordrecht: Reidel.

Stuewer, R. H. (1975), *The Compton Effect. Turning Point in Physics*, New York: Science History Publications.

Suppes, P., ed. (1979), *Foundation of Quantum Mechanics: The 1976 Stanford Seminar*, East Lansing, Michigan.

Tagliagambe, S. (1972), 'Il concetto di realtà fisica e il principio di complementarità', in S. Tagliagambe, ed., *L'interpretazione materialistica della meccanica quantistica. Fisica e filosofia in URSS*, Milan: Feltrinelli.

Tagliagambe, S. (1991), *L'epistemologia contemporanea*, Rome: Editori Riuniti.

ter Haar, D. (1967), *The Old Quantum Theory*, London: Pergamon Press.

Thomson, J. J. (1904), 'On the Structure of the Atom – An Investigation of the Stability and Periods of Oscillation of a Number of Corpuscles Arranged at Equal Intervals Around the Circumference of a Circle; With Application of the Results to the Theory of Atomic Structure', *Philosophical Magazine* **7**, 237–65.

Toraldo di Francia, G. (1984), 'Lo statuto ontologico degli oggetti nella fisica moderna', in M. Piattelli Palmarini, ed., *I livelli di realtà*, Milan: Feltrinelli.

Toraldo di Francia, G. (1986), *Le cose e i loro nomi*, Bari: Laterza.

Trenn, T. J. (1974), 'The Geiger–Marsden Scattering Results and Rutherford's Atom July 1912 to July 1913: The Shifting Significance of Scientific Evidence', *Isis* **65**, 74–82.

van der Waerden, B. L. (1960), 'Exclusion Principle and Spin', in M. Fierz and V. F. Weisskopf, eds., *Theoretical Physics in the Twentieth Century*, New York: Interscience.

van der Waerden, B. L. (1967), *Sources of Quantum Mechanics*, Amsterdam: North-Holland.

van der Waerden, B. L. (1973), 'From Matrix Mechanics to Unified Quantum Mechanics', in J. Mehra, ed., *The Physicist's Conception of Nature*, Dordrecht: Reidel.

van Fraassen, B. C. and Hooker, C. A. (1976), 'A Semantic Analysis of Niels Bohr's Philosophy of Quantum Mechanics', in W. Harper and C. A. Hooker, eds., *Foundations of Probability Theory, Statistical Inference and Statistical Theories of Science*, vol. III, Dordrecht: Reidel.

van Vleck, J. H. (1971), 'Reminiscences of the First Decade of Quantum Mechanics', *International Journal of Quantum Chemistry* **5**, 3–20.

von Meyenn, K. (1980–81), 'Pauli's Weg zum Ausschiessungsprinzip', *Physikalische Blätter* **36–37**, 293–98; 13–20.

von Meyenn, K. (1985), 'Pauli, Schrödinger and the Conflict About the Interpretation of Quantum Mechanics', in P. Lahti and P. Mittelstaedt, eds., *Symposium on the Foundations of Modern Physics*, World Scientific Publishing Company.

von Weizsäcker, C. F. (1955), 'Komplementarität und Logik: Niels Bohr zum 70. Geburtstag', *Die Naturwissenschaften* **42**, 521–29, 545–55.

von Weizsäcker, C. F. (1983), 'Niels Bohr and Complementarity: The Place of Classical Language', in T. Bastin, ed., *Quantum Theory and Beyond*, Cambridge: Cambridge University Press.

Weiner, C., ed. (1977), *History of the Twentieth Century Physics*, New York: Academic Press.

Wessels, L. (1979), 'Schrödinger's Route to Wave Mechanics', *Studies in History and Philosophy of Science* **10**, 311–40.

Wheeler, J. A. and Zureck, W. H., eds (1983), *Quantum Theory and Measurement*, Princeton: Princeton University Press.

Whittaker, E. (1953), *A History of the Theories of Aether and Electricity. The Modern Theories, 1900–1926*, Edinburgh and London: Nelson & Sons.

Wilson, C. T. R. (1923), 'Investigations on X-Rays and β-Rays by the Cloud Method, Part I – X-Rays; Part II – β-Rays', *Proceedings of the Royal Society of London* **A104**, 1–24; 192–212.

Name index

Alberoni, Francesco, 109n
Allen, Stanley H., 31n

Balmer, Johann, 46f, 50, 52, 57–60, 63, 67, 76n
Barkla, Charles G., 106n
Bellarmino, Roberto, 4
Beller, Mara, 175n, 176n
Berkeley, George, 4
Besso, Michele, 34n, 35n
Black, Max, 92, 109n
Bohr, Harald, 72n, 74n, 77n
Born, Max, 1, 3, 8n, 31n, 32n, 34n, 77n, 109n, 124f, 127, 132n, 133n, 147f, 151f, 154, 164, 172, 175n, 176n, 177n
Bothe, Walter, 100, 125, 128n, 133n, 162
Boyd, Richard, 92–94, 96, 104, 109n
Bragg, William Lawrence, 32n, 106n, 108n
Breit, Gregory, 175n
Brillouin, Léon N., 106n
Brillouin, Marcel, 106n
Bunge, Mario, 4, 8n
Bunsen, Robert, 46

Cassidy, David C., 110n, 174n
Ceruti, Mauro, 35n, 212n
Chadwick, James, 73n
Chevalley, Catherine, 216n, 217n
Christiansen, Christian, 72n
Colodny, Robert G., 213n, 214n
Compton, Arthur H., 112, 126, 128n, 133n, 158, 162, 172f
Courant, Richard, 177n
Curie, Marie, 32n, 106n
Curtis, Leon F., 107n

Darwin, Charles G., 72n, 131n
Davidson, D., 109n
Davisson, Clinton J., 141, 167, 174n, 180n

de Broglie, Louis, 3, 23, 32n, 128n, 163, 166, 168, 172
de Broglie, Maurice, 106n
Debye, Peter, 32n, 66, 141, 174n
d'Espagnat, Bernard, 213n
Dieke, G. H., 32n, 217n
Dirac, Paul A. M., 11, 26, 32n, 35n, 151f, 154, 159, 162, 172, 177n, 179n, 209f, 217n
Drude, Paul, 140, 174n

Ehrenfest, Paul, 32n, 36, 82, 84, 88, 106n, 108n, 109n, 124, 132n, 173, 180n, 212, 217n
Einstein, Albert, 1–4, 8n, 11, 15, 19, 21, 26, 29, 32n, 33n, 34n, 35n, 36, 38f, 43f, 50, 65, 70n, 76n, 85, 90, 97f, 100, 106n, 108n, 109n, 111f, 116–18, 123–25, 130n, 132n, 134–38, 141, 143f, 153, 155, 159, 161, 163, 167f, 171f, 179n, 180n, 183–86, 188f, 191–200, 202–05, 211f, 212n, 213n, 214n, 215n, 216n
Epstein, Paul S., 84
Evans, Evan J., 73n, 76n

Fajans, Kasimir, 73n
Favrholdt, David, 108n, 132n
Fermi, Enrico, 31n
Feshbach, H., 32n
Feyerabend, Paul K., 214n
Folse, Henry, 89f, 104, 108n, 215n, 217n
Forman, Paul, 5, 8n, 108n, 110n
Fourier, Joseph, 150, 177n
Fowler, Ralph H., 32n, 76n, 110n, 125, 128n, 133n, 165, 180n
Franck, James, 20, 109n, 124, 166
French, Anthony P., 71n

Galilei, Galileo, 7, 184

Geiger, Hans, 41, 73n, 100, 125f, 133n, 162
Gerlach, Walther, 166
Germer, Lester H., 167, 180n
Glashow, Sheldon, 2
Goudsmit, Samuel A., 32n, 180n, 217n
Guye, Charles E., 32n

Haas, Arthur E., 71n
Haas, Wander J. de, 106n
Haber, Fritz, 123, 132n
Hansen, Hans, 50
Harman, G., 109n
Heegaard, P., 72n
Heilbron, John L., 5, 8n, 49, 58, 71n, 72n, 73n, 74n, 75n, 76n
Heisenberg, Werner, 2f, 5f, 9n, 15, 22, 25, 29f, 31n, 32n, 33n, 34n, 35n, 90, 100, 102, 110n, 117, 123, 125–27, 132n, 133n, 134–40, 146–66, 170–73, 174n, 175n, 176n, 177n, 178n, 179n, 180n, 181n, 196, 201–04, 206, 208f, 214n
Hendry, John, 33n, 35n, 105n, 128n, 131n, 132n, 174n, 175n
Hertz, Gustav, 20, 124
Hesse, Mary B., 92, 109n
Hevesy, George von, 73n, 76n
Hilbert, David, 77n, 177n
Hirosige, Tetu, 75n
Høffding, Harald, 2, 89, 122, 132n, 166
Holton, Gerald, 2, 8n
Honner, John, 34n
Hooker, Clifford A., 213n, 214n
Hoyer, Ulrich, 73n, 74n
Hume, David, 2, 184

James, William, 166
Jammer, Max, 71n, 74n, 76n, 174n, 178n, 179n, 180n, 212n, 213n
Jeans, James H., 62, 71n, 76n, 106n
Jordan, Pascual, 5, 34n, 151f, 154, 159, 177n

Kalckar, Jørgen, 16, 31n, 33n, 34n, 105n, 179n, 180n
Kamerlingh Onnes, Heike, 106n
Kant, Immanuel, 32n
Kemble, Edwin, 112, 128n
Kennard, E. H., 71n
Kennedy, P. J., 71n
Kepler, Johannes, 152
Kirchhoff, Gustav, 46
Klein, Martin, 71n
Klein, Oskar, 105n, 124, 132n
Klibansky, R., 215n
Knudsen, Martin, 3n, 74n, 106n
Kossel, Walther, 109n

Kragh, Helge, 74n
Krajewski, Wladyslaw, 107n
Kramers, Hans A., 31n, 32n, 106n, 111, 113–15, 117, 124–26, 127n, 128n, 129n, 130n, 131n, 132n, 133n, 140–47, 172f, 175n
Kripke, Saul, 93, 109n
Kuhn, Thomas S., 49, 58, 70n, 71n, 72n, 73n, 74n, 75n, 76n, 92–94, 109n, 177n, 179n

Ladenburg, Rudolf W., 109n, 129n, 141, 143, 174n
Lakatos, Imre, 4, 8n, 110n, 130n
Lanczos, Cornelius, 107n
Landé, Alfred, 109n, 110n
Langevin, Paul, 32n, 106n
Langmuir, Irving, 32n
Laplace, Pierre Simon de, 27
Larmor, Joseph, 72n, 106n
Laue, Max von, 36
Lauritsen, T., 71n
Lorentz, Hendrik A., 39f, 42, 71n, 72n, 82, 106n, 140, 143, 174n, 184f, 212n
Lyman, Theodore, 47

Mach, Ernst, 2, 184
MacKinnon, Edward, 176n, 178n
Madelung, Erwin, 77n
Marsden, Ernest, 41, 73n
Maxwell, James C., 19, 38, 42, 69f, 118, 143, 183f
McCormmach, Russell, 75n, 212n
McGucken, William, 74n
McKower, W., 73n
Mehra, Jagdish, 32n, 72n, 73n, 74n, 106n, 109n, 175n, 178n
Mendeleev, Demetrio J., 41
Messiah, Albert M. L., 108n
Michelson, Albert A., 106n, 112, 115, 129n
Miller, Arthur I., 32n, 33n, 130n, 131n, 132n, 212n
Millikan, Robert A., 106n
Moore, Ruth, 108n
Mosely, Henry G. J., 73n
Munitz, M. K., 109n
Murdoch, Dugald, 180n, 214n
Musgrave, Alan, 8n

Nagaoka, Hantaro, 74n
Newton, Isaac, 7, 17, 38, 70, 135
Nicholson, John W., 45, 48f, 54f, 74n, 75n
Nielsen, Rud J., 72n, 106n, 109n
Nisio, Sigeko, 75n

Ortony, Andrew, 109n

Oseen, Carl W., 26, 35n, 152, 177n

Pais, Abraham, 2, 8n, 35n, 213n
Paschen, Friedrich, 47
Pauli, Wolfgang, 3, 5f, 9n, 13, 16, 29f,
  31n, 32n, 33n, 35n, 78, 102, 110n, 123,
  125f, 132n, 139f, 148, 161f, 174n, 176n,
  179n, 180n, 185, 201, 205f, 208f, 211,
  214n, 215n, 216n, 217n
Perrin, Jacques, 74n, 106n
Piazza, Gianguido, 109n
Pickering, Edward C., 76n
Planck, Max, 2, 12, 15f, 18–20, 27f, 32n,
  33n, 36–39, 43–45, 48–55, 57–60, 62f,
  65f, 68f, 70n, 71n, 72n, 74n, 75n, 77n,
  89, 95, 97–100, 105n, 109n, 118, 145,
  159, 164, 166, 167, 172, 180n, 195, 201,
  203, 207f, 211, 215n, 216n

Podolski, Boris, 186–89, 191–94, 197–200,
  212n, 213n, 214n
Poincaré, Henri, 184, 212n
Popper, Karl, 3f, 6, 8n, 214n
Poynting, Giovanni E., 113f
Prigogine, Ilya, 35n
Putnam, Hilary, 2

Quine, Willard von Orman, 183, 212n

Rayleigh, John W., 62, 71n, 76n, 169
Rechenberg, Helmut, 73n, 74n, 109n,
  175n, 178n
Richardson, Owen W., 32n, 82, 106n
Richtmyer, F. K., 71n
Ritz, Walter, 47, 77n, 95
Robotti, Nadia, 74n
Röntgen, Guglielmo C., 51
Rosen, Nathan, 186, 188f, 191–94,
  197–200, 212n, 213n, 214n
Rosenfeld, Léon, 31n, 32n, 72n, 73n, 75n,
  76n, 186, 212n
Rozental, Stefan, 73n, 212n
Rüdinger, Erik, 73n, 75n, 105n, 175n
Russell, A. S., 73n
Russo, Arturo, 180n
Rutherford, Ernest, 36, 38–54, 59, 62, 65,
  68, 70, 71n, 72n, 73n, 74n, 75n, 76n, 95,
  106n, 128n, 166
Rydberg, Johannes, 47, 59, 67f, 77n

Schilpp, Paul A., 8n, 32n, 174n, 212n,
  213n
Schrödinger, Erwin, 3, 14f, 23, 29, 31n,
  32n, 33n, 104, 124, 132n, 154, 163–66,
  172, 175n, 176n, 178n, 179n, 180n, 181n,
  203, 214n
Schwarzschild, Karl, 84
Selleri, Franco, 212n
Serwer, Daniel, 110n, 174n
Shimony, A., 32n
Siegban, Manne K., 106n
Simon, Alfred, 133n
Slater, John, 89, 111–16, 118, 120, 123–26,
  127n, 128n, 129n, 130n, 131n, 132n,
  133n, 140, 142, 146, 172f, 175n
Sommerfeld, Arnold, 23, 71n, 76n, 77n,
  84, 96, 128n, 138, 141, 174n, 179n
Speziali, Pierre, 34n
Stark, Johannes, 96, 138
Stengers, Isabelle, 35n
Stern, Otto, 166
Stolzenburg, Klaus, 31n, 127n, 128n, 130n,
  132n, 133n, 175n
Stonej, George J., 46
Stuewer, Roger H., 128n, 133n
Suppes, Patrick, 178n

Thomson, Joseph, J., 40–43, 50f, 71n, 72n,
  73n

Udden, A. D., 106n
Uhlenbeck, George E., 32n, 217n

van Aubel, E., 32n, 106n
van der Waerden, Bartel L., 127n, 130n,
  174n, 175n, 177n
van Vleck, John H., 114, 128n, 175n
Volta, Alessandro, 10

Wechsler, Judith, 33n
Weiss, Pierre, 106n
Wessels, Linda, 178n
Wheeler, John A., 178n
Whittaker, Edmund, 174n
Wien, Wilhelm, 71n
Wilson, Charles T. R., 32n, 128n
Wollaston, William, 46

Zeeman, Pieter, 96, 106n, 110n
Zurech, Wojciech H., 178n

General index

analogy
 between atom and mechanical model, 145
 between quantum mechanics and theory of relativity, 159
 between quantum theory and classical mechanics, 102–03
 correspondence and, 103
 formal, 83, 121
 symbolic, 127
atom
 helium, 59
 ionization of, 49, 54–55, 57
 quantum theory of the hydrogen, 39, 55, 61, 79
 radiative behaviour of, 68, 80, 91, 95

Balmer's formula, 47, 50, 52, 57–60, 63
Bohr and Sommerfeld's rules of quantization, 138
Bothe–Geiger experiment, 100

c-numbers, 152
causality, 19, 26, 78, 90
 and determinism, 207
 restriction or violation of, 101, 122, 127
commutative property of multiplication, 150, 152
complementarity, 3, 4, 5, 7, 16, 27, 37, 79–80, 89–90, 101, 104, 118, 161, 163, 170, 173, 185, 198–99, 210
 and description, 78, 160
 as a pseudo-principle, 4
 between space-time and causal description, 173
Compton effect, 122, 126, 158, 162
concepts
 conditions of definition, 168–69, 173
 operationally defined, 6, 79, 102, 140

Copenhagen interpretation, 4, 10, 159, 200, 211
 as a variant of bad philosophies, 6
correspondence
 between processes of transition and components of motion, 88
 between symbols and concepts, 135, 150, 156
 symbolic, 144
correspondence principle, 22, 62, 81–82, 86, 88–89, 94, 99, 103–04, 111, 114–18, 126–27, 139–41, 145–47, 150–51
 heuristic content of the, 30

description
 causal in space and time, 22, 25–27, 79, 81, 116, 168
 classical model of space-time, 25, 70, 86, 89, 91, 146
 continuous or discontinuous aspect of, 90
 dependent upon the observer, 207
 of atomic processes, 49
 of individual experimental situations, 160
 of quantum or discontinuous processes, 99, 111, 126
 of statistical type, 23
dispersion
 negative dispersion, 144
 phenomenon of, 140–43
 quantum theory of, 144, 146
dualism
 and the definition of classical concepts, 167
 as apparent problem, 173
 of waves and corpuscles, 90, 153

Ehrenfest's adiabatic principle, 84

238

Einstein's
  coefficients of probability, 141, 147
  criterion of reality, 194
  theory of relativity, 38, 136, 185, 192, 211
Einstein–Podolski–Rosen paradox, 186, 192
  completeness condition, 187–88, 192, 197
  criterion of reality, 188–92
  locality hypothesis, 192
electron
  binding process, 51–54
  Davisson and Germer experiment on diffraction of, 167
  elastic collisions between light quanta and, 112
  electronic theory of metals, 39, 40, 89
  image of the electron's orbiting motion, 30, 142
  orbits, 52, 61, 68, 83, 95–96, 101, 103, 139
  radiative stability, 38, 79
Epstein–Schwarzschild theory, 84

Franck and Hertz's experiment, 124
frequency
  general law of, 80, 82–83, 85, 139, 150
  optical, 55–56, 62, 80
  optical and mechanical, 54, 59, 62

γ-ray microscope experiment, 158, 161
Geiger–Bothe experiment, 125

Heisenberg's uncertainty relations, 5, 25, 29, 90, 153, 159–61, 170, 172–73, 201–04, 208
  as loss of knowledge of a part of the system, 203

incompleteness of quantum mechanics, 161, 186, 192–93
indeterminate interaction, 24, 79, 197–98, 200, 203
  quantum of action, 196
interaction between radiation and matter, 37, 49, 59, 82, 85

Kramers' dispersion theory, 117
Kripke's causal theory of reference, 93

Ladenburg's formula, 143
language
  and reality, 207
  everyday language, 136
  figurative language, 13, 25
  formal languages, 92, 135

imprecise and symbolic language, 137
  natural language, 135, 157
  of classical physics, 79, 135
  translation of, 137, 156, 159, 208
laws of conservation, 24, 26, 85
  statistical validity of, 81, 120
  violation of, 120, 122
light corpuscles, 154
light quanta, 29, 80, 97–98, 100, 112, 114–16, 125, 148
light quanta hypothesis, heuristic value of, 116
Lyman ultraviolet series, 47

matrix algebra, 150–51
matrix mechanics, 22, 100, 127, 154, 165
measurement
  definition of physical quantities and procedure of, 195
  disturbance of the system, 195
  indeterminate interaction, 195, 196, 201
mechanical
  description of, 18–19, 80, 84
  disturbance of the system, 197
  frequency of the electron, 54, 62–63, 67
  instability, 43
  model, 100, 102, 140
  model of stationary states, 95–96, 102
  model of the atom, 29, 42, 45, 94, 117, 148
  stability of atomic orbits, 41, 49–51, 84
metaphor, 91–93, 96
  primary and secondary subjects of, 92–93
  theory-constitutive metaphors, 92–94, 96, 104
model
  as articulation of the principle of correspondence, 102
  as purely logical tool, 120
  heuristic function of the mechanical, 121, 138, 152
  of orbiting electrons, 94, 102, 140
motion
  harmonic components of, 86–87, 103, 145
  of the atomic particles, 18, 20, 30, 49, 70, 80, 83–84, 96, 149
multiperiodic system, 84, 86, 96, 144, 146

Nicholson's theory, 45, 48–49, 54, 55

observability
  conditions for the object's, 158
  independence of the event from its, 198
observable
  behaviour of microscopic objects, 37

properties of the stationary states, 139
quantities, 66, 138–40, 143, 151, 155
observation
  discontinuous change of energy and
    momentum, 160
  limitations of, 160
  subjective character, 26
observation and definition
  complementarity, 200
  idealization of, 78
observation conditions of, 27, 78, 196
  and possibility of definition, 171, 195
observer role, 7, 197, 206

paradox, 27, 183, 200–01, 207
  dual nature of radiation and matter, 154
  indivisibility of the quantum of action,
    185
  wave–particles, 185
Paschen infrared series, 47
perturbation theory classical, 141
phenomenon
  complementarity, 209
  concepts of physics, 14, 89, 90, 104
  continuity, 165
  discontinuity/individuality, 12
  indeterminate interaction, 205
  individuality/indivisibility/wholeness,
    13, 15, 24, 196, 200, 205–06, 209
  observation/measurement, 6, 25, 27,
    158, 194, 202–03, 206, 210
  Pauli on, 206
  physical reality, 197
  redefinition, 193, 194
  space and time picture or description,
    101, 126
photoelectric effect, 19, 51, 98
picture
  atomic radiation, 85
  atomic structure, 18–19, 25, 41
  continuous picture of radiation field,
    111, 114
  quantum transition, 117
pilot waves, 113, 116
Planck's
  black-body theory, 19, 36–38, 44, 48,
    51–53, 62, 64–65, 68, 89, 97
  law of temperature radiation, 65, 66,
    118, 144
  oscillators, 50, 54, 60, 62, 97, 99
Poynting's vector, 113, 114
principle
  of conservation, 80, 90, 112, 119, 125,
    167, 168
  of conservation in individual processes,
    101
  of wave superposition, 167, 168

wave superposition and conservation
    principles, 169
probability
  coefficients of, 21
  primary probabilities, 208, 209

q-numbers, 152
quantization
  atom/atom model, 19, 30, 39, 48
  harmonic oscillator, 44, 53, 62
  integral of action, 84
quantum discontinuity, 59, 70, 78, 89–90,
    147, 154, 158
  and theory's intuitive content, 155
  and uncertainty in our observation, 158,
    163
  of atomic processes, 7, 37, 70, 154, 205
quantum kinematics, 148–49
quantum multiplication rule, 159
quantum numbers
  limiting region, 68, 81, 86–87, 103
  principal, 86
quantum postulate, 13, 15, 24, 29, 63,
    78–79, 83, 139, 195
  physical reality, 165
quantum processes, 7
  in separated atoms, 125–26
quantum rules, 30, 139
  for stationary states, 38, 53, 68

radiation
  absorption negative of, 144
  dual nature, 166
  dual nature of radiation and matter, 5,
    201
  emission and absorption, 20, 66, 79, 83,
    114
  emission of radiation, 50, 54–55, 57–58,
    61–62, 82
  mechanism of, 20, 48, 60, 63–64, 85
  observable properties, 19
  probabilistic/statistic processes, 29,
    112–13, 168
  quasi-classical processes, 49
  spontaneous emissions, 118
  statistical equilibrium, 98
radiative instability, 43
rational transcription, 104, 147
Rayleigh's theory of spectroscopes, 169
Rayleigh–Jeans law, 62
Röntgen rays, 51
Rutherford's atomic model, 36, 38, 43,
    50–52, 59, 62, 65, 68, 70, 95
  and Thomson's model, 51
Rydberg's constant, 59, 67, 68
Rydberg–Ritz principle of combination,
    47, 95

scattering of X-rays, 41, 112
Schrödinger's wave function, 104, 190, 191
  probabilistic interpretation of, 154, 185
Sommerfeld's rules of quantization, 84, 96
space-time co-ordination, 24, 78
  causality, 12, 79, 169
  laws of conservation, 25
  observable quantities, 149
space-time description, 69, 168
  causality, 90
  causality and principles of conservation, 173
  limits to, 202
  model, 7, 30, 139, 142, 152, 156
  model discontinuity, 101
space-time pictures, 26, 80–81, 90, 127, 148
  classical concepts, 79
  quantum processes, 81
spectral lines
  elements, 20, 36, 46–47, 48, 59, 63–64, 99
  hydrogen, 45, 51–52, 56, 67
spectroscopic laws, 18, 20, 49, 64, 66, 91
spectrum and motion, 103
spectrum of the star ζ-Puppis, 59
Stark effect, 96, 138

theory of transformations, 154
Thomson's atomic model, 41–42
  and Rutherford's model, 50
transition processes
  as a resonance effect, 164
  in distant atoms, 115, 119
  independence, 114

individual, 21, 104
  probability, 87, 103, 116, 118–19
  spontaneous, 87
  stationary states, 20, 30, 55, 57, 61–63, 70, 79, 82, 85, 87–88, 95, 99, 101, 103, 111
  system of oscillators, 142
two-particle experiment, 192
two slits experiment, 201

virtual equivalence, 118, 120, 142, 144
virtual oscillator, 30, 89, 100–01, 117–18, 120–21, 123, 139–41, 143–44, 146, 148
  model, 118, 120, 122, 142, 146
  model, heuristic function, 141
  model, principle of correspondence, 120, 122
virtual radiation field, 111, 115, 119, 121, 124, 142
  transition processes, 118–19
visualizable model, 147, 194
visualization
  quantum processes, 203
  reality, 207
  stationary states, 102
  symbolic, 164
visualization/visualizability, 6, 15, 19, 25–26, 102, 151, 155, 162, 171

wave mechanics, 23, 30, 154, 165–66
wave representation of light and of matter, 168
wave theory of material particles, 166

Zeeman effect, 96